RELUCTANTLY ROGUE
ROYALS GONE ROGUE

ERIN NICHOLAS

ROYALS GONE ROGUE

The Series

Reluctantly Royal (Torin & Abigail)
Reluctantly Rogue (Jonah & Linnea)
Rags to Royals (Cian & Scarlett)
Recklessly Rogue (Henry & Ruby)

About the Book...

The gorgeous, brilliant woman I have dirty dreams about every damned night?

She's my best friend's fiancée.
She's supposed to be queen someday.
She's off-limits.

But I can't walk away.

I'm supposed to protect her.
Maybe even be her friend.

I should not be lusting after her.

And I absolutely *cannot* fall in love with her.

But I can't forget that one spontaneous, stolen kiss. I can't stop taking care of her. I can't stop wanting her secrets. I can't get over her smiles, her laughter, her happiness. I can't get over *her*.

So, while my head knows she can't be mine, my heart doesn't care.

And if it comes down to choosing between her or...*everything*...I won't have to think twice.

A Brief History of Cara & The Royal Family

In 1848, Tadhg O'Grady was an Irish sailor accompanying King Frederick VII of Denmark to the Faroe Islands. Their ship was attacked by pirates, and the ships were sunk. Fifty people perished, but Tadhg rescued three men, including King Frederick.

The king was so grateful that he gave Tadhg the southernmost island where they were pulled to shore.

Tadhg named the island Cara, the Irish word for friend.

The O'Gradys have ruled the small island in the North Atlantic ever since.

THE ROYAL FAMILY

Tadhg O'Grady (pronounced Tige—like Tiger without the closing 'r' sound)—first king of Cara.

King Diarmuid (pronounced Deer-mid)—King of Cara. Took the throne when he was 39 after his father died suddenly of a heart attack. He has ruled for 43 years. But he is now 82 years old and has had three heart attacks.

Queen Roisin (pronounced Row-sheen)—79 years old. Has ruled with her husband ever since he took the throne. Has equal power as long as he sits on the throne.

Prince Sean—only son of King Diarmuid and Queen Roisin, father of Torin. Killed in a car accident 21 years ago.

Princess Ábria (pronounced AH-bree-a)—Sean's wife, Torin's mother. Still holds the title of princess but has no formal power since her husband's death.

Prince Declan—Sean and Ábria's first child, Diarmuid's eldest grandchild. Was in line for the throne until his abdication 14 years ago. Lives in the U.S. where he has built up a multi-billion dollar company. Has not returned to Cara.

Prince Torin (pronounced Tore-in)—second son of Sean and Ábria. Now next in line for the throne because of Declan's abdication. He also abdicated 12 years ago but returned 2 years ago and rescinded his abdication.

Princess Fiona—Sean and Ábria's third child and only daughter. Abdicated at the same time as Torin. Lives in the U.S. with her husband and children. She is a wild-life animal rescuer and runs a sanctuary for rescued and neglected animals. She is on good terms with her family but has no intention of returning to Cara permanently.

Princess Saoirse (pronounced Sear-sha)—Fiona's daughter. Now 12. Diarmuid's only great-grandchild. Is in line for the throne after Torin until/ unless he has children.

Prince Cian (pronounced Kee-an)— Sean and Ábria's fourth and youngest child/son. Abdicated at the same time as Torin. Lives in the U.S.. Has basically followed Fiona ever since they left Cara.

OTHERS

Jonah Greene—Prince Torin's bodyguard and best friend
Colin Daly—Princess Fiona and Princess Saoirse's bodyguard and friend
Henry Dean—Prince Cian's bodyguard and best friend
Iris Lee—Prince Declan's bodyguard and best friend
Linnea Olsen (pronounced Li Nay uh)—woman arranged to marry Torin
Alfred Olsen—King Diarmuid's best friend, Linnea's grandfather (deceased)
Astrid Olsen—Linnea's sister
Alex Olsen—Linnea's brother
Miles Stafford—Astrid's PT and best friend (and bodyguard)

THE DRUNKEN POKER GAME THAT GOT OUT OF HAND

Twenty-five years ago, Duke Alfred Olsen, King Diarmuid's best friend, and Diarmuid got very drunk one night while playing poker. As they often did. This night however, Diarmuid was out of money. You might ask how a king runs out of money. And that is a fair question. That no one has been able to answer and that Diarmuid won't address even to this day.

But, as the story goes, because he had nothing left to bid, Diarmuid needed 'something of value' to stay in the game.

So he bet one of his grandsons.

Yes, a grandson.

Not even a specific one. He had three and any one of them would do. Of course, the one that would be king someday was most valuable.

And what did Alfred intend to do with this grandson if he was to win?

Marry him to off to one of Alfred's granddaughters, of course. He has two.

And Alfred did win.

And Alfred's oldest granddaughter, Linnea, was informed at age four that she would grow

up to be a princess and then, someday, a queen!

Linnea embraced this news as any four-year-old would—as if it was gospel—and grew up to be a sophisticated, polished, intelligent, beautiful woman who would make an excellent queen.

But what she didn't know until she was seventeen and her would-be fiancé fled the country, was that the entire agreement—all fifteen words of it, including their signatures—was written out on the back of a playbill, and the words are smudged by spilled whiskey.

Still, the family lawyer has informed everyone who asks (and that is a great many people) that it's completely legal and enforceable since the men both signed it in front of witnesses.

Of course, that lawyer is also a very good friend of Alfred's and owes him money from another poker game. And is the son of a judge.

The most important fact in all of this, however, is that in Cara, there's no need for lawyers and judges. King Diarmuid is the law. So the "contract" is enforceable in the stupid, archaic way that anything having to do with royal families is enforceable: with expectations heaped onto everyone from an early age, much manipulation, a lot of money, and a pretty good dose of guilt.

So now that Declan has left Cara, and Torin is set to be the next king, he and Linnea are "engaged". At least as far as both families are concerned.

Whether Torin and Linnea like it or not.

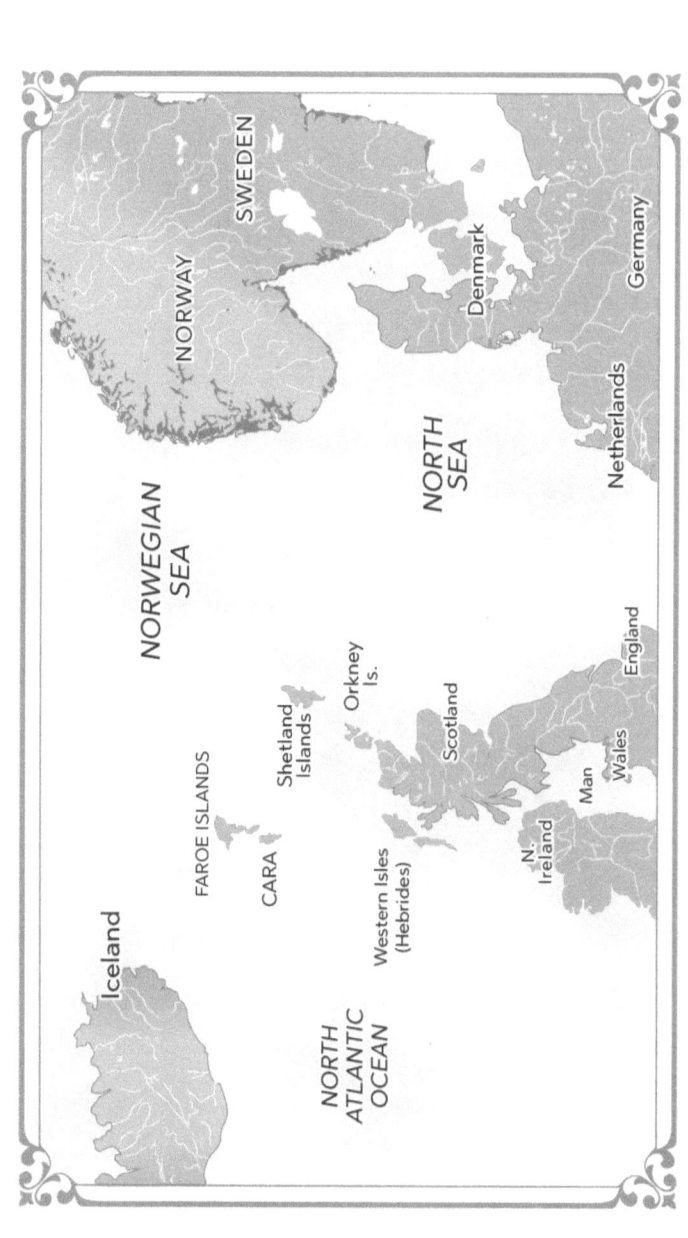

"I'm scared of walking out of this room and never feeling the rest of my whole life the way I feel when I'm with you."

— Baby, "Dirty Dancing"

48 HOURS AGO...

CHAPTER 1
JONAH

I've been having sex dreams about my best friend's fiancée.

Very fucking dirty sex dreams.

I'm extremely displeased by this.

But no amount of reminding myself she's taken, can never be mine, is completely off-limits seems to help.

And it's all I can think about as said best friend swings and jabs at me.

We're just going through the motions. I make Torin do this periodically to try to keep him on his toes when it comes to self-defense. He'd much rather run and hike, and head to his ranch and ride his damned horses. But I insist that he at least pretend to know how to throw a punch.

Not that he *really* needs it. He's now surrounded by security twenty-four-seven.

And he's living on a remote island in the North Atlantic where everyone loves him.

No one here really wants to kill him. Or even hurt him.

Except maybe his grandfather, once in a while.

And me on the rare occasion I think about the fact that he is supposed to marry the only woman to *ever* make me think for even a moment of being disloyal to my position. Or, worse, my friend.

He swings and I sidestep.

I really should let him hit me. Maybe that would make me feel better about the things I've thought about doing to his future wife...

Torin lands a punch right to my jaw and my head snaps back.

Okay, that was an accident. But it hurt. And I deserved it.

I step back and shake my head. "Nice shot, Your Highness."

He frowns, dropping his hands. "How the fuck did I do that?"

There's only one way—I'm distracted. And feeling guilty. "My amazing training," I tell him.

He scoffs. "You've been training me for eleven years. I don't think that's it."

I lift a brow. I don't think we should discount that *entirely*. I'm very fucking good. But he's scowling. He's definitely not himself today either.

"What's wrong with you?" I wipe my hand over my sweaty face.

"Nothing. Haven't you heard? I'm a fucking prince. My life is full of rainbow-shitting unicorns."

Okay, wow. He's never been exactly *enthusiastic* about his role as Crown Prince of Cara. That's no secret to me. But Torin is annoyingly optimistic the majority of the time because he's convinced that things usually go his way, eventually. Because...things usually go his way, eventually.

I probably only need one guess as to why his mood is crap today. "What did your grandfather do or say?"

"Linnea and her family are coming for dinner tonight," he says.

I suck in a quick breath, able to disguise it as exertional breathing. Fuck. This dinner-with-the-soon-to-be-fiancée-thing happens periodically, of course. But it never gets easier.

On either Torin or me.

In fact, it's getting more and more difficult.

But it's better when I have some warning.

This will be the first 'and her family' dinner since my birthday a month ago. The night I stepped over the line and...well, fucked everything up completely.

She's been to the palace twice since then. I saw her, of course, but I avoided being in any room alone with her as if death was waiting on the other side of the threshold.

Or worse—the only woman I've ever fallen in love with.

But having her family here makes it feel more like Torin's in-laws are coming over and reminds everyone that King Diarmuid is getting impatient with Torin's reluctance to make their engagement official.

"You shouldn't be surprised," I tell him, to remind myself that I shouldn't be either.

"I'm not surprised. Just fucking annoyed. I had to practically *plead* with him to get him to attend the dinner with Dr. Hill and Senator Waite. They were here to discuss how Cara can help advance green energy initiatives around the world, for fuck's sake, and he wasn't interested. But *he* doesn't care that *I'm* not interested in dinner with Linnea's family."

It wasn't Torin's pleading that had gotten the king to

that dinner with Hill and Waite either. Linnea had talked him into it.

"Come on," I say, beckoning to him. "I get a better workout with a punching bag."

If Torin would take another decent swing, then *I* could take a decent swing.

And I'm not admitting it out loud to anyone, but I kind of want to hit my best friend right now.

"I'm not in the mood," he tells me, wiping the back of his wrist across his forehead.

I roll my eyes. "Listen, Your Highness." I know he hates when I call him that. "Even princes can get fat and slow."

"Fine." The future king squares up. We began circling each other, taking small, soft jabs.

He lands a hard jab to my shoulder, and he grins.

I don't think he knows that talking about Linnea is a sure way to distract me, but he'll figure it out soon enough if I don't focus.

I swing toward his face, and he doesn't duck fast enough. I clock him on the cheek.

I am, of course, one of the very few people who can hit the Crown Prince of Cara.

I am the *only* person who can hit him without being hit back by someone bigger and stronger. Because anyone else who hit him would be hit *by me*.

He frowns and rubs his cheek. "Hey."

"You really think that if you're in a fight, they're going to just let you bitch and moan about your personal problems?"

"Fuck off. Thought my personal problems were kind of in your wheelhouse."

If only he knew just how in my wheelhouse *this* particular problem of his is.

"We can talk after you land three punches."

He will never land three punches on me, and we both know it.

"This is *training*, not mortal combat."

I roll my eyes that he even thinks this is close to any kind of combat.

"It's even better *training* if you have consequences for fucking up." I swing again, missing on purpose, but he definitely does not duck in time. "Torin, pay attention!"

"We need to find her a new fiancé."

This time my fist lands against his jaw solidly.

I wouldn't admit that it was intentional. I'm not sure that it was. But I didn't pull it back, I didn't swing to miss, and I knew that he wasn't going to duck.

Okay, maybe it was a little intentional.

He takes a step back, rubbing his jaw. "Knock it off."

"We're not having a meeting here. We're training."

"We're *working out*. I need to talk this out."

"No, you don't."

That plan is a terrible idea. He's just being pissy because it's starting to sink in that he's not going to get his way. The king is not stepping down until Torin marries Linnea. Period.

My fist flexes inside my glove. Fuck, I want to swing.

The sooner he marries her, though, the sooner the dirty fucking dreams will stop.

Surely.

Because *then* my brain will finally accept the truth that she's his, that she can *not* be mine, and it will stop torturing me every damned night.

Telling myself that now isn't working. Every time I think it, there's that niggling voice that says, *but it's not offi-*

cial. He hasn't proposed. He doesn't want her. She doesn't want him either. Kissing her was not cheating.

"Okay, so it wasn't cheating. It was still a bad idea. Because eventually she'll marry him and I cannot spend the rest of my life reliving that kiss, the taste of her, the feel of her, the *sound* of her…

"Dammit, fight me," I tell him, harshly. I *need* to work out. I need to hit things. If he's not going to let me hit him —probably a good call really, considering he's the guy who's going to be calling Linnea 'my wife', whether he wants to or not—then I need to go find another of the bodyguards to work out with. Or a punching bag that I truly can just pummel.

"No." He drops his hands. "I need to talk to you about this and this is the only place no one bothers us."

It's true. The rest of the staff doesn't come down here. They're probably afraid that I'm going to make them work out. Or that I'll hit one of them. No one else is allowed to spar with Torin, so they'd have to work out with me.

And the room is relatively soundproof.

"The only solution is to find her someone else," he says. Repeating the ridiculous idea.

"I assume you're talking about Linnea," I say. I wonder if he ever notices the hitch in my voice when I say her name.

Probably not. I'm sure that my best friend has no idea that I'm in love with his fiancée.

I've never been in love before so Torin would have no idea what that looks like on me for one thing. For another, he would never expect something like that to happen. Linnea and I are a very unlikely match. And nothing can ever come of it. I'm sure it hasn't even occurred to him.

"Of course I'm talking about Linnea. Who else would I be trying to set up?"

His sister is married, his niece is too young, and I can't think of any other women in his life that would be important enough to him to be looking for a boyfriend.

"Put your damned hands up," I say in a clipped tone no one but his grandfather gets away using with him.

He puts his gloves up in front of his face, but he frowns. "I'll keep going. If you talk to me about this."

"I'll talk to you about this if I can be swinging at your face while I do it."

"Why are you acting pissed?"

"Because this is a terrible idea, but I know you're going to insist on pulling me into it somehow."

Iris Lee, the lead of the royal bodyguards, who reports to the boss about our activities and itineraries, is *not* going to like this. The boss is going to hate this. The king is not going to allow this.

Torin's going to end up getting me fired. Or banished from this country. Or both.

We circle on the mat and he jabs at me halfheartedly.

I roll my eyes. We keep moving. At least we're not sitting in button-down shirts and ties in his fancy office where I'm reminded that he is not just my boss, but a very powerful man. A man who is obligated to do certain things, not by choice, but by birthright. He has to marry Linnea. And I have to stand by and let it happen.

Being Torin O'Grady's friend is easy. Being *Prince* Torin's friend is turning out to be more difficult than I'd expected.

I jab at his face and he doesn't duck, but he blocks my move.

"She's never really been given the chance to see that things could be different," Torin goes on. "If she finds someone to actually fall in love with, I think she would change her mind. And I think Diarmuid would care. I don't think he would want her to be unhappy with me if there's a possibility for her to be happy and in love."

I feel my heart suddenly pounding so hard, I need to shake my head to try to clear my ears. "You really think they would both rethink everything if she *fell for* someone else?"

Jesus, why are my palms suddenly sweating?

"Yes," he says. "I really do. And—I have an idea."

Hearing him say those four words, I have two simultaneous reactions—excitement and dread.

Torin's ideas are always big and bold. And about half the time, they're good.

The other half the time, they cause me huge problems.

I shove a hand through my hair. "Fine. I'm listening."

"We set her up on some dates. We become her matchmakers. We find some guys who would be perfect for her, arrange for her to spend time with them, tell them to romance her, and show her some other really fantastic possibilities."

I just look at him for a long moment.

When I realize that's it, that's the idea, I say, "So...then what?"

He grins. "We give her permission to fall in love."

"Permission to fall in love?" I repeat.

"That's all it will take. She's a rule follower. Bound by duty. Loyal to our grandfathers. But, if she's given permission to open her mind, to have new experiences, to see what else is out there...I think she'll realize that she absolutely does not want to be stuck here with me."

I snort. Torin can definitely be self-deprecating. It's one of my favorite things about him. But his ego is not small or in any way wounded.

But, then I actually think about his idea.

Dammit. If Linnea fell in love with someone else, someone who was *not* my best friend and the man I intend to spend my life working for, it would be...much better.

Not only would it be better for her, it would be better for Torin.

Neither of them should have to live in a loveless, passionless marriage.

And God knows it would be better for me.

Fortunately for them, the arranged marriage between them, set up by their grandfathers when they were only toddlers, is not public knowledge. While people have certainly noticed, and commented, that the families are close and that Linnea and Torin would make a fantastic couple, there has been no actual gossip about them being romantically involved.

Yet.

It would take the smallest leak from the palace to make that story blow up and spread like wildfire.

"So what do you think?" Torin asks, rubbing a towel over his face. "It will work, right?"

What do I think about him finding a husband for the woman I'm in love with?

Like it might be the best idea he's ever had.

Just wanting to fuck her would be one thing. I could get that out of my system with other women.

The love thing is turning out to be a much bigger issue.

Who knew?

Not me.

I've never been in love before so this is all new to me. Not being able to do a damned thing about it is making me fucking insane.

Getting her out of my life—my line of sight, far enough away that I can't smell her, can't hear her laugh, can't listen to her talk passionately about issues and policies, can't hang on every word she says about her thoughts and feelings—is probably the best solution.

Finding her a better man, who will appreciate her and love her and take care of her in a way Torin never will and in a way no one will *allow* me to, is a fan-fucking-tastic idea.

"I think it makes sense."

He looks at me in surprise. "Yeah?"

"Definitely."

He blows out a breath that is clearly full of relief. "Man, I really thought you were going to tell me I'm a dumbass."

I don't say anything.

Because my best friend doesn't want the most amazing, gorgeous woman either of us has ever met. The woman who would be a perfect queen for him.

My best friend *is* a dumbass. Just not for the reason he thinks.

CHAPTER 2
LINNEA

When I was four years old, my grandfather got me a fiancé.

Yes, a fiancé. As in a man I would someday marry.

It was kind of like getting me a puppy. But easier.

The fiancé was free, didn't require any shots, and we didn't have to housebreak him.

More accurately, my grandfather *won* me a fiancé-in-the-future. In a poker game with his best friend.

His best friend needed one last big bet and put up one of his grandsons.

Then lost.

But this wasn't just some guy my grandfather arranged for me to marry. No, this guy was a prince. A puppy with a pedigree, if you will.

A real, honest-to-God prince. Who would one day be king.

I wish that was all the start to some amazing, too-outlandish-to-believe fairy tale.

It's not. It's my real life.

And now, twenty-seven years later, I'm sitting in that prince's office, listening to him explain to me all of the reasons why I should go on a date with not one, but two, other men.

"He's handsome, well-educated, wealthy, charming, interesting..." Torin frowns. "At least you seemed to find him interesting when you met him."

I nod. "Of course I did. The things James is doing in green energy research and development are very interesting."

Torin seems pleased with that. "And he's very interested in you."

Yes, Torin's mentioned that. Three times now. Apparently, Dr. James Hill called Torin and asked for my personal contact information because he'd like to see me again. Personally.

We met several months ago in D.C. at an energy summit and then Torin invited him to Cara, our tiny, remote island in the North Atlantic, to further discuss a partnership between James's company and our country. Cara doesn't have much, but we do have a lot of wind and a lot of water, both of which are key in green energy production. Not to mention that there's a lot less red tape here.

That all was that James seemed interested in. I had no idea he liked me as anything more than an advisor to the king.

Then again, I have no experience when it comes to men and flirting and dating.

I cast a glance in the direction of the other man in the room.

Torin's bodyguard and best friend is sitting in another of the upholstered armchairs in front of the prince's desk.

He looks huge in the chair. He looks huge everywhere, honestly. He just is huge.

He's six-four, broad and muscular, and his shoulders and arms stretch the black suit jacket he's wearing enticingly. His dark hair and dark beard make him look even more formidable. As do the tattoos on his arms and shoulders. Not that I can see those right now. But I know they're there. I can't *unknow* a lot of things about Jonah. Like how his protectiveness makes me feel safe. And how easy he is to talk to. And how he sees things about me no one else ever does. And how funny he is when he lets you behind his walls. And how husky his voice gets when we're standing only a few inches apart. And how his big, strong hands feel cupping my ass...

Even if not knowing all of those would make my life easier, I can't stop knowing them.

He has one ankle propped on the opposite knee and his arms resting on the arms of the chair. I assume he's trying to look relaxed. But he's clearly not. His jaw is tight, his hands are gripping the padded chair arms, and he hasn't said a word, or even made eye contact with me since we came into Torin's office.

Of course, he hasn't made eye contact with me all night. Or spoken a word directly to me.

He actually hasn't spoken directly to me since the night just over a month ago when he pushed me up against the wall in the kitchen and kissed the hell out of me.

Which seems inordinately rude.

How dare he kiss me like *that*, knowing everything he knows about me, and then act as if he can't even stand to look at me?

So the kiss wasn't good. What was he expecting? It was my first kiss. And he *knew that* going in.

Yes, I'm thirty-one-years-old and I had my first kiss a month ago.

But I've been *engaged*, for all intents and purposes, my entire life. Who would I have kissed?

Not the guy who is so intent on *not* marrying me that he's actively trying to set me up on a date with another man who lives across an ocean, that's for sure.

But Jonah knew that I wasn't going to be good at kissing and he still kissed me. Or let me kiss him. Honestly, thirty-five days later I'm still fuzzy on who kissed who. He lowered his head, but we were definitely talking about it leading up to that point. I'd made it very clear what I wanted. He's the only one I've ever confessed my never-been-kissed status to. He *knew* I wanted him to kiss me. And if it was terrible, he could have at least given me some pointers after. That's what a friend would have done. Maybe some "next time don't act so freaking desperate" or something. Something *helpful*. Instead of avoiding me as if I have a communicable disease.

Or as if he knows I'm falling in love with him, and he needs to shut that down immediately.

Obviously, I need to shut that down.

I've been working on it.

Him acting like a jackass is helping.

But he can't know how I really feel about him.

Can he?

I'm not *that* easy to read. I don't think.

Besides, I'm intelligent. I completely understand our situation. It doesn't matter that I'm in love with him. I'm engaged to his best friend. And loveless marriage or not, I can't exactly get away with sneaking around on Torin. I'll be the queen, for fuck's sake.

"So will you have dinner with him?" Torin asks, pulling

my attention away from the big, broody man next to me who has to be *trying* not to look at me.

He's always looked at me before. In any room, any circumstance, whenever I seek Jonah out, he's always watching me. I love his eyes on me. Having him purposefully not looking at me now makes me feel cold and...hurt. Yes, definitely hurt.

And pissed.

We're friends. Or so I thought. But he's just going to sit here, not look at me, not say a word when Torin is sending me away like this? Knowing everything he knows about me, after declaring that part of his job is to take care of me, he has no opinion on this?

Or maybe his opinion is very, very clear.

He thinks this is a good idea.

I look at Torin and nod. "Yes, I'll have dinner with James. And Christian."

I'm so fucking sick of my life being manipulated by others. By *men*.

You'd think knowing who you were going to marry and what your job—hell, your entire life—would be since you were four years old would make things simple, wouldn't you?

That has *not* been my experience.

The O'Grady men and their friends, including my grandfather, and now Jonah, have been messing things up for me—messing *with* me—for long enough.

Torin grins. "Wonderful. I'm so glad that you see this as the best solution for everyone."

I nod. "Spending time with a brilliant scientist, and inventor, who is worth billions and who wants to bring his research facilities to Cara? Who wants to hire our people and put us at the table for international talks on everything from ecology and conservation to science and tech? That seems like a great idea. Not to mention *also* spending time with a young, charismatic progressive American senator, who is making waves in Washington with several creative policies for working families and education. It's all quite brilliant. Thanks for setting it up."

My tone is a bit sarcastic but I'm not entirely bitter. These *will* be great meetings, with interesting conversations, and I'll enjoy furthering my relationships with these men.

I just won't be marrying either of them.

Torin sighs. He's gotten to know me well over the past two years that he's been back in Cara and his grandfather has gotten more determined to make our engagement official.

For years, the arranged marriage that came out of our grandfathers' poker game was something of a family joke. For the O'Gradys. It never was for my family.

Torin has learned in the past twenty-three months that I'm smart, stubborn, and not at all intimidated by him.

"These are supposed to be *dates*, Linnea," he says, sounding weary now.

Gee, I'm so sorry that me having a backbone and knowing what I want is inconvenient for him.

"I understand that's what you want."

"These men are great matches for you," he says. "And if you get to know them, really give them a chance, you *could* actually fall for one of them."

I swallow, and resist looking to my left. I don't want to see Jonah's reaction to the idea of me falling in love.

Because I don't want to see that he doesn't have a reaction.

That would hurt. It shouldn't, but it would.

"I really do think my grandfather would care about that," Torin continues, his voice gentler. "He loves you."

That's what Torin is betting on here.

That if I were to truly fall in love with someone else, King Diarmuid would care about that, would want me to be happy, and would let Torin and me out of the arranged marriage contract.

He might be right.

King Diarmuid does love me. He also likes me a lot. More than he likes his own grandson, to be honest. Because I've *been here*. I've been in Cara representing the palace and the country. I've been devoted and, dammit, I'm very good at what I do.

But what Torin keeps forgetting—or is refusing to truly understand—is that I don't want out of the arranged marriage.

Because marrying Torin is how I get to be queen.

I'll be an amazing queen.

At least for the country.

For Torin...well, maybe not so much. But sacrifice is part of the job.

"I said I'd go," I tell him. I lift my shoulder. "Obviously, I can't promise you more than that. If you want a guarantee that I'll fall madly in love, or even that I'll sleep with either of them, or both—"

Jonah clears his throat and finally shifts out of the rigid posture he's been holding.

I still don't look in his direction.

Yes, Jonah also knows I'm a virgin. He's also the only one, other than my doctor, I guess, that knows that.

And he'd better keep that to himself.

I go on, my gaze stubbornly on Torin. "I won't promise anything."

Torin blows out a breath and runs a hand over his face. "Jesus, Linnea, I would never expect you to sleep with them." He drops his hand. "Of course, if you *want to*, that's your prerogative. But just...yes, go to dinner. Try to approach it as more than a business meeting though? Please?"

I roll my eyes.

"You're fantastic," he says. "But I'm not in love with you. And you're not in love with me."

I nod. "You're right."

"Do you want me?" he asks. "Are you attracted to me?"

Out of the corner of my eye, I see Jonah shift on his seat again.

I make myself focus on Torin. "No, I'm not."

He nods. "Well, I want that. I think we both should."

"What?"

"Love. And sex."

"I get it," I tell him. As I have before. "And if we were regular people, I would agree with you. But being king and queen is about much more than what you and I want."

"Why can't I be king, with all that entails, and have true love?" he asks.

I swallow. "Do you think having both is possible? Really? What you're going to do with your life is a unique, and very demanding thing that will require more from you than most people can imagine. There are only certain people who would make a good partner for you. The chances of those people also being your true love are... nearly impossible."

His expression softens. He leans back, suddenly actually looking relaxed. "I danced with a woman *once*, almost two years ago, and haven't been able to stop thinking about her."

I lift a brow. He's never told me this. Jonah's never told me this.

I want to look at the big man next to me so badly. I want to know if he knows about this woman.

But looking at him feels risky. It feels like something I shouldn't do.

Torin continues. "I also want all of the best things for Cara. I intend to be the best king this country has ever had. But knowing that I can feel that for someone makes me believe that even a king can have love. And if not, I'd rather rule without a queen." He leans in. "I can have advisors. I can have close confidants. I can have the best people around me. Like you. I will always listen to you, Linnea. But I do not need to have a queen who I don't love."

I take a deep breath.

I've also gotten to know him in the past twenty-three months. He's also stubborn. And always thinks he's right. And he thinks he wants to be king.

I know the Constitution of Cara inside and out. There is no requirement for the ruler to be married.

Probably simply because no one ever imagined the king, or queen, wouldn't want to be.

But if Torin has a wife, she has equal power. As long as an O'Grady sits on the throne, his or her spouse has equal power. Of course, he's going to be careful with who he gives that title to. It will have to be someone he trusts. Someone who he can see as a true partner.

"This is important to you," I say. "That I go on these dates?"

"Yes," he says. He glances at Jonah. "I actually had picked out a few other men as well, but I got vetoed."

I lift a brow. "Vetoed?"

"Jonah thought it was a bad idea."

Jonah Greene is probably the only person on the planet who can veto Torin on anything and make it stick.

"He thought you should start by dating men you've met before and have a pre-established connection with."

So Jonah *has* been a part of concocting this plan.

Well, that's what I needed to know, I suppose.

I tip my head. "How many is 'a few' others?"

Torin lifts a brow, obviously surprised I asked. "Ten."

"You came up with *ten* men you thought would be good matches for me?" I don't know if I should be flattered or appalled that my fiancé could come up with so many other people to set me up with.

"I realize that you could have a hundred dates by tomorrow night if you simply put a profile up on the internet," he says, holding a hand out to Jonah.

He says it so matter-of-factly that I don't know if he even means it as a true compliment so much as he just thinks it's a fact. Which is nice, actually.

"Thank you."

"But you can't date just anyone," he says, taking the folder Jonah hands him.

I note Jonah's heavy sigh as he hands over the material.

"The man who will be a good partner to you will have to, of course, be of a certain…caliber," Torin says.

Both of my brows are arched now. "Caliber?"

He hands me the folder. "Of course. Probably a thousand mechanics and fishermen and farmers would show up, falling over themselves and one another, to simply take you to dinner. But the men who are actually your type are on a much shorter list."

I look down at the folder in my hand. My should-be fiancé made a list of men he thinks I should date.

This isn't strange at all.

"I know you haven't had a chance to really date," Torin says. "I know that you've always had this thing between us hanging over your head. So I think you need a chance to go out and meet a bunch of amazing men who will think you're amazing. To see what it's like. To see if someone else can make you feel..." He trails off and swallows.

"The way the woman you danced with made you feel?" I ask.

"Yes."

I don't roll my eyes. The whole soulmate, love-at-first-sight, one-true-love thing just doesn't feel real to me. It's hard for me to believe in that. But, hell, I've never ever looked at another man with even a tiny romantic thought in my head. I've always been...off-limits, I suppose, for lack of a better word. Maybe I've been missing out. Maybe I really will feel differently if I go out with a man *without* considering myself engaged.

I flip the folder open, curious despite myself.

I scan over the names. I recognize six of the ten. Besides James and Christian, there's another politician, a wealthy entrepreneur, a pro football player, and a billionaire who owns...I don't remember exactly, but I know who he is.

"They're the cream of the crop," Torin says with a smile.

"I appreciate that," I say.

Torin grins. "Jonah crossed three of them off immediately. Even before we discussed that it would be better to start with the men you already know."

I look over at Jonah, noticing, then trying to ignore how my heart rate speeds up. "Why?"

"Embezzlement, asshole, asshole," Jonah says shortly.

I narrow my eyes when he *still* doesn't look at me. "But James and Christian are fine?"

"No," Jonah says.

"He did a full background check on them both," Torin jumps in. "Before they came to Cara, of course, but then he did an even deeper dive."

"But they're not okay?" I ask.

"He wanted to cross James off," Torin says. "But not for a good reason. He's fine. He's safe. Nothing illegal or nefarious to be found."

I'm still watching Jonah. "Then why?"

"He's boring," Jonah says simply.

I stare at him. I'm not sure what to say.

Torin just chuckles. "And really rich. Jonah doesn't like anyone with money."

I smile at that. "He likes you," I point out.

"That's debatable many days," Torin says. He gives his best friend a grin.

Jonah doesn't argue.

"And when he likes me, it's despite my money. And in part because I don't particularly relish having my money."

Ah. That makes sense. Jonah was assigned to be Torin's bodyguard—and obviously became his friend—during the time Torin was away from the palace and all of the glitz and glamour that came with being a prince. While he'd lived in the U.S., Torin and his siblings had lived as "regular people." No one had known about their royal heritage until Torin returned to Cara.

I look down at the list of influential, wealthy men Torin has put in my lap. Literally.

I'm...intrigued.

And I have no intention of actually marrying any of them, but maybe going out with a man who actually *wants me* would be nice before settling down for a lifetime with one who doesn't.

"So how would this work? I call James and Christian up and ask them out?" I ask Torin.

He smiles. "They're both *waiting* for that call. I can let them know you're happy to meet them. Or you could call, or email. They'll be very happy to hear from you."

Yes, see, that's nice. It's nice to think that these men find me interesting enough to want to have dinner with me. It's nice to think about two accomplished, handsome, intelligent men, who could no doubt date anyone they wanted to, *wanting* to spend time with me. Especially considering I'm currently sitting in a room with two accomplished, handsome, intelligent men who really, really, *really* don't.

"I'll call Astrid and see when she can meet me and then I'll let them know," I say.

"Astrid?" Torin asks. "Why?"

"Because I don't want to go to D.C. and do this alone."

"You won't. Definitely not," Torin says. "Jonah will go with you."

My head whips around to look at him.

His jaw is clenched but he simply nods. "Fine."

This is absolutely *not* fine.

I am not flying across an ocean to go on my first date *ever* to placate my *fiancé* with the *man I'm in love with*.

Holy. Crap.

"No," I say firmly. "I need my *sister*. I'll need help with my hair and picking out clothes and advice...before and after. Debriefing. Girl talk. Just...no. It has to be Astrid."

I'll have to actually dress for these dates, I suppose, in case we're photographed. It will have to look like I'm trying. So Astrid can help with that. I know how to dress for business meetings, cocktail parties, royal engagements, the theater, weddings...surely a date falls somewhere in the midst of all of that. But I'm not sure. I definitely need Astrid for this. Though I'll have to finally confess to her that I've never dated. But she won't judge. It will be fine.

But it cannot be Jonah. Not only because these "dates" are going to actually be business meetings wrapped up in a little bit of "so this is how it feels to be appreciated, as a woman, by a guy who isn't being forced to spend time with me by his grandfather" but because I can't fly for *seven hours* on a private plane, just the two of us, and then spend time in D.C. with Jonah Greene.

He's uncomfortable. He regrets the kiss. He thinks I'm a pathetic, needy woman who mistakes physical attraction for love and takes a simple birthday kiss and turns it into a life-altering experience.

I'm not those things but he wouldn't know that since he hasn't *spoken one word to me in a month*.

But most of all, while these are business meetings to me, Jonah sees this as a chance to get me married off for real.

Torin's shaking his head. "Jonah is perfect for this."

"How? How is Jonah perfect for this?"

"Obviously you'll just pay to have your hair done and you'll have a stylist help with picking out new clothes. Jonah will have my credit cards," Torin says. "And he can definitely give you advice. He's a *guy*. Getting a male perspective will be even better than Astrid's."

I stare at Torin.

My fiancé is also going to pay for new clothes for my dates with other men.

How nice.

And the man I'm in love with will be giving me advice about how to act and talk and react to these men.

"Just go to dinner and be yourself," Torin says, obviously trying to give me a pep talk. "But add in some flirting."

"I don't know how to flirt."

He looks at me like I just said the sentence in Arabic. "What?"

I lift a shoulder. "I don't flirt."

"What? How?" His frown deepens. "You're a beautiful, intelligent, interesting woman. How can you not know how to flirt?"

"I *talk* to men. About business and common interests. I don't need to flirt." I lift a brow. "I've been kind-of engaged."

"But..." Torin looks at Jonah with a confused look, then back to me when his friend says nothing. "Can you ask someone how to do it?"

"How to flirt?"

"Yes."

I roll my eyes. "You know, as my fiancé, you should be happier that I haven't flirted with a bunch of other men."

Torin rolls *his* eyes.

Then Jonah mutters something under his breath, then says louder, "Jesus Christ, seriously?"

Both Torin and I look at him.

"What?" Torin asks.

"She doesn't need to know how to fucking flirt." Jonah shoves up from his chair but looks down at me, making eye contact for the first time.

The impact of his green gaze locking on mine rocks through me. My nerve endings light up.

"Do you still have that green dress you wore to dinner in October?" Jonah asks.

I blink at him. Green dress? October? But then the memory clicks and I nod slowly. "Yes."

"How about the maroon one? The long one with the low back."

I nod stupidly.

"Wear those. The same heels. The same lipstick." Then he pivots and stalks toward the door. "Wear your hair down, be yourself. And laugh at least twice. About anything. Just let them hear you laugh. That's all you need to do. But be prepared for them to ask you on another date at the end of dinner." Then he lets himself out of the room, slamming the door behind him.

I stare at the dark wood for several long seconds.

Then I finally look back at Torin.

He looks very pleased. "Great. You'll let the guys know you're coming this weekend then? You can use my plane to travel, of course."

Don't let the door hit you in the ass on your way out.

"I..." I take a breath. I have no reason to say no. Dammit. "Yes. Fine. I'll email them both tonight." Cara is five hours ahead of D.C. so James and Christian will see the messages, and possibly even respond, before I wake up tomorrow.

Torin pushes up from the desk and claps his hands together, grinning. "This is going to be so great."

I just nod.

Yeah, great. So fucking great.

11 MONTHS AGO...

CHAPTER 3

JONAH

I roning naked shouldn't be hazardous.
    I do it all the time.

I've never burned anything. Not shirts. Not fingers. Certainly not my favorite body part.

Sure, hot things near that part of me *could be* dangerous—considering its size—but since I only iron my shirts in my bedroom by myself and I have excellent fine and gross motor skills, I don't worry about it.

Usually.

Then again, I also don't have people bursting unexpectedly into my room while I'm doing it, causing my hand to jerk.

Usually.

But when my door suddenly swings open when I'm mid-swipe, I do jolt, and the hot iron twists toward my mid-section, and I let out a "Fuck!"

This causes the woman—who not only carries herself, speaks, and looks like a future queen but who will actually *be* a future queen—to stop three steps inside the door suddenly.

My grip tightens on the *hot* iron, and I carefully set it down *away* from my crotch as I watch her head snap up, her gaze jerking up from her phone.

She doesn't scream. Or even gasp. She just straightens and says, "Oh," as she registers the fact that there's a man in the room.

A naked man.

Then, her gaze travels down from my face to my chest. Then, my stomach. Then, the ironing board that's not entirely blocking her view of the rest of me.

I suck in a breath and blow it out.

"Duchess," I say, inclining my head.

I know who she is, of course.

She also knows me. Or she should. We've met, anyway.

Though I guarantee I know more about her than she does about me.

"What are you doing in here?" she asks.

Her gaze has *not* returned to my face.

I don't move to cover myself. But I also don't step out from behind the ironing board.

She came into *my* room uninvited, so I'm not diving for cover. I walk around naked in my living quarters all the time. But I'm not going to parade around naked in front of the future queen of Cara. Who is also my best friend's fiancée.

"I'm ironing my shirt," I tell her.

"In *my* room?" she asks, with a frown.

"In *my* room, actually."

"This is the guest room I always use," she says.

Her eyes are still on the ironing board, and because of my height, I know she can see about half of my cock.

She's not even blushing.

Which I definitely make a note of and file into my mental "Lady Linnea Olsen" file.

I know a lot about this woman.

Her lack of boyfriends, suitors, and lovers is one of the facts I've committed to memory. Not necessarily on purpose. What can I say? It stood out to me.

Part of my job is knowing details about her. Eventually, after she marries the prince, she'll be my responsibility, too, so it's important I know things about her. Things like how she takes her coffee, her favorite restaurants, who her best friends are, and the status of her relationship with her parents.

So I take in details right now. Out of habit. She's wearing fitted, silky-looking black pants that flare at the bottom, a gold belt that emphasizes the curve of her hips and dip of her waist, and a cream-colored blouse. Her shoes are one-inch black pumps. Her deep brown hair, with the copper highlights, is down, falling to her shoulder blades, loose, curling softly around her shoulders. Her green eyes are made up perfectly with liner and mascara. Her full lips are a perfect pink color, probably from the cosmetic line I know is her favorite.

She's polished, sophisticated, and perfectly put together from top to bottom. Just like always. Just like a woman in her position should be.

And noticing the details of her hair, eyes, and lips, the fit of her clothing, is my *job*. That's all.

No one should know more about the prince and future princess than the head of their security team.

"I use this room to freshen up and change before dinner whenever I'm here."

"This is my room now."

Finally, her gaze meets mine. She draws herself even taller and tips her chin up. What can I say? The woman is regal as fuck.

"And who are you exactly?"

Yeah, she *should* know who I am, but it seems she hasn't paid attention. Of course, my job is to be in the background, noticed only if needed.

"Prince Torin's head of security," I say. "Jonah Greene. This room is the closest to the prince's, so it's where I'll be staying. The guest room is now the next one down the hall. On the left."

Torin has been living in Cara without me for a year. It makes sense that this room was given to guests. It's the biggest and nicest unoccupied room. But, since I'm now a permanent resident, and it *is* the closest to his, it's mine as of two weeks ago.

"I'd offer my hand, but I'd have to move from behind this ironing board and get closer," I tell her. "And I wasn't expecting to...entertain in my room just now."

Linnea Olsen isn't a princess or queen...yet...but when King Diarmuid made her grandfather a duke and gave him land and responsibilities in Cara, his entire immediate family was bestowed titles. So she is a duchess, and I really should at least shake her hand.

Her gaze drops again to the board and what's behind it, and now, finally, her cheeks get a little pink.

"That's not necessary," she says.

I do *not* smirk, but fuck, I want to. If this were *any* other woman at all, I would.

She's staring at me as if she's never seen a naked man before.

And honestly, that's possible.

And I really want to know if I'm the first and only.

And I *really* shouldn't wonder about that.

"Do you need help finding the guest room?" I ask when she doesn't move.

Until she moves, I really can't.

"The room you say is next door?" she asks. "I think I can find my way."

Is that a little bit of sass I detect?

It's very possible. Torin has told me stories. It sounds like Linnea is as pleasing as sunshine and sweet tea on my grandmother's front porch in July in front of...well, everyone. But behind closed doors, with the man her grandfather arranged for her to marry, she's sassy and even downright snotty. According to the man whose grandfather arranged for *him* to marry *her*, anyway.

Yes, I take what Torin tells me with a grain of salt. But I do believe that Linnea is less than sweet and subservient to him.

"Are you waiting for an escort then?"

"Are you offering? You're not exactly dressed for it. Or for anything."

I could think of a couple of things I'm "dressed" for.

"Just had to ask since you got lost finding the guest room this time," I point out.

"I told the staff I didn't need help. I suppose they assumed I knew there had been a location change."

I know that Linnea has been to the palace several times. Even before Torin had moved back, she was a fixture at the king's side. This bedroom is probably more hers than a 'guest room.' I should probably feel bad about taking it from her. But I don't. I need to be close to Torin. And I'm living here twenty-four-seven now while she hasn't moved in permanently.

Yet.

"I suppose so. Making assumptions can be dangerous."

It can be. I need to constantly remind those under my protection to think of their safety. God knows Torin is more likely to leap before looking and depend on me to get him out of whatever trouble that causes. But I know from all of my research that Linnea Olsen is *not* spontaneous or flighty or rash.

She narrows her eyes slightly. "It was a simple mistake."

I realize that as my friend's sort-of-fiancée and my possible future employer, I should tread lightly. Hell, I should probably tread lightly just because I'm a nice guy, and she's a lady. But she can't get rid of me. That is fully under Torin's purview. Well, okay, technically, until Torin wears the crown as king of Cara, King Diarmuid can overrule him. I could definitely be fired. Or banished from the island. And Lady Linnea is one of the king's favorite people. He absolutely likes her more than he does even his own grandson.

But I'm not too worried.

If Linnea marries Torin, we'll spend a lot of time together. In all kinds of situations. We'll get to know each other well. She's also going to have to learn to listen to me. Trust me. Tell me things that might be a little personal. Maybe a lot personal. The chances of one of us seeing the other naked eventually are pretty good.

But she doesn't have to like me.

"I guess I'll be going then," she says, turning on her heel.

"I'll see you downstairs at dinner, Duchess."

And then, all at once, she's tripping and falling. I watch, almost confused. She has to have tripped over her own shoes. There is nothing on the floor. That section of the smooth stone doesn't even have a rug. But still, she's suddenly on her hands and knees.

Out of instinct, I'm by her side in an instant.

I wrap my hand around her upper arm. "Are you all right?"

She shakes her head. Then takes in a quick breath.

"Are you hurt?" I ask, more firmly.

"Of course I am!" she snaps.

"Where?"

She turns to look at me, her mouth open. Then her eyes drop and widen, and she quickly looks away.

Right. I'm half kneeling next to her.

Naked.

Anything she didn't see behind the ironing board before, she does now.

I blow out a breath. Well, I guess I've made an interesting first impression.

"Did you sprain an ankle? Hurt your wrist?" I ask, making her focus.

"Bruised knees," she mutters. Her eyes are stoically forward.

"Okay, you'll get over that." I stand and haul her to her feet. I don't know why, but I feel strangely cheerful.

"Yeah," she agrees. "I'll get over *that*."

And then I chuckle before I even realize that I'm going to.

"You're *laughing*?" she asks, frowning at the doorway rather than at me.

"This is funny."

"It's not."

"It is."

She's still staring straight ahead. "How?" she asks.

"Women often *laugh* when they're with you, and you're naked?"

I chuckle again. "Oh, definitely not." I watch as her jaw tightens. "What's funny," I tell her, ''is that the shirt I'm ironing is what I'm planning to wear tonight to dinner. When I first expected to see you."

There's a beat as she absorbs that. Then I see the corner of her mouth twitch. She shrugs out of my grasp. "I'm sure my mother will appreciate you coming to dinner with a shirt on."

Damn, I almost laugh out loud.

"Do you need help walking to the door?" I ask.

She sighs. "I'm going to say no. Then pray that's true."

I watch her walk away. She does *not* look back. But I'm guessing she's picturing the sight behind her.

CHAPTER 4
LINNEA

The shirt looks really good. Crisp. Well-pressed. I can't see much of it underneath the black jacket and black tie he's wearing, but I'm having difficulty looking away from it.

Of course, I know why that is.

Because I know that he pressed it himself. And what it's covering up.

And I can't *unknow* that.

That's not the kind of thing you forget.

But I also can't stop thinking about it. Not even for ten minutes, it seems. The images of Jonah completely naked, standing unfazed in front of me, crossing the room, kneeling, helping me up...

Burned. In. My. Memory.

That could be very problematic.

Even more problematic is that when we were introduced when I arrived in the dining room for dinner, he smiled at me, told Torin that we'd already met, then gave me a wink behind my fiancé's back. A *wink*. Behind my *fiancé's* back.

Jonah seems perfectly at ease. I saw him naked earlier. Now we're having dinner with my family and Torin's. That happens to include the *king and queen* of our country. But he's acting as if it was no big deal.

That has me almost more rattled than the actual scene upstairs in the guest room. In *his* room, more accurately. I was in *his* bedroom while he was completely naked.

This man is Torin's bodyguard. And best friend. He'll be around a lot. Basically constantly. For the rest of my life.

My sigh is internal only, but it's very real.

The first man I see completely naked—or even partially naked—in real life had to be the guy I'm going to spend as much time with as I will with my *husband*.

The husband I've known my entire life, who I've been sort-of engaged to for a year now, and who has *never* made me tingle, not even once.

I know how this works. Jonah Greene has been Torin's bodyguard for the past twelve years. He has essentially pledged to serve in the role for the rest of his life. His life and loyalty belong first and foremost to Cara and its future ruler.

This means that once Torin and I are married, I will be spending time with the first and only man to make me aware that I do have body parts that respond to the opposite sex completely outside of my conscious control.

I honestly hadn't believed that happened before today.

But it does.

There is, evidently, such a thing as pure lust, after all.

And I feel it for Jonah Greene.

Not *felt*. Feel. Currently. Even when he's dressed.

It's clearly not about some kind of intellectual connection between us. We've barely spoken. It's not about a friendship or any kind of emotional relationship. We don't know one another at all.

It's all chemistry.

Holy. Crap.

I mean, I've always suspected I was heterosexual. I've never really had any lusty thoughts or feelings for any women I've met. But the most I've ever felt for a man was 'oh, he's good-looking'.

I'd kind of started thinking I was maybe just asexual. Which was fine. I was destined for an arranged marriage with a man that my grandfather had chosen for me when I was four years old. So being wildly attracted to someone else at any point would have been inconvenient.

But nope. Not asexual.

Very, very capable of sexual attraction to a man, it turns out.

At least *one* man…

"Does that work for your schedule, Linnea?"

I pull myself out of my thoughts and make myself focus on the people around the dinner table. Dammit, the king just asked me a question about my schedule.

"I…" I take a breath and admit, "I'm sorry, Your Majesty, I didn't hear what you asked me."

King Diarmuid seems confused by that. Which makes sense. I'm never distracted.

But Jonah is sitting directly across the table from me. Torin is at the end of the table, opposite the king. Jonah is to his left. I'm to his right.

And oh God, this is how it's going to be. Forever.

"I asked if it would work for your schedule to accompany Torin to the energy summit in Washington, D.C., at the beginning of September?"

I glance at Torin. His jaw is tight. He doesn't look at me. I don't roll my eyes, at least not outwardly.

"Yes, the hockey season starts for Alex in October so he'll have some events in September, but I can spend a weekend in D.C."

My brother is a rising hockey star, and I'm his agent. Just as I am for my sister, Astrid. She was once a gymnast predicted to not only be Cara's first Olympian but our first gold medalist as well. A horrible fall and spinal cord injury during the qualifying round ended that dream. But I've ensured the world has seen her strength and resilience through her recovery and rehab. She's now a sought-after inspirational speaker, an advocate for athletes with disabilities, and a children's book author.

My siblings are independent and have names of their own. They don't have to lean on our family name or legacy, and they definitely aren't at the mercy of the royal family of Cara for their success and security.

Exactly as I intended.

I'd like to think that I would have been a huge cheerleader for them both and would have helped them become big stars regardless of, well, anything. But being raised to believe that I had only one path and that I had no choices in my own life and future—and then being jerked around by the people who were supposed to be a part of that future—made me *determined* that my siblings would be in positions where they could determine what they wanted their lives to look like.

"Wonderful," Diarmuid says. "I think having you and Torin there together will be—"

"No." Torin interrupts with a single, firm word.

I sigh.

So does the king.

Jonah leans back in his chair.

We were all expecting this.

I watch Jonah with interest, though. This is the first time he's been present for a "family dinner" with the O'Gradys and me, my parents, and my grandmother.

We've been having these once-a-month dinners for years. For a very long time, they included my grandfather, the king's best friend.

And none of the king's grandchildren.

They had all abdicated their titles and were living in the U.S.

The good old days.

Sure, *my* future plans were in limbo during that time, but my grandfather kept assuring me that everything was fine and was going to work out. I'd delusionally believed him and let myself imagine a time when the eldest grandson, Declan, returned home, reclaimed the throne, and got down on one knee to make our engagement—the one I'd been imagining my whole life—official.

Instead, Torin, the second grandson, is the one who came home.

And he's not in love with me. Which evidently bothers him.

He's being a real pain in my ass.

Because *his* wanting to marry for love directly conflicts with *my* goal—to be queen of Cara.

"Torin," King Diarmuid says with clearly forced patience. "You and Linnea are the best representatives to attend the summit."

"I can represent Cara. She doesn't need to come," he says.

"She's been to these summits before on our behalf. You haven't."

It's true. The king has trusted me to meet with other world leaders and speak for Cara on a number of occasions. Considering his heirs were all *gone* for a *decade,* he needed someone to step up. And I've been training to be queen all my life.

I give Torin a cool look. "I've probably already met a number of people who will be there. We've been discussing ways to bring green energy to the island for about three years now."

Torin frowns as he looks at me. "Why's it taking so long?"

I frown back. "Spoken as someone who doesn't understand how this all works."

"I don't—" he starts.

But a low voice says, "Hey."

My gaze shoots across the table to Jonah. He hasn't changed his posture. I don't even know if anyone else at the table heard the 'hey'. His eyes are on Torin.

He was *warning* the prince?

I watch them.

Torin glares at Jonah, but he doesn't finish what he was about to say. Instead, he looks at me. "Let's discuss the summit further. I'd like to hear what you know."

I give a nod. "Fine." What am I supposed to say? It's not like I can tell him he can't go to the summit. He *is* the prince.

He scoots his chair back and stands. "We'll have coffee in my office," he says to no one in particular.

Jonah also stands. His gaze settles on me.

I *feel* it before I see it. It's heavy and warm.

Which is ridiculous.

I look up and meet his emerald gaze.

God, green is my favorite color.

I'm very proud of myself that my gaze remains on his. Because the intensity in the way he watches me makes me instinctively want to look away. And because my traitorous, newly awakened lust sensors want to take in the rest of him, I can see now that he's standing.

"I'm going to assume that means it's yes to the summit in September," Diarmuid says.

I take the opportunity to look at *him*. He doesn't like when people leave a dinner, a meeting, or even a conversation without *him* dismissing them.

"Cara will be represented," Torin says.

Again, I don't roll my eyes visibly.

It's obvious Diarmuid notices the noncommitment in the answer.

"She's very good," Diarmuid says.

He's clearly talking about me. I don't love the third-person reference as if I'm not here.

"She's exactly the kind of representative we need," he continues. "In the past, our princesses and queens have had less presence in international affairs than the princes and kings, but the world is changing. Having her speak for us reflects well on our values and ideologies."

"You mean, the people at the energy summit tend to be more progressive thinkers and leaders, and they'll like knowing that while Cara might be a monarchy, it's not run by a misogynist?" Torin asks.

"Torin," I say, before I can bite my tongue. "That's not fair."

Though honestly, I need to be sure my future husband knows that I won't be biting my tongue.

"He thinks you reflect well on our values and ideologies," he says. "Isn't that how that sounds to you?"

I stand, smooth the front of my dress, and turn slightly so I'm facing Torin directly.

"I *do* reflect well on our values and ideologies," I say. "I'm a product of our education system, so my superior knowledge and ability to articulate ideas and plans, not to mention my fluency in three languages, reflects well on that.

"*My* values and beliefs about how important it is that Cara do our part to save the planet and contribute to the effort to clean it up reflect Cara's stances, both morally and politically.

"And my charm, wit, and ability to communicate with all kinds of people reflect my upbringing within my family and yours.

"So what it sounds like to me, is that the king thinks I, a lifelong citizen of Cara and a member of his family, will be a great representative to this summit. As a person. Regardless of the fact that I'm a woman."

Torin is staring at me.

I feel Jonah is also watching me. But while I can see surprise from Torin, I don't get the impression Jonah is surprised.

I take a chance and glance at him.

He looks amused. And pleased. Which seems strange. And there's something else in his expression that I don't understand. I can't name it.

"I think it's time to go to your office," he says to Torin.

"I agree." Torin turns and stalks out of the room.

CHAPTER 5
JONAH

Well, dammit. She's beautiful, has a good sense of humor, and is sassy as fuck.

The way she just stood up for herself in front of Torin was a fucking turn on.

That's not helpful.

I can't be turned on by my best friend's fiancée.

Even if he doesn't want her to be his fiancée, that is not a good situation.

I follow them out of the dining room, down the hallway, up the grand staircase, and down another hallway to Torin's office. He walks slightly in front of her, which is a dick move that I will point out to him later.

We all get it. He doesn't want to marry her. He doesn't have to be in love with her. But he *does* have to treat her well. Torin O'Grady is not an asshole. He's actually a really great guy. But he's in a situation that makes him feel out of control by the one man who can push his buttons, making him act like a jerk.

This isn't about Linnea at all. And I think she knows that, at least on some level. But Torin has to stop acting like a jackass.

At least toward this woman.

In general, I try to keep his jackass tendencies in check, but there's something in particular about him being a jerk to this woman that rankles.

Maybe it's because she is as much a victim in this situation as he is. Her grandfather was in on the stupid poker game that resulted in their arranged marriage as much as Diarmuid was. Just because she's a better sport than Torin doesn't mean that she doesn't deserve to be treated with respect.

So I walk next to her. Not just because it's polite, but because it also keeps me from looking at her ass.

Yes, I looked at it when she was walking out of my bedroom. Sue me. I was standing there naked, and she's a gorgeous woman with a nice ass.

I won't make that mistake again. Like checking her out in the black sheath dress that hugs her curves even better than the silky pants she'd had on earlier. And the fucking heels she's wearing tonight. These are three inchers, and I still know that if I stood right next to her, she would not quite reach my shoulder.

I step to the doorway, not needing to open it for her, but gesturing for her to precede me into the room. Because I'm a fucking gentleman.

She glances up at me, then quickly away.

She's been doing that all night. Sitting across from her at dinner, I couldn't help but notice how she would steal glances and quickly look away as soon as I met her gaze.

She was picturing me naked.

There's no doubt in my mind.

Of course she was. I would've been doing the same thing if I had been the one who walked in on her ironing her clothes in the nude.

Not that I would ever do that. I know who is staying in every single room in this palace, and at any given time, I know if they are actually *in* those rooms or not. I'm head of security. I take my job seriously.

There will never be a time when I walk in on Lady Linnea naked. At least not accidentally.

I shut that down right away.

There's no time I'm going to see her naked *purposefully,* either.

Definitely not that.

Whether or not Torin wants to be married to her, is in love with her, or even eventually somehow gets out of this engagement, it would be completely inappropriate for me to start anything with her.

As if she would even consider that.

I'm a bodyguard. I might be a step up or two from…I don't know, "the help", maybe…but I am definitely not the guy a duchess is going to be getting romantic with.

I shut the door behind us and watch my best friend cross to his desk. He sighs, shrugs out of his jacket, and rolls up the sleeves on his shirt. He loosens his tie and unbuttons the top button as if he's just horribly uncomfortable in general. He comes around the front of his desk and leans back on it, placing his hands on either side of his hips, clearly trying for a casual pose. Finally, he makes eye contact with Linnea. Who was standing perfectly still, her fingers linked in front of her, dressed impeccably and looking very—yes, I'm going to say it again—regal.

"I apologize if I insulted you," he starts.

I'm proud of him.

She tips her head. "I appreciate that."

"Of course you are an excellent representative for Cara."

She doesn't say anything. She doesn't need to. That's just a statement of fact.

This woman has lived in Cara for the past eleven years, while Torin has been in the United States. She's been doing the things that Diarmuid would've liked his *grandchildren*, the heirs to the throne, to be doing. She is the youthful face of the leadership in the country. To the people of the country as well as the world.

Cara is a tiny country that most people didn't even know of until Astrid and Alex Olsen became famous. Their fame is thanks to Linnea.

But she has studied world politics, history, and political science. She's met with world leaders from the countries of Europe that Cara trades with. She's established a relationship with the royal family of Denmark, Cara's closest ally. She's friends with the Prime Minister of the Faroe Islands. She is ready to be queen. She'll be excellent in the position.

Even Torin would admit that. That's not his beef with her at all.

"I can go to the summit myself," Linnea says. "You don't need to come."

Torin frowns at her. "I'll be going."

She lifts one shoulder. "Fine. We'll both go."

"*You* don't need to come."

"But I think we both know that's not true," she says calmly. "I've made the contacts there. I can introduce you."

"I'm capable of introducing myself."

"It will make them more comfortable to know we're working together and that I've filled you in on all of our prior discussions and where things stand."

Torin lifts a hand and pinches the bridge of his nose.

"She's right," I say. He knows it, but he so desperately wants Diarmuid to start seeing *him* as a leader, his pride could easily cause him to make all this much harder than it needs to be. Linnea can help him start several steps ahead.

He blows out a breath and drops his hand. He looks at her. "You have to stop encouraging my grandfather."

Now she does that thing where she draws herself up taller. "What do you think I'm encouraging him in?"

"You're encouraging him to see us as a couple."

"Your grandfather has seen us as a couple since you were five and I was four and our grandfathers got drunk playing poker together." She sighs. "Well, since Declan left anyway."

"I think he actually was really hoping we'd all stay away and Saoirse would take over," Torin mutters.

Saoirse is Torin's niece. His sister had her out of wedlock just after leaving Cara. She's the only O'Grady heir to not officially abdicate her title. If Torin hadn't returned home, she would have been next in line after Diarmuid stepped down. Or died. Which was a real concern after his third heart attack.

The biggest problem is that Saoirse is only eleven.

And the only time she's spent in Cara has been over the holidays.

"Maybe," Linnea agrees.

"You could tell him you don't want to marry me."

She crosses her arms. "But I do want to marry you."

Torin sighs.

I get the impression they've had this conversation. They've been here for a year together. I just got here.

When Torin first came back to Cara to rescind his abdication, the general wisdom was that he no longer needed me. I had been assigned to be his bodyguard while he was in the United States. I was chosen to play the part of his best friend and college roommate. Which I did. I also now have a master's degree in political science with a minor in criminal justice. And no student debt. But coming to Cara to keep him safe on a remote island in the middle of the North Atlantic, where there were already scads of security, seemed...unnecessary. And I'm an American. My family and friends were all in the States. Except for Torin. So I stayed behind.

The thing is, Torin has been my focus for a decade. Not just the guy I protected, but he'd become my best friend. More like a brother than anything.

Needless to say, Torin and I only lasted a year apart. He was restless and feeling frustrated. I was without direction. *He* had been my purpose. I came to Cara after only thirteen months. Gave up my life in the U.S., moved away from my family and the rest of my friends, to help Prince Torin become the best king, leader, and international influence he can possibly be.

And now I'm here, feeling the very familiar mix of exasperation and affection that I have felt for this man since the moment I met him.

"You mean that since we first talked about this, and you got to know me better, your decision to marry me hasn't changed?" Torin asks Linnea.

She shakes her head. "Marrying you is still the way for me to become queen. And I still want to do *that*."

"Still power-hungry, I see," he says. But there's no heat behind his words. I don't think he actually believes that she's power hungry.

She drops her hands, takes a deep breath, and blows it out. "I told you before, we'll get married, you'll become king, and then you can change the rule about the fact that an O'Grady has to be the one actually sitting on the throne. Change that rule, and you can leave again. I'll be left in charge. And we all know everything will be fine then."

Right now, Torin's mother, Ábria, is still recognized as a princess of Cara, but she has no official power since her husband, the O'Grady by blood, died. In Cara, the king and queen have equal power while they rule, but when the O'Grady leaves the throne, their spouse steps down as well.

Torin grits his teeth. "Except that I don't want to leave again."

She shrugs. "Then I guess we might as well set a wedding date."

I watch them volley this back and forth.

So he wants to be king, she wants to be queen, and the only way for that to happen is for them to get married. Which Torin doesn't want to do.

I think he's crazy. This gorgeous, intelligent, sassy woman who will actually be an incredible queen is willing to marry him. How terrible would that really be?

"What's the real problem here?" I ask.

Strangely, Torin and I have not talked about this. Not in depth. He told me that he doesn't want to marry her. And I've been picturing a snotty, bitchy woman who won't let him make any choices and thinks she's better than him.

That is not the impression I now have of Linnea.

I don't think he's opposed to marrying her because he doesn't like or respect her. Something else is going on.

"I want to do this now. I will be a good king."

"Not without help."

He takes a step forward. "And that's it. You believe everything my grandfather has told you. That I need your help. That I can't do this on my own. That you're the key to all good things for Cara."

She takes a step closer to him. "Yes. You haven't been here in *ten years*. You don't understand this country. I have been here. I have been dedicated. I have been learning. This has been my entire focus since I was four years old! Even when I thought I was going to marry Declan, he left, and I was in limbo for a decade until you came back, and then I suddenly had to shift my entire mentality around *this*, I have not wavered."

Torin takes a second to respond. Because...she's right.

"So you think you would be better at this than I will," Torin says.

"At leading Cara?" she asks. "Absolutely."

Torin takes another step closer, and my body tenses.

"I want the throne," he says firmly. "It is *my* family's legacy. *I* want to do this. And I want *him* to give it to *me*. Not to you. Not *us*. I want him to give it to *me* because of *me*."

Linnea studies him for a moment. I can read the tension in her body. But I'm struck by how she seems to be searching his eyes.

Then she says, "You have a lot of work to do then."

Her words aren't harsh. They're...true.

But Torin scowls. "Linnea—"

He takes another step forward, and that's it. I step in. "Enough." I don't say it loudly, but I say it firmly.

Their eyes snap toward me. Torin is frowning. Linnea's eyes are wide.

"You both need some time to cool off."

Torin looks at her, then back to me. "We've been having these conversations without you for a year."

"Well, I'm here now."

"You have an opinion about this, I take it?" Torin asks me.

"You know I do."

"Let's hear it."

Fine. He knows I don't hesitate to tell him what I think.

"You need to start showing your grandfather that Cara's best interest is your priority. Everyone knows Linnea going to that summit with you is in Cara's best interest. Take her with you. If you're worried that everyone at the summit will think you're a couple, why? Don't act like a couple. Act like a professional team. Split up. Talk to different people. Mingle, network. As long as you're not holding hands and kissing in the hallways, why would anyone think anything different?" I watch him process all of this. His shoulders start to relax, and he shifts his weight back on his heels.

I go on. "If she's been representing Cara all of this time, no one's going to jump to the conclusion that she's there as anything other than that now."

Torin takes all of that in, as he usually does when I advise him.

Linnea's gaze bounces back and forth between the two of us. Obviously, Torin and my interactions are new for her.

Finally, Torin nods. "Fine."

I'm not surprised. Torin very much respects my opinion, plus he depends on me to be objective in situations where he is not. And with Linnea Olsen, he definitely is not.

Linnea looks at him in surprise. "Fine? So I'll be going to the summit?"

Torin leans on his desk again. "Yes. That's what's in Cara's best interest."

Clearly, she was ready for a bigger, longer fight. But she nods. "All right. I'll clear my schedule."

She looks at me, seeming not sure what to say. Then she just tells me, "It was nice to meet you tonight, Jonah."

I really try, but I cannot help the smirk I give her. But I just nod my head without saying anything.

Then she steps around me and says, "Goodnight, gentlemen."

I wait until the door shuts behind her to laugh. "If she thinks you're a gentleman, I hate to think what the other men in this country are like."

Torin runs a hand through his hair. "Fuck. I do not handle myself well around her."

I nod. "Clearly."

"I keep forgetting that the only people who know about this arranged marriage are our families. I feel like it's weighing on me constantly."

"All that's weighing on you are your grandfather's expectations and judgments. And my friend, you deserve some of them."

He scowls. "That is not supportive."

"Telling you the truth is always supportive. It's going to take time to earn your grandfather's trust back. Linnea has his trust. It makes sense that he wants her at important meetings representing Cara."

"And it makes sense that he thinks that we need to *marry* so that she can actually be in charge?"

It does. He knows her and trusts that her ideas line up with his. The queen can do everything her husband can when it comes to laws, policies, and orders.

"Maybe," I tell him, honestly. "Until you can prove differently."

"I'm trying."

I nodded. "I know."

"Do you think I can prove it before he walks me down the aisle?"

I shrug. Probably not. The plan is for Torin to marry Linnea. I don't know how Torin can get out of this. But that's not what he wants to hear and it won't help at the moment to point that out. "I guess you better hope so. I didn't realize that your pseudo-fiancée was actually on board."

"Well, she's on board with being queen."

"Smart lady."

"*You're* supposed to be on my side," he nearly growls.

"Me pointing out facts doesn't mean I'm *not* on your side. I'm just saying she loves her country, she's been preparing to be queen, and she thinks she'd be good at it, so she's willing to do what it takes. You can't say that doesn't make sense."

"Why would she want to marry someone she's not in love with? We have no chemistry. She doesn't want to kiss me or fuck me. She really wants to live a life with a man she has no feelings for? No passion?"

That is a very good question. And Linnea Olsen kissing and fucking is *not* something I should spend a lot of time thinking about.

CHAPTER 6
JONAH

I'm reading in my room when I hear a knock on my door. It's nearly midnight.

"Yes?"

Sean, one of the main security guards inside the palace, pokes his head around the edge of my door. "You said you were to be notified if the prince or duchess left their rooms."

I set my book to the side. Dammit. What's Torin doing? "Yes."

"Lady Linnea is in the garden."

My heart thuds at the mention of her name. Fuck. That's not good.

"The garden?" I'm already getting out of bed. "Why?"

"She's going for a walk. I think she's perfectly safe," he hurries to tell me. "But you did say—"

"Yes. Thank you."

I was more worried that she'd be pissed off and try to go home tonight. But I do feel the need to check on her.

I understand that she and Torin have been having these disagreements ever since he returned. I understand that they believe they understand each other. That's great. I also understand that of the two of them, *she* feels more at home here in Cara, in the palace, and with the royal family than Torin does.

So why do I feel the need to go and be sure she's all right?

It's my job. Ensuring Torin doesn't make rash decisions or, when he does, that I mitigate the consequences, is second nature by now. And until their arranged marriage is officially over and done, Linnea is an extension of Torin in my mind.

That's what I tell myself anyway as I make my way downstairs, across the first floor, and out the French doors that lead into the solarium. I cross that space quickly as well and let myself out into the gardens that extend behind the palace. What starts as an elaborate flower garden turns into a hedge maze filled with benches, fountains, sculptures, and a butterfly farm. I don't know how far into the garden she's gone, but I know the layout and I'll simply keep going until I find her.

But I only make it to the first fountain.

She's sitting on the edge, watching the water spray up and fall in the white lights.

I take a moment to study her. A moment I know deep down that I shouldn't take.

Because she's beautiful and she looks sad, and those are a bad combination for a man who's already trying very hard not to notice or react to her beauty.

She's wearing a long silky robe, and she's barefoot. Which makes me frown. She should definitely have more clothes on than this. What does she have under that robe?

And why the fuck isn't she wearing shoes when she's outside? That's not safe.

"Duchess," I say softly, not wanting to startle her.

Still, she jumps slightly and swings to look at me.

"Oh. Jonah." She presses a hand to her chest. "I thought I'd be alone out here."

"Our security team is too good for you to really be alone at all while you're here," I tell her, moving closer.

She grimaces. "Not sure how I feel about that."

"You should feel safe."

"I also feel a little surveyed."

I incline my head. I won't argue. She's being watched. That's just a fact. How she feels about it is how she feels about it.

"Are you all right?" I ask. I take her lack of clothing and shoes to mean she's not going to be leaving the palace and that she just needed fresh air. Still, she looks vulnerable, and something inside me won't let me leave her.

She gives a short laugh. "Well, no. Not exactly. But I'm not in danger, or sick, or anything, if that's what you're asking."

"I'm asking if there's anything I can do to make you feel better. More secure. Happier."

She studies me. "Do you want to talk for a minute?"

"Do you want me to talk for a minute?"

The corner of her mouth curls. "So deferential."

If she ends up Torin's princess, she'll find out that is, in fact, not the case. At least, not all the time. I'm in charge. But I'm respectful and give in where I can so that Torin—and she—will not feel like I'm a demanding asshole all the time.

I can be laid back. I can have a good time. I know when to let Torin go and make a stupid decision or do something he'll definitely regret later. I resign myself to doing clean-up instead of prevention sometimes. I can't keep him under my thumb at all times or none of this will work long term.

But because I give him leeway, he knows when I say no, I mean no.

She'll learn too.

"I just want to make things as good for you as possible," I tell her honestly. "If you need someone to listen, I can do that."

She studies me. Then nods. "I do."

I move forward and sit next to her on the stone ledge surrounding the fountain. I leave more than a foot between us. I'm in joggers now and a Henley. It's almost July, and in Louisiana, I'd be in shorts and a tee. Or maybe shirtless. Louisiana is a fucking swamp. Literally. It's in the nineties right now during the day and humid as hell. But in Cara, the high tomorrow will be fifty-four degrees and right now it's about forty-six.

"Are you cold?" I ask her.

She shrugs. "I'm okay."

I don't believe that she's not feeling the chill, but she's from here, so maybe this doesn't feel cold to her. I turn toward her slightly and say, "What's on your mind?"

"You're Torin's best friend."

I nod.

"Maybe you can convince him to leave and let me lead Cara."

Ah. She doesn't want to share deep secrets. She wants an ally.

"I'm not going to do that," I tell her.

"Why not?"

"Because Torin wants to be king. And because I believe he should be."

"You think Torin should be king?" Linnea repeats.

"I do."

"Just because he wants to be?"

"Because he'll be good at it," I say. "It's his destiny."

Her brows arch, but she doesn't argue. "Do you think we should get married?"

There's a trickier question. They should because that's the plan. I know that the plan has always been to join the O'Grady and Olsen families. I know that the plan changed from Linnea and Declan to Linnea and Torin about twelve years ago. But that was the plan as of when I started as Torin's right hand. I also know that Alfred always believed that Torin would be the better king than Declan and believed that eventually Torin's leadership and loyalty would lead him back to Cara.

So when I first started, before I *knew* Torin, when he was just a job, before I cared about him, before I loved him like a brother, I knew the expectation was that he would return to Cara, marry Linnea, and take over the throne.

The plan made sense to me. I was all in.

He was going to be the king, Linnea was going to be the queen, and Diarmuid and Alfred's families were going to be united permanently. Their power, money, and gene pools would become one big, wonderful, influential family that would do great things for the world.

But then I did meet Torin. And I started to care about him. And he did become like a brother to me. And now I do care if he's happy.

So if Linnea can't make him happy, then no, I don't think they should get married.

But I finally say, "I do." Because, as Linnea herself pointed out, the plan is greater than any one person or couple.

And it's not like he'll be miserable with her. She's gorgeous, intelligent, strong, and will help him do amazing things. The kinds of things he *wants* to do.

Part of his resistance is simply because marrying Linnea is what his grandfather wants, and Torin is rebellious.

He needs to get over a few things.

"And you've told him that?" she asks.

"I haven't."

"Why not?"

"He hasn't asked me."

"You only give your opinion when asked?" She shakes her head. "See? Deferential."

I most certainly do not only give my opinion when asked. But in this case, my opinion doesn't matter. Torin wants the crown, and he has to marry Linnea to get it. It's really that simple.

He'll complain. He'll stall. He'll try to find a way out of it.

But eventually, he *will* marry her.

"Can I ask you a question?" I ask.

"Of course."

"Do you *want* to marry *him*?"

"I want to be queen."

"That isn't what I asked you."

"All right. No. But that might be in part because I don't know him."

"Do you think there's a possibility that you could like him? Or even love him? If you get to know him? And then possibly want to marry him? Is that what you're hoping for?"

She sighs. And I realize that I am tense waiting for her answer. It would be best for everyone if they liked one another. It would ultimately be the best thing of all if they loved each other. For them to be married, fulfilling the ultimate goal is the main objective, but would it be nice if everyone could be happy? In love? Glad it happened? Probably.

So why is my gut knotted with the idea of my best friend being in love with this woman?

I should want them to be in love.

"I've never been in love," she says, quietly. But she's not acting shy. More thoughtful than anything else. "I have no idea if I want that."

I stare at her for a long moment.

We have met in the past. Torin has spent holidays here in Cara, at the palace, with his family. And Diarmuid, committed to this plan to marry the two of them, has invited Linnea's family here when Torin's been home.

But again, I don't think she remembers me. She may know my name, because I have been a part of the entourage for so long, but we don't know one another.

I decide to be upfront with her. It shouldn't be a secret to her that I know a lot about her and that over the next few years, having a lot of opportunity for close proximity, I'm going to know her well.

No time like the present to get her used to the idea.

"I know that you've never really dated. Certainly never had a serious boyfriend."

Surprise does flicker across her face. But she's a very smart woman. And she's been in this world, with the royals and the upper echelons of society, long enough that it doesn't take her long to connect the dots.

"You've done an extensive background search on me?"

"I basically know everything about you."

She nods, clearly processing that. "I see. At least you know facts."

"Yes. Facts."

"But you don't know how I feel about those facts."

"I would be very interested in knowing your feelings about those facts, actually."

She tips her head and seems to be thinking for a moment. Perhaps, trying to figure out why I would want to know all of her feelings.

Indeed, I don't actually need to know them. The facts are enough. But understanding Torin and why he does the things he does definitely helps me be better at my job.

"All right. I think it might be easier if I'm *not* in love with Torin."

I frown. "Why is that?"

"Because I have a job to do. So does he. We'll be leading this country. I think we'll be more objective about that, able to have honest *discussions* about decisions that need to be made, if we don't have a lot of other emotions and expectations involved."

I watch her face. She sounds and looks as if she's truly discussing a new professional position rather than her marriage.

"You really don't want to have deeper feelings for your *husband*?" I press. Then I go even further. "And the father of your children?"

She does flinch then. But she shakes her head. "I'm so tired of having my emotions wrapped up in the O'Grady men," she finally says. "I've just decided to focus on the job."

"You do have emotions involved here, then?"

"I *did*," she corrects.

I ignore the stab of what I can only assume is jealousy at hearing that she had some feelings for Torin, even if they were in the past.

"Go on," I urge.

She turns toward me. "I was told when I was just a little girl that I was going to be marrying a prince and that I would someday be queen of Cara."

I nod. I know all about the poker game that her grandfather played with Torin's grandfather that led to their arranged marriage.

"How did you take the news?" I asked her.

"I was thrilled," she says with a smile. "At the ripe old age of four, and for years after that. My family made me promise that I would never tell the secret, but whenever my friends were playing Princess and Queen, I knew that it was going to be real for me. And when I got to the age to start noticing boys and having crushes and romantic feelings, I knew that I was destined to marry Declan O'Grady. So, when people talked about him and how charming and charismatic and handsome he was, I absorbed it all into my impressionable young heart. I knew that someday he was going to be my prince. Literally."

I nod. This all makes complete sense. And I've literally never given it any thought.

"Which means very early on in my teenage crush years, I imprinted on Declan. I never even looked at another guy. I convinced myself I was in love with him. Whenever I imagined my future romances, it was always with Declan. I never let myself think of any other boy in a romantic way. And, of course, my family never would've let me date anyone else anyway. I was promised to Declan." She pauses and frowns. "And then when I was fifteen, imagine my shock and hurt when Declan left the country, abdicating the throne."

I frown. "I never thought about that."

She nods. "I don't think anyone in the family did. Well,

my mother was devastated. She had latched onto Declan in the same way. She was sure that her daughter would be queen. Anything and everything Declan did was amazing in her eyes. Then suddenly, he was gone. We went to my grandfather, wanting to know what had happened. He and Declan had always been close. My grandfather told me not to worry. That everything was going to be okay. But he could never assure us that Declan was coming home."

I nod again. I know that Alfred helped Declan invest in his original business and was part of the reason for Declan's success now. The two men had always stayed friends up until the very end of Alfred's life.

"After a year, I went to my grandfather in tears, wanting to know if I could move on. He said I could definitely move on from Declan. He was not coming back. My heart was broken. But my grandfather assured me that I was still going to be queen. He knew that Torin was going to be a wonderful husband for me. So I had to suddenly shift all of my thoughts and feelings, after years of believing it would be Declan, to Torin. Which was difficult," she tells me, meeting my gaze directly.

I can't help but chuckle slightly. "It was difficult to have feelings for Torin?"

She nods. "I've known the O'Grady boys all my life. Our grandfathers were friends. As were our parents. We spent a lot of time together growing up. Torin was always kind of a little shit."

I laugh harder. "Really? In what way? I'm not saying I don't believe you. I just want details."

A smile tugs at her lips. "He just was always pushing boundaries and testing the rules. He's always been rebellious, and he loves to be right."

I roll my eyes. He hasn't changed at all since childhood it seems.

"We used to get into debates about the monarchy," she says. "He used to argue that the King of Denmark never should have given the island to Tadgh O'Grady in the first place. That he should have made him a duke in Denmark, or just given him a chest of gold for saving his life. That giving the man an *island* could have actually been a test, and King Frederick might have expected Tadgh to fail. To try to settle the island and die doing it."

I shake my head. But that sounds just like Torin.

Cara had come to be under the rule of the O'Gradys after Torin's great-great-great grandfather, Tadgh, an Irish sailor, saved King Frederick the Seventh's life when pirates attacked their ship while sailing from Denmark to the Faroe Islands. The king gave Tadgh the island as a thank you.

"I, of course, argued that test or not, Tadgh and the rest of the people made it work so it doesn't matter now and that Cara deserves to exist and to continue on as it always has. I can't believe he now thinks he can convince me that he *wants* to be king," she finishes with a mutter.

"So the arguing between the two of you is nothing new," I say.

"Absolutely not," she confirms. "When he found out that the arranged marriage had shifted to *him* and me, he started picking even more arguments. About history and politics and world events, always trying to trip me up and prove that *I* wasn't fit. He always wanted to debate that a representative government was better than a monarchy."

I'm grinning. I know that he tried to convince his grandfather of that very thing just before he abdicated. "I take it you didn't agree with getting rid of the monarchy?"

"Actually, I never said that a representative government

was a bad thing or that there isn't room in Cara to have more citizen input," she says. "But I did have issues with his proposition for the transition. It was too fast, and it was sloppy and would have left a lot of holes in how things are taken care of now."

I feel my eyes widen. I've heard Torin talk on and on about government structure for years. But I've tuned him out a lot of the time. It's mostly ranting.

Now though, I want to hear Linnea talk about it. For hours.

"How are things taken care of now?"

She looks surprised, but she says, "Well, it's not as if Diarmuid literally handles every single program and issue in the entire country personally and on his own. He has people overseeing various aspects of life. Education, healthcare, and so on. And those people are tasked with understanding the issues, talking to people, gathering information and ideas, and presenting solutions."

"That sounds representative. At least, kind of."

"It is," she agrees. "And Torin's plan didn't have a transition for those people. Everything was about electing people into new positions. Which I understand, but you have to ease into things, respect the people who have been there doing the work and know more than you do, and understand that not everything functions in real life the way it looks on paper."

I can't help it, I like her. I like that she's smart, that she cares this much, that she knows what the fuck she's talking about. But mostly I like that she'll push back against Torin and tell him when his ideas need work.

"Torin needs people like you around him," I tell her.

The earnestness in her expression shifts to something else. A true frown.

"He does," she agrees. "But...well, you can imagine that I went from a crush from a distance on the older, broody, handsome Declan to thinking I was going to have to marry this annoying, pretentious boy that...I wanted to hit with a baseball bat."

I understand. "I've *actually* hit him with my fist. More than once."

"That must have felt good."

"It did," I admit.

That gets another small smile. "He needs people like you around him too, I suspect."

"He does." I pause. "But as you were arguing with him and being annoyed by him, you were adjusting to the idea that you were going to marry him," I say, realizing it as I say it out loud.

She nods.

Of course she did. She believes that's her duty.

"And then he left," I say.

She blows out a breath. "Then he left. And even though no one but my family knew about the arranged marriage, I was humiliated. I figured I was part of the reason he was running away. And then he was gone for *ten years*. And I kept waiting to hear that it was all over. I could move on. In fact, I *tried* to move on. I went to college and thought, fine, I can date now. I don't have to worry about this anymore.

"But it was so ingrained in me, and I worried about Cara, and I was close to Diarmuid, and I knew he was worried and hurt. And I just could never shake it."

She frowns, and I can *feel* her frustration.

"I would try to go on dates," she says. "But I just could not let myself get close to the guys, thinking that at any moment, things would change and they would say, 'Linnea, all your dedication and hard work has been noticed. We want you to be queen. We changed all the rules, please come home and take the throne'. Or—" She sighs.

I watch her face, fascinated by the play of emotions over her features. Her frustration is clear, but there's also a hurt there. She gave up a social life all through high school and college because she believed she had a higher calling. I want to run a finger over the tiny wrinkle between her brows and smooth it away.

"Or I'd imagine one of the O'Grady boys would suddenly come home and I'd be called back because of the stupid arrangement. Even when I was *twenty,* I was still caught up in that. Because it was *so* important to my grandfather and Diarmuid. And I didn't know if it was it going to be Declan or Torin or Cian. Everything was always up in the air. I have felt in limbo for over a *decade.* And then, sure enough, Torin waltzes in the door as if nothing's happened and we should all just be grateful he's back. So I'm here, ready to do the job, ready to *help* him. And he acts like *I'm* this huge problem."

Wow.

She's right about all of it.

My best friend is such a jackass sometimes.

"I know all of this sounds pathetic. But since it started when I was so young, and my family has been fully committed to it, I just can't shake it. And I do believe that I will be a wonderful queen. So, here I am, all wrapped up in this, annoyed as hell at Torin, convinced I will be better at it than he will, and no, I just can't make myself care that there's no love or passion or even lust between us. The job of being queen is bigger than that to me. If he and I have to give that up for the greater good of Cara, then we should be willing to do that."

And that hits me as sad and just wrong. Not for the first time, but stronger now.

This woman has given this mess her focus for her entire life, and Torin needs to at least respect that.

"Duchess," I say, my voice a little raspier than I expected. "We're going to figure all of this out. For everyone. It's going to be okay."

I want to make it even better than okay.

Which could be a problem. Because the goal is Torin on the throne and the O'Grady and Olsen families united. Everyone being 'better than okay' isn't in the fine print.

She gives me a smile that seems sad. I hate that.

"I know *he* is your responsibility. It's not your job to make *me* okay," she says.

Technically, it would be. If she was engaged to Torin. But the knot in my stomach is telling me that *that's* getting further and further away from happening.

And yet...I can't shake the *need* to say, "I'm still going to be sure you are."

Our gazes lock and we just stare at each other for a long, heavy moment.

Then I say, "Time to go back inside, Your Grace."

She swallows, then nods.

I escort her all the way back to her bedroom door. Right next to mine.

"Thanks for the talk," she says, stopping before her door and turning to me. "Maybe I shouldn't have spilled all of that to you, told you how annoying I find your best friend. The future king."

I smile. "You can talk to me about that any time. Trust me. No one knows how annoying he can be better than me."

She smiles, a true, genuine smile. "Thank you. That's...a relief. I can't say those things to anyone else."

"Any time." And I mean that.

Then she says something terrible.

"As you know, I haven't had a lot of men—okay, *any* men—walk me to my door. I don't know what to do now."

And that's all it takes for my imagination to flash with thoughts of pressing her against the door, tunneling my fingers into her hair, taking her mouth...

I have to clear my throat. "You say goodnight, then you go inside," I say. Firmly. For myself, if not for her.

She nods. "Okay. Goodnight, Jonah."

Fuck, her saying my name, her voice a little soft and husky...

Dammit.

"Goodnight, Duchess."

And as I turn away and go to my door, it's not lost on me that my room puts me *between* her and Torin.

But I refuse to think of that as symbolic.

It doesn't mean a thing.

CHAPTER 7
LINNEA

My phone lights up with another social media notification from the podcast I follow. The podcast *Wait 'Til I Tell Ye* passes on the news and gossip—especially the royal gossip—from the island and even does stories on things like pet adoption drives, skincare tips, and home decorating ideas during their three-hour daily show. They're not recording tonight, but they're posting on their social media channels because the two hosts, Lindsey and Jen, are down at the pub tonight.

The pub where Torin and Jonah are celebrating Jonah's birthday.

Wait *'Til I Tell Ye* post:
Lindsey: He's usually behind the scenes, but tonight, ladies, Prince Torin's bodyguard, and best friend, Jonah Greene, is celebrating his birthday! Come on down for a birthday shot on the Crown Prince!

I smile as I set the hot cookie sheet on the cooling rack.

Needless to say, whenever Torin is out in public, he gets plenty of attention, but it sounds like Jonah is, appropriately, the star tonight.

He's always in Torin's shadow and I'm so happy that Jonah is getting some special attention from Torin. I know that Torin cares about and appreciates Jonah, but I'm very glad he's showing that publicly. I'm sure Jonah tried to talk him out of it. I'm sure he's trying to brush it all off. I'm sure he gave in only after other members of the security team assured him that they were on top of everything and he could just relax.

I wish I could be there.

I push that thought to the back of my mind.

There's no reason for me to be there. It wouldn't make sense. Explaining why I'm there wouldn't be worth it. Yes, Jonah and I are friends, but connecting those dots for people would lead to revealing how much time I spend at the palace with the prince and his bodyguard and would, no doubt, lead to speculation about Torin and me that would annoy his royal highness.

I roll my eyes. Wouldn't want that.

My phone pings again, and I lean over to read the new notification.

It's a text from my sister.

> Astrid: Tell me two nice things about Miles because at the moment I can't think of even one thing I like about him.

I laugh and reach for my phone. It's just after three p.m.

in Portland. The time and the mention of Miles means that she just finished a physical therapy session.

Astrid adores Miles. He's been her PT since day one in the hospital after her injury, and they're best friends.

> He's hilarious. He's helped you recover. He puts up with your sassy shit. There, that's three.

Where I have to be composed and always polished, Astrid is feisty and speaks her mind. Especially since the fall. The fall that happened from the uneven bars in the middle of her routine during the qualifying round for the Olympics. She was in the lead. She was absolutely going to make the team. Everyone believed she was on her way to the gold.

And then suddenly, she was lying on the floor. And there was a stretcher. And an emergency room. And surgery.

Now she moves a little slower, and she has pain and it's frustrating for her. It also kills me a little every time I notice it.

It's why *I* love Miles. He helps her. He coaches her. He doesn't let her frustration and attitude get to him. He keeps her going.

> Omg, don't ever tell him you think he's hilarious. You will get stupid jokes and memes and GIFs from him for the rest of your life.

I laugh.

> Thanks for the warning.

> So what are you doing right now? Are you in bed yet?

It's just after eleven, but she knows I'm a night owl. We often text at this time of day—late for me, mid-afternoon for her.

I look down at the six gigantic cookies I just pulled out of the oven in the deserted palace kitchen.

The six gigantic cookies that will join the other six gigantic cookies that are cooling on the counter. Which will join the other *twelve* gigantic cookies I've already decorated.

Just one of these cookies is equivalent in size to three regular cookies.

But I've made two dozen.

And the finished ones absolutely look like they were frosted and decorated by someone who has never frosted or decorated a cookie before in her life.

Because that's exactly what's happened here.

But it's fine. It's completely fine.

It's probably fine.

My sister isn't going to believe what I'm doing, so I snap a photo and send it along with, *baking cookies.*

I look at the cookies as I await her response.

Yes, this is fine.

Probably.

> Who is this and why do you have my sister's phone? And how do you know Miles? Because hilarious is stretching it, but you're right about him putting up with my shit.

I grin, feeling a few of the butterflies in my stomach over the cookies calm a little.

> I didn't make the dough or frosting. They were shipped here. I just followed the directions.

> I can tell you're at the palace. Why the hell would you be making your own cookies when you're there?

> Diarmuid wanted me here for some meetings tomorrow.

I live two hours from the palace and, while I could have made the trip in the morning, I enjoy coming early, having dinner, staying over, and enjoying a more relaxed morning before the meetings start.

I've done this dozens of times.

But I was especially eager to come this time.

Because I'd planned this surprise for Jonah's birthday.

> That doesn't explain the cookies. That actually makes it weirder.

> These are for Jonah's birthday.

> Jonah? Torin's bodyguard?

> Yes.

> Why?

> It's his birthday.

> You said that. Why are you making him cookies for his birthday?

> He's my friend.

I've never had a man who is a friend before. I have *a lot* of acquaintances. But no real friends. Not like Astrid is with Miles.

Well, until now.

In fact, in the past nine months or so, Jonah has become my best friend. I don't know how he would feel about knowing that, but he knows things about me no one else does. Especially about one important area of my life. My love life. My sex life.

Or lack thereof.

He knows that Torin and I aren't in love. He knows we aren't sleeping together. And he knows that I'm not sleeping with anyone else either. He just...knows. Those are things I haven't *had to* tell him.

But I *have* told Jonah things I can't tell anyone else.

I can't tell my mother when I'm pissed at Torin. I can't tell her that Torin does *not* want to marry me. She wants to believe Torin is perfect—as a future king and my future husband.

I can't tell Diarmuid when I'm frustrated with Torin's reluctance toward...everything. Because *I* want him to think Torin is getting more responsible and taking things seriously. Because he has to be king. At least long enough to change the law that says an O'Grady must sit on the throne.

I can't tell my friends or sister that I'm not attracted to my pseudo-fiancé. They'll think I'm crazy or that I'm just being stubborn. Torin is handsome, charming, funny, and intelligent. He seems like the perfect man. Every single media piece written about him goes on and on about all of those things. I might be the only woman in the world who *isn't* attracted to him.

But I can talk to Jonah about all of these things. Because he knows Torin. He knows our situation. He knows that neither of us wants to be *married* to the other and that we're at a stalemate about what happens next.

I stand, tapping my finger against the marble countertop, waiting for her response. It's taking a really long time.

> That's…interesting.

I frown. It is?

> How so?

> Is baking a new hobby for you I didn't know about?

> No. I wouldn't say that.

> Did you make Torin cookies for his birthday?

I chew on my lower lip.

No, I didn't make Torin anything for his birthday but… I'm not sure Torin and I *are* friends. Engaged to be engaged, yes. Friends? Not exactly.

> No.

> Did you make the king cookies for his birthday?

> No.

> Did you make Dad cookies for his birthday?

> No.

> Did you make Torin's butler cookies for his birthday? Or any of the other bodyguards?

Fuck. This sounds bad when she spells it out like that.

> No.

> I see.

> I'm not friends with any of them.

> You don't care enough about Diarmuid or Dad to make them cookies?

I don't reply to that.

I look at the cookies spread out over the marble countertops in the palace kitchen.

I probably went overboard.

Jonah is a big guy with a big sweet tooth—and I promptly shut down any further thoughts about his size and the fact that I've noticed it repeatedly over the past several months. But it's difficult *not* to notice it. His height—six-four. The size of his hands—big enough to span my entire lower back as he guides me through doors and crowds. And logically then, big enough to span most of my ass. Or my breast...twice.

I lift a hand and rub my forehead. I *have* to stop that. I can't think about how easily he could lift and carry me. How big his feet are. How wide his shoulders are. How deep his voice is.

Okay, his voice isn't about his size. But I also really like it...

> How good of friends are you and Jonah?

I can't tell my sister the things Jonah and I talk about. She doesn't need to know. She would worry if she knew I was prepared to enter a loveless, sexless marriage.

> We just spend a lot of time together. He's always with Torin. And we've gotten to know each other. I just thought this would be nice.

> It is nice.

I stare at the cookies.

I probably shouldn't be making him cookies.

But he *is* my friend. And he loves these cookies. Sure, I made too many, but is there such a thing as doing too much for someone you care about?

And...I want to do something for him that makes him smile *that* smile. The one that he doesn't let show very often. The one that makes him seem more approachable, I suppose.

He's always so in control, so in charge, so decisive and sure. But every once in a while, he relaxes and lets his guard down. Like when it's just him and me and Torin, and Torin and I aren't arguing, and we're outside of the palace, and we're just hanging out.

That doesn't happen often, but, for instance, when we were in D.C. for the energy summit, and Torin and I had both had successful meetings—separately, of course—and the three of us were having a drink in Torin's suite, and we were all happy and on the same page.

Jonah was relaxed then. He was happy. He wasn't refereeing between Torin and me. He wasn't on guard, thinking about our safety, or taking care of either of us, making sure we had our phones, coats, water, coffee, or anything else we might need.

We were just all...us.

Then he smiled. A relaxed, regular-guy smile.

And I want to see that smile again and again.

I press my hand to my stomach as I think about the *other* smiles of his.

There's the one that we exchange sometimes when Torin gets on one of his rants about something. It can be his grandfather. It can be some decision the U.S. president made. It can be something his younger brother did. Torin is a passionate guy. There's very little that he doesn't feel strongly about.

There's also the smile Jonah gives me when he's standing nearby as I'm meeting with someone or 'chatting' with someone important at a cocktail party. I'll catch his eye, and he'll give me a smile that seems part encouraging, part impressed, and part...proud.

It always makes me feel like there's a warm bubble expanding in my chest and then bursting open and flooding me with tingles.

Does it really make me feel that good to know my *bodyguard* is *proud* of me as I meet with leaders from various areas of science, business, and public policy? Something I've been doing for years on my own? But yes, it does. Jonah is paying attention, and he thinks I'm doing a good job.

And then there's the smile he gives me when I first walk into a room.

Any room. Any time. No matter what the situation. No matter how I'm dressed. When we're both in the same room, we seem to search each other out, and the first moment we make eye contact, he always gives me the same smile. I can't really describe that one, but the warm bubble and feel-good tingles in the professional settings feel like a spark of static electricity compared to what that smile does to me. That smile makes me feel like I touched a live wire and got a jolt of heat and power that spreads a lot further than just my chest.

A lot *lower* than just my chest.

I swallow.

Dammit. This is not good. I know that.

But I can't help it.

Dirty thoughts about my future husband's best friend are inappropriate. Dirty thoughts about *my* future bodyguard—and hell, he's my *current* bodyguard whenever I'm with Torin—are just plain torturous.

Isn't it just perfect that I finally find myself attracted to someone, and he's probably the most off-limits man I know?

Dammit. I really shouldn't have made him all these cookies, should I?

This is basically like twenty-four colorful disks of sugar screaming *I want you and like you so much*.

Astrid finally replies.

> Have you kissed him?

I stare at her message. Why would she ask that? Why would she jump to that all of a sudden? And why are my cheeks hot?

> No!!!!

> But you've thought about it, right?

> No.

I'm lying, of course. I've thought about it a lot.

> Liar.

> I did.

> You've thought about kissing Jonah???

> Lol! No. I kissed Miles.

> What???!!

> Of course I did. He's good-looking and funny and we're together All. The. Time. And he takes care of me, makes me feel safe, all of that. So yeah, I kissed him one time. But it was just kind of...misplaced affection. Hero worship or something. Don't worry. It will be like kissing your brother.

I read her message three times.

Oh...wow.

First, she kissed Miles once.

I had no idea.

But it wasn't good. Or at least, it wasn't anything that turned into anything.

Okay, so that's...good.

Yeah, that's probably good. She's right. If she felt that way about Miles, then it's no big deal that I feel *affection* for Jonah.

And it's fine that I made him cookies.

We've been meeting in the kitchen for late-night snacks every time I'm at the palace overnight. We talk, we laugh, we share stories about silly things from our childhood to serious things like how we feel about politics.

So tonight I did something a little more because it's his birthday. No big deal.

If Torin had ever met me in the kitchen for a late-night snack, maybe I would have made him cookies for his birthday too.

> Hey, you okay?

>> Yes. Thanks for telling me about you and Miles. You made me feel like I'm not crazy.

> <heart eye emojis> I'm glad I can help you for a change. You know everything and are perfect at everything.

I feel the pang of missing her squeeze my heart. Then I turn my phone to snap a photo of my worst cookie decorating attempts. I send it to her.

>> Not perfect at everything.

> Oh my god...okay, I love knowing that there is actually one thing you clearly suck at.

I laugh.

>> I need to finish horribly frosting these cookies.

> Fine. I'm leaving you alone now, before I say anything inappropriate about how nice Jonah's cookies probably are, because Miles is here and he'll tell me to stop being a brat. Because he's got nice cookies too, but I'm telling you, I'm glad I never slept with him because he's annoying as fuck.

I laugh, and then I shake my head. God bless Miles Stafford.

> I love you.

> Love you too.

I pull up Miles' number and text him.

> She's extra sassy today. She probably needs extra laps or reps or whatever.

His response comes within a minute.

> Miles: <eyeroll emoji> An extra five miles on the run, you say? Well, okay.

I laugh. Then laugh harder when I get Astrid's next text.

> Astrid: Traitor. I hope your vibrator runs out of charge right before you get there.

I set my phone down, and once again look over the plethora of cookies I have before me.

Jonah knows very well I didn't make Torin cookies for his birthday. Or the king. Or anyone else. He knows everything I do.

So how in the hell is Jonah going to walk in here and *not* immediately know that I have a crush on him?

I'm sure he thinks I'm a little pathetic anyway. I've been pawned off on a man who doesn't want me, and I'm actually *agreeing* to it. Not because I have a crush on Torin or want him to love me or anything, but I've been avoiding other men, saving myself for...what?

Ugh.

I need to get rid of these cookies.

But as I'm reaching for the tray I decorated first, I pause.

Jonah's been here in Cara for over a year. Away from home. Away from so many things that he's missed. He always smiles nostalgically when he talks about home. I don't think he regrets coming here, but that doesn't mean he doesn't miss being there.

And thinking about that smile makes me pick up the bag of chocolate icing and start swirling it onto the bare chocolate cookies.

Because...I want another one of Jonah's smiles tonight. The happy, surprised smile that I've seen only once before, when Torin told him they were going back to the States just before Christmas.

He's never surprised. He always knows what's going to happen because he's in charge of what's going to happen. He makes the plans. He gives the orders.

But this will surprise him.

And I *do* want to stay here in the kitchen until I see him. It's his birthday. I want to at least wish my very-good-friend-who-can't-be-anything-else a happy birthday.

My phone pings again, and I lean over, almost expecting it to be another message from Astrid.

Instead, it's a notice from the podcast.

. . .

Wait 'Til I Tell Ye post:
   Jen: It was so nice of all you ladies to give the birthday boy a kiss! 😉 Thanks for being so generous. LOL! I know he's feeling very good about this next year now! 😊 Thanks for coming out for the celebration tonight!

I frown and lean in closer to read that again. Wait, what? Jonah was getting birthday *kisses* at the pub?

That's...not what I imagined when I pictured them out on the town.

I also don't like the flutter of jealousy that invokes.

I can't be jealous of Jonah getting kisses from other women.

If I were to kiss him...which I am *not* going to do...it would be like kissing my brother. Just like Astrid said. So why should I care if he kisses other people?

It doesn't matter at all.

He's my *friend*.

That's it.

Jonah is the closest I have been to a man outside of my own family in...ever.

And the only man *inside* my family that I've been close to was my grandfather.

My brother Alex is great. But he's my younger brother. I've always felt responsible for him. I don't confide in him. I take care of him.

I was close to my grandfather, but it's been years since we talked about my hopes and dreams and worries and plans. Even before his dementia got bad and he couldn't really talk about it all.

Jonah is the first person I've really confided any fears or worries to in a very, very long time. I've prided myself on seeming confident and composed and ready for whatever lies ahead.

He knows better.

I like our friendship. I like feeling like he's taking care of me. I like the way he watches me when I enter a room. I like the way that I can search a room for him and find him, his eyes on me no matter where we are. I know that I can text him at any time of the day or night, and he'll respond. I like knowing that tonight when he gets home from the pub he will stop here in the kitchen.

Because I know he knows I'm at the palace tonight. Jonah *always* knows things like that. Even though he and Torin were out and didn't join us for dinner, I know he knows I'm here.

We've developed some easy habits that I'll admit are comforting, but they also cause butterflies.

Like right now. It's eleven twenty and I can hear footsteps coming down the hall.

"Duchess, you're here."

I turn to find him leaning against the doorway. His hands are tucked in his pants pockets, and he has a goofy smile on his face.

Okay, I like *that* smile too. It's new. Ish. It's his I'm-really-glad-to-see-you smile. But it's a little bigger and wider than usual. Maybe because there's no one else around.

"I'm here," I say with a smile. "I didn't know if I'd see you."

"I came back early, hoping you'd be here. In the kitchen."

That makes my heart flip. Eleven *is* early to leave the pub. But he came back hoping I'd be here? See…how am I not supposed to have a crush on him?

Dammit. I have a crush on my fiancé's best friend. That's not good.

CHAPTER 8
LINNEA

I turn to face him, bracing my hands on the counter behind me. The island is between us, but I still drink in the sight of him. He's wearing blue jeans, and a long-sleeved black shirt that molds to that chest and those shoulders...

Yeah, there's nothing wrong with my hormones.

"I'm glad you came back early," I tell him.

He hasn't noticed the cookies yet. They're taking up all the counter space, but he hasn't looked away from me yet.

My heart starts thudding faster in my chest.

He pushes away from the doorway and takes a few steps toward me. He does not walk a straight line.

I feel myself grinning. "I take it you had a few birthday drinks?" He's obviously more than a little tipsy.

He makes it to the huge island in the middle of the kitchen and braces his hands on it. But he's still looking at me. "People were very friendly."

I feel a little stab of jealousy again thinking about the 'friendly' kisses, but I laugh. "Did you have a good time?"

"I did. But I wanted you to be there."

I feel my brows arch. Wow, maybe the liquor has loosened his tongue a bit. He never says things like that. "Really?"

He nods. "But you're not a pub girl, are you?"

"Well, that's a pretty big assumption," I tell him. "I actually go to the pub a lot. When my brother and sister are in town, we're there almost every night. They're local celebrities, you know. And they're definitely pub people. I love the pub. I go for lunch on a regular basis. Molly does a great job."

He sinks down onto one of the stools on his side of the counter and leans in, his brow furrowed. "Who's Molly?"

"The owner of the pub."

"Oh," he says, his head bobbing. "The sweet one. Black curly hair."

"No, that's Shannon. Molly's daughter."

He snaps his fingers. "Right." He pins me with a gaze that's surprisingly steady. "You know the people that own the pub?"

I smile at his amazement. "I know the people that own all the businesses in town. Did Shannon make you the special birthday drink?"

"The one with lime juice?" he asks.

"Yes."

"Three of them," he says. Then shakes his head. "Probably two too many."

I chuckle. "Molly made that one up. Decided to give it away to the birthday boy or girl. But she made it *very* strong and kind of nasty. She didn't want people to like it. She wanted them to get drunk fast and move their birthday celebrations back home."

He grins, and it's wobbly and adorable. This man is incredibly handsome, and he always has an intense air about him. He is always in charge, always knows every detail of what's going on around him, and I swear I don't take a breath that he's not aware of, but right now all of his inhibitions are down and he's just happy and feeling good. I like this side of him. Too. I like the other side of him a lot as well. Dammit.

"I'm not sure that's working out for her," he says.

"It doesn't always, and it annoys her. But you're probably too big for just one drink to affect you much."

He lifts a brow. "I'm too big?"

"You're..." I stop, realizing maybe I shouldn't be talking about how big he is. Because that always takes my mind into dangerous territory. "So tall," I finish weakly.

He laughs. "I can definitely hold my liquor. I've been drinking with three crazy Irishmen and a Brit for a decade."

God, I love his laugh. I grin. I've done some research of my own. I know about Colin, the other Irishman besides Cian, and Henry, the Brit. They are Fiona's and Cian's bodyguards. It seems all the men are good friends. Three more people he left behind to come to Cara.

Jonah's studying me. "If you *are* a pub girl, and you know all the people, why didn't you come down?"

"Torin doesn't think we should be socializing together. People might start talking."

Jonah shakes his head. "But it was *my* birthday."

"You didn't invite me."

He leans in, resting his forearms on the countertop. "Would you have come if I'd invited you?"

Good question. Torin really has tried to make a point

that we should not be seen socializing. He thinks it would be too easy for people to make the jump that there's something more going on between us. I think he's overreacting, but it's fine. We don't need to socialize now. There will be plenty of that required once we're married.

But looking at Jonah now, I nod. "I think I would have."

"Linnea—" He takes a deep breath. Then he sits up straighter. "What is that smell?"

I grin, then turn and take one of the finished trays of cookies from the countertop next to me. I pivot back, presenting them to him, nervous and excited. "Surprise."

His mouth falls open. "Are those *Well, Frost Me*?" He says the name of the cookie company reverently.

I nod. "Yes."

"But...how?"

"I called and talked to them. They couldn't ship cookies already assembled. They might have gotten broken or messy. But we arranged for them to ship me the dough, icing, and the other decorations in refrigerated containers. So I baked and decorated them here."

His eyes move from the tray of cookies to my face.

"These are my favorite."

"I know."

"I haven't had these since I left the U.S.."

"I know."

"How do you know?"

I think about that, but I shrug. "I'm not sure. I guess I heard you and Torin talk about them. I know that you miss them a lot. Just like you miss your favorite coffee and pizza and your gym, and your friends and family, and bowling."

He staring at me as if he's never seen me before.

"You know all that?" He says it softly, almost as if he doesn't mean to say it out loud.

I set the cookies down in front of him. "Yeah."

"And you went to all this trouble."

"Well, you gave up so much to come here. To help Torin. You gave up almost *everything*," I say.

This has struck me several times in the time I've known him. Yes, when he and Torin have gone back to the states, which does happen periodically when Torin gets restless or frustrated, Jonah is able to see his friends and family, and probably gets the pizza and coffee that he's missed. But he does spend large chunks of time here in Cara, far away from all of the things that he loved and grew up with. "Besides," I add. "It's your birthday."

He's staring at the cookies, but then he lifts his head.

"You are...extraordinary."

I scoff and dip my head. "Come on. They're just cookies."

"They are. But they're cookies that took you paying attention. And then going to a lot of trouble."

"You go to a lot of trouble for me all the time."

"It's my job."

I lift my head and meet his gaze. "Is it?"

Of course it is. But a little part of me feels almost hurt that he would brush off the things he does for me simply as being something he's paid to do.

But there's a bigger part of me that knows that that's not entirely true. I don't know where that confidence comes from, but I know it. There are little things he does for me all the time that show he's paying attention. That he's taken inventory of things that I like and need. Even without me having to say a word. Do I believe that Jonah Greene is exceptionally good at his job? Yes, of course. But do I think he goes above and beyond for me? Yes.

And has that given me confusing feelings when I let myself think about it too much?

Absolutely.

Which is why I don't think about it often.

But right now, it's staring me in the face.

"You do this for a lot of people," he finally says.

"What do you mean?"

"Like at the pub," he says. "You don't just know who Molly and Shannon are, but you actually know things about them, don't you?"

I frown, confused. "Of course."

"You probably know several people who go there regularly, too. And you know things about them as well."

He's not wrong, but I don't say anything. I just watch him.

"Like the kitchen staff in here. The first time we ever met down here at night, you told me facts about the people who work here. And not just their names or what they do here, but facts about their families. What they're good at. Things they do outside of the palace."

I swallow and grip the edge of the counter. I don't know why, but I feel warmth swirling through me. "So?" I ask. "I know things about them. That's not a big deal."

"Yes, it is. Because you see them. You pay attention. You talk to them. Everyone you meet is just a person. There are no separations or classes or levels."

I frown. "Of course not."

He laughs slightly. "You're a fucking duchess, Linnea. But you don't act like one. I mean, you do," he says, shaking his head as if that isn't coming out quite right. "You carry yourself like royalty. You speak and dress and eat and fucking get in and out of cars like royalty. But you still know that your driver takes his coffee with two creamers and two sugars, the butler at the front of the palace has a nephew who loves hockey—and you got him a puck signed by your brother—and that Frieda, the woman who takes care of your room when you're here, is allergic to cranberries, so you never have her bring you anything with cranberries to your room, not even the cranberry scones or the cranberry tea you really love for breakfast."

I'm staring at him. How does he *know* all of this?

"Ren actually likes his coffee with two creamers and *one* sugar," I finally say.

Jonah laughs softly and shakes his head. "Exactly. You see people. You get to know them. You care about them."

I look at him, taking in what he's saying. I accept it. He's right. I love to learn about other people. "I guess my own life feels very simple. Kind of boring."

He scoffs. "You're a duchess. You're related to a hockey star and an almost Olympic gold medalist. Your grandfather's best friend is a king. You're engaged to a prince."

I shake my head. "Well, first, all of that is about other people. The people around me. And my life feels like a blank white sheet of paper. Everything that's interesting has been written by somebody else. Everything that you just talked about are circumstances that came into my life because of someone else's decisions. I helped Alex and Astrid, but it's their talent that's taken them to where they are. My family's heritage has nothing to do with me. Even my engagement is because of my grandfather."

He doesn't say anything for a moment. Then he asks, "If that's how you see it, that's what makes you interested in other people?"

"Other people have had experiences that I haven't. That I never will. They know trades that I know nothing about. They have hobbies I've never tried. They've been places I've never been. Some of them have children. I haven't done that."

"Yet," he says. His voice is low, and it's almost as if he said it to himself.

I don't comment on that. "People also have different relationships. Some people are extremely close to their parents in a way that I'm not. Some people have six older brothers. Some have been in love a dozen times. Some have fallen in love only once and have been with that person for fifty years." I smile. "Everyone has a different experience, and yes, I do find that interesting. I love to hear their stories." I prop my hip against the island. "Did you know that Anna was raised in Ireland?"

"The head of this kitchen?" he asks.

I'm not surprised he knows the names of everyone in the palace.

I nod. "She divorced her first husband after only three years of marriage and decided she was never going to get married again. But then one day, she literally bumped into a man on a sidewalk, spilled her coffee down the front of him, they fell madly in love in a weekend, and he whisked her off to Cara. She fell in love with the country and wanted to stay, but wanted to work. She's an extraordinary baker. So one day, she made her best cakes and cookies at home, came to the palace, and insisted she *had* to see the queen. Of course, they weren't going to let her in, but Princess Fiona was home and was in the front of the house. She came running to see what the commotion was about, and when she saw the cookies, she said *she* would take Anna to the queen. Of course, they had to be sure nothing was poisoned or anything like that, but Anna ended up having tea with Princess Fiona and Queen Roisin. Roisin hired her personally on the spot, and she's been here ever since. Her job seems so simple on the surface, but if you talk to her, you find out that every time there are guests, someone offers her a new job in *their* palace or home. Anna is madly in love, has beautiful children, and has a job that allows her to be something she's incredibly passionate about. And she's got amazing stories."

He's watching me with a huge smile.

"What?"

"And you're fascinated by her," he says. It's not a question.

I nod. "That experience, everything that she's done in her life, is something I will never experience."

"Getting divorced and spilling coffee on someone?"

"Taking a huge chance on my passion. And crashing into my soulmate out of the blue and falling head over heels like that."

The smile falls away from his face, and he takes in a sharp breath.

I want to ask so badly what he's thinking. But decide not to.

Something about it feels dangerous.

"These cookies are not as pretty as when they decorate them in the store, but you have to try one. I followed their directions perfectly, so they should at least taste good."

He also seems to shake the moment off. He looks down at the tray in front of him. "How many different kinds did you make?"

"Well, I know the store has six new cookies every week, and they rotate what's on the menu."

He nods. "That's part of the fun. You're never sure what you're going to get or when your favorite might come back up."

"So, when I explained the situation, I was able to talk

her into sending us all the cookies they're going to have this month."

His eyes round. "Who did you talk to?"

"The CEO."

He freezes. He blinks. Then he asks, "You talked to the CEO of *Well, Frost Me*?"

I nod. "Yes."

Slowly he nods. "Of course you did."

I put a hand on my hip. "Who should I have talked to?"

"I just…I guess I assumed you called a store and talked to the manager."

"I didn't know if a store manager would be able to do what I was asking. I knew the CEO would."

"And of course you were able to sweet talk the CEO."

I don't know why he's acting like this is some great feat. "When you need a question answered or something done, it's efficient, for everyone involved, to go to the people best able to answer the question or do the thing."

He smiles. "Of course, you're right, Duchess."

I frown, but say, "Besides, I wasn't sure what your favorite was. I know you really love chocolate, though."

There's something in his eyes as he looks at me now that makes a swirl of heat ripple through my stomach. I press my hand to my stomach, as if trying to quell it. Though I'm not sure I want to. I like it.

But again, there's a sense of danger, something hanging in the air around us.

"You know I like chocolate."

"Of course. It's pretty obvious."

"Every meal we have eaten together, except for the few where we've been traveling, Queen Roisin has been there," he says.

I'm not following. "Yes?"

"I don't think the queen knows that I prefer chocolate desserts."

Yes, well, the queen probably doesn't have a crush on her grandson's bodyguard. Nor does she love to watch him drag the tines of his fork between his lips or lick extra sauces from his spoon.

I clear my throat. "Well, I know Queen Roisin prefers lemon desserts," I say, trying to downplay the fact that I know details about him.

He nods. "Yes, she does."

I'm guessing he knows that because of reading something about her rather than because he just noticed.

He reaches out and plucks probably the ugliest cookie from the tray.

"That one?" I say with a laugh. "That was one of the first I did. I got better."

"Duchess," he says. "The fact that you did this at all makes me want to eat the ugly ones first. They might be the most delicious."

"Why would that be?"

"Because I can imagine you standing here, frowning, your lips pursed, concentrating so hard as you try to get it perfect. You always do everything right. I love the fact that this was a little outside of your comfort zone, and yet you did it for me."

I suck in a little breath. There's something in his voice, his eyes, or maybe both, that heightens that feeling of danger. And excitement.

His eyes stayed locked on mine as he takes a big bite. Then his eyes slide shut, and he groans. He chews and swallows, then looks at me. "Holy shit. I've missed these so much."

I can feel how wide and goofy my own grin is now. "I'm so glad you like them."

"I fucking love—" He breaks off. "This is amazing. Thank you."

"Of course." I almost say it's no big deal or no problem, or don't mention it, but I really like how much he likes this.

He gets up, goes to the refrigerator and fills a glass of water. He comes back and hands it to me, then takes his seat again.

I looked at the glass in my hand, then up at him. "Did you mean to get this for yourself?"

He looks at the water almost as if he didn't remember getting it. "No, that's for you."

He's always doing this. No matter where we go, he's always pressing glasses or bottles of water into my hand. He also seems to always have a shawl for me, no matter where we are. They don't always match what I'm wearing—most often he has my favorite jade green one—but it seems that whenever I might get chilly, he's there, draping one around my shoulders.

I've never asked him about this. Tonight seems the right time. "Why are you always giving me water?"

"Because you need it," he says around another bite of chocolate cookie.

He's already almost through with one entire giant cookie.

"I know that you know a lot about me, but you can't know when I'm thirsty, Jonah."

"No, but I know you get recurrent UTIs. Water is important for avoiding those."

I pause, realizing I'm lifting the glass of water to my mouth. I set it back down with a thunk. I'm staring at him. "*What?*"

He pushes the rest of the cookie into his mouth, wipes the corners of his lips, chews, and swallows. "You get chronic UTIs. You need to drink more water. You also need to drink less coffee, but I'm working on the water first."

As I'm staring at him, I realize that I've actually not had a UTI in about seven months.

That has to be a coincidence.

Right?

I feel my cheeks heat. "How do you know about the UTIs?"

He reaches for another cookie. The second ugliest. "I know everything about you."

"Including my personal medical history?"

His eyes come up to mine as he takes a bite out of the strawberries and cream cookie. I made a few of each of them, though I did make more of the three chocolate varieties.

"I have to know all about you to take care of you, Your Grace," he says.

His voice is low and rumbly, and it affects my stomach like everything else has.

I cling to the idea, however, that he knows something very personal and somewhat embarrassing about me.

"That feels invasive."

He nods. "I'm sure it does. I don't discuss it with other people. And it's strictly so that I can make sure you're healthy." He pauses and dips a finger in the chocolate frosting on his cookie. He lifts it to his mouth and licks it off.

I am startled by the way it makes my stomach, and okay, lower muscles too, clench.

I *definitely* don't need to go to my doctor about hormonal issues.

"But you only had one since I've been here," he says. "And that was over seven months ago."

I can't deny it. Obviously, he knows the truth.

And it's a good thing I haven't had an infection.

"And you're taking credit for that." I cross my arms over my stomach.

He nods. "Yes, I am."

"I can't believe you studied my personal medical history."

He shakes his head. "I don't study it. There are things that I check for. Things I need to know on a regular basis while I'm with you, while traveling. Some of it I find out as we're going along."

"Things like?"

"Like that your last gynecologic exam was perfectly fine and normal."

I feel my mouth drop open. "You looked at my last GYN exam?"

"Didn't look for it or at it specifically. I skimmed over it while I was looking at other things."

I honestly don't know what to say. "I guess I didn't realize how well you would know me."

He nods. "Very well. But you can trust me," he said, his voice gentling. "I only know what I know so that I can take care of you."

See, that should probably not make me feel all warm and...aroused.

Fine, it makes me feel aroused. It shouldn't. It is invasive. The man is not my doctor, boyfriend, father, or anyone else who really needs to know these intimate details about my life.

But maybe he is.

He's supposed to be keeping me safe and healthy. I

think that the entire security structure around the royal family of Cara is a little overdone. Cara is a small country with very little reason for anyone to want to harm or even extort any of the royal members, but the king is adamant about their safety being taken extremely seriously. And I'm, sort of, one of them.

"Do you know all these things about Torin?"

"Of course."

"The king?"

He inclines his head. "Yes."

"Okay, I'm not mad."

The corner of his mouth tugs slightly just before he takes a bite of cookie, maybe trying to cover up his smile.

"You think it's funny that I might be mad?"

"No. I think it's funny that you think I might care that you're mad about this."

"You wouldn't care if I was mad?"

He sets the cookie down and brushes his hands together. "Your Grace, my job is to make sure that you're safe. Healthy. Happy. That you have everything you need. Whether that makes you mad, or not, is not a concern."

I study him. He means this, I can tell. And it's a very strange mix of emotions I feel.

"Does that mean that you will help me get out of marrying your best friend?"

CHAPTER 9
LINNEA

His brows arch. "So we're off the healthcare issue?"

"Well, you're saying that your job is to make sure I'm happy and have everything I need," I say. "I think I need one less fiancé."

"But you also think you need the throne." Despite how many drinks he had tonight, he pivots easily within the conversation.

I nod. "Any ideas how I can have both of those things?"

He shakes his head slowly. "No." He pauses. "But I've been working on it."

My eyes widen. "Really? You've been working on a way for me to have the throne but not have Torin?"

"If you think that I've been plotting some kind of assassination or kidnapping, you would be wrong."

I laugh. "I don't want him to die."

"I *have* been thinking about how to get you both what you want, though."

"But there really isn't a way," I say. "We both think we

want the throne. But neither of us wants to be married to the other."

He nods. "So far, that's where we're at."

For some reason, my heart is pounding.

Maybe it's just because I finally have someone taking me seriously.

He's not just hearing that I want the throne. He's not just hearing Torin and me complaining about not wanting to get married. He really wants us to be happy. What we want is as important to him as the greater good.

"Thank you," I finally tell him.

"For what?"

"For listening. For caring." I pause. "For being my friend."

He takes a deep breath, then blows it out. "You don't have to thank me for that."

"Right. It's your job."

"No." He pauses. "It's...my pleasure."

Oh.

Damn.

I like that.

"Well, you make me feel..."

He straightens on his stool and his eyes are suddenly laser-focused on mine. There's a heat, and intensity there.

"What do I make you feel, Duchess?"

I swallow hard. "Important," I say, my voice almost breathless. "Taken care of. Just...good."

He closes his eyes and I see his fist clench on the top of the counter.

For a moment I'm concerned. I round the edge of the island. I stop right in front of him and put my hand on his leg.

He sucks in a quick breath as his eyes snap open.

"Sorry. Should I have not said that?"

His eyes seemed to drill into mine. Then they drop to my mouth. Tingles cascade through my body.

He swallows hard now. Then he says, his voice husky, "No, Duchess. You probably should not have said that."

Something inside me tells me to step away. To put space between us. Maybe even to run.

But I don't do any of those things. I stand right there.

His entire body is tense, completely still.

"Why shouldn't I tell you that you make me feel good?" I ask.

A sound comes from his throat, almost like a groan. Then he swallows. And pins me with a direct gaze.

"Because I don't want anything more than that."

Heat washes over me. I suck in a little breath. "Then it's good that you make me feel good," I say softly.

Jonah tips his head back, looking at the ceiling. This time, his groan is very audible. "Duchess," he says, his voice tight. "You're killing me."

I don't understand everything that's happening, but I feel a little thrill at his words. A surge of power goes through me.

"How am I killing you?" I ask.

He sucks in a deep breath, then brings his head up to look at me. "You're my best friend's fiancée. My *boss's* fiancée," he adds.

Yep. Astrid and I just talked about that.

Still, I hear myself say, "Not officially. No one's proposed."

I'm not sure *why* I say those words. We both know it's as good as an engagement. Kind of. Without the emotion. Which actually makes it a pretty bad engagement.

"*He* should be the one making you feel good."

I tip my head to the side. "Well, that would be very nice. But that is not the situation we're in."

He just looks at me, his gaze roaming over my face, as if cataloguing every single detail. I swear he counts every one of my eyelashes.

Finally, he says, "I got a bunch of kisses at the pub for my birthday."

"So I read online," I tell him.

"Torin said it's a tradition."

"Well, Torin is the prince. I suppose he can make a new tradition if he wants to."

"That's what he said."

I give him a little grin. "But I don't think Torin was being the prince. I think he was being your wingman."

He doesn't grin as I expect him to. He looks at me very seriously suddenly. "It's one of the reasons I wished you were there."

I freeze. Then I straighten. "You..." I have to clear my throat. "You wished I was there because you were getting kisses for your birthday?"

I really think he's admitting this, at least in part, because of the liquor in his system. Jonah is usually too controlled to say things like this.

He nods. "I thought maybe you'd kiss me. And it would be okay. Because we were in public, and Torin was egging it on, and it's my birthday. We'd have a million excuses."

My gaze drops to his mouth and I realize that I absolutely would've kissed him. I would've been very glad for a reason.

An excuse.

"Because we need an excuse," I say quietly. My gaze is still on his mouth.

I watch his lips as he says, "Yeah. We do."

"Because if we don't have an excuse, and we just kissed, that would mean…"

"Something else," he fills in.

My gaze bounces back to his.

He's watching me with what I now know is heat. I've never had a man look at me like this, so it does feel strange. But I recognize it. It's like an instinct. I don't have to have experienced it before to know it.

I wet my lips. I suddenly want to know what it's like to kiss Jonah more than I've wanted anything in a very long time.

"There's something else I know about you."

"I thought you said you knew *everything* about me."

He nods. "I do. Facts anyway. But as you pointed out the first night, I don't always know how you feel about them."

"What do you know?"

"That of these boyfriends you've had—"

"I've never had a boyfriend," I interrupt. "I've gone on a couple of dates."

He swallows. "Right. I know that at the end of those dates, they didn't kiss you."

I feel my brows pull together. "How do you know that?"

"Does it matter?" He shrugs. "We have a collection of notes about you. They come from a lot of places. I suspect you told someone at some point. But—" He pauses, then blows out a breath. "I've read every fucking word anyone's given me about you."

Shock, and pleasure, and more heat cascade through me.

I press my hand to my stomach. I don't know how he, or anyone, knows about my dates. Probably a college acquaintance. I may have even told my mother or grandmother. They were always so concerned about my dating status and my relationships with other people. They were always worried about how it would affect my future with Torin. I might have assured them that I hadn't even kissed anyone else.

And no, it didn't matter how Jonah knew this.

"It's true."

"So you've never been kissed?" His voice is rough.

I know this is very hard for people to believe. I am a composed, sophisticated, thirty-one-year-old woman. And I've never been kissed.

"It's true."

He stands up from the stool. We are only inches apart. And I have zero impulse to step back.

In fact, I want to step closer. Jonah is a safe place for me. I know his body will be strong and warm, and I'll feel completely safe with him against me. I would love nothing more than for him to pull me into his arms and hug me.

He makes me feel secure. He makes me feel special. He knows my biggest secrets—that I am engaged to be married to a man who doesn't want me and that I'm considering it because I want to be queen. He knows that I have ambitions that mean I will agree to a loveless—possibly sexless—marriage.

If Torin and I decide to have children, we can do it without having sex with one another. We can do it with in vitro fertilization.

And if we do, Jonah will know that.

Hell, he knows about my recurrent UTIs.

He'll probably know how many times Torin and I kiss. If we ever do.

This man really does know everything about me. All the really weird, kind of messed up stuff. And yet he's still standing here, gazing down at me as if I'm something precious.

"How have you never been kissed?" he asks, as if in awe.

So, okay, fine. He can know this too.

"Have you ever had my grandmother's Danish layer cake?"

He blinks, clearly not following my seeming change in subject. "Um...no."

"It's this traditional cake that is layers of vanilla cake, pastry cream, and raspberry jam."

"Okay," he says.

"Lots of people make them, but my grandmother's is the *best*. Absolutely. I used to *beg* her for it on my birthday and any other special occasion I could think of. But, about eight years ago, her back got bad enough that it became too hard for her to stand and do a lot of baking, especially anything that took a long time or had a lot of extra steps. So she passed the recipe and instructions to my mom and my aunt. But it's not as good. No one's is as good. And I miss it. I would never expect her to do it for me now, but I still crave that cake the way she made it."

He's just listening. When I stop, he asks, "Is that somehow about kissing?"

"Do *you* ever crave my grandmother's Danish layer cake?" I ask.

"No."

"Because you've never had it," I tell him. "You can't miss something you've never had."

I see understanding dawn in his eyes. Then he shakes his head, almost as if he's sad. "You've avoided kissing because...of Torin?"

I lift a shoulder. "Well, it was because of Declan when a

boy tried to kiss me when I was fourteen, and I punched him in the nose. But after that...yeah. It was Torin."

"Dammit," he mutters.

"My grandfather kept telling me it was all going to work out. So, in the back of my mind, or deep in my heart, or something, I couldn't stop thinking that I was basically engaged. And I guess I knew that my marriage might not have love and passion. So, I didn't want to fall in love. Or have amazing kisses. Or sex. Because that way I wouldn't know what I was missing."

"Jesus, Duchess," he breathes out, almost as if he's in pain.

"So, I might not have kissed you at the pub," I tell him, now thinking about it. "I wouldn't have known what to do. I've never kissed anyone. I've definitely never made a move on anyone."

He steps in close. Nearly on top of me, and he lifts a hand to cup my face. "You wouldn't have needed to kiss me. I would've absolutely used the excuse to kiss you."

My eyes widen. "Even though I'm your boss's fiancée?"

"Yeah, well...it's my birthday," he says, his voice husky and deep.

His eyes are on my lips.

My entire body feels like it's jumping and tingling.

I've never been kissed. But oh my God, I want to be.

By Jonah Greene.

And no one else.

I reach up and cover the hand that's cupping my face.

"It's still your birthday," I tell him. It's still before midnight.

"But we're not at the pub."

"Did Torin say the new tradition is for only in the pub?"

"I guess he didn't."

"Then it's not breaking any rules if you kiss me here."

But the thing is...it's probably breaking several rules, actually.

"Still...*fuck*," he mutters. He drags his thumb along my jaw. "You've been avoiding it all this time."

"I have." I lean in. "But it's never been difficult to avoid before."

"Duchess," Jonah says, his low, deep voice rolling over me with a rumble.

"Yeah?"

"You're. Killing. Me."

I smile. "Until this moment, I thought that was a bad thing."

The corner of his mouth twitches. "You don't mind torturing me now?"

"I made you cookies."

"You did."

"Your *favorite* cookies."

"You did."

"Maybe you're just saying thank you for that." His thumb moves over my skin again, and tingles explode.

"You know what?" he asks.

"What?"

"That sounds like..." He leans in, his lips nearly against mine, his warm breath coasting over my lips. "...a very fucking good excuse."

Then his lips meet mine.

Just a gentle touch. Pressing sweetly, softly.

But he's so big and warm, he seems to wrap around me. The hand that's not touching my face steals to my lower back, and he pulls me up against him.

He's *hard* and big and *hot*.

I can taste the chocolate on his lips. His scent also

surrounds me. It's a combination of the chocolate and sugar but also a scent I've learned to associate with him. I don't know if it's cologne or his soap, but I always know when he's near because I can smell him.

But more than anything, it's just the feel of him. Him being this close and wanting to be this close to me. The intimacy of this act that I've never shared with anyone else.

Without thinking, I reach up and fist my hands in the front of his shirt. Then I hear a quiet, husky moan and it takes a moment to realize that it came from me.

That sound seems to unleash something in Jonah. He gives an answering moan and then I feel him sliding his hands into my hair and gripping loosely. Then he licks his tongue along my bottom lip.

Fire seems to shoot through me. I feel my nipples tighten, my pussy clench, and my entire body feels like it's melting. I grip his shirt tighter, and I can't hold back the louder moan that climbs up from my chest.

I feel his fingers tightening in my hair and a groan rumble through his body. The fact that I can feel his reaction to me is even more heady than hearing it.

Then suddenly, he's lifting his head, looking down at me, breathing fast.

"Fuck," he breathes. Almost as if he's just now realizing what we're doing.

Instinctively, my hands tighten in his shirt, keeping him close.

I stare up at him, then say the first thing that comes to mind, "More."

"Duchess..." The term has always sounded slightly affectionate.

Well, maybe *after* the first time in his bedroom when I

saw him naked. There was a hint of amusement and maybe a touch of condescension then.

But ever since then, it has seemed almost a term of endearment.

Now it sounds dirty.

And I love it.

I nod my head. "Please."

Now he *looks* as if I'm killing him.

Again, the little thrill of power and pleasure shoots through me.

"Jonah," I say softly. "*Please.*"

He stares at me. Not moving. Not speaking. But I feel his fingers flex in my hair.

My heart is racing, and I'm breathing fast.

Then he growls, "Fuck it."

The next thing I know, he's backing me up against the wall, and his mouth comes crashing down on mine.

This kiss is different. It's not soft and gentle. It's hungry. It's hot. It's consuming.

Both of his hands are tangled in my hair, holding my head still. His mouth opens over mine, and I can do nothing but open in response.

But why would I do anything else? I want to be consumed.

I want to be closer. I want him closer. I want everything.

His tongue strokes deep, sliding along mine, making all of my nerve endings spark to life.

My body heats, my nipples pull tight, my stomach clenches, my pussy throbs.

I want his hands everywhere. It's as if I have this ache, deep down somewhere I can't exactly name, and I know I can't reach, and I know that Jonah is the only one who can get rid of it.

His hands coast from my head down to my ass, and he lifts me, pressing me against him.

I haven't kissed, and I certainly haven't made out, or more, but I'm very aware that the part of his body pressing against my stomach right now is not normally that big and hard.

I remember that part of his body. I've *seen* that part of his body. I think about it far too often. And I'm really enjoying feeling it now.

I'm affecting him. A lot.

I *love* that.

My hands go around his waist and I grip his back, holding him tightly. I arch closer, going up on tiptoe, trying to get more of me against him. But I can't. I'm too small, too short.

He makes another growling noise, this one sounding almost frustrated. I feel his hands go under my ass and then lift. And just like that, I'm up against the wall. My legs wrap around his waist automatically, my ankles hook behind him. None of this needs any conscious thought, it's just what my body wants.

And then I realize why. That big hard part of him presses between my legs perfectly, and oh my God, *yes*.

So I have to say it. I pull my mouth away. "Yes, Jonah."

His mouth drags over my jaw and down my neck, his beard causing goosebumps to break out all over my body. Then he presses a kiss against the curve where my neck meets my shoulder.

"Jesus, you feel so fucking good."

"You too."

"I knew you would."

I love that he's thought about this.

"You're so sweet," he rasps against my neck.

His hands flex on my ass, his cock rocks against my clit, and *God*, I need more of that. He nips my neck and heat streaks through me. I let my head fall back against the wall so he can have more of my neck to...do whatever he wants to.

"So fucking hot," he mutters. "I can't believe—"

Then it occurs to him that we're doing something I've never done before.

I know that's *exactly* what just hit his conscious mind.

Not that it's a new thought, but it sinks in.

Dammit.

I knew it would eventually. If he knows that I have not had a UTI in the last several months, and he's taking credit for that, he's going to remember that I've never been kissed and remember every detail about how I react when he's the one to finally do it.

I feel the moment when his sense of responsibility and loyalty come back to him.

He pulls back, looking down at me.

"You okay?" he asks.

I give him a wobbly smile. "Yeah. Really good."

But also kind of bad. Because I realize I know him pretty well by now, too.

And he's not going to do this again.

He takes a deep breath and blows it out, then lets me slide to the floor.

He looks at me for a long moment, lifts his hand, and tucks a strand of hair behind my ear. Then he steps back and runs a hand over his beard before tucking his hands in his back pockets.

I stoically keep my eyes on his face rather than scanning over his body to that very prominent part that I liked having up against me far too much. I can close my eyes and remember the details of his body naked. I've done it many times before. But I keep looking at his face instead.

"You see what I mean about my grandma's cake, then?" I finally ask.

He nods. "I really fucking do."

Yeah. I am definitely going to miss having this.

"Happy birthday, Jonah," I finally say.

"Thanks, Linnea."

Typically, the use of my title would be more formal and my name more intimate, but the way Jonah says Duchess always sounds affectionate, and a little hot, whereas he never calls me Linnea when we're alone. His use of my name now makes me sad. I get it. He's putting up a barrier.

And that's probably a good idea.

I don't think I've hated being engaged before now as much as I do right now.

And I've really hated being engaged before now.

TODAY...

CHAPTER 10
IRIS LEE
DECLAN O'GRADY'S BODYGUARD, HEAD OF ROYAL BODYGUARDS

I know the guys prefer to communicate via our group text.

Actually, I know they prefer to communicate via their own group text that they think I don't know about.

But I make them get on video calls every once in a while.

They don't like calls where I can *see* them, because I am a master at reading facial expressions and body language.

Especially the expressions and body language of Jonah Greene, Henry Dean, Colin Daly, and Miles Stafford.

I absolutely clean them out at poker.

"You're going to Washington, D.C., with Linnea, without Torin?" I ask Jonah.

We've gone around and everyone has given a status update and what the next couple of weeks will bring for everyone.

Jonah shifts on his seat. "Yes."

He's being especially short in his answers. Which means there's more going on here.

The guys think of me as an older sister. Some might think I'm more like a mother-figure to them since I give them assignments and I'm the one they check in with and call when they're in trouble and need to be bailed out. Sometimes literally.

But one, at thirty-two, I'm not old enough to be any of their mothers. And two, mothers would lay down their lives for their children.

I love these guys, but four times a week I dream of firing them all and never seeing or speaking to them again. Ever.

Annoyed older sister definitely works though.

"Why?" I ask.

"She has some meetings. And Torin asked me to escort her."

That's weird. And he knows it. I scan the other faces on the call.

Colin is the hardest to read, and right now he's trying to be stoic. But he knows something.

Miles looks interested, but I don't think he actually knows anything about what's going on here.

Henry, on the other hand, is an open book. He's smirking. At Jonah.

"What are the meetings?" I ask.

"She's meeting with James Hill." He pauses. "And Christian Waite."

That catches my attention. I know the names, of course, and the history of the prior meetings with them.

But Henry is still smirking.

"Why isn't Torin going along?" I ask.

It's not like Torin has anything pressing to do in Cara. The king isn't giving him any specific responsibilities and history would show that Torin takes every opportunity to come back to the United States.

"Because he..." Jonah sighs.

It used to be a little easier for these guys to lie to me, but I've known them all for a very long time now. I don't know why they even try now.

"Jonah, what's going on?" I press.

"Torin wants her to go alone. James and Christian both want to see her...personally. They reached out and Torin agreed to...set them up. These will be..." He rolls his eyes. "Dates."

I frown and then lean in closer to my monitor. "Excuse me? *Dates*? Like romantic dates?"

"Yes."

"She's engaged."

"Not technically."

"She's supposed to marry Torin," I say firmly.

Jonah's sigh is heavier now. "You know he doesn't want that."

Yes, I'm aware of the pouty prince. But we all agreed he'd just have to get over it. "It's been almost two years. She's amazing. She's perfect to be queen. What the hell is his problem?"

I can see Jonah gritting his teeth. "We've talked about this," he says shortly.

Yes, we have.

And as frustrating as it is to me—and it is very fucking frustrating to me—I know it is equally frustrating for Jonah.

His friendship with the prince is, for the most part, a good thing. Just like my friendship with Declan helps him trust me to make decisions that will not only be good for him, but will make him happy. Eventually.

The same goes for Henry and Cian—though Henry definitely puts Cian's happiness above the bigger picture more than the rest of us do.

Jonah and Torin are the same. Jonah has, at times, pissed Torin off, of course. But the goal of getting Torin on the throne of Cara and married to Linnea Olsen must always come first. And Jonah sleeps well at night, knowing that is how Torin will ultimately be happiest and most fulfilled.

Sometimes we all have to remind him of that.

None of us are doing this on our own.

"I can't believe Linnea is agreeing to this," I finally say. It does no good to berate Jonah for Torin's stubbornness.

"She's going along with it because she sees these meetings as a good chance to further relationships with these men for Cara's sake," Jonah says. "She's looking at these as business meetings."

I sigh, feeling a bit of relief at that. At least Linnea is still doing what is expected of her.

"You can't condone this with Torin, though," I tell him.

Jonah is quiet for a moment. Then he says, "But, it's Christian Waite. And he reached out first. He likes her."

I frown. "So?"

"So this could actually turn into something."

"We don't want that."

"Why not?" Jonah volleys back. "This could be good for her."

I don't say anything. I know what he's getting at.

Yes, Torin, Declan, Fiona, and Cian are the royals, but the Olsens matter too. Linnea's happiness matters. It mattered to Alfred. It matters to us. Astrid's and Alex's do too. But it would be very difficult for anyone to convince me that Linnea Olsen wouldn't be happiest as queen of Cara.

"The guy's going to be the president of the United States someday," Jonah says.

"*Maybe*," I say.

"Come on," he says. "You know the odds are *very* good."

He's not wrong. Politics are tricky of course, but all of the data we've got—and it's a lot—points to Christian Waite being right on track for the highest position in one of the world's most powerful countries.

"She's going to go out with James Hill though, too, right?" Colin asks.

"Yes. But nothing will come of that," Jonah says.

I lean closer to my screen, interested in this in spite of myself. "How do you know?"

"I know her," he says. "They'll talk about his energy program and she's into that, but there won't be any chemistry between them."

He seems completely confident.

"But there will be with Waite?"

Jonah nods. "I think so."

"He's still not Torin," I point out. "That's *not* the plan."

"In a lot of ways, he could be *better* than Torin," Jonah says. "Another powerful man in our circle? How is that *bad*? She'd have influence over different things. We could spread our influence even wider."

I roll my neck. "This isn't the plan," I say again. As if anyone is listening.

"Plans can adjust," Henry says.

I glare at him. He's the one who has, so far, done the worst job of sticking to the plan. "The plan has *already* been adjusted. A few times."

"And the world hasn't ended," Henry says with a grin. "Maybe "the plan" needs to relax a little."

When he says "the plan", Henry means the man who pays all of our salaries.

But the *actual* plan was Alfred Olsen's happy, hopeful vision for all of the grandchildren.

He loved them dearly. He knew they were born with incredible privilege and opportunity that shouldn't be squandered. And he believed in them. He knew they had big hearts and lots of varied talents and passions and was convinced that given time and the space to figure themselves out, then supplied with the right resources, they would all find their path and make the world a better place.

He supplied those resources. And kept King Diarmuid at bay during the years they were all growing up and finding themselves.

He and Diarmuid were old friends, and I have to believe the king trusted him implicitly and he was simply unable to *not* believe in the things Alfred preached so wholeheartedly.

Hell, it took Alfred only ten minutes to convince a highly trained, incredibly cynical, kind-of-bitchy FBI agent who had believed her life's mission was to take down all the billionaires to leave her job and work right next to an asshole, know-it-all billionaire every single damned day.

But I simply couldn't resist a man who had the heart of Fred Rogers, could give a speech like Churchill, and looked like Santa Claus.

And in the past ten years, he and these families have made me believe in things like benevolent billionaires and compassionate royals and altruistic politicians.

So now that that amazing man is gone, it's my job, and mission, to keep this bunch together.

I lean in. "You were all hired knowing the plan. You all *believed in the plan*." I take a breath. "We were supposed to have a king and queen, a human rights activist, a billionaire philanthropist, a politician, a social media influencer, and a sports star all out there using their power, influence, money, and resources to make the world a better place. They were supposed to be examples of how money and power can be *good* things and used for *positive* progress. The O'Grady and Olsen families were supposed to..." I take a breath as I run out of words.

"Shame everyone else in those same positions into being better?" Colin supplies.

I nod. "Yes. In part." If they can do it, then other billionaires and sports stars and political leaders can fucking do it too. "They are supposed to grab headlines and magazine covers and interviews and dominate in as many influential spaces as possible. *That* was Alfred's vision and what we're all supposed to be doing here!"

"We *are* doing that," Miles argues.

I glare at him.

"We *are*," he says. "Torin is back in Cara. Fiona is an activist. Declan is a billionaire philanthropist. Astrid is an influencer. Alex is a rising star in hockey. Cian is..."

We all look at Henry as Miles trails off.

Cian is a playboy who spends part of his time as a swamp boat captain, part of his time as a volunteer firefighter, and part of his time working at an animal park. At least when he's not partying and flirting and having a really, *really* good time.

But he's naturally charismatic, and generous, and his superpower is making people feel comfortable and accepted. He'd be an amazing...anything. If he'd just get serious.

"He's talking about heading the summer festival committee," Henry offers.

"A summer festival *committee* in a tiny bayou town—" I stop myself. I take a deep breath. I will not talk about the things Cian is not doing.

I'll talk about the things the *rest of them* aren't doing. "Torin is back in Cara, but we all know he could jump on a plane and bolt again at any minute. Fiona is an advocate for *animals,* not people. And yes,"—I put my hand up before anyone protests— "she's great at it and animals are important too, but that wasn't the expectation. Astrid was going to be a social media influencer and then she got hurt and now...well, none of that has gone according to plan, either."

"Not her fault," Miles says, his voice low with warning.

Yes, I know better than to criticize Astrid within earshot of Miles. Her pit bull will growl and bark and even bite if he needs to in order to protect her.

I roll my eyes. Astrid is in no danger from me. Miles knows that.

"Instead of happy and sunny and fun, she's now grumpy and feisty, that's all I'm saying. It's just a little different 'vibe' and following than we'd expected."

"She's been through hell," Miles growls. "But she's still showing up and advocating for healthcare changes and for accessibility for disabilities and bringing awareness—"

"I know," I snap. Jesus, I've heard him exalt Astrid's accomplishments numerous times. I'm well aware. "It's just an example of the plan going off the rails."

"You and your fucking *plans*," Miles says. "You and the boss need to let up a little. Life doesn't always go exactly the way you want it to. Alfred knew that. He knew when to let up and give things some time. You've put a lot of weight on the shoulders of *human beings*. Even if they're not perfect, that doesn't mean they're not making a difference."

I can't win this argument with him. I never have any of

the times we've had it. I don't even need to try. Miles knows me. He knows I don't actually mean it that way. He's just protective of Astrid and...I want him to feel that way. That's what makes us good at our jobs. We love the people we're taking care of. That's great.

His feelings for Astrid just also make me stupidly jealous and I need to shut this conversation down before I give anything away that I don't want him to see.

I focus on the other problems with our "plan" that is feeling more and more like a big ball of tangled up string instead of the beautifully spun tapestry it was supposed to be.

"The royals are all doing things their own way and now Linnea is going on a date with a man who is *not* the one she's been arranged to marry. She was the *most* reliable one," I say. I focus on Jonah. "Linnea needs to be queen. Torin needs her. Take her to D.C. if that's what everyone wants, but you bring that girl home *single*."

Then I hang up on all of them.

CHAPTER 11
JONAH

This woman is magnificent.

Linnea Olsen is good at everything.

Even giving the silent treatment.

She does not want me on this trip, but instead of throwing a fit, she decided we were going to make the seven-hour flight from Cara to Washington, D.C., overnight.

It's brilliant, really. She was able to avoid me by reading and then sleeping most of the flight.

And I didn't push things. I didn't try to make conversation. I sat as far away from her as I could. I also tried to keep myself occupied with other things.

I ignored the fact that her very casual travel outfit of loose blush-pink pants, matching zippered hoodie and tee is still silky and perfectly pressed and expensive looking. That even with her hair pulled up into a high ponytail and no makeup on, she's still stunningly beautiful. And that being in close confines with her, just the two of us, late at night, dressed down and relaxed, reminds me of our late-night kitchen talks.

Because I'm trying to preserve my sanity.

I realize my method of ignoring and denying is not perfect, but I'm a desperate man.

I miss her like hell.

I know facts about her and what she's been doing. But I miss talking to her, I miss getting her *feelings* about the facts I'm privy to, and I've collected facts I probably shouldn't be privy to—like that she went to the doctor two weeks ago for a UTI since I haven't been around to make her drink water. Now I'm pissed about that too.

I miss hearing her laugh. I miss hearing her sassy remarks under her breath that no one else catches. I miss her searching the room for me and her shoulders visibly relaxing as soon as she sees me. Her shoulders have been tense and her mouth pinched when we've been in rooms together over the past month. And I haven't been brave enough to stand close enough to hear her muttering under her breath. Because then I might catch a whiff of her perfume. Or put out a hand and catch her when she trips over one of the rugs, which would require touching her. Which would make me think about how perfectly her ass fits in my hands.

I almost broke a tooth clenching my jaw, and my hand, when she tripped two weeks ago.

And her fucking mouth. That I couldn't keep from looking at before is now taunting me in a new way. I don't like the angry set to it that's been present since...that night.

Now that I actually know how soft and sweet and addicting it is, I'm really definitely...fucked.

I crossed the line. And I fucking want to cross it again. That line and about a hundred others.

And it would really only take one word from her.

Maybe not even a word. A sigh. A moan. Her hand on my chest, her fingers in my hair, certainly her mouth against mine.

For the first time in my life, I lost myself.

Kissing Linnea, I forgot who I was, what was important.

My entire world narrowed to a single focus. That woman.

And it was just a kiss.

Yes, it was a hot kiss. Maybe the hottest of my life. But still just a kiss. If I ever got her naked, if I ever had her legs wrapped around my waist, if I was ever buried inside her, God knows what I would do. Or what I wouldn't do. What I would give up. What I would forget.

It scared the shit out of me.

This trip is a bad idea. For so many reasons.

Iris isn't happy about it. The king is displeased with Torin for not coming along.

And none of them even know that I want to ravish the woman I'm supposed to be escorting on dates with other men.

I also want to hug her, rub her back, make sure she has cranberry scones every morning, and take her bowling.

Normal little things that would let me just *be* with her. Just us. Just two regular people spending time together.

And that's almost more dangerous than the ravishing.

It's just the two of us, for the most part, for the next ten days. We are far from Cara. No one in the U.S. really knows who we are. Yes, she'll be spending some time with people who are easily recognized and followed to some extent. Certainly, when she's with the senator, there is a chance for photographs. And it won't take long for people to figure out who she is. Her connection to Astrid and Alex is enough to make her pseudo-famous, and her additional connection to Cara is enough to make any sighting of her with a U.S. senator very interesting.

But if the two of us walk down a D.C. sidewalk to a coffee shop, no one's going to notice or care.

And that's dangerous.

Because if I hold her hand or pull her into my side with my arm around her waist, or press her up against a wall and kiss her, no one will blink. No one will make note of it, no one will report it back to anyone. Iris will never know.

I've been able to rein in my emotions while we've been in Cara, in the palace, around all of the eyes and ears who know that me kissing and touching her is not allowed.

No one here knows that.

I pull the door to the hotel open and hold my breath as she steps past so that I don't inhale her scent.

She gives me an irritated look.

It's better this way. If she thinks I'm being an asshole, then she'll keep me at arm's length, too.

That is a really good idea. The more space between us, the better. But it's also better if I don't listen to her get passionate about some subject she's excited about. It's better if I don't hear her laugh. It's better if she doesn't tell me that she's worried about these dates and doesn't know what to do.

The last thing I should, or can, do is help her date another man.

Thank God she doesn't need my help.

I was not exaggerating when I said all she needs to do is wear one of those fucking dresses and smile at the guy. James Hill and Christian Waite will be falling over themselves to get closer to her.

The fact that she's inexperienced and so damn genuine

turns me on more than anything about any woman I've ever met before.

And I'm sure other men will feel the same way.

I always thought I liked women who knew what they liked and wanted in the bedroom.

But judging by my nighttime fantasies, and the number of times I've had to wrap my hand around my cock over the past several months, that's not actually true.

Linnea Olsen and her inexperience with men, her innocence with kissing, and anything more, taps into a deep, primal part of me I was not aware of.

Perhaps it's the protector in me that is never fully satisfied, but I want to be the one to show her all the things she's been missing. All the pleasures there are to have, all the things her gorgeous body can do, all the things our bodies can do together.

And the idea of someone else showing her those things makes me want to put my fist through the wall.

This trip is a really bad fucking idea.

"Checking into the presidential suite," I tell the woman behind the desk.

She nods, taps on the computer, then looks up with a frown. "Mr. Greene?"

I know. "Yes. And Miss Olsen."

"Yes. We have been trying to get a hold of your contact."

I feel my neck tighten. There's a problem. Fucking perfect. The palace staff—specifically, Torin's assistant, Samuel—made these arrangements. I haven't arranged a hotel room in probably ten years.

"Our contact was in bed," I tell her.

"We just wanted to let him know there is a slight problem with your room. Nothing major," she rushes to add. "Just a minor inconvenience."

I scowl. "Such as?"

"It is a full suite, with a living area, kitchenette, and dining area. There are two bedrooms and two bathrooms. However, one of the bathroom's showers is being repaired. We thought it would be finished by now, but they got behind."

I feel the tension creeping up my neck into my head. "Then move us to a different suite. We require two bedrooms and two bathrooms."

"I will be able to do that in a couple of days. But our other suites are occupied until then."

I stare at her. I'm not used to inconveniences. Honestly, for the royal family, things just seem to work out. I know intellectually that isn't true, and they have a whole staff that handles inconveniences so that it *seems* that everything always works out. Still, *I* don't handle things like travel arrangements or itineraries, so everything seems to just fall into place for me as well.

"That will be fine." Linnea says to the woman.

"It's not," I say firmly. "We require two bedrooms and two bathrooms."

Linnea looks up at me with a frown. "And they can't accommodate that right now. So we'll make do."

"Actually, I will get a hold of someone," I say. "They'll move us to a different hotel."

The woman behind the desk looks distressed. "I am so sorry, Mr. Greene. Please let us try to make this right. I can have repairmen in there today. It's just the shower that's not working. Everything else in the bathroom is fine."

I feel Linnea's hand on my arm squeezing gently. "That is not necessary." She looks up at me. "There's one working shower. Two bedrooms. We have more than enough space. We'll be fine."

Fine. That is absolutely not the word I would use.

Sharing even a shower with this woman is a terrible idea. Torture, in fact. I will have to smell her bath gel, shampoo, lotions, and perfume. Not to mention, seeing the towel she wrapped around her body and trying not to picture her body wet, slick, glistening...

Like I am right now.

Fuck.

I am absolutely picturing her wet body wrapped in only a towel.

I squeeze my eyes together and pinch the bridge of my nose.

I'm not going to argue with Linnea in the hotel lobby. We can deal with this upstairs.

"Show us to our room, please," I say curtly.

"Of course. Right away," the woman says. She shoots Linnea a grateful smile.

Of course, Linnea is handling this with grace and ease.

Because this actually isn't a huge deal.

If it was Torin and me traveling together, I wouldn't think twice. Hell, Torin and I have shared a *sleeping bag* in the past. It was not a good night, and I don't want to repeat it, but we both lived through it.

And fuck, now I'm imagining sharing a sleeping bag with Linnea. And she's still wet and wrapped in only a towel.

A bellman hurries over and takes our bags. I don't need help getting our bags upstairs, but I decide it's a good idea to have an extra person in the elevator with us and in the room for the first few minutes until I can get my shit together.

I follow him to the elevator. As the door swooshes open,

out of habit, I put my hand on Linnea's lower back, then immediately snatch it back as if I've been burned.

But now I'm definitely standing close enough to her that I can smell her perfume and can study the wisps of hair that have pulled loose from her ponytail and are lying against her slender neck.

The ride up seems to take forever, but we're finally walking through the door of the suite.

"Where would you like your bags?" the bellman asks Linnea.

"I'll take the room without the shower," she says. "Whichever that is."

"Absolutely not."

The man stops in his tracks at my firm words.

Linnea looks at me with a brow lifted. "It seemed like a big deal to you."

"It *is* a big deal."

"Why?" she asks, tipping her chin up and meeting my gaze directly. "I can use the tub and take a bath. You can have the shower."

I cross to the man, peel off some bills and hand him his tip. "Thank you. I've got it from here."

He gives us both a nod and slips out the door.

I turn to face Linnea, deciding to be completely up front about our situation. If I lay it all out, maybe she'll realize that this trip is going to be tough, and we need to keep our distance.

"Sharing a bathroom is more intimate than we should probably be. It means people walking around in towels and things."

She rolls her eyes.

I lift a brow.

"We can always dress inside the bathroom. They're

enormous." She turns away and grabs the handle of one suitcase in each hand and starts toward one of the bedrooms. "But don't worry, Jonah. I'm a big girl. I know how to keep my hands to myself. You don't have to worry about me trying to sneak a peek or throwing myself at you."

Her words take a moment to sink in, but when they do, I do the one thing I absolutely should not do.

I reach out and touch her.

I step forward and grasp her arm, pulling her to a stop and turning her. "*What?*"

"I'm just..." She presses her lips together and I, of course, have to look.

Those damned lips haunt me.

"I'm sorry," she says, making my eyes bounce back to hers. "I'm sorry for your birthday. I hate that it's ruined our friendship. I hate that so much. I *promise* it will not be a problem while we're here."

Fuck. Our friendship. She thinks that she did something wrong. "Linnea—"

"And I hate when you call me Linnea."

"That's your name."

"But you say it differently than other people do."

"I do?"

I do. I know what she means. I just didn't realize it was so obvious.

"You do. And I know that you've been trying to avoid me because of how I acted on your birthday. But I promise you, even if I'm inexperienced in how these things go, I am a mature woman who is very intelligent. I understand that you don't want that to happen again. Message received. No worries. I can control myself."

I stare into the big green eyes that I have been trying to avoid for weeks.

Then my gaze drops to the mouth, that, despite trying to avoid it in real life, I have dreamed about every night.

"Duchess," I say, my voice husky and low. "What do you think happened in that kitchen, exactly?"

She hasn't tried to pull away from me, and now the tip of her pink tongue darts out to wet the lips that I have imagined doing very inappropriate things to.

I force myself to look back into her eyes. "Answer me."

It is clear that we are not on the same page. And we need to get there. This trip will be torturous for me, but I refuse to make it uncomfortable for her. Or worse, painful.

What she said has me sure that she absolutely does not understand my reaction in the kitchen a month ago, and though I am opening a gigantic can of worms, I cannot let her have a mistaken impression of what went on that night.

"Two friends were having one of their usual late-night talks, one was drunk, the other was...stupid and overreacted," she says. Her cheeks are a little pink, but she meets my gaze directly.

Of course she does. This woman was born to be a queen. Or at least raised to be one. She's not going to look away even when embarrassed.

"No," I say softly. My grasp on her arm loosens slightly, but I find my thumb dragging back and forth over her inner elbow.

"You had a lot to drink. You were getting kisses for your birthday from a lot of women. We were joking and teasing. So we kissed." She lifts a shoulder, obviously trying to make it seem like no big deal.

How I fucking wish it was no big deal.

"And then I took it too far. I went too far. Yes, I blame my inexperience, but I'm very sorry that I was too..." She stops and swallows. "Enthusiastic."

Jesus. Christ.

I shouldn't say what I'm tempted to. It won't necessarily make things easier between us.

But I have to be honest with her.

And maybe, if I'm completely transparent, she'll understand why I've been trying to put distance between us. Maybe she'll fucking *help* put some distance between us. Maybe she'll go on these dates and actually be open to the idea of finding someone else. Maybe she'll decide that she does not want to put up with mine or Torin's bullshit anymore and will realize she doesn't want to live within those palace walls with the two of us dumbasses.

"Your enthusiasm was the hottest thing I've ever experienced," I tell her.

Her eyes widen.

"You did not go too far. You did absolutely nothing wrong."

She studies my eyes as if looking to see if I'm sincere. I let her look. Because fuck, if nothing else, she has to understand how I feel.

It should drive her away.

Maybe that's the one hope here.

"What? You liked that?"

"It was so much more than like," I tell her.

"You're just saying that to make me feel better."

I blow out a breath and shake my head. "It would be so much better for both of us if, somehow, I was turned off by you and what happened that night, Duchess.

"It would be so much better if that had been disgusting, and I didn't want to be close to you. But instead, I think about it every fucking day. And all night long. I not only want to repeat it, I want to keep going."

I move closer. "I want to go so much further. You have

no idea what you do to me. But it is such a bad idea. The only reason I pulled back was because otherwise I would've had your pajamas on the floor and your naked body up against that wall, and we would've crossed a line that I'm not sure we can come back from. At least from the kiss, I thought maybe I could reclaim my sanity. That I could walk out of that kitchen and sober up and get some distance and realize that it wasn't what I had built up in my mind."

I shake my head and my voice drops even lower. "But that's not what happened. I want you. All the time. So much that I have had to try to avoid you, not even look at you, to keep from doing something really stupid."

The pink from her cheeks has now spread down her gorgeous throat. She's breathing fast. She's staring at me. And she's not saying a thing. She is also still not pulling away from me.

Finally, I drop my hand. "So that is why we should not share a shower."

"You're afraid of losing control around me?" she asks.

And the gorgeous thing looks absolutely fascinated by that.

God, getting close to her, making her trust me, telling her she can always be honest and open with me, is going to be my downfall.

She is going to be curious about everything and ask me these questions, not understanding the effect it has on me.

Unless I tell her.

"Yes. You drive me crazy. I am constantly on the verge of doing something *really* stupid. Just being here together alone is a really fucking bad idea. But I'm gonna try my damnedest to be a good guy, to be a good friend and employee to Torin, and a good friend to you. I *want* you to have these experiences with dating other men. I am here to keep you safe, to guide you through this, and make sure that you take it seriously. For everyone's sake."

She shakes her head. "I don't want to."

"Please, Linnea." I know I sound a little desperate. Probably because I am. "Please do this."

Her eyes fill with hurt, and I feel it jab me in the heart. I actually brace my feet so that I don't weaken.

"You're really okay with seeing me with someone else?"

"I want you to be happy," I insist, avoiding answering her question directly. "I want you and Torin both to be happy. I want you to have love and passion."

"I want to be queen."

I shake my head. "Everything you want about being queen is about making things better for your people." I know her. I know that she hasn't let herself imagine something else, but I do understand what it is about being queen that appeals to her.

She's loving and generous and kind and sees the position of queen as a way to help.

It's one of the reasons I've fallen for her.

"You want to have a say in how the palace serves and helps the people. But you already have that. You are already a princess to Cara in all the ways that matter. The king and Torin both respect and listen to you. They always will. The people love you and trust you. You will always be an ambassador for Cara. You will always be able to travel the world and represent the country and bring innovation and new ideas and improvements to the island. You don't need to marry Torin for that. You can have it all—influence for Cara *and* love."

She's studying my face and I know what she's going to say before she even says it.

"You and I—"

"No." I cut her off. I can't listen to her say out loud that she wants anything with me. "You know that can't happen."

"But—"

"Torin told you the list of men who are qualified to be with you is short. I'm not on it."

"Jonah—"

"No," I interrupt her again. "I know what my place is. I've chosen it. I want it. I am very good at what I do. I also get to influence and improve people's lives by making sure Torin is the best king he can be. I have his ear too. I want to be by his side while he reigns. But I'll never be a prince. I'll never be a billionaire. I'll never be a senator or a prime minister or any of the other things you could have."

She hugs her arms over her stomach and swallows hard. Then she takes a breath.

"Will you be my friend?" she finally asks. "I've *hated* us not talking. Not spending time together. I want you as a friend. And a confidant."

I want so fucking much more. I know this. I've acknowledged it. But the thoughts, and the way they tighten my chest, still sneak up on me. "Always," I say sincerely. "That's why we're doing this. You're going to find someone worthy of you. Better than Torin. Someone who can love you."

She takes a deep breath. "I don't know how to do this. I was serious when I said I know nothing about dating."

"I will help you with that." *Even though it's going to kill me.*

That makes her look a little sad. Yep, definitely going to kill me.

"It won't be easy for me, Duchess." I definitely say that word differently than I say 'Linnea'. "I don't want you to think that. It will be hard for me to see you with someone else. If things were different, if we were different people, this would all be...very different."

"In what way?" she asks.

We've come this far. We've been honest, we've laid out that there are feelings, but there's nothing we can do about them. She knows the purpose of this trip, and where I stand. So I figure there's no harm in saying, "I wouldn't have pulled back the night in the kitchen. And the past month, instead of avoiding you, I would've had you in my bed every night."

She sucks in a quick breath. She lifts her hand and plays with the necklace at her throat. Her gaze goes to my lips.

I work on standing perfectly still.

Finally she says, "I was right, you know."

"Which time?" I ask with a small smile.

"I was right to avoid having even a taste."

Then she grabs her bags, turns, and heads into the bedroom, closing the door behind her.

CHAPTER 12
LINNEA

I shut the bedroom door behind me. I roll my suitcase to the closet. I tip it over and start to unzip it. But mid-unzip, the adrenaline hits. My hand starts to shake, and I have to straighten and press my hand to my chest so that I can take a deep breath.

Holy. Shit.

Jonah is not mad at me. He's not uncomfortable because I acted like an idiot.

He wants me.

He's been avoiding me because he wants me and can't do anything about it.

He said that if we were anyone else, I would've been in his bed every night since that night.

Holy. Shit.

I cross to the bed and sink down onto the mattress. I keep working on my breathing. My heart is pounding and my whole body feels hot.

No one has ever said anything like that to me.

No one has ever looked at me the way Jonah looked at me just now.

I've never had a man's *voice* make my panties wet.

Oh my God. Jonah Greene wants me. The only thing keeping us apart is the fact that I'm engaged to his best friend.

I frown. That's not even it. Torin and I aren't actually engaged, and no one knows it better than Jonah. He's not staying away from me because of some bro code or because Torin is madly in love with me and it would break his heart if Jonah and I had feelings for one another.

He's staying away from me because he's the prince's bodyguard.

Nothing can happen between us. He's right about that.

If we're hoping King Diarmuid would want me happy and would allow me to break off the arranged marriage with Torin for someone else, the odds of him thinking Jonah is the one to throw it all away for are slim.

Even if I can see myself with him.

The way we share smiles across crowded rooms. The way he brings a pashmina along for me even on the nights I'm sure I'll be warm enough, and then I'm always grateful to have it. Our late-night talks in the kitchen. The fact that he knows intimate details about me and that immediately made me feel safe rather than violated. I know I can tell Jonah anything. And not only will he keep my confidence, but none of it makes him think differently about me.

He understands my life.

He knows how to act at balls and meetings with international figureheads, and even around my family. He understands what I want. I don't care about the crown, the jewels, the fame. He understands why I want to be queen.

And if I wasn't queen, but just an advisor or ambassador, he understands that too, and would support me and would be awesome by my side. He wears suits like other men wear blue jeans and T-shirts. He has the manners, understands the social norms, can absolutely conduct himself in any social situation.

He could fit into my world seamlessly.

Except that he's committed to Torin.

Torin is his assignment. Torin has to come first. Unless Jonah leaves his assignment as Torin's bodyguard, which...I would never ask him to do. I admire his work. I know he's important to Torin's success. Torin is who he is today, in part due to Jonah's presence in his life and I do believe that Jonah is someone who will be integral in making Torin the best king he can be.

Not to mention that Jonah will literally need to be by Torin's side.

If Jonah has to choose between me and Torin, he'll have to choose Torin.

That would kill Jonah. That would cause tension between him and Torin. It might affect how he does his job.

And then there's the current king.

Diarmuid is old-fashioned, for sure. But some of it would be misplaced affection and protection on his end as well. He would want me to be with someone who had the means to support me and give me everything in the world. And yes, he would like my partner to be a good partner for Cara.

Jonah is a bodyguard. As much as Diarmuid loves me, I know that he would not think a bodyguard was good enough for me. Not as a romantic partner, anyway.

Still, I know Diarmuid likes Jonah. Trusts him. In fact, I believe that he would trust Jonah's opinion over Torin's in some cases.

Fuck.

I press my hand to my chest. Of course, I would have to start having feelings—romantic and sexual—for someone and it would have to be someone it could never work with.

It really would've been better if the feelings were unrequited. If I had made a fool of myself in the kitchen. Or if Jonah had never told me otherwise anyway.

Knowing that he wants me is even more of a turn-on. The desire I feel for him right now is nearly overwhelming. I want to go back into that living room and beg him to kiss me again.

My whole body is humming with it.

I take a deep breath. Then another. Then I make myself stand up.

Jonah is my friend. He cares about me. He wants me, but he realizes that we can't be together.

But he has taken my feelings about Torin, and how I feel about Cara, seriously.

So I have to trust him.

If he thinks that something good can come out of me going on these dates with James and Christian, then I'll believe him. I will at least give it a try.

That means I need to take a shower and get ready for tonight.

And maybe, since I developed feelings easily for Jonah, maybe I can develop feelings easily for one of these other men. Maybe I've just been too stubborn, too wrapped up in the things I thought I should do or shouldn't do. Maybe once I let these walls down, I'll find that romance and desire are all around me.

There's a soft knock at my door.

I suck a breath. If Jonah comes in here right now and wants to kiss me, I am absolutely letting him.

"Yes?"

"Are you decent?"

Does he want me to be decent? "Yes."

The door opens and Jonah leans in. "I'm going to head down to the gym for a workout. Would you like me to shower down there or—"

"No, I'll use the shower and everything now and then you can have it when you get back."

He clenches his jaw, then nods. "Okay. Sounds good. Do you need anything before I leave?"

I'm shocked at the inappropriate thoughts that go through my mind. Things I could ask him for. Things I could say I need. I shake my head. "No. I'm fine."

"Call me if that changes."

A little part of me, a part that is very unfamiliar to me, thinks that it would be fun to call or text him with a flirtatious offer. Just to see if he would come up in the middle of a workout and give me something I *need*.

I almost laugh out loud. As if I would even know what to ask for.

I really want another kiss. I also know that that's innocuous compared to other things.

I'm not even sure how to put the other things to words. Certainly not out loud to an actual human man.

Again, I just nod.

"Okay, I'll be back soon," he says, then turns and pulls the door shut behind him.

I let out a long breath.

Man, if it's easy to feel how I'm feeling right now around other men, I am going to be a bundle of nerves, emotions, and hormones for the next ten days.

But I don't actually think that will be a problem.

I don't know much about men, dating, sex, and

romance, but I have a feeling that all of this between Jonah and me is unusual.

> How do I look? Is this okay for drinks tonight?

Almost two hours later, I send the text and the photo of me in front of the full-length mirror in my hotel room to my sister.

I showered and then dressed in casual clothes to sit in the living area with my computer while Jonah cleaned up after his workout.

When I came back into my bedroom, I could smell his soap and aftershave hanging in the air.

I took in huge lungfuls.

I love the smell of him. Yes, it makes my heart beat faster and my nipples tighten and my skin feel tingly. But those are pleasant sensations in a way. I feel more alive and almost...daring.

We're in the U.S.. No one from Cara is here. I don't have to mind every single thing I do or say like I feel I do when I'm at the palace.

And the way I react to Jonah's scent in my bedroom and bathroom makes me wonder if he had a reaction to being in my bedroom or the scent of my shampoo and soap in the shower.

And I hope so.

That's probably problematic, but I can't stop myself from thinking about it. And that I *want* him to have a reaction.

It's as if now that I know he has feelings for me, that he *wants* me, I can't stop wanting him to want me even more. That's not kind. That's not sympathetic.

But I've never had a man want me before. At least not like this. A man like Jonah. One who really *knows* me, but wants me anyway. And one who I want too. One who could have any other woman. One who is good and loyal and noble so is holding back, yet still makes me feel desirable and admired and safe.

> Damn. You look great. You're so hot with your hair down. I don't know why you don't wear it that way more often.

I smile at my sister's response.

I'm in the green dress Jonah told me to bring. My hair is down, and I'm wearing the lipstick and the heels he mentioned.

I look good.

And I feel nauseous.

She's right. I don't wear my hair down often. It's much more businesslike and sophisticated up.

I smooth my hands over my hips and turn to check myself out from behind.

I suppose this dress is sexy. I think the last time I wore it, I had a jacket over the top.

But I definitely would not have worn my hair down.

I take a deep breath.

My phone pings again with another message.

> Where are you?

> Hotel in D.C.. About to have drinks with James Hill.

> The billionaire?

Yes. We met at an energy summit a few months ago.

> Oh, damn. You can't wear that. He'll think it's a date.

My sister knows all about the arranged marriage situation. Of course. She is part of the family and this has been part of our family's story since before she was born.

But she doesn't know the details. Like how I feel about it. I've always made sure my family thinks I'm fine. I don't want them to worry. I also haven't shared with anyone how Torin feels about it.

She wouldn't just worry if she knew Torin wasn't committed to me. She'd tell him exactly what she thought of that. And she would not think—and say—*nice* things.

I'm older and have done everything I can to make Alex's and Astrid's lives easier. And their own. It's important to me that they get to make all their own decisions. Where I have had to work to be deferential, I've encouraged Astrid to be the opposite. She's independent, speaks her mind, knows that she is not only right to have her own opinions, but should voice them whenever possible.

She's taken all of that to heart. Astrid can be a bit of a handful.

So I have not shared with her that things are not smooth sailing in my life. She gets very protective, even being eight years younger than me.

I hesitate, take a breath, then type,

> It is a date.

> <wide eyes emoji> Does Torin know?

> It was Torin's idea.

> I'm confused. <Confused face emoji>

I start typing. I type the whole thing out. I cannot tell her this in person or even out loud over the phone. But it feels good to let her in on my secrets. I tell her that Torin doesn't want to get married, that he thinks I need to date someone else because I've never had that chance, and that I am going out with two men while I'm in D.C. for the next few days. I mention Christian as well.

There's a long pause after I send the paragraphs' long text.

I could've sent it in chunks, but I know Astrid would have responded to each one individually and it would have driven me crazy. I wanted to get it all out at once.

But now I have to wait for my sister to process the information I've just given her.

Finally she responds.

> Wow.

That's it. Just three letters. One word.

I chuckle.

Then my phone rings. I was expecting this. But now that I've told her everything upfront, this will be easier.

"Hello?"

"This was *Torin's* idea?"

"Yes."

"Are you kidding me? He's such an asshole."

I sink down onto the edge of the bed. "He's not.

There's just no chemistry between us. That's not his fault. We were both signed up for this without our consent. Now he's giving me a chance at something else before it's too late."

"But you're amazing. How does he not know that?"

"I think he thinks I'm amazing. In certain ways. But you can't make someone fall in love with you. Or even want to sleep with you. It's just something that happens or doesn't."

She's quiet for a few seconds. "I guess," she finally admits. "But this is crazy. He's sending you off on *dates*? Are you okay with this? Do you want to go on these dates?"

"I am *willing* to go on the dates," I hedge. "If nothing else, these men are interesting, and can be great contacts for Cara."

"There it is. God, you're always thinking about Cara. I want to know if you are attracted to either of these men."

"They're both handsome."

"Not the same thing. "

"I know. I'm not sure. When I've been around them before, I haven't been thinking about that at all. I guess it's good to find out if I am?"

"I guess." She does not sound convinced. "This is all really weird."

"I agree." I hesitate, but I want to say the rest of this because I really want her reaction, and her advice. "I'm a virgin, Astrid."

There is a long silence on my sister's end of the phone.

"Really?" she finally asks. She doesn't sound judgmental. That's the best thing about my sister. She definitely doesn't judge. "I guess I'm not surprised by that. You haven't been out with a lot of guys. And you're very..."

I lift a brow. "Very what?"

"Proper." She laughs. "A nicer word would probably be classy."

I smile. "Uptight, you mean."

"Concerned with rules and how things are supposed to be," she counters.

"Well, that's true." I sigh. "I've only been kissed once."

"Wow," she says.

"Yeah." I almost tell her it was Jonah, and it was just a month ago, then decide that maybe I am laying a lot on her at once. Besides, I'm not sure it matters.

"Are you attracted to Torin?"

"No," I say easily. "But I decided a while ago that it didn't matter."

"Of course it matters!" I can picture her shocked face. "You're planning to *marry him*."

"Marriage is about a lot more than physical attraction."

"But that has to be a part of it. Otherwise, you should just be friends. Or co-workers, or whatever."

"He needs a queen. I want to be queen."

Astrid sighs, as if I'm just being stubborn. "But not wanting to sleep with him is going to make having babies with him kind of hard. Maybe not impossible, but definitely not pleasant."

"There are ways."

"Oh. Come on! Sure, being queen is a cool deal but no sex? For the rest of your life?"

"Sex isn't the greatest thing in the world."

"Spoken by someone who's never had it," Astrid says.

"You do not think sex is the greatest thing in the world," I say with a little laugh. Then I frown. "Wait. Do you?"

"Well, it's way up there when it's done right," she says. "Seriously, it bugs me that you've never had sex. Not to mention great sex. And that you're resigning yourself to marrying a guy who you don't even want to have sex with. That's crap. You're making a huge decision without all the facts."

"My life is weird. I think we all know this." But now I have a niggle in the back of my mind.

Because *kissing* has moved up my list of great things and if that can happen, maybe it can happen with sex too...

And maybe I should find out.

That's dangerous, of course. Because it's possible I end up really liking it and still married to a guy who doesn't want to do that with me and then I'm stuck wanting to do it but not getting to.

On the other hand, maybe I will fall in love with someone else.

I have to admit that it's definitely possible. I've fallen in love with Jonah. Easily. Rather quickly.

Maybe it won't be that difficult at all. Maybe James or Christian will sweep me off my feet. Maybe, if I really let down my guard and let myself consider this, there will be sparks.

Maybe they can make me not care about being queen.

"What if..." I start.

"Yes?" Astrid asks, eagerly.

"What if I did want to find out what all the hype is about?"

She laughs. "Well, you're not engaged. That's the first thing you need to start telling yourself. You've lived for a long time as if you are. But Torin's never asked you and you've never said yes. And he's actually sent you off to date other men. So there's no cheating here."

I swallow. "Okay. Right. You're right. I'm not engaged."

"Then," Astrid goes on. "Definitely wear that dress and go on this date. Go on a few dates. Hang out with men you're attracted to. You will not have trouble finding guys who are willing to help you find out if you like sex."

I'm smiling and rolling my eyes. "And what if I don't? What if it's not good? Then I can go back to Cara and say 'hey, I tried', and then be queen?"

Astrid laughs. "Well, I have good news. You can teach men to have good sex."

"What?"

"Sure. I mean, no one's good at it the first few times. Everyone has to learn. And every partner is a little different. So you can help the guy get better. You can't write it all off if it's not amazing the first time."

"Has that happened to you?" Now I wish Astrid and I had talked about sex long before this. This is definitely one of those times when I feel like she's the older sister.

"Sure. I've been lucky more often than not, and the guys have definitely known what to do. Which is awesome. They helped me figure out what I liked. But there were a couple who I really liked but who weren't *quite* there, and I was able to coach them along. A really great guy wants it to be good for you, so he's definitely willing to learn what you like. But *you* have to know first. You need to have sex to figure out what you like and what does it for you. And what *doesn't*. It's a lot like figuring out your favorite wine. You have to drink good *and* bad stuff to know what gets you excited."

I think about that. This makes sense. And gives me some hope. Still, I say, "It would be easier just not to have sex."

"Easier. And fucking sad," Astrid says. She's quiet for a moment, then says, "Okay, you told me something very vulnerable and I'm gonna tell you something now."

I frown and sit up straighter for some reason. "What?"

"I don't tell you all this crap because I know it worries you. But we're having a moment here," she says.

"Astrid, just tell me."

She sighs. "Okay. Sex has been really hard for me since my accident. My sensation is weird because of some nerve damage, and...it's painful. My joints and muscles around my hips and pelvis are all crazy, and I just can't enjoy things like I used to."

I feel my stomach knot. Her accident played on repeat in my head for weeks afterward whenever I'd close my eyes. I can perfectly picture the moment when my baby sister hit the floor and the excruciating seconds afterward when she didn't move. "Oh my God, Astrid. I'm so sorry."

"I know. And it's not something I wanted to talk about. I was definitely hoping it would get better. But it's not. My doctors aren't very helpful either. Typical men. I'm working on some things, but the point is, sex isn't fun anymore. It's not pleasurable. And dammit, I miss it. Seriously, Linny, you've got to have some good sex. Don't live a life without it. I promise you, you *are* missing out."

My sister hasn't ever been in love that I know of. At least nothing that's ever lasted. So for her to say this, that she's loved sex and misses it, even without the love part, must mean there really is something there I should try.

"I am going to think about all of this," I promise.

"Great. I'm kind of excited that you're going on dates. You've never gotten to do that. You should get to do some normal things. You've given up a lot for Cara, and for our family. And even if you've liked some of it, or even most of it, your situation is so weird. You should get to have some fun along the way."

I laugh. "You don't think being a princess and then a queen will be fun?"

"Yeah, yeah," my sister says. Our family might be the only ones who are unimpressed by the idea of royalty. "But you're going to take it very seriously," she says. "I hope there's some fun along the way. At least the pretty dresses and parties. But it's gonna be a job for you. I know you."

"Well, of course it is. People's lives depend on us."

Again, she's quiet for a moment, then says, "You know, you're already doing that job. You don't really have to marry Torin. You've already made so many things better in Cara."

My eyes widen. "You're the second person to say that to me today."

"Really? Did Torin say it?"

"No. Jonah did."

"Torin's bodyguard? The birthday cookie guy, huh?" Astrid asks. "That's interesting. When did he say it? You said today?"

Just thinking about the fact that he's in the next room makes my heartrate kick up. "Yes. He's here with me, in D.C.. He came along as security and to drive me around and all of that." I leave out the part about how he's here to make sure I actually go on these dates.

"Really? It's just you and Jonah?"

"Yeah. Why?"

"No reason," my sister says, with a strange tone in her voice. Then she laughs. "Other than, I'm guessing Jonah Greene knows a thing or two about how to give a woman an orgasm."

I audibly gasp. "Astrid!" I feel my cheeks flush.

I have certainly had these thoughts about Jonah. Many lusty thoughts. But I had no idea my sister would've thought of Jonah that way.

She laughs again. "Seriously? That man is hot. There is no way he doesn't know his way around a woman's body. If

James and Christian don't wanna help you out, or you don't want them to, Jonah's the guy, Linny. I'm telling you."

"Yeah, and he's my future husband's best friend and bodyguard."

"I will bet you one thousand dollars and a pair of the next tennis shoes I endorse that you will have sex, love it, and decide to absolutely fall in love with someone else because you will want to keep doing that. So you won't be marrying Torin and you won't be running into Jonah."

My cheeks are hot and I'm so glad we're not on a video call right now or Astrid would know immediately that I've had all of these same thoughts.

"I can get a pair of the next tennis shoes you endorse without your help," I say.

Astrid laughs. "And let's say you *do* decide to marry Torin. Jonah is very dedicated and loyal. He's a great friend. He can just chalk up anything he does with you as helping make sure his best friend's wife is all in."

"Astrid!" I exclaim. My cheeks are burning now. "That's..."

"Don't tell me he doesn't want his best friend having great sex with his wife."

"Astrid," I say firmly. "That's completely inappropriate."

And *very* dirty.

"I know." I can picture her huge, unapologetic grin.

I'm definitely flustered now. And if I keep talking to her about this, she's going to catch on that I've already had some of these thoughts about Jonah. *Not* in relation to "helping Torin out", but that if Jonah has already made me a huge fan of kissing, he could probably be a fantastic tutor in...other things.

"I need to go and finish getting ready for my date. "

"Okay. That's a good idea. If Jonah ends up being your sex tutor, it might be better if you marry James. Then you won't accidentally end up pulling him into a linen closet in the palace—"

"*Goodbye*, Astrid."

"Goodbye. I love you! Have *fun*. And I mean that!"

I hang up on my sister and press my hands to my hot cheeks.

Oh, I know she means it.

The problem is...now I can't stop thinking about the kind of fun she thinks I need to have.

And with whom.

CHAPTER 13
JONAH

I told her to wear the green dress.

I was right.

And so very, very wrong.

She looks amazing. Too fucking amazing. James Hill doesn't know what's about to hit him.

She will have a date every night as long as we're here and maybe a marriage proposal before we leave.

Fucking great.

I straighten from where I am storing the bottles of water I had delivered in the fridge.

"You look amazing," I tell her sincerely.

She licks her lips. "Thank you."

I tuck my hands in my pockets. "Your hair is up, though." I specifically told her to wear it down.

She's always a knockout, but her hair down is sexy as fuck.

She needs to walk in there tonight looking like this is a

date, not a meeting. Hill has seen her hair up. He needs to know that she considers this a *social* get-together.

She lifts her hand to finger the hair gathered at the back of her head. "I had it down. Then panicked."

"There's no need to panic. He'll be excited to see you. You'll take his breath away."

She chews on her bottom lip. "I think I need to ease into this."

"Is that why it's drinks only tonight? And why you invited his assistant?"

Her eyes widen.

Before she can say anything like 'how did you know that', I remind her, "I know everything, Duchess. I needed the itinerary, so I knew what we were doing. I needed to get a table near yours at the restaurant."

She blows out of breath. "You're treating me like I'm Torin. I don't need security right beside me the entire time."

"Maybe not. But I'm also along to make sure you do what you agreed to. Which is good, considering you're already *not* doing what you agreed to."

She straightens. "I'm seeing James."

"You're having drinks instead of dinner. And his assistant is coming. Obviously, he now thinks this is a business meeting."

"I want to talk to him about some of the labor projections we discussed when he was in Cara. He said he could hire almost a hundred workers at the research facility he's proposing. I want to know if that's a firm number now that he's had time to think about it in more detail."

I love how important Cara and its people are to her. It's one of the most beautiful things about her. But it can't be the *only* thing important to her. *She* needs to be important to her.

It shouldn't be this hard to convince someone to make themselves happy.

And she needs to stop reminding me that she's intelligent and creative and dedicated and truly has the heart of a public servant. Because it's already hard enough to not cross the room and press her against the wall when she's wearing that damned dress.

"You can talk to him about that any other time," I tell her.

"It will make conversation tonight easier," she insists.

I blow out of breath. "I know you're nervous. And of course, talking about things you have in common is a great idea. But you need to do it alone with him."

"I can't expect him to have specific numbers off the top of his head. That's why he has an assistant."

"So you don't need specific numbers tonight. Talk to him in general. His assistant can forward things tomorrow." I take a few steps closer to her. "Call him right now and tell him that Stacy can stay home." Yes, I even know his assistant's name.

Linnea swallows. "What if we have drinks and talk business tonight? It will be the first time seeing each other in a couple of months. Then, if I feel comfortable, we can make plans for dinner another night while I'm here."

I give her a small smile. And shake my head. "I realize that you're used to negotiating with people and getting your way. But you forget, I'm used to Torin. He tries to negotiate and get his way all the time. I'm immune."

"You're immune to good ideas and compromise?"

"I'm immune to giving in when my ideas are better."

She sighs.

I take another step closer. "Besides, you're in the green dress. This is a dinner date dress."

"I wore this in October," she reminds me. "To a reception that was social, but also business. *Not* a dinner date."

"And you about gave a dozen men a heart attack and caused the staff to have to clean up several puddles of drool."

She smiles. "No, I didn't."

"Practically."

"Maybe it's just you that likes this dress."

"I like this dress *a lot*," I confess. "But I'm definitely not the only one. I was watching. And, though I find it hard to look away from you, I do notice other people in the room with you."

She blushes lightly and I so badly want to cup her cheek. I clench my hand instead.

"I could change," she offers.

I take the final step. I know exactly what to do. I have a great idea about how to convince her that she wants to go on the date. Or rather, remind her. The only problem is it's going to be hard on me. But that's the job. Making sacrifices to be sure that my protectee is safe and happy and that things go according to plan.

I lift my hand and cup the back of her neck. With her hair up, her neck is bare and her skin is silky and warm. I trace my thumb up and down the side of her throat, loving the way she catches her breath, and her eyes fall to my lips.

I draw her closer. I put my mouth against her temple.

"Tonight is supposed to be a *date*. It needs to be romantic. Sexy even. You need to see if you can have a deeper connection with James."

I drag my jaw down her cheek and along hers. When I get to her mouth, I say against her lips, "The business will be there tomorrow, Duchess. Tonight is for different adventures."

Then I kiss her.

This entire trip is going to be torture.

Watching her with other men, being in the same vicinity as her and not being able to touch her, or touching her and having to pull back.

It won't matter. All of it's going to be difficult. So, I might as well have a few seconds of enjoyment, right?

Especially if it's for the greater good.

She sighs against my lips, her mouth opens slightly, and I take advantage. I lick my tongue over her bottom lip, then slide it over her tongue. I taste her fully. She tastes like toothpaste. Then when she sighs again and arches closer, the lust between us has its own sweet flavor.

I run my hand from the back of her neck up into her hair, finding the bobby pins that are holding her hair up. I pluck them out, one by one, dropping them to the floor. Then I pull the ponytail holder loose. Her long, dark tresses tumble around her shoulders, and I sink my fingers into her thick hair, cupping her head and tipping her so that I can taste her even more fully.

My other hand finds her ass, lovingly hugged by the green silk she's wearing.

This dress fits against all her curves. It has a wide neckline that shows only the hint of cleavage. It's sweet and completely modest, but teases at the beautiful body underneath.

Just as she's starting to go up onto tiptoe to get closer, I release her mouth.

I stare down at her.

"Don't you want more of that?" I ask her huskily. "Don't you want to feel this with whoever you're with? Don't you want to find someone who can make you feel like this *and* talk to you about green energy and making Cara better?"

She blinks those beautiful green eyes at me, trying to focus, trying to remember where we were prior to the kiss.

I can't help it, that makes every inch of my ego swell.

Which goes well with the swollen cock behind my fly.

I can handle that. I can handle wanting her and not being able to have her. If it means that she goes out and finds someone that can make her look the way she's looking right now, I can do this.

She deserves this.

A wrinkle furrows her brow as she finally realizes what I'm talking about. She pushes against my chest and I let her go. She steps back.

"Dammit, Jonah," she says. "That's what that was? Just a reminder?"

"A reminder that you like this. Another little taste of cake."

She wets her lips again and then lifts her hand to her hair.

"And now my hair is down."

"I am right about this. You need to go into this like a date."

"And hope that James can kiss like you." She presses her hand against her stomach and stares at me.

"Are you going to find out?" I ask her. "Are you going to let him kiss you?"

That's what I want. At least that's what I tell myself.

She takes a deep breath. "I don't know yet. I haven't thought about it."

I shake my head. "Liar. You've thought about it."

"I don't know if I want to kiss *James*."

I frown. "If you don't want to, then definitely don't. I don't expect you to do anything you don't want to do. But I do want you to think about if you want to kiss him while you're with him tonight. Don't just look at him as someone who has something Cara needs."

She swallows. "We're still just having drinks, but I'll tell him Stacy doesn't need to come."

I sigh. Linnea is still going to try to compromise with me, though. "Fine. But you're having dinner with him before we leave D.C.."

She pulls out her phone. "If I don't want to, then I definitely won't. Because you won't expect me to do anything I don't want to do."

She just throws my words back at me casually as she looks down at her phone and starts typing a message.

Right.

She's right.

And inexperienced with dating or not, she's no pushover.

I should really remember that.

And I thought dealing with a rogue prince all these years was difficult.

CHAPTER 14
JONAH

At the restaurant, I take a seat at the table next to James and Linnea's. This is a very upscale French restaurant, so the tables are not right on top of one another and there's plenty of space for them to have a private conversation. I don't intend to eavesdrop. I just need to be there in case she needs anything. Specifically, in case she tugs on her left earlobe. That's the sign we came up with if she needs to leave.

She also knows that she better use that ear tug carefully.

No, I don't want her doing anything she's not comfortable with, but she needs to give this a chance.

I sincerely doubt she's going to need to leave. James Hill is a very nice man. Professional. About eight years older than Linnea. And I'm sure he's dated. He knows how to handle himself with a woman.

Still, there is no situation I would not rescue her from, even if she's only nervous.

I order a drink and an appetizer.

I've never developed a taste for French food. I'll grab something later or have something delivered to the hotel.

I'm sitting out of James's line of sight, but where Linnea can see me. We have other hand signals besides the ear tug. Mostly signs for me to give her. Like me loosening my tie to signal she's acting uptight and needs to relax. Or me smiling to remind her to smile. Me shaking my head to tell her that no, she should not talk about Astrid and Alex any longer. Real complicated codes like that.

There are a million things she can talk about other than her famous siblings. There are things about *Linnea* that are interesting.

They are about halfway through their entrée and she starts to reach for her left ear. I catch her eye and shake my head.

She's bored, but she doesn't need rescuing. They've been talking about the latest thriller novel that's been sitting at the top of the New York Times list. They've both read it and other novels by the author. See? They have some things in common. They both also know some online personality who teaches kids about science on social media —Bill someone—and they've exchanged anecdotes about meeting him.

I have to fight a smile, though. She is trying, and I must admit, Hill isn't a fascinating conversationalist.

This is why I wanted to cross him off the list.

Still, he's great practice for her. He's intelligent, and they do have things in common. They haven't talked a lot about green energy, though they did get onto a long tangent that I had to finally give her the sign to wrap up.

She has learned a little bit about some of his colleagues,

and that he has been in talks with Canada about some of his research and development.

She shot me a look when he said that, and she seemed less panicked about the conversation and more concerned about what that would mean for Cara.

I'm amazed at how well I know this woman. I can tell her different kinds of smiles, and her different kinds of panic.

I gave her what I hoped was a reassuring look and indicated that we would talk about it later.

I'm sure she's still distracted by that.

"James, will you excuse me? I need to run to the ladies' room." She's already pushing her chair back and standing.

"Of course," James says, coming partway to his feet.

"Thank you. Just be a minute." Then she shoots me a look.

Clearly I'm supposed to come with her. To the ladies' room. I sigh.

I wait until she's out of sight, then I wipe my mouth and push my chair back, fishing my phone out of the inner pocket of my jacket.

My waitress is by my side immediately. "Is everything all right?"

"Yes. I just need to take this call. I'll be back."

She smiles. "I hope so."

She's been flirting all night. I give her a small smile that is friendly, but not encouraging. Then I head in the direction of the restaurant lobby with my phone to my ear. James knows I'm Linnea's driver tonight, and I don't want him to think anything strange is going on.

She's standing outside the restrooms in the short hallway just around the corner from the lobby.

"What are you doing?" I ask.

"I don't want to kiss him."

I lift a brow. "Okay. You had to tell me this now?"

"Yes. Because I need to talk to him more about Canada. But I don't want to go on another dinner date with him. And I don't want to kiss him. So I wanted you to know so you can stop glaring at me."

"I'm not glaring at you."

"But you will when I start talking about Canada."

I take a breath. Then nod. "Okay. Fine."

I should not feel relief that she doesn't want to kiss him. I should be frustrated. I should feel this is a setback.

I don't.

"Also," she says. She's watching me, chewing on the inside of her cheek.

"What?"

"If he tries to kiss me later, how do I dodge that without offending him?"

"Just...turn your head so he hits your cheek," I tell her. "Don't pull back, but...you've had your cheek kissed a million times."

"I have. But not by someone who was going for my mouth."

I smile. "Fair enough. Just turn a bit."

She steps closer to me. "Can I practice with you?"

Both of my brows lift. Then my eyes narrow. "Practice *avoiding* my kiss?"

She smiles. "We should do that, right? Since this is all so wrong between us?"

She says 'so wrong' with just a touch of sarcasm and I find myself stepping forward. "It is wrong."

"Well, wrong isn't really accurate. It's complicated, sure. But we're not breaking any moral rules. Or any laws. Nothing like that."

This is *not* good. I need her on my side here. I need her to be in agreement that us not being involved beyond friends is the right thing to do.

Because I'm not sure I'm strong enough to do this alone.

"The king would never let me have you."

Her eyes widen. And there's heat there. She runs her tongue over her bottom lip. "The king isn't here."

"You're asking me to have a fling with you while we're here?" I ask her bluntly. "Where the king won't know?"

"Well, I thought—"

"No."

"Jonah—"

"*No*," I say more firmly. I take another step closer and now anyone walking by will know that we are not just casual acquaintances. "Because I won't want to give you up."

"Oh." She says it softly. Almost as if she's touched by it.

And I have to know... "What are you thinking right now?"

"How nice it is to be wanted."

My chest tightens suddenly and almost painfully. I wasn't expecting that. "You..." I have to clear my throat. "You have to know you are."

"I feel...appreciated," she says. "Often. I feel needed, too. The king, other members of his advisory groups, citizens, my family, all make me feel important. It's not that. But wanted, like this, the way you make me feel, is very new. Very unique."

Well, fuck.

I want this for her. I want her to feel wanted. Beyond her job and the things she's given up and is willing to give up for other people, the things she's capable of doing, I want her to feel wanted just as she is.

I lift my hand, cup her face, and lean in.

Our lips meet and I take the moment to kiss her. Sweetly. At least as sweetly as I'm capable of kissing this woman when even her smile across a room can set me on fire. I slide my hand down her side and over her hip, finally feeling the silk of this damned dress, warmed by her body underneath.

I give her hip a squeeze and lift my head. "You were supposed to turn, so I only kissed your cheek."

"I forgot," she says softly, her breath warm against my lips.

"No, you didn't."

"No, I didn't. I didn't want to turn away from you."

My heart squeezes. I press my lips quickly to hers again, unable to resist, then I step back. "You have to go back to your table."

She nods. "To talk about Canada and the energy project."

And I feel myself nodding. Because I don't give a fuck if the rest of her conversation with James Hill is about business. She's not falling for him.

And I'm far too happy about that.

CHAPTER 15
LINNEA

An hour later, I sigh as I slide into the front seat of the black rental car.

Jonah shuts the door, and I watch as he rounds the front bumper.

God, he's hot.

He's such a great kisser, too.

Guys who look like that should be great kissers. It's only fair.

As if I know anything about great versus bad kissing.

But if I thought kissing James would be like kissing Jonah, I would have been all over him, and somehow I *knew* it wouldn't be. Nothing in me tingled. Nothing in me got hot when James looked at me.

How can I just know that it would be different?

Jonah gets in and starts the car.

"So you were right about James being boring," I tell him. "*But* he is willing to look over my plan to keep Cara competitive with Canada for the energy project. So the dinner wasn't a waste." I pause. I want to tease him. Poke at him. Flirt? Maybe? Is that what this is? But I want to get a reaction out of Jonah. "And I *did* get a hot kiss tonight, anyway."

He doesn't respond immediately. I glance over and see the muscle in his jaw tense. It makes me smile. It's a reaction and I know now that it means I'm getting to him. In a good way.

"You're going to keep Cara competitive with *Canada*?" he asks, ignoring the mention of the kiss.

I smile. "Yes."

He glances over at me as he pulls out of the parking garage and into traffic. "Of course you are. That's awesome. How?"

"I'm not sure yet. But when I do, James will look at the plan."

"You don't have a plan yet?"

"Well, no. I just found out that Canada is also in talks with him about taking his research facility there."

Jonah chuckles. "You'll figure it out."

That makes me feel warm.

"When does he need to know?"

Soon. So I need to get to work. "He's flying to Canada next month. They're beating us on labor costs and I don't love the idea of bringing those down, to be honest. I want our people paid well. So we need to give James's company something else that makes Cara more attractive. The real key is getting the king on board, of course. He didn't really like James when he met him."

"Really?" Jonah looks surprised.

"No. But he told me he trusted me. If I like James, Diarmuid will listen to him."

Jonah just smiles at that. And yes, it's a good feeling

knowing that I have the king's trust. I've earned it. Diarmuid knows that my intentions are always to do what's best for Cara.

"Diarmuid does agree this is a great project to bring jobs to the island." I turn in my seat to look at Jonah. "In fact, this new plan to woo James could be something great for Torin to present to Diarmuid."

Jonah looks at me again. "You'd let Torin present it?"

"He needs something to show Diarmuid that he's serious about being king. That he has good, solid ideas and that he's able to work with international influencers."

"But it will be your idea."

"Torin can help me. We'll discuss it. He can add to it."

"The king will know you're a part of it."

I shrug. "That's okay. But we can tell him that Torin sealed the deal."

Jonah clears his throat. "That's really great of you."

"Well, maybe if Torin can prove that he's doing a great job and is really dedicated, and that we can work together even without being married, the king will let up on the arranged marriage. Maybe then it won't matter..." I trail off as I feel Jonah's gaze on me.

"Maybe what won't matter?" he asks. His voice is rough.

I swallow and stare down at my hands. "If Torin can show he's ready to be king and we can prove our professional relationship is strong, maybe it won't matter to the king who I fall in love with."

In my peripheral vision, I see Jonah's grip on the steering wheel tighten.

"You didn't eat much at dinner," he says, as he pulls to a stop at a traffic light.

Wow. Okay, I put that out there and he's just going to

avoid it entirely. And not even subtly. But he gripped the steering wheel. "I guess I don't like veal as much as I thought."

"Are you hungry?"

I think about it. I was focused on Canada and how getting the project to Cara could help us out of the arranged marriage and how that could mean Jonah and I could have a relationship. That is all way more important than eating.

But now that he's asked, I realize I am. A thought occurs to me, and I reach out and grab his thigh. "Can we get pizza?"

He looks at me. "Really? You want pizza?"

"I want the pizza that you love when you come here. To the U.S. I mean. Do they have that kind here in D.C.?"

His leg muscle tenses under my hand. "They do. One of my two favorites, anyway."

"I want to try that," I tell him. "You rave about it, so it must be amazing."

He looks over at me again and puts a hand on top of mine. He smiles. "I don't know about that. But it is something I always try to have when I come."

"Then let's do that."

He drives for two blocks without responding, then he seems to make a decision and nods and takes a left. "Okay. We'll get pizza." He's quiet for a couple more blocks, but he keeps his hand on mine.

"I'm sorry that you haven't had a great story," he finally says.

"What do you mean?"

"You love collecting stories from people. People who are living different lives from yours." He chuckles. "Which is just about everyone in the world. But I know that you tried to engage our stewardess in conversation on the plane. Her story about how she became a stewardess for the royal family was also boring."

I nod. "It really was. How is that possible? How can her story not be interesting? And James tonight. How do you become one of the richest men in the world, interested in innovation and technology that could change things for entire countries, maybe even the whole world, and your story about that is boring? He's really just a guy who saw a need for something and decided to make it. Which is great. The work he's doing is wonderful, but it's like he found out that people wanted to have bright purple bridges, so he went and painted a bunch of bridges purple. It's nice, but it's not really that interesting."

"I agree. Surely he's met some really fascinating people along the way. Or had a few weird things happen in the research. Or *something*," Jonah says. "He could at least have told you those things."

"Yeah."

Jonah turns into the parking lot of a restaurant.

"We're here. Mike's. Let's go get you some pizza."

I have to move my hand, but he comes around to open the car door for me, and he settles his hand on my lower back as we head inside.

As we're waiting at the small red and white checkered table in a corner for our pizza and cheesy bread to come out, Jonah pushes a big glass of water toward me, then leans back in his chair. He props one ankle on his opposite knee and lifts his bottle of beer to his lips. He takes a drink as he watches me sip from my water.

After he swallows, he says, "You know, you should probably ask a royal bodyguard how he went from a regular kid in North Carolina to best friend and bodyguard to a prince in a country that he'd never even heard of. That might be an interesting story."

I look at him. Then I actually think about that. I lean in. "You're right. There is no straight line between North Carolina and the Royal Palace in Cara."

He smiles and lifts his bottle again. He's dressed in a dark suit, as he often is, his hair is styled perfectly, his beard trimmed, and he's wearing a watch that cost more than probably most of the cars in the parking lot. Still, he manages to look at ease, and like a regular guy in many ways.

It's his attitude. His air. He never acts better than anyone and I swear he can fit into any situation or crowd.

I prop an elbow on the table and rest my chin in my hand. "So how did you become a bodyguard for the royal family of Cara?"

"I grew up in Durham, North Carolina. My mom was a lawyer and then a judge. My dad was a stay-at-home dad as soon as my mom graduated from law school. Prior to that, he ran my grandpa's hardware store with him in a little town outside of Durham."

I reach into my clutch for my phone. I pull it out and open a browser window.

"What are you doing?" Jonah asks.

I look up. "Looking up North Carolina and Durham. I know nothing about it."

He gives me a smile, and it makes my belly swoop. It's warm and affectionate, and he looks almost as if he expected my answer and is pleased by it.

I smile back. "So, how did you get from Durham to Cara?"

He grins. "I was in college, studying criminal justice. Thought I'd follow in my mom's footsteps. I was going to be a cop first, then look at law school. So I took a bunch of poli sci classes and world history classes. Loved them. Excelled at them. I was actually invited by one of my poli sci professors to this book club that met monthly. It was an interesting mix of some younger guys, past students of his, and also men in various fields—business, law, politics. They just got together, talked about books, current events, and inevitably the conversations drifted to things like politics and history. I loved it. I felt so flattered to be there."

"Wow. He really saw something in you," I comment. Jonah is quiet and absolutely is in the background when he's with Torin. That's the job. But I've seen them interact one-on-one. Jonah absolutely holds his own with the prince. They have lively discussions about any number of topics. Jonah is intelligent and articulate and knows as much about Torin's role and all of the nuances to it as Torin does.

I know Torin sees how incredible Jonah is. I'm also very glad this professor and members of this impressive 'book club' did.

He goes on. "One day, after a really big test, that professor asked me to stay after class. I thought maybe I'd bombed the exam or something. Instead, he introduced me to someone from the U.S. Secret Service."

My eyes widen. "Oh. Wow."

He nods. "He was more connected than I realized. One of the men in the book club had been an advisor to a senator at one time. There was a big D.C. network that I wasn't aware of. Anyway, my professor had talked me up and, long story short, they asked if I had any interest in applying. I gave them an enthusiastic yes. That was a little above and beyond what I'd imagined, honestly, but when they asked, it just clicked. I knew immediately that I'd love to be a part of something like that."

"That makes sense."

He looks curious. "It does?"

"Of course." He's watching me as if what I'm saying is significant, so I go on. "You're drawn to big things and able to immediately see something as special, but you're okay with not being able to tell anyone about it.

"You kept Torin's identity—hell, Fiona, Saoirse, and Cian's too—secret for a decade. You know that people who are doing the big, out-in-front, public facing work have scores of people behind them who never get recognized. But you know those people behind the scenes are just as important. You know the leaders in front *need* those people and you're comfortable knowing you're doing vital work even without any fame or fanfare.

"You can't even really flash your badge. You don't wear vests with three big letters emblazoned across the front or shout out your identity when you storm into a room. You're very confident just *knowing* you're doing something big without everyone else needing to know. You're perfect for Secret Service."

He stares at me for another several seconds. Then he clears his throat. "Thank you."

"Of course." I smile. "Though I guess you're not as behind the scenes as you thought."

"What do you mean?"

"I see you. So did these people."

His gaze turns more intense, and I feel the air around us heat.

I swallow hard. "So, did the U.S. Secret Service assign you to Torin?" I ask. I want every detail about Jonah.

"No. I never was in the U.S. Secret Service. They were

just the contact Cara made. They said they'd been approached about a special assignment and were looking for someone like me. My age, with my interests and competency. So, I came to D.C. for a sit-down with some very high-up people. One of them was from Cara, though I didn't know it at the time. After my interview, they filled me in on a prince from a small, barely known country who had abdicated the throne, but needed a companion and bodyguard who could pass for his best friend and roommate at college."

"You gave them an enthusiastic yes about that, too?"

He shakes his head. "The prince sounded like a pompous asshole."

I laugh.

Jonah grins. "I wanted to meet Torin first. And I wanted to do it without him knowing who I was. So I showed up at a college party, befriended him, and we hit it off immediately."

I laugh again. "You just got drunk together?"

"Nope. We had a few drinks. But we sat up until four a.m. around a fire pit debating the various forms of government and how empires have risen and fallen throughout history."

I shake my head. "Oh my God." *That* I can easily picture.

"Yeah. I knew then that I could hang out with him for the next few years. So I asked him to go bowling the next weekend with me and some buddies."

"Bowling?"

"Absolutely. It's a great way to get to know what someone is really like."

I'm fascinated. "Did he agree? Wait, did you have buddies?"

Jonah laughs. "I had Secret Service 'buddies' who

played the part. And yes, he did agree. Torin had never been bowling before and he's always up for trying new things." Jonah studies me for a moment. "You two have that in common."

I nod. "Growing up in Cara, we don't have a lot of 'new and different'. I'm guessing the other O'Grady kids were the same. I know Alex and Astrid were. They wanted to try all kinds of new things when they got to the U.S.."

"Definitely," he agrees.

"So how did the bowling go?"

"It told me exactly what I needed to know," Jonah says. "I followed him around for the week, without him knowing, of course, and observed him in class and with other people. I realized he was basically a good guy. But the bowling sealed it. Exactly as I knew it would."

"What does bowling tell you about a person?" I ask.

"Okay, well, bowling is a sport that few people are really good at. But it's an activity that most people can have fun doing if they have the right attitude. So first and foremost, it tells me about someone's ability to enjoy doing something they're not good at, and to laugh at themselves. It also attracts a wide variety of people. A bowling alley will have young and old, all walks of life, people who are healthy and strong, and people who aren't and struggle. There are people who bowl for a sense of community and belonging, and people who bowl just to hang out with a group they're already a part of." He shakes his head. "It's actually very cool how many different types of people bowl."

I'm watching him, completely caught up in just listening to him talk. "I've never bowled. I know nothing about it. But you've sold me."

He smiles. "My plan for Torin and bowling was to see

how he responded to not being good at something, how he treated a variety of people, how he reacted to losing, to being jealous, and to being unrecognized. I was pretty sure no one there would know who he was, and I wanted to see if he was serious about wanting to be a royal in hiding."

"And how he reacted to being jealous?" I ask. "What's that mean?"

"Oh, I fully intended to flirt with whoever he flirted with."

I laugh. "You were sure he'd be flirting?"

"Have you met Torin?"

I nod, still grinning. "And did he pass all your tests?"

"He did. He was charming to absolutely everyone, he talked a very cute girl into teaching him to bowl since he sucked so bad, he helped an older guy out in the parking lot when he saw he had a flat tire, and he never seemed to care a bit that no one knew who he was."

I love this story in part because I do love hearing that Torin has always been a good guy, but I love seeing Jonah talk about his best friend. The affection and connection there are so clear.

"I'm surprised Torin knew how to change a tire," I say. "I have no idea how he would have learned that. That's not really something the royals ever have to do."

"Oh, he didn't change it," Jonah says. His eyes are almost *twinkling* with amusement. "I said he helped the guy out. By getting *me* to change the tire."

I laugh loudly, then cover my mouth. "That makes more sense," I admit.

Jonah is grinning widely. "Yeah."

"And the cute girl? Did you flirt with her?"

"I most certainly did. Got her number too."

"And he didn't care?"

"Well, he got her number *too*, and decided to make it into a competition. We both called her, even took her out, planned to see who she chose in the end."

"And?"

"She didn't want to choose. She tried to talk us into a threesome after only two dates with each of us."

My eyes go wide. And my cheeks get very red, I'm sure. Not out of embarrassment, but because... "Good for her."

His grin drops to more of a smirk and his eyes narrow slightly. "It didn't happen."

"No?"

"I don't share."

I swallow hard as the heat in those words slide through me.

"Neither does he."

Got it. "So who did she end up with?"

"Neither. She dumped us."

I shake my head. "Wow."

"But that day I told him I was pretty sure I'd be seeing him naked someday, anyway. He laughed and said I was great and good-looking, but not his type. The next day when I walked into the meeting where he was going to meet his bodyguard, the look on his face was priceless."

I laugh. "How many times have you seen Torin naked over the years?"

"Countless times."

I tip my head. "How many times has he seen you naked?"

His eyes lock on mine and there's heat there that I can feel swirl through my body. His thumb strokes across the back of my hand. "I have no idea."

"I bet he knows. It's a very memorable experience."

"Duchess," he says, his voice low and full of warning.

Just then our food arrives. He lets go of my hand and leans back. I miss his touch, but I also want to try this pizza.

I take a bite and moan. "Oh my *God*."

"Duchess," he says again, with that same low warning in his tone.

I look up. "What?"

"No moaning."

"But this is so good."

"You sound like you did when I kissed you."

I smile. "This is just about as good."

He shakes his head. "Nope."

I laugh and take another bite. But after I chew and swallow, I ask, "How about you?"

"How about me what?"

"How does kissing me compare to your favorite pizza?"

He sets his piece down, wipes his mouth, then leans over and swipes his thumb over the corner of my mouth. He lifts the little smear of pizza sauce to his mouth and sucks it off his thumb. "I'd give this pizza up to kiss you again in a heartbeat, Duchess."

I like that a lot. I lean in. "Well, good news, you don't have to. You can kiss me whenever you want." I pucker up.

He smirks and lifts the pizza. "I didn't say I wanted to kiss your mouth."

I gasp and my cheeks get warm.

He looks very proud of himself.

So, I just say, "Okay."

He chokes as he tries to swallow. After coughing, he says, "You have to stop."

"I'm practicing flirting. How am I doing?"

"Fine." He blows out a breath. "Good. Except that's a little direct."

"You're the one who was direct first."

He nods. "Okay, fair enough. Christian probably won't talk about...that."

"Kissing other parts of me than my mouth, you mean?" I ask, nibbling on my pizza crust.

Jonah shifts on his chair, and I grin. "Yes. That."

"I like when you do it," I tell him. "It makes me hot and tingly."

Jonah freezes in reaching for his beer. "Jesus, Linnea." He frowns.

"What? Isn't that the point? Wouldn't you be disappointed if you talked about kissing me and *I* didn't get hot and—"

"Okay," he cuts me off. "Right. So I need to stop too."

"Please don't." I don't mean for my voice to get soft and husky. It just happens.

His stare is direct. And hot.

"We shouldn't talk about these things. Even in practice."

"You're the perfect one," I tell him. "I trust you. You can tell me what I'm doing right. And wrong."

"You're not doing a damned thing wrong."

"No?"

"No." He shifts on his chair again. "You're being honest and open and curious and that's damned hot."

Oh. Good. I smile widely. "Then why stop?"

"Because it makes me want things I shouldn't want."

"But," I say, continuing even when he shakes his head. "I have never made a man want anything from me before. Nothing from *me* as a woman. Not on purpose, anyway. I've made them want things from Cara and the king, of course, but not *me* personally. And I really like it. And you want me to really like it," I remind him. I've discussed and negotiated with heads of state, business tycoons, and scholars. I can make a compelling argument to *anyone*. "You want me to want more *cake*. You want me to get caught up in all of this. I didn't feel it with James, but I feel it with you. So I should keep exploring it in the hopes that it's so good, there's no chance of me settling for things with Torin."

His jaw clenches. He watches me without speaking. Then he says, "Well, this is a good change of attitude before you go out with the senator tomorrow night."

I frown. "I don't know if it will feel the same with Christian."

"Why not?"

"I've met him before and never felt tingles."

"You met me a long time ago and didn't feel tingles."

"That's not true."

His frown deepens. "Excuse me?"

"I did feel tingles when I met you."

He narrows his eyes. "When was this?"

"When I walked in on your naked ironing. That was actually the first time I'd ever felt tingles like that. It was the first time I'd ever seen a man naked, too. In real life."

"In real—" He breaks off as one of the waitresses comes over and offers to box up the rest of our pizza. "Yes, thank you," he tells her. He also hands over his credit card to settle the bill. When she moves off he says, "Well, that doesn't count."

"Why not?"

"That wasn't the first time we met. You met me long before that. And not only did you *not* feel tingles, you don't even remember it."

"When did we meet?"

"The first Christmas Torin went to Cara after abdicating. He'd been in the U.S. for about three years."

I remember that. And now that I think about it, I remember there being a number of people with Torin. Fiona and Saoirse were there. Her bodyguard, Colin. Cian and his bodyguard, Henry.

"That holiday was especially overwhelming. I was afraid Torin was coming back to rescind the abdication. There was so much tension with Diarmuid and everyone. And I was there only for a day. And I was trying very hard to *avoid* Torin. Which, I suppose, meant avoiding you." I frown, thinking back. "But I do remember noticing all of you. The bodyguards, I mean. You were all intimidating, but it was interesting having new guys around and..." My gaze snaps back up to his. "*You* were trying to keep me away from Torin, too!" Now I remember. "I was trying to sneak off to one of the guest rooms to hide out away from everyone. And you and Henry stopped me in the hallway. You said I wasn't allowed on the third floor. Which was bullshit. I was allowed everywhere. But you wouldn't let me pass."

He smiles. "You do remember. And no tingles."

"No. I was too busy being annoyed." I lean in. "By the way, I got up to the third floor. I know that entire palace inside and out. Including the secret passageways."

He laughs. "I'm not at all surprised *now*. But you didn't bump into Torin. That was our job. Keeping you apart."

I roll my eyes. "He was so worried I'd throw myself at him and beg him to marry me."

Jonah nods. "Pretty much."

"Ugh."

"Yeah. Well, you avoiding him made our job of helping *him* avoid *you* a lot easier."

"You're welcome. And we saw each other again at other holidays," I say. We did. I remember now. But I always did the same thing—tried to avoid Torin and tried to avoid seeming interested at all lest our families start wedding planning.

Jonah nods. "Of course." He leans in. "And no tingles."

"Okay," I concede. "But I *do* feel the tingles now. Even before we kissed."

That wipes some of the smugness off his face. "Well, then, you might feel some with the senator. Now that you're...in the mood."

"I wasn't 'in the mood' when I walked into your room when you were ironing. Or all the times you've touched my arm or lower back. Or all the times you've smiled at me, or stood close enough I could smell you, or wrapped a pashmina around me, or—"

"Okay," he cuts me off. Then he shakes his head. "You've felt tingles...all of those times?"

"I have. I ignored them as much as I could, of course, but yes...I felt them."

The waitress returns with the credit card slip and the boxed pizza.

Jonah doesn't say anything else about our conversation as he signs the slip, stands, pulls my chair out for me, and picks up the pizza. He escorts me out to the car, a hand on my lower back.

And yep, there are definitely tingles.

Whether he likes it or not.

CHAPTER 16
JONAH

"You've got to be kidding me."

I'm standing in the doorway to my bedroom, staring at the bed.

Then I look up at the ceiling.

Water is dripping from the ceiling onto the bed. And clearly has been for some time.

"Awesome."

Nearly an hour later, the maintenance men, the manager, and the assistant manager have surveyed the damage, and determined the leak in the pipes they were working on in the shower has extended into the bedroom. They've managed to contain the problem, but they can't fix the pipe or, obviously, dry out my bed in the next hour or so.

They've offered me several options to compensate for the inconvenience. Money, which I don't need. Another room, which I can't take because I need to be near Linnea—okay, maybe *need* is a strong word, but I want to be near her. I don't want to be in an entirely separate room on another floor.

They've offered to move both of us to another room, but the two-bedroom suites like this one are all still occupied. The other options are regular rooms with two beds—not going to happen—or a one-bedroom suite. That one at least has a couch that converts to a bed and would have a wall and door between us. But I'm not making Linnea pack up and move to another room.

"I'll be fine on the couch here," I say. Again, at least there's a wall and a door between us. French doors, to be specific.

"Absolutely not," Linnea says, emerging from her bedroom with her two suitcases. "We'll move to the one-bedroom suite." She looks at me and it is the look she often gives Torin. The one that says, 'I know you're going to fight with me and I'm ready'. "At least then you'll have a full-sized mattress," she says. "This couch is *not* big enough for you." She narrows her eyes. "And I know what you're going to say if I suggest we share the bed in my bedroom."

I clench my jaw tightly.

I glance at the blue velvet upholstered sofa. She's right, of course. It's way too small. It's not designed for sleeping and certainly not for a man my size. It's for…tea or something. Or, more likely, just to look nice I'll never get any sleep on that thing.

I look through the French doors into her bedroom. That bed is plenty big enough for both of us. But no, I'm not doing that.

I study her. She's not taking no for an answer, and she's already packed.

"Fine." I cross to her and take both suitcases. I hand

them off to the manager. "Please take Lady Olsen to the new room. I'll get my things together."

"Yes, sir. Of course." The manager hands the bags off to the assistant manager. "And I'll have some extra amenities sent up."

"That would be great."

We're finally settled in the new room forty-five minutes later. Linnea is unpacked, again. I've stored the champagne, chocolates, and fruit basket they sent up in the kitchenette, and made up the sofa bed.

"This is ridiculous, you know."

I look toward the doorway to her bedroom. She's got a shoulder propped against the doorframe. She's in a long, silky robe. I refuse to wonder what's underneath. At least for more than a few seconds. Her hair looks freshly brushed and I can tell she's just washed her face.

"Everything is fine," I tell her, tossing the pillow I'm holding onto the mattress beside me.

"You could just share my bed."

"Not without touching you," I tell her bluntly.

"I've shared a bed with Astrid a number of times and she's a huge bed hog. I'd survive."

"That's not what I meant. At all. And you know it."

"I wouldn't mind."

"You don't know that." I tuck my hands into the pockets of my joggers. "You've never been touched the way I would touch you."

I don't know why I'm poking at this.

General annoyance, probably. She's so goddamned tempting and I'm trying to be a good guy here, dammit, and...fuck. I want to touch her so badly I'm aching with it. I want to push her away. I want *her* to help me.

She lifts her shoulder in a small shrug. "I like every way you've ever touched me."

My body tightens.

She has no idea the things I want to do to her.

"And I touch myself and like that. Seems like I would like you touching me that way."

Lust slams into me.

Jesus. Christ.

"Linnea," I say low and firm.

"Yes?"

I want to know all the ways she touches herself. Does she really slide her fingers into her pussy or does she just play with her clit? How many fingers? How deep? Does she orgasm that way?

"Go to bed," I tell her.

She looks surprised, then disappointed.

She blows out a breath and turns away. "Goodnight, Jonah."

It won't be. It will be restless as hell now.

"Goodnight, Duchess."

Twenty minutes later, I'm on the mattress, in a T-shirt and boxers. The lights are off, everything is quiet, I should be drifting off.

But there's no fucking way.

This whole night with Linnea, this whole *trip*, is playing through my mind. Every single word.

She thought I didn't want her.

She truly sees me.

She trusts me.

She loves my touch.

She touches herself.

She wanted to share the bed.

Maybe the hardest one to forget, even more than the knowledge that she touches herself and likes it, was what she said earlier.

Maybe it won't matter to the king who I fall in love with.

I scrub a hand over my face.

She's a very smart woman. She knows nothing between us could ever be permanent. Even if she thinks she wants one night, or a brief fling, I have to be the one who's strong. I'm the one who understands that emotions can quite easily get mixed up into all of that. I'm the experienced one. It falls to me to keep this from becoming more complicated.

But I'm already fucked.

There are already emotions.

It's already complicated.

A sound drifts to me and I frown.

I still my breathing and listen more carefully.

What is that?

Then a horrible thought hits me.

That is a buzzing sound.

Only a few things make a buzzing sound like that.

And it is definitely coming from Linnea's bedroom.

Oh, hell no.

I take a deep breath and make my voice as calm as I can.

"What are you doing, Duchess?"

I hear her give a little squeak and the buzzing stops. There's no sound for a few seconds, then she asks, "You could hear that?"

"I could hear that. It better not be what I think it is."

There's no answer for a long moment. Then she says, "I'm trying to think of other things that would be making this noise. What do you *think* it could be?"

She's killing me. "You could tell me it's a handheld massager and you're using it on your neck."

Another long silence, then she says, "It's not."

I squeeze my eyes shut and curse under my breath. "You can't even lie to me about it?"

"I don't think I want to lie to you about it."

"Why not?"

"Because I'm curious about your reaction to knowing that I have a vibrator."

I groan and dig the heels of my hands into my eye sockets.

Is it her innocence that is making her talk like this? Or is it because deep underneath, she's actually a siren who wants to torture me?

Very likely the latter. She knows what she's doing.

"I don't need to know about your vibrator, Duchess."

"You know everything else about me. You know about my UTIs. You know my last OB/GYN appointment went well. You know a lot of things about this general part of my body."

I groan again. "Those are very different."

"Well, I guess you know this now too."

Then the buzzing starts again. My brows slam together. "Knock it off," I bark.

"What?"

"You cannot lay in there and use that, knowing I can hear it."

"Why not? I'm in my bedroom. I'm not bothering you. "

"You are most certainly bothering me."

"Why? This isn't loud enough to actually keep you awake."

I grind my teeth together. Then I suck a long breath in through my nose and let it out. "Because it's making me hard. And I'm not going to be able to sleep with a hard-on."

There. If we're just going to be all out in the open about everything, she can know that.

"So you *do* have a reaction to this," she says.

"Jesus Christ, Linnea," I finally say. "The fact that you're getting yourself off with a vibrator in the room a few feet away from me? Yes, I have a reaction to that. Stop it."

"I can't. I need this."

"You *need* this?" I repeat. I shouldn't. I should absolutely not continue this conversation.

"Don't you have headphones or something? Or you could go for a walk. Go down to the lobby. Or just pace out in the hallway. I'll come out and get you when I'm done."

Sure, that's just what I need. To know exactly how long it takes her to get herself off with her vibrator.

"You can't resist? For one night?"

Now I definitely want to know how often she uses that vibrator. And yes, how long it takes her to get herself off.

And if she has more than one vibrator. And what kind they are. But she said she touches herself. So sometimes she uses her fingers...

I reached down and press my hand over my aching cock.

Fuck. This is all so bad.

"I need to know what I like," she says softly.

But I hear it clearly. I think about her answer for a moment, then shake my head even though she can't see me. "What do you mean?"

"Well, for one thing, I'm wound up and need some release. For another, Astrid and I were talking earlier, and she made some really good points about knowing what I like and don't like about sex."

I give up any possible chance of actually going to sleep. I shove myself up to sit and scrub my hand through my hair. "I thought you've never had sex."

That knowledge has tortured me for months.

She better have never had sex.

That thought is not okay. If she's going to *marry* someone else, she *will* have sex and I have nothing to say about it. None of this should be any of my business.

But...somehow it is. I want to know what she likes and doesn't like too. I want to know that whoever she's with is treating her well. I want to be sure he's good enough for her. In *every* way, and yes, goddammit, that includes the bedroom.

"I haven't," she says. "Not with another person. But this is the only way I can do anything tonight. I guess," she adds. "This just seemed like a good place to start while it's all on my mind."

The buzzing noise has stopped. Thank God.

"A good place to start what, exactly?" Now I'm torturing myself. But how exactly should I end this conversation, anyway?

"Astrid agrees with you. That I'm missing out having not had sex. That I don't know what I'm talking about when I say I don't care about it or don't want it. She thinks I should try it so that I know what I'm giving up. And she believes it will help me want to date. She also thinks that I need to figure out what I like and don't like. She says if I find someone I like and am attracted to, but the sex is only so-so, I can coach him and it can get better. But I need to know what I like first. Obviously."

Astrid's great. I like her a lot. She's bold and feisty, and clearly, very self-aware and sex positive.

I also kind of hate her right now.

"So you and Astrid decided you need to get your vibrators out tonight?"

"We didn't specifically talk about vibrators. Though this is the one she gave me for my birthday."

I mutter another curse. I am so curious about what this vibrator looks like and what kind it is. Is it one she inserts, or is it just a clitoral stimulator...I shut all of that down.

"But she talked you into having sex? Before you marry Torin?"

"Yes. She said I'm missing out and that it's not fair for me to get married without knowing what I'm missing. And again, that I could coach any guy—"

"Yes, I caught that part," I cut her off.

We're both quiet for several seconds.

I don't know if I can do this.

I don't know if I can send her home with Christian Waite, the very good-looking, very charming, clearly-enamored-with-Linnea senator she'll be having dinner with tomorrow night.

But what are my options here?

"I was thinking," Linnea says after a moment. "You would be perfect."

I freeze. Literally every muscle in my body tenses. "For?" I ask. Stupidly.

"To teach me about sex. I'm sure you've had a lot of it."

"Hey," I say, offended for some reason.

"Well, you have, right? You've had sex. You liked it. You're good at it?"

I blow out a breath. "I have had sex. I do like it, and yes, I think I must be pretty good at it." All understatements, of course. I've had a lot of sex. I fucking *love* sex. And I'm *damned* good at it.

But sure, I had to learn to be damned good. No one

starts out phenomenal. It takes practice, and paying attention, and being very committed to the craft.

"So you'd be perfect," Linnea goes on. "I trust you. You already know all kinds of intimate details about me. Things that could be embarrassing, but they're not because you never judge me, you never make me feel stupid. So if I was clumsy, or not good at it, you'd be patient. You would take care of me. Like you do with everything else."

All of those muscles that were stiff from shock now tense up out of pure lust.

Would I take care of her? Fucking hell. I would take care of her over and over again.

Linnea Olsen needs to learn about sex? What she likes in bed? How her body can be the source of incredible pleasure? Damn right, I'd be the perfect instructor.

She definitely can trust me. And I absolutely would not judge a single thing. In fact, her inexperience is a fucking turn-on like nothing I've experienced before.

This is also the worst idea anybody's ever had.

"That's not gonna happen," I say. I wonder if she can hear the note of regret in my voice.

"I can't believe you won't help me with this!"

Suddenly, Linnea's voice is much closer. As in right behind the couch.

I turn swiftly. "What are you doing out here?"

"You say you like me, you say you want me, you claim to want to keep me happy, to want to help me with things, but you won't help me with *this*. This very important thing that even you agree I should do. I need to find out what I like, what I want, so that I'll go out and get it. And you are probably the *only* person I can totally trust for this. We're here together, alone, in this gorgeous hotel room, far from home where no one will ever know, and you still won't do it?"

The only light in the room is the pale blue nightlight from the kitchen, but behind her there's a soft glow, possibly from a lamp. It shines right through the flimsy, silky peach colored camisole and shorts she's wearing.

So that's what she had on under that robe.

She never came down to the palace kitchen like this. Thank God.

She has her hands on her hips and actually looks angry. And maybe a little hurt.

Her chest rises and falls as she breathes fast, her breasts pressing against the scrap of silk. The shorts caress the curve of her hips and the upper part of her thighs but leave plenty of creamy bare skin for my gaze to travel down.

And something in me snaps. I know exactly what it is—it's the very thin thread of resistance and sanity that I have been clinging to.

I shove up from the couch, stomp around the end of it, and stalk to her. Her arms drop to her sides and her mouth opens, but without a word I bend and hoist her over my shoulder.

"Jonah!"

I clamp my hands firmly around her silky thighs to keep her steady. And to keep myself from sliding my palms higher.

Soon enough, I'll know what she's wearing under the shorts.

I stride into the bedroom and toss her onto the mattress. Then I strip off my T-shirt.

"Be sure, Duchess."

Her eyes are wide, and she props up on her elbows to look at me.

"Are you..."

I set my hands on my hips.

I'm sure my erection is obvious behind the boxers I'm wearing.

I just let her look at me, big and hard for her. I'm not smiling. I'm also breathing harder. She should feel intimidated.

Of course she doesn't. Her gaze tracks over me, at least as far as my cock. She lingers there, then looks up at my face.

"I'm sure."

"You want to find out what you like," I say. "But you've never done this before. So we're going to do it my way. I'm going to make you come. I'm going to show you all the wonderful things your body can feel. *My way*. I'm in charge. I'm the one with the experience. I'm the teacher here. You are going to listen to me and do what I say."

I notice how she presses her thighs together. She nods. "Yes. Please. I have no idea what I'm doing."

My gaze lands on the vibrator lying on the duvet next to her. It's slim, only about four inches long, and neon blue. I look back at her. "You know a few things."

She knows what I was looking at. "A few things. But I've never done anything with anyone else."

"That changes tonight. In about one minute. So, be sure."

She nods. "I am."

I was an idiot if I thought I was going to leave Washington, D.C., without touching her. This might be the biggest mistake of my life, but I'm only a man. I like to think I am a good man, stronger than most, all of that, but we all have our limits.

Linnea Olsen is mine.

I was right that there is a light on in here. The light in the closet is on. I wonder if my duchess doesn't like full darkness. That works out well because I want to see *all* of her tonight. I cross to the bedside table and click on the lamp.

She doesn't say a word. Where some women protest having too much light, she just watches me. So far, so good.

"The only word you need to stop what we're doing is 'stop'," I tell her. "I'll decide what to show you, what you're ready to try, but if you don't like something, you can stop any of it at any time."

She nods. "Okay."

I glance at the closet again and smile. Oh, I have a fantastic idea. I can't fuck her tonight. Not this first time. There's so much more to show her first. She's a virgin. I cannot forget that. I *have* to be one hundred percent certain that she's ready for *me* to change that. There's no undoing that.

But I'm now sure that once I see her naked and see and hear her come, if she asks me for more, I'll say yes. It kills me to think of someone else being her first.

We are going to have a lot of fun tonight, though.

I stand by the side of the bed, looking down at her. Her hair looks even darker against the stark white of the sheets. Her pajama top has pulled up on her toned stomach and that strip of skin makes my mouth water. Her legs shift restlessly on the sheets.

Christ. Where to start?

She's watching me with wide green eyes, pink cheeks, mouth open as she nearly pants.

We are definitely doing this my way. We're going to find out what Linnea Olsen likes, but if she doesn't like the way I do things, that would be good. And save me a lot of time fantasizing about all the things to teach her. Because from here it gets *so* much better. Or worse.

Guess we'll see.

"I talk," I tell her. "Lots of words. Dirty ones. I love women's bodies. I love exploring, looking, touching, tasting. Sometimes I like it fast and dirty, sometimes slow and dirty. But always dirty."

"Okay."

"You sure?" I am positive. No one has ever said the things I intend to say to this woman.

"Totally sure."

I put one knee on the mattress and lean over. I stroke a hand up her leg. "You're okay with hearing me talk about your pussy? Saying things like I can't wait to feel you come apart all over my tongue? Tell you that I'll bet your sweet, tight cunt is so wet for me right now?"

My fingers are dragging back and forth over her inner thigh and she's watching me raptly.

I palm her thigh and squeeze. "You have to talk too, Duchess."

"Oh. Yes. I want all of that." She licks her lips. "I'm good with anything you say."

I move my hand higher. "You're telling me that I might be telling a future queen that I want her to grind her pussy harder against my mouth?"

She blows out a breath. "Yes."

"So dirty talk definitely goes on your Things I Like list."

I run my hand up under the bottom of her shorts.

No panties. Just hot silky skin.

"Take your top off." I need to see her tits. Now.

She reaches for the bottom of her cami. She wiggles a little as she slips it off over her head, making her breasts bounce.

Fuck. Me.

I'm done.

I don't care who I am, who she is, why we're here, what comes tomorrow. Right now, it's her and me and this bed and no one's going anywhere for a very long time.

She tosses the peach silk somewhere, but I don't bother watching. My eyes are glued to the full, firm breasts with the hard, dark pink nipples.

Of course, her tits are perfect. Everything about her is.

My hand is resting high on her hip, the web space between my thumb and finger fitted right along the crease where her thigh turns into her pelvis. Her skin is hot. And I need to touch her.

"Cup your breasts."

She does without hesitation, plucking at the nipples. She makes a soft moaning sound.

"That's right. Show me what you like."

She squeezes her nipples harder.

Fuck, yes.

"I want to suck on you, Duchess. All over. But starting right there."

She moves one hand. "Yes, please."

I lean over, bracing a hand by her shoulder. "I'm going to take your shorts off," I tell her just as I fasten my mouth on her nipple.

I suck hard, lick, then suck again. I slip her shorts down her legs at the same time.

When she's arching into me and totally bare, I lift my head and look down.

"Fuck," I breathe out. "You're exquisite. "

She's all smooth, lightly tanned skin, perfect curves, and pinkness—sweet, tempting pinkness.

"Touch me more, Jonah," she says quietly, her legs sliding restlessly on the sheets.

"For sure." I cup her breast, loving the way she fills my

palm, and run my thumb over the tip. Then I run my flat palm down her stomach.

Her stomach tenses and I slide my hand across the smooth skin.

"How many of these do you have?" I ask, reaching for her vibrator.

"Four."

I look at her in surprise as I pick it up. "And this is your pick? Your favorite?"

"I like all of them."

"Do you tease your clit with this? Or does it slide inside your pussy? Or a little bit of both?"

It's slim and simple. There's no extra attachment for clit stimulation while it's inserted.

She sucks in a breath. "I mostly like it on my—" She takes a breath. "Clit."

I swear I get even harder just hearing her say that word.

"That's fastest," she adds. "I told you I mostly do it for release."

I turn it on, the buzzing filling the room. "What do you think about while you use it?"

"Sometimes I just pretend it's some guy. Faceless. Nameless. I make up scenarios. Like we met at a party and danced a few times and then he pulled me into a deserted room, because he just couldn't keep his hands off of me any longer. Sometimes we have known each other for a long time, and I've been flirting, and he found out I'm about to get married, and he comes and whisks me away."

Now I'm staring at her. These aren't just dirty fantasies, like some guy going down on her in the shower. These are entire scenarios.

"It's you a lot of times," she says.

I stare at her. "You don't have to say that."

"But it's true. It's been you for a long time."

I want that to be true. God knows how many nights I've thought about her with my hand wrapped around my cock. I'm not proud of it. I've tried not to, but I haven't been able to resist entirely.

And I know she needs to hear that.

"I'll bet I've come to thoughts of you more often than you have to thoughts of me," I tell her, leaning over, and pressing a kiss to her mouth. "You are definitely the star of my greatest fantasies." I kiss her more deeply now, dragging the buzzing vibrator up her inner thigh. "The ways I've made you come in my imagination could keep us busy for days."

"Oh God, Jonah," she breathes against my mouth.

I drag my jaw along hers then down her throat. I place a kiss at the base of her throat, then give into the urge and suck lightly on her skin. I might make a mark. But it will be gone by the time we go back to Cara. Still, I need to be careful. She's going on a date tomorrow night. I can't mark her anywhere that someone will see.

But I want to mark her someplace at least *she'll* see.

I drag my mouth down to her collarbone and then lower to the upper curve of her breast. I lick, then suck, then bite gently. She gasps and arches closer. I bite a little harder then suck again.

"Bite marks are important to mark your territory," I mutter against her skin.

Her hand goes to the back of my head, and I feel her fingers curling into my scalp. She likes that too. Not just the biting but me calling her my territory.

Of course, I will be making note of every tiny thing that gets a response out of this woman.

"I'm going to make you come for the first time with this vibrator," I tell her. "And my fingers."

She nods quickly.

"Then when you're hot, wet, and soft, I'm going to lick you clean and make you come again on my tongue."

She lets out a soft moan. "*Yes.*"

"The only thing I'm not completely sure of yet," I tell her, swirling my tongue around one nipple and then pulling it into my mouth before letting it go with a little pop. "Is if I'm going to spread you out, legs wide, everything open to me, and eat you like a feast, or if I'm going to make you sit on my face."

"Can we do both?" she asks, her voice husky.

I chuckle darkly. "We just might, my naughty, greedy girl."

She moans.

I kiss her again, then tell her, "I can make you desperate for this. Willing to do anything for my fingers, my mouth, my cock. Willing to spread your legs for me whenever I want it." She is definitely not pulling away from me. She's not pushing me away. She is not saying no or stop. She's arching closer, her fingers are digging into my hair, her pelvis is lifting. She loves this.

And I love knowing there's a dirty side to this woman. Selfishly, I never want anyone else to know that. I want to explore every single fantasy, everything that makes her hot and wet and needy. I want to be in charge of all of her orgasms. And I never want another fucking soul to have a clue that this gorgeous, sophisticated, bold, amazing woman has this side. Can be made to beg, can be pushed to the point of only caring about what I can do to this very sweet pussy.

"Do you want to see how many you can get?" I ask her. "Do you want to see how far I can push you?"

She nods.

"Do you trust me?"

"Implicitly."

"Sit up."

She does, and I slide onto the mattress behind her. I position my legs on either side of her and pull her up against me so that her ass is against my cock and her back is against my chest. "Look."

Her eyes focus in front of us. She immediately finds our reflection in the mirror on the closet door.

"You're going to watch me make you come apart. It will help you really see what it takes."

"Oh my God," she breathes.

"Look at you," I say, lifting my hands and cupping her breasts. "So fucking gorgeous. And all mine tonight. Needy for me. Only me."

Her hands come up to cover mine, but I shake my head. "Put your hands on my thighs. Don't move them. Just watch."

She does as I say. I play with her nipples, tugging with my fingers and running the vibrator over the hard tips. She squirms against me but doesn't move her hands.

Then I slide the vibrator down between her breasts and across her stomach, teasing her belly button and then gliding the vibrating silicon from one hip bone to the other.

"Spread your legs. Hook your feet on the outside of my ankles."

CHAPTER 17
LINNEA

I can't believe I'm doing this. For one thing, I am completely naked in front of Jonah Greene. Though, that does not feel as strange as it maybe should. It feels very comfortable. Natural. I think it's always felt inevitable.

Taking my clothes off for him was a no-brainer. I wanted to get naked with him months ago. It's only been building since then, and ever since the idea of him being the one to teach me about sex was planted, it has burrowed deep and grown large.

Now, I'm sitting on a bed, bare naked, spread out, with him behind me, in front of a mirror.

I did not expect this. I didn't expect a front-row seat to all the things he was going to do.

But this is hot. My entire body feels like it's on fire. The tingles I have felt in the past, because of this man are nothing compared to the electricity that is zipping along every one of my nerve endings.

He drags the vibrator back and forth across my lower stomach.

My clit feels every vibration.

I am aching with needing him to touch me there.

I squeeze his thighs and just watch. I'm not going to say a word. He's in charge. And I love it.

I love having someone take control like this. Someone who is purely here for my pleasure.

And *that* I definitely feel.

He's not even naked himself, but he's hard as a rock and won't let me touch him. He's doing all of the touching. All of the talking. He's doing this for me. I feel like he is slowly unlocking things. Spinning a combination lock, finding each number one by one, to get to the final exact combination that will open everything up.

Jonah doesn't have to say it. He is taking care of me. This is what he always does. I don't think he's able to be any other way.

So whatever he wants to do, however, he wants to do it, I am here for it.

"Look at you," he rasps in my ear. "I want to touch and lick and suck and bite every inch of you all at once."

I shiver again at the idea of him biting me—I had no idea that would be a turn-on. But I want to be marked. By Jonah. I want to be owned by him. I want to be his.

I tip my head back to rest on his shoulder, letting my eyes slide shut. "This feels so good."

The buzzing stops. My eyes open.

"Keep those gorgeous eyes open and on us," he says. "You close your eyes, it all stops."

I swallow and nod.

The buzzing resumes, with him dragging it down over

my mound, making small circles, but still not low enough to hit my clit.

He runs a hand down one of my thighs. "Right here," he says as he gives me a little pinch and I gasp. "I'm going to mark you right here." It's a spot high on my inner thigh. Obviously, no one but me will ever see it and it makes a hot swirl of need go through me.

"Oh yes," I say, unable to keep the words in.

He gives me a very pleased smirk in the mirror.

His hand travels up, and he finally cups my pussy. "Want to mark this too."

With his hot hand cupping me and the vibrator just above my clit, my entire pelvis clenches, and I feel myself get even wetter.

"Oh, God," I half moan, half gasp.

"Definitely will take a little nip here," he says, pinching one of my outer folds.

It sends a shock of sensation through me. Then he tugs, opening me.

"Goddamn, Duchess, your pussy is so gorgeous," he rasps.

I don't know what to say to that. I don't know if that's a compliment that you say thank you to. Which is fine, considering I don't have any oxygen in my lungs to form words.

Then he drags the vibrator down over my mound, my clit, pausing there only momentarily, and then down to my opening. He circles it with the tip.

"So wet, so needy. You need some pressure here. This little thing isn't gonna do any good," he tells me.

I shake my head from side to side, only vaguely registering what he's saying. He's saying something about me needing more down there, and that is true.

I haven't had sex before, but I know how it works. This empty aching inside? I very much want Jonah to use his cock to make that feel better.

"Need more," I tell him.

"Oh, I know, baby, I'm going to give you what you need," he says.

He circles my opening and then slides the vibrator partway inside. I whimper. The sensation is nice, but it's definitely not enough. Then he turns the vibrations up.

I grip his thigh. "Jonah!"

"I've got you," he promises. "You just let go and feel. Whenever you need to come. I'll tease you later."

I don't know what that means, but I shift against his hand and the vibrator. It's not enough though. I want the vibrations against my clit.

"Move it up," I plead. "My clit. Please."

"God you're magnificent," he tells me against my neck, his beard against my skin sending sensation skittering down my arm and across my chest, tightening my nipples further. "I love that you'll tell me what you need."

"You need to listen," I say, squeezing his thighs.

He chuckles against my neck, then moves the vibrator. Suddenly it's pressing against my clit.

"There?" he asks.

"Yes," I gasp, with pleasure and relief.

"You still need more," he says against my ear. "You need to be filled up."

I nod.

"Do you have a vibrator that does that? Something that really fills you up and gives you what you need? A nice thick one to stretch this pretty pussy?"

"Y—yes."

"Good, then this will be just fine." He slides his middle finger into me.

I can't help myself. I move one of my hands off his thigh and down to grip his wrist. To keep him there. "Jonah!" I gasp.

"Jesus, you're so tight. So wet for me."

"Yes," I agree, though I'm not registering all of his words perfectly.

"Eyes on me," he says gruffly. "Watch. Watch me stretch you open. Watch how you take my fingers."

My gaze immediately goes to the image in the mirror. My hair is tousled, my skin is flushed, and I'm lying against Jonah, my legs spread open. I barely recognize myself. But I love the image. I look overcome with lust.

But even more, I like the look on the face of the man holding me. Lust is also all over his features. He looks hungry and raw. But he is also watching me with a possessiveness that takes my breath.

Our position is intimate, and my body is completely on display, yet he's holding me almost protectively. One of his arms is banded around me, holding me firmly against him. Yes, that hand is pressing the vibrator against my clit, but that almost feels possessive as well. As if he is hell-bent on giving me this pleasure, on being the first, on uncovering all of my secrets.

I watch as he adds a second finger. The visual along with the stretch is delicious. Yes, one of my vibrators is about that large. I don't use it often, preferring the quick orgasm the clit stimulator gives me. But when I'm really into a fantasy or need a little more, I use that one.

But then Jonah does something the vibrator definitely does not. He starts moving, thrusting in and out, curling his fingers, then pulling his fingers apart to stretch me.

I gasp, then moan, squeezing his wrist hard.

"My job is to be sure you have everything you need, remember?" he asks gruffly. "I want to be sure you know just how good you *can* feel. So you want it and *demand* it. So you make sure you get what you need every fucking time."

He rubs against my inner wall, right over my G-spot. I gasp again and arch into his hand. "Oh my God!"

"Tight, hot, wet. All for me, isn't it?" he asks against my ear, then drags his beard up and down my neck.

"Yes, yours, oh my God," I babble, writhing in his arms.

"Give it to me, Duchess. Give it all to me. It's mine. This first orgasm with a man's hand on this sweet pussy. I want it."

I come hard. Hot pleasure spills over me, and I cry out his name.

"That's right," he mutters. "That's fucking right."

He eases the vibrator away, but his fingers still stroke slowly in and out. He lets me come down and only then does he ease his fingers out.

I realize his other hand is splayed possessively over my stomach and he's holding me tightly to his body.

"So. Fucking. Gorgeous," he tells me.

Then, in the mirror, I watch as he lifts his hand to his mouth and sucks on his fingers.

My eyes widen.

He chuckles. "That's the part that surprises you?"

"I just—"

He brings that same hand to my mouth. "Open."

My cheeks blaze. "What?"

"Open your mouth, Duchess."

With his other hand, he presses his thumb against my chin, urging my mouth open. Then he slides that middle finger along my bottom lip, then partway into my mouth.

"Suck," he says simply.

I do, my eyes locked on his in the mirror. I mostly taste the saltiness of his skin, but there's maybe another slight, unfamiliar flavor.

The sucking seems to affect Jonah, though. He presses his very hard cock into my ass.

"That was number one," he says, sliding his finger out of my mouth. "You were perfect. Can all of that go on your Like It list?"

"Definitely," I tell him with a smile.

"Then time for number two."

"Number two what?"

"Orgasm."

And before I can say a word, he's sliding down to lie on his back, and gripping my hips to turn me to face him.

"Come on up," he says.

"Up?"

"I decided how I want you. Grab that headboard."

I look at how he's lying, then look at the headboard.

"What—"

Hands on my hips, he pulls me up his body. "Pussy on my mouth, hands on the headboard."

Oh. God.

I move my knees to either side of his head and grip the headboard. Mine at home would be much better for this. The ones in the palace would be as well. But this will have to—

"Oh!"

Jonah pulls me down firmly—all the way down until I'm literally sitting on his face—and runs his tongue from my entrance to my clit in one long, firm lick.

"Damn, you are delicious, Duchess. Already addicted."

Then he does it again. And again. And again.

I just hang on. All of my weight is on Jonah. He's doing all the work, moving my body with his hands on my hips and making magic happen with his mouth. I think I say his name a couple of times. I know I say God's.

Especially when Jonah sucks on my clit. And when he thrusts his tongue inside me. And for sure when he flicks it back and forth across my clit.

Then I give a very loud, "Fuck!" when he nips me.

I look down to see him grinning up at me. "Told you, bite marks are important."

"That's yours now, huh?" I ask, my heart hammering. The throaty, breathless voice doesn't sound like mine.

"Yes." He squeezes my ass. "It is."

I keep watching, mesmerized as I watch his mouth, feeling his beard against my thighs, his tongue and lips and yes, a little bit of teeth again on my clit and seemingly every other inch between my legs.

His big hands are holding me tightly and I feel safe and definitely claimed, and…worshipped.

And I swear that's what shoots me over the delicious edge of another orgasm.

This man is worshiping me.

"Jonah!" My hand goes to his head, my fingers tangling in his hair as my thighs tighten around his head and I press down as the pleasure rolls over me.

A few seconds later, I feel Jonah's big hands lifting me up and back off his face.

He chuckles. "Need a little oxygen, Duchess. What a way to go, but if I suffocate, we can't do that again."

"Oh, sorry!" I start to shift to the side, meaning to slide off him, but he grips my thighs.

"Where're you goin'?"

"Just off of you."

"I very much want you *on* me." He pulls me back so I'm straddling his chest.

"This is...kind of an awkward position," I tell him, but I smile. I'm not sure he even heard me. He's staring at my pussy.

"Hello?" I wave a hand in front of his eyes.

He catches it and pulls my palm to his lips for a kiss. "Just marveling at my new favorite view."

I laugh. "You literally just had your face *in there*."

"And loved every second," he says. "But couldn't really *see* it."

That makes me laugh harder. This is all so ridiculous. "Come on, this close up, they must all look pretty similar."

"Not true at all and it doesn't matter," he tells me firmly. "This is *you*."

"What does that mean?"

His eyes are on mine now. "You're my dream girl, Duchess. I've never..." He clears his throat. "I've never known a woman this well or this long before..."

"Being this close to her pussy?"

He frowns. "It's more than that. You're different. I want to know all of you and yes, physically too. I'll admit I've pictured you naked many times. I've imagined more than just seeing you naked, too. But the reality is so much better. So much...bigger."

"*What?*" I laugh.

"Bigger emotionally," he says quickly. "Not *bigger*. Jesus, you're perfect. It's just blowing my mind that I'm here with you. Touching you. Able to look and touch. Able to make you come."

Yeah, this is bigger and he's going to start overthinking this any second. Like in the kitchen on his birthday.

And I'd rather not be naked straddling his chest when he pulls back.

I start to cover myself with my hand, trying to decide how to...dismount...in the most graceful, least humiliating way.

He catches that hand too and shakes his head. "Mine."

"Jon—"

Suddenly I'm on my back, both of my wrists held in one of his hands over my head.

His nose is nearly touching mine. "I said, mine."

Then he slides down my body, kissing my lips, my throat, both breasts, my ribs.

When he's down far enough that he can't hold my wrists together anymore, he growls, "Don't move your hands, or I'll put you over my knee and make this gorgeous ass bright pink."

I shiver.

He gives my stomach a little nip. "You're not ready for that, but reaction noted." Then he continues down my body until he's at my pussy. "Spread your legs for me."

I do.

"Good girl."

Oh, damn.

He notes that shiver too, I'm sure.

He settles between my thighs and spreads me open with his thumbs. I feel my face blush as he studies me so up close. Then he gives me a long lick.

After two orgasms back to back, I'm very sensitive and I gasp his name.

He grins up at me, but I swear it looks devious rather than amused.

He slides down another few inches. With his eyes on

mine, he leans in and licks my inner thigh, then sucks. Then sucks harder. Then bites.

I gasp as heat floods me.

That's going to leave a mark.

On his territory.

He kisses the spot, then shifts higher again.

"Jonah, I—"

But I don't complete that thought. Or even remember what it was as he proceeds to lick and suck and finger me to *another* orgasm.

Spread out. Like a feast.

He did it both ways. Just as I asked.

And when I come down from it, he kisses me deeply and says, "Mine."

CHAPTER 18
JONAH

> Henry: Of course this got all complicated. You got the angsty royal.

> Jonah: I did? Torin is more angsty than Declan?

> For sure. Declan's an asshole, but he's consistent. He's always the same. Fiona too. She's the passionate one, but she's always known who she is and what she wants. She causes trouble, for sure, but her drama is more external. Like raiding some asshole's farmstead in the middle of the night to rescue a bunch of animals or going to Congress to testify about laws and regulations.

In spite of everything, I smile as I read that. He's exactly right.

> And Cian?

> <grinning emoji> Cian is just happy to be here.

> Where's here?

> Wherever he is at the moment.

I laugh. Henry got the easiest of the four royals. Easiest of the five if we count Fiona's daughter Saoirse. She's a great kid, and we all helped raise her from the day Fiona had her, but she's a sassy little thing.

> You've had more broken bones than me, though.

> True. And enjoyed getting every one. Cian's not necessarily easy all the time, but he's an optimist. He's a fucking Suzy Sunshine, and it's hard as hell to be mad at him. And hell, as the youngest, there's always been no chance his pampered ass is sitting on any thrones.

All also true.

> You think Torin's the difficult one?

> We all do. The guy is always worked up about something. Mostly good things. He's passionate and smart and wants to make the world a better place. But he's always thinking about where he fits into that, and what he should be doing. My God, he abdicated because of a moral dilemma regarding the monarchy. And then he went home so his niece didn't have to be queen. He's loyal and a genuinely good guy, but yes…angsty.

I can't argue with any of that.

> So you banging his fiancée is very on brand for you two. That's dramatic AF.

I sigh. I needed to tell *someone* about what was going on with Linnea. No one outside of the palace even knew we were here in D.C. together. Typically, all the bodyguards stay in touch about travel and "assignments", i.e., where our protectees dragged us off to and why.

But this was the first I'd told anyone. And I'd only texted Henry and Colin rather than the whole group.

> We did not have sex.

> That is not true. The things you did were sex, my friend.

> No. It was all…

I sigh and shove a hand through my hair. And delete what I started typing. Henry's right.

> But I did not 'bang' her.

> Do you really think that matters at this point?

> Yes. That's one line we haven't crossed yet.

I hit send before I realize I should not have added the 'yet'.

> Yet.

Dammit.

> We haven't crossed that line. She wanted to. She would have. I didn't. That has to count for something.

> Yeah. It counts for you're in love with her. Which makes this an even bigger deal.

I stare at his words. I'd made the mistake of telling Henry a few months ago that I didn't mind accompanying Linnea and Torin to the energy summit in D.C. because listening to her talk was always fascinating. And that I didn't like how Christian Waite looked at her. Henry immediately accused me of having feelings for her. And I denied it too quickly and too adamantly.

Then I'd told him and Colin about kissing her on my birthday.

They're my best friends next to Torin. They know things about my job that Torin doesn't know. They know that this is a problem.

So I texted them this morning so they could remind *me* that it's a problem.

Because I don't know if I can let her go now.

> If I'm in love with her, why didn't I take the chance to sleep with her? When that's what she wanted? Before someone else gets the chance?

They've known as long as I have that Torin doesn't want to marry her and that she's only marrying him to be queen, expecting that he'll change the rules and allow her to keep the title and crown after he steps down.

That is, of course, *not* the plan that Alfred and Diarmuid laid out, and that our group is intent on seeing through. So I had to share the situation with my friends and colleagues in the hope they had some idea about how to make this work.

Their solution? Make Torin marry her. But *don't* let him change the rules.

Yeah, easy for them to say.

> You can take any random girl home and fuck her and it doesn't really mean anything. But the stuff you did with Linnea last night was more than fucking. And you know it.

Yeah. It was. He's right. If I wasn't in love with her, I probably could have resisted the entire thing, honestly. Or, I could have just taken her v-card, showed her what it was like, made it good so she'd want more, and then happily sent her off on her date tonight.

Instead, I barely peeled myself away from her warm, naked body this morning and am going over scenarios to keep her away from Christian Waite.

Which is the *opposite* of my mission here. It's somehow *worse* than the opposite of what Iris told me to do when she said to bring Linnea home single.

I'm not going to marry her, but I'm certain Iris didn't mean for me to fall in love with her. Or to become her sex tutor.

Fuck.

Okay, I have to somehow convince Henry that this is fine. Because then I can convince myself it's fine.

> This doesn't—

But I'm cut off by an incoming text from Colin.

> Colin: And then you slept with her right? You spent the night with her in your arms, right up against you, and you woke up like that. And now you're done for, my friend. Done. For. You're not getting over that.

Well, I guess that answers my question about if Colin is even reading this group text.

And he would know best about this.

Henry is a woman-loving playboy, just like Cian. The two of them have a hell of a good time. He's never been in love. I'm sure of it.

Colin is another story. He took a job as the temporary bodyguard for an up-and-coming singer who had gotten herself a stalker. Hayden is now Colin's wife.

> I guess you could give some advice about falling for the woman you're just supposed to be protecting. One who is supposed to be off limits.

> Colin: Hayden was never off limits the way Linnea is. Linnea is a part of something much bigger that you can't mess with. Her being Torin's queen has always been Alfred's plan.

The knot in my stomach tightens. I know all of this. Colin is simply voicing all of the things I've been trying to ignore or rationalize. It's pissing me off.

> We can't force her to marry him.

> Colin: Maybe not. But they'll use guilt and manipulation and whatever else to try. And if you are the reason she doesn't, the boss will fire you and Diarmuid will throw you out of the country. Then YOU won't be there for Torin the way you're supposed to be. Torin needs both of you.

> Henry: Once Torin's king, he could hire you back, though. So there's that.

Yes, there's that.

> Colin: That could be years. And without Jonah and Linnea there helping him, Torin might lose it and abdicate again.

And there's *that*.
I sigh. Fuck.

> She has a date with Christian Waite, the senator, tonight.

> Henry: Oh. Fuck. Sorry, man.

I frown. It's not as if it's a given she'll fall madly in love with Waite.

> Colin: Good.

It is absolutely the opposite of good. At least for the guy who's head over heels for her.

> Henry: It's good? What if she falls for Waite? That means she doesn't marry Torin and doesn't become queen.

I hate the way 'falls for Waite' tightens my chest.

> Colin: No, that's not ideal, but it's better than her and Jonah. If Torin is determined not to marry her, then we still need to get him on the throne. Whatever it takes.

> Henry: How?

> A program that will do something huge for Cara. Something that will be really impressive. That will show the king Torin is ready. He doesn't need Linnea babysitting him. He can do this on his own. That's what he really wants: to be taken seriously. To have his grandfather recognize HIS talents and passions.

> Henry: Iris won't like that. She's all about this marriage thing.

Yeah, she is. That is the first priority. I know. But...once Torin's king, *he* can make—or change—the rules. That is my glimmer of hope.

My mind is spinning. Linnea is working on this

program with James. She said she'd let Torin present it. She wants the king to take Torin seriously too. She knows that's what they both need—Torin to know the king trusts him and the king to know Cara will be in good hands.

If Torin can take over the throne without being married first, he really could change all the rules. The arranged marriage won't matter. He'll be able to choose his bride, when and if he wants to.

And Linnea and I can be together. If that's what she really wants. What she *chooses*.

And we can both stay in Cara as advisors to the king.

> Don't say anything to everyone else about any of this, but Linnea has a plan. We need to see what happens.

Colin: To go back to Cara and marry Torin?

> No.

Colin: <eye roll emoji> Then you better hope this is an amazing plan. Because if not, you need to take that girl home and give her back to your best friend.

Henry: The way you put that makes this sound very sordid.

Henry: I like it.

I roll my eyes. Henry's grandmother calls him a scamp. There are moments like this when I think she's spot-on.

> Torin and Linnea aren't going to happen.

> Henry: But Linnea and someone else might?

I fucking hate the idea of her with someone else, but... she deserves to have a choice. She deserves to finally, for the first time in her *life*, decide for herself what her future looks like.

Her entire life has been dictated by other people and what she's planned and expected has changed at least three times based on the *choices* other people got to make—first Declan, then Torin.

This time *she* gets to choose.

> Whatever Linnea wants, I'm going to make sure she gets.

> <wide-eyes emoji> <sweating face emoji> <winky face emoji>

> Colin: Well...damn.

I look up as the bedroom door opens. I close out of the text conversation and pocket my phone. I really have nothing more to say to them anyway.

"Morning," I greet Linnea as she steps out into the living area. She's showered and dressed in silky lounge pants and a matching top, much like the ones she always wore to the kitchen at the palace.

I'm immediately hard.

Everything from last night flashes through my mind and I swear I can still taste her on my tongue.

She gives me a smile that's shy and makes me even harder.

"Morning."

"I had breakfast sent up."

"Oh, that was very nice." She looks at the table by the window that's set with a full coffee service, as well as scones, fruit, and a platter of bacon. "I went ahead and showered. I didn't know if testing how I feel about shower sex was on the list this morning."

I cough in surprise. I was not expecting her to be so forthright first thing in the morning. Heat hits me low and hard, but I grin. I love that my Duchess is comfortable flirting with me right away the morning after. Or maybe she really was just curious about what was on the "Like It" checklist today. I love that she can talk about this with me. Yes, she is used to speaking her mind to most people, but I don't think she would be like *this* with just anyone.

She trusts me. She knows that my role has always been to take care of her, and that I have her best interests at heart.

"Oh, we'll check on shower sex," I tell her, rising and pulling out one of the chairs at the small table near the window. "But there are plenty of other things on the list, too. The shower can wait. Come here. I've got cranberry scones for you."

She crosses to me with a soft smile. Obviously, she's pleased that I'm open to discussing more things on her sex checklist, too, and that we're going to explore more of them today.

I'd love to take her back into that bedroom and spend the day just learning every erogenous zone, every sigh, every gasp. But I also want to make this fun and playful. She's never dated either. I want to fix that too.

"I wasn't sure how we would act this morning," she says, stopping next to me instead of taking a seat.

I reach up and slide my hand under her hair, cupping the back of her neck. Then I draw her close. I lean in, my lips hovering over hers. "We're going to act like we had one of the hottest nights of my life together last night. And like we're going to have a really fun day together today."

She gives a happy sigh. "So you don't want to go back to trying to resist? Telling me to stop talking about how you make me feel?"

I can't. I can't resist her. I have to be the one to take her out, make her feel special and pampered, treat her the way she deserves to be treated.

I have to help her discover *everything* she wants and should expect from a man. Not just in bed, but everywhere.

That hit me sometime between kissing her cheek as I slid out of bed and ordering her a new dress for today.

I want her to know what it's like to be wanted. To be cherished.

She hasn't had mind-blowing orgasms, and she wants to know what that's like, but she also hasn't been romanced. And she should definitely want that as well.

She deserves all of that.

And if I can't be the man doing it for the rest of her life, I am, by God, going to make sure she knows to demand it from whoever is.

"I'm not going to be resisting you anymore, Duchess," I tell her softly. "I can't."

I kiss her. It starts soft, but the heat builds quickly and soon I'm tipping her head so that I can claim her mouth fully.

She's gripping the front of my shirt and arching into me when I lift my head nearly a minute later.

"Breakfast first."

She nods and licks her lips. "I also need to work just for a little bit. I came up with some ideas for James's project. I want to send them over to Torin and get his input."

I let go of her and nudge her into the chair, then slide the chair to the table. "That's wonderful. I love that you're going to share this with him. I hope you and Torin can come up with something."

I want that so fucking much. If they can come up with something to impress the king, it could change everything.

"Great. It will take maybe an hour. I'll write some things up and send them over to him, and then we can have a quick call."

I also love that she's willing to share this with my friend. Torin's great, and I know that he will listen to anything Linnea presents him. He's also very excited about the energy initiatives he's been hearing about. But he gets very worked up when it comes to having to deal with his grandfather. Sometimes those emotions can keep him from being fully rational and patient.

"I also had some clothes sent up," I tell her as I pour coffee and slide a scone onto a plate for her.

She looks at me with surprise. "Clothes?"

"We're going to play tourist today. I assumed you hadn't packed anything that would be appropriate for just walking around and blending in."

She smiles and shakes her head. "But I've already seen D.C. a few times. I've done all the museums and monuments."

I smile. I have too. "Not like this."

She gives me a thoughtful look. "Okay."

I don't think she has any idea how hot it makes me when she just goes along with my plans.

"How did you know my size?"

I lift a brow. "Duchess…"

She waves her hand. "Right. You know everything about me."

"I do. Plus, I had my hands all over your body last night. I promise you that I could guess within a half-size now."

She blushes prettily and laughs. "Fair enough. I'm impressed."

"So eat. And drink lots of water," I tell her, tapping the end of her nose. "Then work fast. I have a lot planned for you today."

CHAPTER 19
LINNEA

"I think this is amazing," Torin says over the phone. "Thank you for this."

"You don't have to thank me. I think this is going to be fantastic. It will create so many jobs, plus show our people that we're interested in creative, new ways to make work actually *work* for families and that we understand and are committed to helping with work-life balance. These kinds of incentives for our workers can make us competitive with the labor costs Canada is offering James."

"I agree. It's innovative, progressive, and a win-win. But I *do* appreciate you taking the lead with James. I didn't expect this trip to be about work, Linnea. But he obviously likes you better than me."

I laugh. "Well, I'm glad you're happy about that. So you're not upset when I tell you that I'm not interested in dating him."

Torin sighs. "All right. A fantastic new energy program

for the country *and* a new fiancé for you was probably too much to ask."

My cheeks heat and my eyes find Jonah across the room. He's lounging in one of the chairs, typing on his phone.

Obviously there were no marriage proposals last night, and he hasn't said anything about me canceling my date tonight with Christian, but last night was amazing. I can't imagine going out with another man after having Jonah's hands and mouth all over me.

I don't care what my sister says, there's no way sex is always like that.

We didn't even have *sex*. A detail I'm very aware of. Jonah never even got completely naked. I would very much like to correct that as soon as possible. But I enjoyed every minute last night. I have never felt more wanted, more beautiful, or more taken care of in my life. There is no way that is common with every single man.

"You are seeing Senator Waite tonight, correct?" Torin asks.

"I am."

"Well, fingers crossed you have a fantastic time."

I laugh. It will never not be strange that my current fiancé is so excited about me going on a date with another man.

"You'll be one of the first to know how things turn out," I assure him.

I'll definitely need to discuss how I feel about your best friend with you. But I can't do that over the phone. And I can't do it before I discuss those feelings with that friend.

"I'll go over everything you're sending me, and maybe I'll try to get James on the phone. But I will present this to my grandfather before you get back." Torin pauses. "If that's okay?"

"Of course. I think you should take this to him. I think he needs to see you with important ideas and programs for Cara, and the ability to negotiate to get what Cara needs. We definitely don't have enough resources on our own to keep our young people on the island and to keep building our economy. Your grandfather knows that. While he might not fully understand green energy and embrace the idea, if we can talk in terms of jobs and international goodwill, he'll appreciate that."

"International goodwill," Torin repeats. "I'll remember that. That is important to him. He wants Cara to be seen as a country that others can look to as a leader, and one that can cooperate with a number of different groups for lots of different purposes."

"Exactly. Our small size and government structure *are* advantages when it comes to putting programs and ideas into place quickly and pivoting when things come up, like this thing with James," I say, trying to emphasize the point to Torin as well. "If you can manage to say something like that, it would make Diarmuid very happy."

"You mean acknowledge that there are good things about the monarchy?" Torin asks with a chuckle.

I grin. "Yes. And you know it's true. There are pros and cons, of course, but being able to make decisions quickly is definitely in the pro column."

"Fine. I'll see if I can work that in," Torin says.

"And," I say, "try the other-countries-will-look-at-little-Cara-as-a-major-leader-in-an-important-field angle instead of the scientific or ecological stuff."

The king cares about ecology, of course, but he's an eighty-two-year-old man and it's easier to just speak directly to the things that are most important to him.

"I'll give it my best shot," Torin says. "Okay with you if I call James?"

I'm flattered that he even asks. He's the prince. I am simply his advisor. My job is to make these connections between him and people like James, and if Torin wants to call the other man, he certainly doesn't need my permission. It's truly very respectful of Torin to ask.

"Of course. I think that's a great idea."

"What do I say if he asks about you?" Torin asks.

"Why would he ask about me?"

"He might ask if you mentioned your date last night. Remember, he called me to get your number."

"Do you want to tell him that I just didn't say anything?"

Torin chuckles. "I'm not sure that will make him feel any better, but yeah, at least I have plausible deniability."

"I'm sorry if you feel in the middle of this." I glance at Jonah again. Speaking of awkward situations for Torin, I wonder what he will think about me and Jonah being together.

I think he'll be fine with it. He doesn't want me himself, and he loves Jonah. If Jonah and I are happy, Torin will be happy.

Though it won't solve the problem of getting him on the throne. Diarmuid doesn't think he's ready, and the king has been counting on me being there to make sure everything goes well.

"Well, I didn't expect you to end up with both of them, so obviously at some point one of them was going to be disappointed."

"I guess that's true."

"I'll let you go. I hope you have a good time tonight. Tell the senator hello for me."

"I will."

We disconnect, but my stomach is suddenly uneasy. I have a date tonight. With a man other than the one I slept with last night.

With a man who is probably very close to perfect for me.

If I'm not going to be married to a prince, a senator would also be a good fit. Of course, assuming we get along and are attracted to one another.

But I can't stop thinking about Jonah. Of course, because of the things we did last night. *Of course* I'm thinking about all of that. It was…amazing. I was disappointed to wake up alone in bed this morning. It was all so new for me and better than I ever imagined.

But also, just *Jonah*.

Take away the magical tongue and the dirty talk and the hands that know exactly how to touch me, and he's still such a good fit for me. He sees sides to me that no one else does, that no one has ever even bothered to. And he likes them all. Taking care of me seems to give him pleasure, and I love knowing that he's there for me.

I can easily imagine traveling the world, on behalf of Cara, with Jonah at my side. We would discuss policies and new ideas, he'd listen to me brainstorm, ask questions, tell me honestly when I could push harder to do more, but he would also be proud of me, and would be very generous with the praise and compliments when I was doing a good job.

With enough 'good girl's' from that man, who knows what world problems I could solve?

He would never see the things I do as just good for Cara. He understands why I do what I do, and that it gives me pleasure and fulfills me as well. He would want that for me.

I hit SEND on the email to Torin with my ideas outlined and my notes about what James told me last night. He can take it from here.

I turn on my chair. "I'm done. Ready to go."

Jonah looks up. He's dressed in blue jeans, a black T-shirt that fits across his chest and shoulders in a way that makes my mouth water. Vivid images of his bare torso last night spring to mind. I didn't get nearly enough chance to run my hands, and mouth, over his body. I would very much like that opportunity. Soon.

"You just need to go get dressed," he tells me.

I feel butterflies flutter in my stomach, replacing the nerves.

I don't remember the last time someone bought me clothes. I've never had a man buy me clothes.

I'm also excited to see what he has in store for us today. I love D.C.. But I have seen all of the monuments and museums before, and I am very interested in how Jonah is going to make it different.

"Just give me a few minutes," I tell him.

I go into the bedroom and shut the door, though I realize that's silly considering how much of me he saw last night. Very close up.

I giggle thinking about it. Then I giggle about giggling. I am not really the giggling type. But Jonah makes me happy. Almost giddy.

I've never dated, so I'm going to blame all of this on the fact that there is a sixteen-year-old girl still inside me who is experiencing all of this for the first time.

I reach into the gift bag that is sitting on the mattress. He had someone else pick this out, but he knew the size and I'm sure he gave them specifications, considering he has a very distinct idea about how I need to be dressed today.

Though he's right that I didn't bring any casual clothes appropriate for tourist activities. I have lounging in the hotel room clothes and dress up to go out at night clothes. I really thought those were the two things I was going to be doing here.

I pull out a dress. A sundress. I hold it up in front of me and grin. It will hit me about mid-thigh. The wide straps will cover my shoulders but will leave my arms bare. It's white with little red cherries scattered all over it. It's very feminine, very cute, and I have to admit, kind of on the nose. But I'm blushing and grinning at the same time. I reach back into the bag and find a little red cardigan to go over the top.

The weather here is beautiful, but it is only April, so it's not hot yet by any means.

If we're going to be walking around a lot and playing tourist, I also realize that I'll need to wear comfortable shoes. I know it's no coincidence that the shoes I wore on the plane will go perfectly with this outfit. It will be cute, casual, and fun.

I love that those are the words to describe going out with Jonah.

I slip the dress on and debate whether I need a bra or not. The material is not thick, but it's not see-through either and the bodice is fitted. I decide to forgo the bra, and shrug into the cardigan. I head into the bathroom so I can quickly pull my hair up into a high ponytail. Jonah has seen my hair in several different styles over the past year, but I very rarely wear it in a simple ponytail. I decide to skip make-up, adding just a little mascara and some shiny lip gloss. I study myself in the mirror and like what I see. I look happy. Excited.

I get to just hang out today with someone I like very

much. I don't have to meet with anyone important. I don't have to worry about how I look. I don't have to be ready to negotiate or prepared to think on my feet in case someone asks me a challenging question about the palace's stance on an issue. I don't have to win anyone over.

The guy in the next room likes me. He knows me well. And likes me anyway.

This is going to be a great day.

We take our seats in the National Air and Space Museum's planetarium.

So far we've strolled through the museum holding hands, talking casually, showing each other our favorite exhibits, and comparing notes on our favorite things about D.C..

It's been light and fun and definitely different from my previous trips. I haven't felt this relaxed on a trip in years.

Or this...desired.

Jonah hasn't stopped touching me since we got out of the town car that brought us to the National Mall.

It's been casual and completely appropriate.

Holding hands was sweet, and something I've never done with anyone else. It felt completely natural with Jonah. He's also looped his arm around my shoulders as we looked at exhibits, or when we were standing in line. At one point, he stood behind me, with his arms wrapped around me. He's rested his hand on my lower back when escorting me through a crowd or just now as we were choosing our seats in this auditorium.

I've loved all of it. Public displays of affection are definitely on my Like It list.

Jonah takes up a lot of space, his leg pressing against

mine, his arm crowding mine on the armrest between us. I don't mind. I love touching him. I love when he's touching me. I press closer, leaning into him.

We're sitting toward the back and there are several rows between us and the group of grade schoolers who are taking in this show with us.

Jonah shifts, placing one big hand on my thigh just above my knee. Tingles explode and I lean closer, pressing my shoulder into his.

He starts drawing a lazy circle with his index finger on the inner portion of my thigh just above my knee. I give a little hum of pleasure and he shoots me a look.

I meet his gaze and don't say anything. But I do move my knees apart slightly.

He gives me a half grin. "Good girl," he says softly.

My eyebrows rise. I don't really know what this is all about, but I like it so far.

The lights dim and almost immediately Jonah's hand slides up my thigh under the edge of my skirt.

Okay, this is fun.

As the program begins and everyone leans back in their seats to gaze upward at the night sky overhead, Jonah's hand continues up my thigh.

"So now we're going to find out if you like getting naughty in public when you might get caught," he says quietly. "And if you can stay quiet."

I press my lips together as his fingers brush across the crotch of my panties. I grip the armrests.

"What do you think?" he asks, his voice low and husky.

I nod.

"You like the idea that someone might see my hand up under your sweet little dress?"

I swallow and nod again.

We're alone in our row, and there's no one seated right in front or behind us. There is a couple in the same row but across the aisle and several seats in. And, of course, it's very dark in here. Still, I do feel a thrill dance through me, thinking about what someone might see if they looked over.

"There's a kid who works here back by the door," Jonah says. "He's probably barely old enough to drink. But he was checking you out when we walked in. I'll bet he'd love a look at you spreading your legs and having a finger fucking this sweet pussy."

I gasp. His words shock me, but so does the stab of heat they bring.

I'm *not* an exhibitionist. I'm certain of that.

But as Jonah slips his finger under the elastic edge of my panties and strokes over my clit, I look around. And I'm not so sure I'd stop him if someone walked by.

"There's no one by the back door," I whisper.

Jonah's finger teases my clit, then slides lower, dipping just inside me and making me have to bite back a moan.

"Hmmm," he says, clearly unbothered. "He must be walking around, making sure everyone is behaving."

My pussy clenches.

I'm shocked by that.

Jonah slips his finger deeper. "You're so wet, Duchess."

I nod even though I'm not sure he can see me in the dark. I have a death grip on the arms of this chair.

"That's so hot and so naughty." He slides his finger deeper and I have to consciously work not to moan. He moves his finger in and out. "I wonder if I could make you come right here, right now."

His thumb circles my clit, and I have to press my lips together even harder.

"You won't make me stop, will you?" He moves his finger in and out again. "You'll let me do whatever I want to this pussy. You know how good I can make you feel. You don't care where we are. If I tell you to spread your legs, you will."

I lean over and put my face against his shoulder, breathing out and giving a quiet moan that is muffled by his shirt.

He chuckles, sounding smug. "Exactly. I can get you to do anything. I am putting fingering in public on your Like It list."

I see movement out of the corner of my eye and realize that he was exactly right and one of the workers is coming up the aisle.

I tense.

"Oh no," Jonah says gruffly. "I'm not done."

I moan into his shoulder again, and he strokes me even as the kid moves closer.

"I don't know if you can stay quiet though, Duchess," he says. "You do love to cry out my name."

I desperately want to moan his name now. And beg for him to add another finger and move faster.

His thumb rubs over my clit. "Lift your head if you don't want him to wonder what's going on. Sit up nice and straight. Like a lady."

I can hear the amusement in his tone. He's enjoying the fact that he can make me so needy.

Hell, I'm enjoying that too. The kid is coming closer and I sit up, trying to make my posture look normal. That's difficult with a huge hand between my legs. Jonah rests his head on my shoulder, playing the part of a cuddly boyfriend.

The whole time his finger is moving in and out, his thumb is circling, and I feel an orgasm winding tighter.

The kid moves past our row and I let out a long breath.

I let my eyes slide shut and lean back, ready to let the orgasm take me under.

But Jonah stops and slips his hand out from under my dress.

"Hey," I protest softly, grabbing his wrist. "That's not nice."

"It's very nice. We added something very fun to your list of things you like." He leans in and presses a quick kiss to my lips. "You're welcome."

I'm sitting there, stunned, trying not to focus entirely on the pulsing between my legs, when the lights come up. Jonah grins, and takes my hand, pulling me to my feet. "Let's go see what else this museum has to offer."

I'm distracted as we make our way through more of the museum, even more aware of every single touch, every time Jonah presses a kiss to my temple or the top of my head, every time his hand brushes over my hip, or my back, or my stomach.

Was he touching me like this before? Was he kissing me like this? Or is he getting even more handsy? Is this part of a little game he's playing?

We're standing looking at an airplane that I could not tell anyone a single fact about, when he leans in and says in my ear, "Go to the ladies' room."

I look up at him. "I don't need to go."

He meets my gaze directly and repeats, "Go to the ladies' room."

I narrow my eyes, but I can see a little mischief in his expression. I'm intrigued.

"Fine."

I turn and start down the hallway, but he calls after me, "You have your phone, right?"

I pat my pocket—yes, this dress even has pockets. "Of course."

"Good."

I step into the nearest women's restroom and wait. I don't know what to expect exactly, but I pull my phone out, assuming that has something to do with it.

A moment later, a text from Jonah flashes on my screen.

> Jonah: Go into a stall.

I do, butterflies swooping. We're going to sext. I've never done that.

> Me: I am.

> Take your panties off.

I stare at the screen. Oh boy. I reach up under my skirt and shimmy out of my panties.

> Okay.

> Prove it.

Oh.

Boy.

I take a breath. Obviously the way to prove it would be with a photo.

Can I send a photo of my pussy to a man's phone?

Then I have another idea. I hold the panties up and take a photo of them dangling from my fingertips.

> Cute. Now let me see your cute finger in your cute little cunt.

I gasp as my eyes go wide.

He really just texted that to me.

And I'm hot all over because of it.

I love this man.

It's the strangest time for that thought to hit me. But it's true.

He's fun. He makes me laugh. He makes me hot. He makes me proud—of myself and of him. He makes me brave. He's the first one to make me actually consider something other than the life that everyone else laid out for me so long ago.

So can I do this risky thing that he's asking me to do? This playful, hot, fun thing that he's doing for me? Sure, I think he'll enjoy the photo. I am sure he's turned on and thinks this is fun, too. But he's also doing all of this for me. To find out what kind of sexy fun I like. To find out what kind of sexual relationship I want to have. He's helping me realize what I want and what I need to be happy and to feel desired and fulfilled.

With that, I prop my foot up on the toilet, flip my skirt up, and slide my finger down over my clit. I take a photo of that first, careful to keep the very unsexy toilet out of the frame.

Then, I slip my finger into my pussy.

I'm wet. For Jonah.

And I take a photo of me fingering myself for this man.

I can't believe I'm doing it, but I hit send, and then give one of those joyful, giddy giggles.

I wait for a moment, dropping my foot back to the floor.

Then another few seconds.

When half a minute has gone by, I finally text him.

> Did the photos come through?

> I am just having a hard time doing anything but stare at my phone.

I laugh. We are in the National Air and Space Museum. He's standing out there, surrounded by normal people just going about their day, with no clue about what crazy stuff the big handsome man is looking at on his phone...

Then I gasp. What if someone walking by looks over his shoulder and sees his phone?

They'll see...*me*!

Jonah is the only one I want to ever see that part of me. He's the first and I want him to be the last.

That also seems to hit me from out of the blue. I realize that the general plan is for me to have at least a couple of other men in that general vicinity, but I no longer have *any* interest in that.

Why would I when Jonah Greene can do the things he can do?

> No one else better be able to see your phone!

> There's no way in hell I would ever let anyone else see this.

Strangely, that warms me. He's so protective of me. And I believe him. I believe that he wants to keep that to himself.

And that possessiveness also makes me hot.

> We can add sexting to my list.

> I am shocked.

I laugh. He's getting to know me and I love that.
Clearly, I love being a little naughty, playful and fun.
I can't wait to see what's next.

> Do not put your panties back on. Bring them to me.

I shiver. Yes, sir.
Oh, I wonder if Jonah would like to be called sir...

CHAPTER 20
JONAH

She is everything I expected her to be and then some.
She has gone along with everything and has enjoyed it immensely.

I have been walking around harder than I have ever been in my life. And yet I've been having more fun than I've had in a very long time.

She's laughing, her cheeks are flushed, but she has a confident, sexy air about her that has never been there before.

Lady Linnea is figuring out that she's sexy as fuck.

Besides letting me finger her in the planetarium and taking very naughty photos for me when I asked, we also did a naughty professor-student role-play where I was her displeased professor and she was my grad student who was supposed to have a new display for me to examine and approve today.

She didn't have the exhibit up in time and as punishment, I got to take her into a dark corner behind one of the existing exhibits and finger her just to the edge of orgasm.

I've been edging her all day.

She's starting to get frustrated. As much as she's enjoying this, she's also wound up.

And I'm about to see if there's something else to add to her list, right under role-playing.

"You seem a little irritated," I comment as we walk to the Museum of Natural History.

"I'm wound up." She looks around and then whispers. "I need an orgasm, Jonah."

"Hmmm, well...maybe you should demand one."

She looks up at me. "What?"

"Let's see if *you* like to be in charge. Why don't you tell me what to do?"

She stops walking. She studies me. "Really?"

"Yeah. We know you like it when I'm in charge. We've found a bunch of fun things you like. But maybe you like to be the boss sometimes."

She thinks about that for a few seconds. Then she nods. "Okay." And she starts walking again.

I grin. O-fucking-kay.

Seventeen minutes after we enter the museum, we're in the hall of fossils.

We're standing in front of a dinosaur skeleton, not saying a word, when she turns to me and says, "Take me back to the hotel."

I open my mouth to, I guess, protest. But then I realize, I'm not an idiot. She wants to go back to the car and I'll take her. For whatever reason.

"Okay."

I take her hand and we head back out the front doors.

The car picks us up five minutes later.

We're quiet. I told her she's in charge, so I don't want to speak first. I smile though, wondering what she's planning.

When we get to the hotel, she waits for me to open her door and help her out, but we still say nothing as we take the elevator up to our room.

I open the door and let her pass in front of me.

She heads straight for her bedroom. She glances over her shoulder though and says, "Come on."

I let the door close behind me and swallow hard. I've put her in charge. Am I truly prepared to do *anything* she asks? What if she asks me to fuck her?

But I realize that I will absolutely do anything this woman needs me to. If she wants to take charge, and that is the ultimate ask, there's no way I can deny her.

I pause in the doorway to the bedroom. Linnea kicks off her shoes, and shrugs out of her sweater, letting it drop to the floor. Then she moves to the bed. She pauses by the bedside table, opening the drawer, and taking out the vibrator.

My heart kicks hard and my entire body tightens.

She climbs onto the bed and leans back against the pillows, partially propped up. Then she pulls up her skirt.

Because her panties are still in my pocket, she's bare.

She meets my gaze.

"Remember, this is your fault." Then she turns on the vibrator.

I start forward, but she stops me. "You can watch from there."

I gape at her. I was not expecting this.

I am torn between being incredibly turned on, being completely frustrated, and being intensely proud of her.

This woman is discovering her sexuality, her power, and she is already using it.

"You're going to do that all yourself, Duchess?" I ask, tucking my hands into my pockets.

"Yes. You've been teasing me all day. I'm going to take care of myself now."

She moves the vibrator along her inner thigh up toward her pussy.

I lick my lips. "You're amazing."

Her eyes flare with surprise. I assume she expected me to be annoyed.

"You have no idea how fucking hot you look right now. I can jerk off to this image for months."

She trails the vibrator over her mound. Then nods. "Why don't you start now?"

My eyebrows rise. "You want me to jerk off while you get yourself off?"

"I haven't seen your cock since the day you were ironing. After everything you got to see last night, that seems unfair."

I straighten and lock my gaze on hers as I shrug out of the gray hoodie I've been wearing and toss it to the floor. "You're complaining about last night? I didn't do quite everything you wanted?"

A smile ghosts her lips. "I wouldn't say that. Just in retrospect, I realize I missed out on a few things I was hoping for."

I reach back and grab my T-shirt between my shoulder blades, yanking it over my head. I toss it on top of my hoodie. "I am so sorry you were less than fully satisfied."

Now her smile grows. "Oh, I was pretty satisfied. I just really want to see you naked."

I lift a shoulder. "You're in charge right now."

Her gaze drops to my fly. "Let me see."

Now she's trailing the vibrator slowly back and forth across her clit. I know that she's just working herself up. She's going to need more direct intense vibration to get off. And I love that I know what she needs.

I unbutton and unzip, opening my fly and pushing my jeans down over my hips. I push my boxers out of the way. My cock has been hard most of the day, so it's a relief to free it from the denim confines. I fist it, nearly groaning at how great that feels.

She blows out a breath. "God, that's hot."

My gaze drops to her pussy. "Get to work. "

"Hey, who's in charge right now?"

I stroke up and down my cock twice, firm and slow. "Tell me what you want, Duchess."

"Come with me."

"Give that pussy what it needs then," I say, my voice gruff.

She moves the stimulator directly onto her clit and turns up the vibrations. She gives a low moan and starts moving in slow circles. She's been on edge all day so I don't think this will take long. She slides it down into her pussy, then back up over her clit. I keep stroking long and firm, then faster as I watch her climbing closer to her orgasm.

"You're the most fun I've ever had, Duchess," I tell her. "You're fun, daring, sweet."

She's breathing hard and she lifts a hand to one breast, teasing her nipple. "I loved today," she tells me.

For some reason, it seems so appropriate that we are

saying nice, sweet things even as we are mutually masturbating.

This is maybe one of the hottest moments I've ever had.

She keeps working the vibrator over her clit and I stroke my cock harder and faster.

"Tell me you're close, Duchess," I say, my jaw tense.

"So close," she says breathlessly.

"Need to see and hear you."

"Jonah," she gasps. Then she gives a little whimper and says my name again.

"That's right, just like that," I urge.

I'm barely holding on. I want her to come first, but I'm so close.

And then it hits her. She cries out my name, and her thighs tense, her hips lift, pressing up against the vibrator firmly.

And I let myself go. I come, spilling into my hand, my eyes fixed on her.

My head drops forward and I take a huge, shuddering breath.

I hear the vibrator switch off and I look up. She's slumped back, her head resting against the pillows.

"Better?" I ask.

She looks up and grins. "Much."

I head into the bathroom and clean up, then come out with a warm washcloth. I lean over her, grasping her chin and kissing her deeply as I wash between her legs.

I toss the washcloth in through the bathroom door and sit down on the edge of the mattress.

"I meant what I said. Today was awesome. I had the best time."

"Me too." She reaches up and runs her hand over my beard. "Can I tell you something?"

"Anything." I turn my head and press a kiss to the center of her palm.

"I appreciate you letting me be in charge. But I like it a lot better when you are."

I'm surprised. "I thought you'd like it. It seems like in so many areas of your life, you don't actually get to be in charge."

She nods. "I appreciate you thinking about that. But the thing is, everything else, when other people are in charge, it's all about them. So, I don't always like it and I do wish I could call more shots. Like today with Torin. He was asking me how I thought he should handle the presentation to his grandfather and was listening to my suggestions. He even asked my permission to call James." She smiles. "That was really nice. And unusual. But with you, it's different. Because when you take charge, it's not about you. It's about me."

I feel my chest tighten. I lift her hand to my lips and kiss it again. "I'm so glad you know that."

"It's obvious. You're always doing things for me."

"Always." *Because I love you* is right on the tip of my tongue, but I can *not* say it.

Not yet.

It's too soon. Too many other things need to happen and fall into place.

But soon.

Very soon I can tell this woman everything I feel.

"Also, I was thinking," she says. "About the date tonight."

"I still think you should go," I say before she can say anything else.

"I knew you were going to say that."

"Linnea, you need to go. For you. You need to have some

choices. I want you to know how that feels. No matter who you pick at the end, I want you to know that you had a choice. You haven't had a lot of those."

She gives me a smile, one I haven't seen before. There are emotions in her eyes I can't quite name.

"Thank you." Her voice is a little wobbly. "That means a lot to me."

"*You* mean a lot to me." That's as close as I can get to spilling my emotions tonight.

"Well, if you think I should still go, then I think there is one change I want to make."

"Okay. Whatever you want."

"I want to go bowling. "

I was not expecting that. "You want to go *bowling*?"

"I do. I've never been, and I know it's something you like. But even more, after you told me how you took Torin bowling to figure out what kind of guy he is, I was thinking, that would be the perfect way to figure out what kind of guy Christian really is."

I think that over. I love this idea. She's amazing. "That's a fantastic idea. I'll find out where there's a great bowling alley. We can make sure his security team has time to check it out. I'll get in touch with his people."

"I already texted him. And he agreed. He's working on the security and everything on his end."

I laugh. "See, you do kind of like being in charge sometimes."

She laughs. "Maybe. Except when it comes to you." Her voice gets softer. "I really like when you're in charge."

I lean in and kiss her. "Don't be getting all sexy with me. We need to get ready for the big bowling night."

But it takes everything in me to force myself to stand up from the edge of that bed and walk into the next room, away from the woman I am convinced I am fully in love with.

And who I'm accompanying on a date with another man tonight.

A man who her fiancé, my best friend, would really like her to end up with.

Fuck. This is going to be really complicated.

CHAPTER 21
LINNEA

It surprises no one, least of all me, that Christian Waite is an exceptional bowler. Not that I ever would have wondered about that if it wasn't for this date. Who wonders if someone is a good bowler? But if anyone had ever asked me if I thought he would be, I would have said yes. He simply exudes competence at everything. Though, I suspect, even if he was a terrible bowler, everyone would walk away from this event thinking he was amazing.

He's that guy.

Everybody likes him. He won his district with an unheard of seventy-eight percent of the vote. His opponent pulled out things like Christian wanted to spend too much money on social programs, and he's not a military veteran. But that was about all they had to criticize him on.

They also tried to get some traction with him not being married, but it was very difficult to paint him as "not a family man." He's from a big, loving family. His parents, four sisters and their adorable families, his nieces and nephews and brothers-in-law, all show up to his campaign events and there are a million stories in the press from people who knew him growing up and know the Waites as a close, supportive, wonderful family.

He's good looking, charming, able to be self-deprecating, even while being talented, sophisticated, and witty.

He's basically Ryan Reynolds.

If Ryan Reynolds were a U.S. senator.

Of course, Ryan Reynolds could be a U.S. senator quite easily. Even though he's Canadian. He could probably run a very successful write-in campaign *and* convince Congress to change the entire constitution to make it official.

The small crowd that has gathered around the end of our bowling lane suddenly erupts into cheers, and I pull my thoughts from Ryan Reynolds. I realize Christian has knocked over all ten pins. Again. Or is it twelve? I haven't picked up much about bowling except that the more pins you knock over, the better.

I smile and clap along with everyone else and shake my head as he turns, grins, and waves as if he didn't expect to knock them all over. Again.

"Your boyfriend is really good at this."

I roll my eyes at Jonah. He's been referring to Christian as 'my boyfriend' all night. The guy who just masturbated in front of me, while I was masturbating, two hours ago, is calling this other guy my boyfriend. I'm annoyed by that, but I'm trying not to show it. I like the little note of jealousy in Jonah's tone and expression. And because I've never, *ever* had anyone be jealous of me before, I want more of it. I know it's childish. I know I should be above this. But I'm also bowling for the first time, eating chili cheese fries for the first time, and wearing black skinny jeans for the first time. And I like *all* of that. So I'm going to just enjoy having two men both want my attention tonight too.

Of course, I'm bowling because of Jonah. And he's the one that brought me the chili cheese fries. He's also the one that sent the stylist out to get me some 'date night' outfits and then immediately rejected all of the skirts, the shorts, and finally settled on the jeans. So *all* of this is because of him.

Of course it is.

I'm beginning to realize that all of the things that make me feel good have to do with Jonah.

He's sitting next to me, one ankle propped on his opposite knee, his arm stretched out along the plastic chair back behind me. He's waiting his turn and I watch him watch Christian.

"You act surprised he's beating you," I say to him. "As if you're not letting him win."

Jonah shrugs. "When you throw strikes one right after another, it's not hard to win."

"Then why aren't *you* throwing strikes one after another?"

Jonah studies me for a moment, then he gives me a half-smile. "Because it's more important for him to win than for me to win."

I knew it. I knew Jonah was letting Christian win. That is so like him.

"So he looks good in front of his fans?"

"Or at least in front of someone he hopes will become a fan." Jonah gives me a pointed look.

So Jonah is trying to help Christian look good in front of *me*? "I don't know enough about bowling for him to impress me that way."

"Neither of you is really here for the bowling," he says, his gaze drifting to the people in the area around us.

I look around too. Of course a lot of these people know who Christian is, but I think that's mostly because Emily is here with him. Emily is clearly a PR person whose job it is to be sure people know—and love—Christian, even if he's not the senator from here and these aren't his constituents. He has bigger aspirations, and it's in his best interest for more people than those in New York to know and like him.

"How many of these people do you think Christian's people invited to be here?" I ask Jonah quietly. "About thirty percent?"

He chuckles. God, I love that low, deep sound.

"I was going to say fifty."

He's probably right.

"But not Tami and the girls," Jonah adds, his grin growing as his gaze lands on the women in the lane next to ours.

My eyes shift to the woman with the bright blond hair who just threw up her hands with a, "Fuck yeah!" as she spins away from the lane where she just got a strike. She's bowling with her sister, best friend, and mom.

I grin. "No. Not Tami."

Tami and her group are pissed about the circus around Christian, actually. I saw them whispering and frowning when we first came in and was next to Christian when Tami approached him.

"My friend Mona said you paid her a thousand dollars *not* to bowl tonight," Tami told him, hands on her hips.

Christian had given her a big smile that made him even more handsome. I'd watched Tami blink and her frown fade a little just because of that smile. I'd rolled my eyes. I've been around guys who have those kinds of smiles for years. Torin has a smile like that.

"The owners of the alley said everything was booked." He'd looked down at me and then back to Tami. "But I needed a lane so I could spend time with this beautiful woman. You understand, don't you? She's worth it. I promise."

Tami had looked me up and down. "Four thousand dollars?"

Dang, he'd paid *each* of the bowlers scheduled for that lane a thousand dollars?

But Christian had nodded.

She'd whistled. "So are you a hooker? Or the queen of England?"

I'd simply laughed. "Not either of those." Though when I looked up at Christian, he'd given me a cute wink.

"A lot closer to one of those than the other," he'd teased.

"Well, honey, *now* I need to know more about you." And Tami had linked arms with me and taken me over to talk with her and the other three women she was bowling with.

I'd looked back and seen Christian just grinning after us. Then I'd looked for Jonah. He'd been watching me with a much different look. A warmer, more intense look. But he'd definitely been watching me. Just as I'd known he would be.

"Christian was really good about the bowling. And he was charming with Tami. And about her monopolizing me for the first thirty minutes," I say to Jonah now.

He nods. But his eyes are soft as he says, "I'm sure he was thinking that he'd pay twice as much if that's what it took to get you to go out with him."

I feel my cheeks heat. "So you heard that?"

"I did." He pauses. "But I knew about it ahead of time.

Scott told me the alley was booked. I told him that they just needed to show up and offer one of the groups an incentive. It's not league night, so they weren't bowling for any standings or anything. I thought Waite could finagle concert tickets or a White House tour or something, but they just went straight to cash."

"It was *your* idea?"

He lifts a shoulder. "Yeah."

"How did you know it wasn't league night?"

"Saturday night is for families and dates and stuff. Leagues are during the week."

I study him. "And you wanted to see how much Christian wanted this to work out. The bowling was my idea and he could have used the booked alley as an excuse not to do it, but instead, he found a way to make it happen."

I know Jonah. When I first suggested bowling tonight, Jonah could have told me the chances were good the alley would be booked. Instead, he wanted to test Christian.

"Well, his people did anyway. With help," Jonah says with an eye roll, tipping a bottle of soda back.

I smile as I watch him swallow, the strong muscles of his throat mesmerizing me. I want to lick him right there. "But he still did it," I say absently. "I'm sure it's his own money. It's not like they can use campaign donations for something like this."

Jonah looks at me again. "You're right, Duchess. He clearly really wanted to make this happen for you." His tone is sincere.

That makes me feel...squirmy. Good, because it's nice that Christian wanted it to work and wanted to make me happy. But also weird to have Jonah agreeing that Christian clearly wanted to make me happy.

"And I know he's glad this worked out," Jonah tells me,

his voice a little softer. "You have been, as usual, charming as hell."

He sounds like he's reassuring me, and I feel squirmy again. I shift on my seat. "Me? I haven't even talked to him much. And I'm a terrible bowler."

Jonah shakes his head. "This is definitely not about how you are as a bowler."

I wiggle on the hard plastic again, then I reach for his soda, plucking it from his hand and taking a long drink. I don't know why, but the idea of Christian wanting me and working to be with me makes me feel strange. Maybe it's because Jonah seems to think it makes sense. And is okay with it. Is helping with it...

But this is why we're here, I remind myself. It's the reason for this entire trip. This was part of his plan with Torin.

But...

I want someone else.

I already knew this, but it's clear in this moment.

Both of these men are making things work so I can spend time with Christian. They're letting me call these shots. They're going with the flow of the evening.

Christian is passing the tests.

But, I still want someone else.

"So *I'm* passing the bowling tests?" I ask. "The ones you gave to Torin without him knowing it?"

Jonah gives me a smile that makes my stomach swoop. "Of course you are."

"How? I haven't helped anyone change a tire and you haven't flirted with anyone I want to flirt with."

"Duchess," he says, in a warm tone that sounds like *are-you-kidding-me*. "You were with Tami and her friends for thirty-two minutes and talked Tami into auditioning for the community theater part she wants and convinced her mom to sell her homemade earrings online."

My eyes widen. "Did you *hear* Tami sing? She's amazing. Of course she should audition." I pull my long ponytail to one side. "And these earrings are beautiful."

Jonah laughs. "And they know nothing about *you*. But you have their stories." He leans in, his eyes filled with affection that makes my skin tingle. "And you told Tami not to go to the director who only wants to cast women under the age of thirty, but to go to his best friend and sing for *him*. Because there's always someone behind the main guy who can convince the main guy to do the things he's not doing."

I lick my lips, my gaze falling to Jonah's mouth. "I'm right."

He nods. "You are. You know firsthand about talking to the people behind the scenes to get shit done."

"I do."

"*And* you bask in finding ways to make other people shine."

My gaze lifts to his. "I do."

"Of course you passed the tests. The test of seeing people for who they are no matter what the circumstance. The test of not needing to have any attention on yourself and not caring if someone else has the spotlight or is better at something than you are. The test of being genuine and amazing and beautiful inside and out." He pauses and lifts his hand, dragging the back of his knuckles over my cheek. "But we didn't need to go bowling. I already knew all of that."

My breath catches in my chest and I open my mouth to reply.

"Linnea!"

Christian's call interrupts us, and I swallow hard. Jonah's hand drops away from my face and I pull in a breath.

I turn as Christian approaches.

Despite this turning into an obvious PR event, I do believe that Christian's smile for me is genuine as he steps down from the upper level where he was talking to some other bowlers—a group of men standing around a tall table with beers and all wearing green shirts that say Balls Deep—and comes to sit on the plastic chair on my other side.

Just like I believed that his greeting was warm and sincere when Jonah and I arrived at the bowling alley. He gave me a friendly, but not too friendly, kiss on the cheek and squeezed my hand and said, "It's good to see you. I'm really looking forward to this."

I believed him. I also believe he's actually having fun.

"I'm glad you're on my team and not the other," I tell him as he leans back against the plastic chair.

He chuckles. "I haven't bowled in years. This was a great idea."

It *was* a great idea. I am learning exactly what I intended to learn.

He has been friendly and genuine with everyone.

The staff who has come around and asked to refill drinks have all gotten direct eye contact and thanks, he has greeted everyone who approaches him with handshakes and warm words, he's posed for photos, and he helped some veterans down the short steps to the lanes where they are bowling next to us, then stood and chatted with them for several minutes.

But, I can't stop myself from finding Jonah, no matter where he is in the huge room.

I love watching him. There's no crowd around him. No cameras. No PR people making sure he doesn't miss anyone. But...he doesn't miss anyone.

He helped a man in a wheelchair get in the front doors and down to the lanes and I was the only one besides the man's family who noticed. He's been talking to two of the veterans off to the side, out of sight of anyone with a camera, and *he's* been refilling drinks and food rather than waiting for the bowling alley staff to do it.

The truth is, both men are handsome, charming, and good guys. I like being around both of them.

But one has political power. He can more directly make changes and help influence policy that can affect people's lives for the better.

The other has to work indirectly to affect change.

One I don't know very well and objectively find attractive, but don't feel a particular spark with.

The other I find I can read easily. And right now, given the opportunity, I would climb into his lap, straddle him, run my hands up under his shirt, and stick my tongue in his mouth.

Jonah gets up and strides toward the lane to take his turn.

Though none of us are taking this particularly seriously —our team is made up of me, Jonah, Christian, and his head of security, a guy named Scott—we're doing pretty well. Christian and Jonah are both exceptional bowlers, and Scott is decent as well. I suck, but it doesn't matter with those three on my team.

As soon as Jonah is out of earshot, Christian stretches his arm along the back of the plastic chairs and leans in.

"I'm so glad you wanted to get together tonight."

I turn, our face only a few inches apart. "I am too. I was very flattered when Torin told me that you wanted to see me again on a more casual basis."

That's all true.

"I think this was a great idea. Bowling is fun and casual and a great way to get to know each other."

"I agree."

"But I am hoping that maybe you'll say yes to going for a drink somewhere after this. Somewhere a little quieter, with fewer people, where we can talk for a little bit."

I study him up closer. He really is very good looking. He's not Ryan Reynolds only in personality, he's classically handsome too and I'm sure he could date any woman he wanted to.

"We could probably do that." I should. This is the whole reason I'm in D.C..

There was no chemistry with James, and I didn't need to see him on a more one-on-one basis. But maybe Christian and I should spend a little time alone.

If nothing else, James and I had a chance to have a serious conversation about the energy project. Christian and I should further our professional relationship at least.

"Great. As soon as we're done with the game," he says.

"Okay." I agree. I've seen what I needed to with the bowling. Christian is a fun, easy-going, personable guy. He does think of others. Sure, it seemed a little bit like a campaign event, but I can't blame him. He is a current, active politician. And he's up for reelection in November.

"I'm not dressed for anything fancy."

Besides the black jeans, I'm wearing a casual pink top. It's a halter, tied behind my neck and leaving my shoulders and arms bare, but I'm wearing a short pink and black cardigan over the top and black flats when I'm not in bowling shoes.

It's cute, but it's not sexy and I know that's no accident. And it makes me smile that Jonah doesn't want me in anything sexy around Christian. I could have vetoed this outfit and insisted on one of the others. There was a dress, a skirt, and a pair of shorts, all of which would have been just as cute and casual but would have shown more leg. But I let Jonah's choice stand. It felt possessive and I can't help it, I liked that.

Besides, I don't need to show off for Christian. At least I shouldn't need to. If he needs to see me in something sexy to be interested, then that's a mark against him. I wanted to see how he reacts to me dressed down and casual. He's seen me dressed up for cocktail parties and dinner at the palace. He knows that I can pull off the classy, sophisticated look.

And apparently the maroon dress with the low back *is* sexy. At least according to Jonah.

"Oh, it doesn't have to be anything fancy," Christian says. "We'll find a small bar nearby. Just as long as it's a little quieter and we can have some one-on-one time."

I hesitate. I don't necessarily want one-on-one time with Christian. But I have a feeling Jonah is not going to go for that anyway. I just nod.

Jonah comes back from bowling a spare, and we're finished.

Christian stands and offers me a hand and I let him pull me up from my seat.

"I'm going to head to the ladies' room to freshen up," I say.

"Great, I'll let everyone know our plans," Christian says.

I glance at Jonah and simply get a quirked eyebrow.

I turn and head for the restroom.

But as I'm washing my hands and touching up my lipstick, it occurs to me that I don't need more time with Christian. I know what I need to know.

He's a great guy. He is someone who could give me some amazing opportunities if I wanted to be on the world stage as more of a leader. He actually has more power and influence in some ways than Torin does. Torin has the ability to enact policy and programs directly, but Christian is part of the government of a much bigger and more influential country.

If all of that—world politics, and influencing policy at the highest level—is what I want, then Christian is someone that I should be interested in getting closer to.

If love, and chemistry, and all of that really isn't important to me—as I've told myself all these years—if I'm truly willing to give all of that up to do something for the greater good, then why not trade a guy like Torin, who isn't interested in marrying me, for a guy who *is* interested in me romantically?

It would at least be worth going on a few dates, right? It would at least be worth getting to know him better. It would at least be worth pursuing.

But something has changed.

I could say it's happened over just the last few days, since Torin presented me with this opportunity to go out and consider someone other than him as a partner.

But the truth is, it's been happening for the past almost year.

Ever since Jonah found me by the fountain. Ever since we started to become friends. Ever since he became the person I feel the safest with, the most *me* with.

And definitely ever since he kissed me.

I've actually let myself consider something else.

Something other than what I've taken for granted all this time.

Something other than what I thought was inevitable.

And now I can't stop.

Instead of a straight path in front of me that was paved a long time ago with only one direction to go, I'm now standing at a fork in the road.

CHAPTER 22
JONAH

"So Linnea and I were just talking about going and getting a drink someplace that will make it a little easier to talk."

I tuck my hands into the front pockets of my jeans and give Christian a nod. "Okay."

Christian Waite is a really good guy. Nice, charming, seems to really care about people, seems enamored with Linnea.

He'd be perfect for her.

I really fucking hate him.

"And I'd appreciate it if maybe you'd hang back," Waite adds.

I lift a brow. "Define *back*."

"I'd like her to come with me alone."

I shake my head. "Not gonna happen. Where she goes, I go."

I don't know exactly what Linnea told Christian about my accompanying her tonight, but I can and will explain to the duchess what I am now explaining to the senator—she's not going to be out of my sight tonight.

"I'm surrounded by security. They'll make sure the place is safe. There's nothing to worry about," Christian says.

"Where she goes, I go," I repeat.

This is not negotiable. And I don't give a fuck if he's a senator. Linnea is my responsibility. He doesn't have to like it.

"Okay," Christian gives in. He's a nice guy. He doesn't seem like the type to get into a big argument or a big fight with me about something like this. Especially when we're both looking out for Linnea. "But it would be great if she and I could get a table alone. You can hang out at the bar or something."

I narrow my eyes. "What exactly are you gonna be talking about? You giving her the nuclear codes or something?"

He grins. "Nothing like that. "

"I am fully vetted," I tell him. "Fully cleared to hear anything she can hear."

Christian studies me for a moment, then says, "You really can't think of anything I might want to say to her that I don't want you to hear?"

And there we go. No matter how business-like Linnea might want to be, Christian is making it clear that *professional* is not how he perceives this time with her.

"Got it," I tell him.

Well, I did want her to know she had choices. Seems like Christian is going to make that clear. And it doesn't matter how knotted up my gut is, or how tight my chest feels, or how much I want to punch this guy in the face. Linnea deserves to have all the men falling at her feet.

She deserves to know that she can choose anyone she wants.

I should appreciate him laying it out so she knows that she can have her pick.

And fuck, there isn't a single person who would deny that Christian can give her things that I can't.

Hell, he can give her things Torin can't. Not the least of which are love, sex, and passion.

It's clear that Christian truly likes Linnea. He's attracted to her. He wants this to be more than just a business relationship or friendship.

This is exactly why we're fucking here. I take a breath, remind myself that both Torin and Iris will be very happy about this, and nod. "I'll hang back. But I need to be there. Close by."

Christian inclines his head. "I appreciate it."

Great. So glad he appreciates it.

Linnea returns and comes to stand with us. "So now what?" she asks.

I grit my teeth as I watch Christian put a hand against her lower back. "That drink."

She looks up at me. "You're coming too?"

"Of course."

I am relieved to see that she smiles at that. "Good."

I'm glad she thinks that's good. There's no way I'm not coming along, but I'm glad I don't have to argue with her about it too. This is the weirdest fucking situation.

I want her to be more confident. I want her to own the fact that she's amazing, sexy, deserving of whatever she wants. The whole fucking goal here is for her to know that she can have something different, something better than what waits for her in Cara.

But just this afternoon, having my hands on her, having

my mouth on her, hearing her laughter, her moans, is making it very fucking hard to remember that part of the mission here is to actually turn her over to another man.

This is really fucked up.

Or maybe I'm just making it fucked up.

Maybe I'm so damn good at my job that I'm losing track of what is supposed to be happening here. Maybe I'm doing such a good job, she's already become exactly what we want her to be—more than Lady Linnea Olsen, arranged fiancée to Prince Torin. Now she's a sexy, confident, kick ass woman ready to take on the world and any powerful man she wants.

It probably shouldn't surprise me that it took only a little over a day to get her to this point.

She's extraordinary.

Of course, it should take only a few hours to show her that.

It takes a while to get Christian out of the bowling alley. People want to shake his hand again, and pose for pictures, and he of course, wants to make a statement about how great it is to hang out with regular people in a regular setting and how much he appreciates a chance to do this and to reconnect and to remember what a regular Saturday night is like. He thanks them for spending some time with him and letting him just relax and helping him kick back with people who are not politicians and who want to talk about real problems and remind him about real life.

I swear to God if I was playing a drinking game and took a shot every time I heard the guy say the words 'real' or 'regular', I'd already be wasted.

But the guy has charm. And it feels genuine. And Torin would really fucking like him.

In fact, if Waite and Linnea end up getting together, I can see a lot of positive cooperation between Waite and Cara. Stuff that would be good for both. Christian could help get Cara a seat at some pretty important tables and into some consequential discussions. Cara, with Linnea's help, could get some interesting projects and programs going that would make Christian look really good when he talks about moving America forward and new policies he believes in when he runs for president.

Because there's no way this guy *isn't* going to run for president.

This could be a fantastic partnership.

So why do I still want to punch the guy?

That question has a very easy answer. And it's incredibly obvious when we get to the bar that's about four blocks away. Waite doesn't wait for me to help Linnea out of the car. He's next to her door, opening it and offering her a hand before I even get the ignition shut off.

This 'casual' bar has a valet service, so I hand my keys over as Waite escorts Linnea through the front door. By the time I step into the dark interior, he's already got her in a dark U-shaped corner booth, and his arm stretched across the back of the booth behind her.

The bar has white tablecloths with glass bowls holding votive candles in the center of each table. Their specialty is martinis, and jazz plays low over the sound system.

The two security guys with Christian take a seat at the bar. I cast a glance at the cuddly couple and catch Linnea's eye, but then head to the bar myself. I order a soda and settle into some small talk with Scott and the other guy, whose name keeps slipping my mind.

It's only about ten minutes before my cell phone pings.

I look down then straighten as I realize it's a text from Linnea.

> Linnea: What are you doing?

> Having a soda

> Why over there?

> Your boyfriend asked for some alone time with you.

> I thought you said I had a choice.

I stare at the words, then I look over at her. Christian's talking to her, and she's smiling and nodding. I looked down at the message again. I did say she had a choice. She could choose between Christian, James, and Torin. But is that what I really meant?

She could choose Torin, but it would be a bad choice. Neither of them would be happy. She knows this. She's already taken James off the list. Are there ten, twenty, one hundred other men that she would have a chance with? No question.

But she's talking about Christian and me.

I know this. And will I give her that choice? Am I on the list?

Yes.

I know it before I even actually form the entire question in my mind.

If she wants me, she can have me.

It's complicated as fuck. It will mess all kinds of things

up. People will be pissed. She and I could lose everything we've got in Cara.

But if Linnea Olsen chooses me, over everything else, over everything she's got and can have...fuck yes, she can have me.

> Yes, Duchess. You have a choice. Whatever you want.

I watch her look down at her phone, then pick it up even as Christian is speaking, and type.

Her message comes in a moment later and my mouth goes dry.

> Prove it.

I study those two words for nearly thirty seconds. Then I tip back the rest of my drink, set my glass down, and excuse myself to Scott and the other guy. I walk toward the table where Linnea is sitting with Christian.

She looks up at me with a smile. I slide into the booth on her opposite side from Waite.

I meet Christian's gaze. He gives me a frown. "Is there a problem?"

"No problem at all," I tell him.

"Linnea and I were just in the middle of something."

"Go right ahead," I tell him. Under the table, I reach over and set my hand on her thigh.

"You were saying something about a gala next month," Linnea says to Christian. "I wanted Jonah to hear the details."

"Yes, I was hoping you would be able to come back and be my plus one," Christian says. "But I don't think your bodyguard needs to be in on the discussion just now. We can always involve him regarding any security measures later."

Linnea looks at me, then back to him with a laugh. "Oh, you think Jonah is my bodyguard? Somebody behind the scenes?"

"Isn't he?"

Linnea shakes her head. "No. Jonah is my best friend. My confidant. He's the one who helps me make all of my big decisions. He definitely needs to be in on this."

She emphasizes the word *this*. I squeeze her thigh.

Hearing her describe me to Christian as her best friend unknots some of the tension in my gut. She's not declaring that I am her boyfriend, or her lover—hell, none of that is true—but telling Christian that I am more than a bodyguard, more than a guy on the periphery, definitely means something.

And it is definitely true.

If someone had *asked* me, I wouldn't have described myself the way she did, but hearing it, the truth hits me. No one knows her the way I do. No one cares about her the way I do. Her family, even her sister, doesn't know all the sides, all the layers, to this woman. It's only me. And I suspect she knows things about me that I'm not even aware of. Things that even Torin has missed.

My heart is now pounding harder, and I have to fight the urge to haul her out of this booth, throw her over my shoulder, and march out of here.

And straight to a bed.

To finally fully claim her. To make her fully mine.

Though, in many ways, she's been mine since she walked in on me naked ironing.

My hand moves up on her thigh. I feel her hand drop to

cover mine and I expect her to push my hand away, or at least down an inch or two.

She doesn't. She drags it an inch higher.

I'm glad for the tablecloths now, I suppose. Though I'm becoming less and less concerned with Waite's thoughts on my relationship with Linnea.

Christian's eyes say that he's understanding there is something much deeper going on here.

"I apologize. I knew Jonah was Torin's head of security. I just assumed he was traveling with you for safety."

"Well, Jonah is much more than that to Torin as well. He definitely leads the security team around Torin and myself, but that's the least of the things he does," Linnea says.

Christian meets my gaze. "I apologize for not understanding the full breadth of your role."

"No problem. I'm really just here for whatever Linnea needs."

She turns, our gazes locking.

I know that statement means more to her than it does to Christian. Exactly the way it should.

"The gala is a fundraising event for conservation efforts," Christian says, pulling Linnea's attention back to him. "It's one of those ridiculous things where attending costs money that should probably be given directly to the charity, but it does drum up publicity for the organization, and gives us a chance to rub elbows with people we wouldn't usually see in a social setting. People are a little more relaxed and friendly. You understand these things."

"And what will it mean if I show up as your plus one?" Linnea asks him. "I assume there will be photos? Reporters asking questions about me?"

"Yes. They'll want to know who the gorgeous woman

on my arm is." Waite gives her a charming, seemingly sincere, smile.

"And what would you tell them?"

My thumb starts stroking over her thigh. Not unintentionally.

If she wants to know what kind of choice she has, this is the perfect moment. Christian Waite is asking her to show up at a major public event, where photographers and reporters will capture her name and give her a title in relation to him. And my hand is on her thigh, stroking, communicating that I am right here, ready to give her whatever she wants from me.

"I will tell them whatever you want me to tell them," Christian says. "But I would very much like to get to know you better in the next month before that time. And maybe by then, be able to introduce you as my girlfriend."

My thumb stops. Linnea's eyes go wide. "I see."

"I figured you would appreciate me being direct," he says.

"I do," she agrees.

Christian is doing a great job of ignoring me sitting right here. He leans in. "I like you," he tells Linnea. "I think you're beautiful, intelligent, interesting, and I think we have a lot in common. I would like to get to know you better, but I have every reason to believe that we could be an amazing power couple. With my connections and future here in the United States along with your connections and past in Cara, not to mention your connections in Europe, I think we could do some amazing things."

"Such as?"

"I'm up for re-election in November. I will most likely win. My party is excited about my future in politics. There's a very good chance that I could be vice president. And someday..."

"President," Linnea fills in.

His smile is actually a bit self-deprecating. "Yes. And like it or not, my chances for all of those things increase if I'm married. I'm not saying I would get married just for that reason, but I do want to marry and have a family someday. And I believe that there are certain women who would be better matches than others for someone in my position."

Linnea tips her head to the side. "So you are looking for women of a certain...caliber."

It is not lost on me that she uses the same term that Torin used when discussing the men he was looking at for her.

"Yes, I suppose you could put it that way. There are certain women who are probably better suited for life married to a politician."

"And you think I might be one of them."

He nods with a smile. "I know so. In fact, I think you would enjoy it. In many ways, you would be a politician yourself. Some first ladies are simply that. A wife. They have a few projects of their own. They do a few public appearances here and there. But mostly they are known for being the first lady. I have every reason to think that you would be as influential, if not more in many ways, than your husband would be."

He's figured her out perfectly.

Linnea Olsen would be a leader. No matter who she's married to, she will be influential in her own way. She could also lead all on her own.

I like the guy in that moment, knowing that he is recognizing and appreciating her for who she is. And I don't blame him for recognizing her for what she can do for him.

Linnea turns to me. "What do you think, Jonah?"

Oh, I see. She's just going to put me on the spot. Just challenge me right in front of him?

I like that she's feeling feisty. Maybe she's enjoying having the two of us vying for her attention. She deserves that. And if that's what she wants, I'll give it to her.

"I think the senator would be lucky to have you on his arm. I think he's exactly right about everything he said. You would be a fantastic senator's wife, and First Lady."

Her eyes widen. "Really?"

"Of course. Just like you would be a fantastic queen of Cara."

Her eyes narrow. This is clearly not what she was expecting me to say. What did she think? That I was going to pound my chest and say, 'no, he can't have you because I want you?' That she'll be a fantastic *bodyguard's* wife?

"Of course, you would also be an amazing speaker. Or author. Or ambassador. Or advocate. Whatever your passion is, you would be amazing at it. You are talented, brilliant, passionate, and there's nothing you can't do. So really, Duchess, it's up to you." I pause, drilling my gaze into hers. "What do *you* want?"

It's not that I'm not willing to fight for her.

But I don't need to fight for her.

She needs to fight for herself. None of this is up to me or Waite. Or Torin. Or Diarmuid. Or her grandfather's last wishes.

It is all up to her.

And goddammit, she is going to understand that.

She stares at me for several long seconds. Then she

takes a breath and turns back to the senator. "Well, it seems that I have some things to think about."

He nods. "Of course. I don't want you to think that if you say yes to the gala, you're committed to anything else. We can go to the gala as friends, acquaintances, whatever you want. But I do want to get to know you better. And if we can do that over the next month and find that by the time of the gala, we can be more, I would be thrilled."

She takes a breath. "That seems fair."

It does. What he's proposing is very fair.

I definitely want to punch him.

"Wonderful." Waite seems pleased. And relieved.

"Meet me for breakfast tomorrow. Somewhere *secure*." His eyes rest on me. "In fact, we could have breakfast at my place. I make fantastic eggs and there would be no security concerns. Not that I want to steal her away," he says to me before looking at her again. "But I can send a car and we can stay in. It would be a chance to get to know each other better without cameras or crowds."

I feel that he's very aware that the words 'steal her away' poke at the possessive bear inside of me.

"That sounds..." Linnea casts a glance in my direction. "Nice."

I know *she* is intentionally poking that bear.

I clear my throat. "We'll talk about the transportation and security, but...that would be fine." It would *not* be fucking fine, but I'm just here for whatever she needs.

I feel my shoulders tightening.

She turns a smile back to Christian. "I'll text you for details."

"Great."

"But for now, I think I should call it a night," Linnea tells Christian.

He's clearly disappointed, but to his credit he nods. "Let me walk you out."

Obviously, she doesn't need this. I'm here. He's probably assuming that I'll give them some space and time to say goodnight "one on one". But I slide out, hold out a hand, and watch as Christian does the same on the other side of the booth.

And the little vixen, who absolutely deserves to have two men holding their hands out to her, waiting for her to give them even the smallest crumb of her attention and time, looks from my hand to his and smiles.

Then she slides to the end of the booth and stands up without taking either of our hands.

I grin as I step back.

That's right. She doesn't need a man.

She gets to choose one because she *wants* one.

"Can you give us a minute?" Linnea asks Christian, stopping a few steps from the table.

He looks back and forth between Linnea and me, then nods. "I'll have the valet bring our cars around."

I dig into my pocket for my tag and toss it to him. "Thanks."

She waits until Christian is out of ear shot, but I watch the feisty brunette who is tying me up in knots.

When he rounds the corner at the front, she looks up at me. "What are you thinking?"

She doesn't say it with any kind of accusation in her tone. She looks and sounds curious. Like she really wants to know what I'm thinking.

"What do you mean?" I ask.

"What are you thinking about right now? About all of this? About Christian. And me."

I frown and shake my head. "I don't know why you're asking. This is about what *you're* thinking."

"I..." She stops and takes a breath. "I haven't done this before. You know that. I've never even gone to the movies with a guy who I wanted to kiss me goodnight. And now I suddenly have two guys. One who is basically asking me if I want to get married and be the First Lady of the United Fucking States and the other with his hand on my leg, who's been playing with me all day, who watched me with my vib—"

I put a hand over her mouth and tug her over to the side, away from all the other tables and the wait staff who are winding through the room.

I tuck us into an alcove with a potted plant that I would bet used to hold a payphone.

She's watching me with wide eyes, but of course lets me put her against the wall and block her view of the rest of the room. The way she trusts me, lets me in her personal space, lets me just do whatever I want to with her is...so fucking hot. And huge. It matters to me that she trusts me this way.

"Jesus, Linnea." I move my hand. "How about we not talk about your vibrator in public?"

"Why? Is that not normal date conversation?" she asks, sarcasm suffusing each word.

I lift a brow. "It's not."

"Is it *normal* date conversation to talk about becoming the future First Lady after *bowling* with a guy *one time*?"

I study her face, then I feel my mouth kick up into a smile. Then I chuckle. Her eyes get even wider.

"*Jonah!*"

"No," I say quickly, but unable to stop smiling. "Of course not. But...for you? Yes."

She blows out a breath.

"Look, Duchess, you're...not normal. In so, so many fucking amazing ways. You are the kind of woman who walks into a damned *bowling alley* and has a man ready to make you, essentially, his queen. However he can. Yes, on date number one. I'm sorry to break it to you, but Torin O'Grady is probably the only man on the planet who is stupid enough to *not* want to marry you."

She's frowning but she's listening.

I can't resist lifting my hand and cupping her face. I drop my voice. "As for your vibrator...*only* a man with superhuman strength could have walked out of that room and I am *not* that man."

She swallows, her eyes locked on mine.

"Do not," I say firmly, "settle for a man who will not make you his first fucking lady *and* give you *everything* you need." I run my thumb along her jaw. "Whatever room you are in. You understand me?"

She nods. "Yeah," she says softly. "I understand."

"So now," I say, dropping my hand and taking a deep breath. "What do *you* think about all of this?"

"I think that Torin will think it's wonderful. I think Diarmuid will like Christian a lot. I think he'll think I'll be a wonderful First Lady. Even my parents will like that."

My chest is tight and I have to clench my fist to keep from reaching for her. "I agree. I think I'm doing a hell of a job on this mission to get you dating someone who can give you everything you want and need."

I was supposed to help her understand that she wanted *more* than what she had with Torin. To understand that she wanted to date and fuck and fall in love.

I've done that. Clearly.

But when I agreed to this job, I hadn't yet admitted that I wanted her to date and fuck and fall in love with *me*.

My phone vibrates in my pocket. I reach for it. I check the screen and my stomach knots. I curse under my breath.

"Is everything okay?" Linnea asks, frowning.

It's Iris. So, no, everything is probably not okay.

Before I can even answer Linnea, another text comes through.

This one's from Henry.

Then another. From Torin.

I frown. It's ten p.m. in D.C. That makes it only seven p.m. for Iris and nine for Henry. But it's three a.m. for Torin. What the fuck is he doing awake?

"I just need to check in with a few people it seems," I say.

"I can go out to the car with Christian," she says.

I don't want her to. But...fuck. There's no reason to say no.

Because, like it or not, there *is* other security around her because of Waite. I've only stayed close because, well, I want to be close to her. She doesn't need me right on her ass all the time. She doesn't need me at breakfast tomorrow. She doesn't need me at the gala a month from now.

She's completely safe with him. Hell, I did the thorough background check on Waite myself. He's exactly who she should be with.

"Okay. I'll be out soon."

She nods and opens her mouth as if she has something more to say. But then she shuts it and just smiles before stepping around me and heading for the door.

I watch her go before I swipe on Iris's message.

> Iris: Saw the social media posts. Linnea is looking very girlfriend-esque next to Waite. That is not the plan!

Great. There are already social media posts from tonight. I'm not shocked. Christian had his PR people there. As Linnea and I guessed, several of the people at the bowling alley were invited there by his staff if not working for him directly.

And I'm sure Iris has tags for Linnea's name set to notify her whenever anything is posted about her.

I don't answer and open Henry's message.

> Henry: You and Waite just going to share her then?

He's attached two photos that also clearly come from social media. They're both from the bowling alley tonight. In one, Waite is kissing Linnea's cheek. It looks like it's from when we first arrived and he was saying hello.

The other is of me and Linnea. We're sitting close on the plastic chairs and I'm leaning over, saying something in her ear. I don't remember the exact moment, but the look on her face has my entire body heating. She's blushing, smiling, leaning into me, and yeah, she looks like a woman who is very into the guy and whatever he's saying.

Into me. And whatever I'm saying.

> Henry: Very progressive of you both. Brilliant solution really. Except for the you getting fired part. But I guess if you're the senator's boyfriend, you won't need the job with Torin?

Henry is such an ass.
I text him back.

> I don't share.

I get a wide-eyed emoji back followed by

> Thought you'd say that. Good luck. Has Iris texted yet?

I ignore that because he knows that of course she has. I sigh and open Torin's text.

I'm almost expecting him to attach photos as well. Instead, his message is completely off topic and I have to read it twice before I can mentally switch gears.

> Torin: How do I tell L that James already committed to Canada? The energy program is a no go for Cara. She's going to be upset.

Well...*fuck*.

Iris is displeased. Henry has photos of Linnea and *me*...which means other people do too. Even if our team scours the internet and pulls anything down, other people have seen them. Whether or not they care is another question, of course. And now the big program that Torin could have used to convince Diarmuid he doesn't need Linnea as his queen is dead in the water. I guess that explains why the prince is up at three a.m. He's been worrying. And brainstorming.

Just...*fuck*.

> I'll tell her.

> Thanks. Fuck. We need something.

> I know. Go to bed. We'll deal with it when we get home.

I open Iris's text again and my thumbs hover over the keys for thirty seconds before I simply text,

> I'm handling it.

Then I close out of all messages and turn my phone off. The only person I need to be in contact with is a gorgeous brunette standing outside this bar. The rest of them can just fuck off for tonight.

I breathe deeply and head for the door. I pull it open, step out onto the sidewalk…

And come up short.

Our cars are at the curb, running, the driver's side door on mine open, the back door on Christian's open.

Christian's men are inside his.

But Christian is still on the sidewalk with Linnea.

Kissing her.

He has one hand on her waist, one in her hair, and he's kissing her. Not just a peck on the cheek or even on the lips.

This is a full-on, I-want-you kiss.

I see red.

My heart starts to pound, my entire body tightens, and my vision narrows until it's just the two of them. I start forward.

But as I take my first step, Linnea pulls back. Christian lets go of her, and they smile at each other.

He says something to her that I can't hear, and she nods, and then they both turn toward me.

Her smile gets bigger when she sees me.

I'm right beside her then.

"I'll talk to you soon," Christian tells her.

"Okay," she answers. "Thanks for bowling with me tonight."

His smile is fucking *affectionate* as he nods. "Any time."

This man should have her. *Fuck*. He's exactly what she deserves.

And all I want to do is shove him away from her, carry her back to the hotel, and tie her to the bed.

And keep her.

I breathe in deeply and unclench the hand I didn't realize had curled into a fist.

"You ready to go?" Linnea asks me.

"Yes." Her eyes widen slightly at my short answer.

My hand goes to her lower back and I nudge her toward our car. I try to be gentle, but I'm seething and I know I need to get a fucking grip.

"Goodnight, Jonah. It was nice to meet you," Waite says behind me.

"Yeah," I answer.

I don't have to be nice. I won't be seeing him much, if at all, after this. Once Linnea is officially dating him, she won't be under my protection anymore. I won't come back to D.C. with her on her dates. I won't go to the galas and the balls. I won't go to his fucking inauguration. I *will* be sending in an absentee ballot though, and I just might not vote for him. And I absolutely won't fucking go to their goddamned wedding.

I put her in the passenger seat—I literally pick her up by the waist and *put her* into the leather bucket seat—and lean over her to fasten the seat belt. I hold my breath as I do it to keep from pulling in her scent.

But then I make the mistake of looking at her before pulling back.

She's watching me with wide eyes, her lips parted, breathing fast. She almost looks scared. But...her throat is flushed.

Her adrenaline is pumping, but this isn't nervous adrenaline.

"Jonah—"

"Are your panties wet now?" I growl.

She wets her lips and nods.

I lean back and slam the door, stalking around to the driver's side. I get in and shift into drive, easing us into traffic.

"Jonah—"

"I need you to not talk right now," I say, low and firm.

"Excuse me?"

I stop at the light that turns red. I risk a glance in her direction.

She's watching me with a frown.

"I just really need to *not* rehash your kiss with Waite, okay?" I tell her. "I don't want to hear about it or have you ask me questions about it. I am *not* going to analyze it for you. You're going to have to call Astrid after all. But no, Duchess, not every man's kiss is going to make you hot and wet, though I suppose it's good that the future president's does."

The light turns green and I'm about to press the gas pedal when I hear her door open. I look over but am too stunned to react as I watch Linnea get out of the car, slam the door behind her, and walk across the two lanes of traffic to the sidewalk.

"What the *fuck*?" I yell. I roll down the window. "Linnea! Get your ass back here!"

She keeps walking, not even looking in my direction.

The cars in the lanes between us are now moving and the car behind me lays on the horn. I lift my middle finger.

"Linnea!" I roar.

But even if she can hear me, she doesn't slow down or look back.

I don't know where the hell she thinks she's going, but she won't get far.

I press the gas and the car lurches forward. I immediately signal, jerking the wheel to the right, and merging into the lane next to me, then the next. If you can call causing the cars behind me to slam on their brakes and call me very unflattering names 'merging'.

I round the corner, speed to the next, round that block and realize…fuck it. I pull over at the curb, not even bothering to note if it's actually legal to park there. I grab my phone, the keys, and make sure I have my wallet, then I take off at a run in the direction she was headed.

Thankfully, she's walking resolutely but not quickly.

I catch up with her a few minutes later.

I walk up behind her, wrap my arm around her waist, and pick her up.

She starts fighting, exactly as she's been trained, but she doesn't have her pepper spray in hand. I'm both irritated and relieved by that.

"It's me, you little hellion. Stop it," I say against her ear, carrying her down the sidewalk to a bench.

She stops fighting but when I deposit her onto the bench and squat in front of her, caging her in with my hands on the seat on either side of her hips, she's glaring at me.

"What the *fuck* was that?"

"That was me refusing to be spoken to the way you were speaking to me," she says, chin up.

If I had forgotten for one second this woman has spent twenty-seven years planning to be a queen, in that moment, she is royal as fuck from the top of her gorgeous head to the tips of her feisty toes.

"No one tells me when I can and cannot speak," she says.

I tip my head. "You're right, Duchess." She is. There are some very specific instances where this woman will enjoy me bossing her around. My body heats with that simple thought and I have to clear my throat. We will both enjoy those instances. But they won't extend to every circumstance, for sure. "I'm sorry."

She crosses her arm, and her leg, kicking me in the stomach—thankfully just above my fly—in the process. She regards me with a cool look I haven't seen in months. And I hate it. I only want warmth and heat from her.

"After *you* kissed me the first time, you stopped speaking to me. And now after another man does it, you decide you don't want to speak to me," she points out. "You seem very emotional about the topic of me and kissing."

"I am," I agree. "I have a lot of very big emotions about that subject."

"Well, you're a big boy and you're going to listen to what I have to say anyway," she tells me. "And I'm a big girl and I am not telling you this because I'm naïve and need you to help me *analyze* this. I know very well what's going on. I'm also not telling you this because I love when you're jealous, though I do. I'm telling you this because it concerns you."

A lot of fucking things *concern* me about this woman. But I blow out a breath and nod. "Fine."

"Christian asked to kiss me."

I grind my back teeth together. "And you said yes."

"I did."

"Okay." It's not okay. She's mine. Everything in me is

screaming at me that she's mine and that every other man needs to back the fuck off. Even if they are future presidents and kings.

I'm so fucked.

Iris is going to kill me.

And Linnea isn't done yet. "Because I wanted to be able to say to you that I only want *you* to kiss me from now on."

My gaze clashes with hers.

She stares directly into my eyes. "I knew that if I'd never kissed another man who I really liked and thought was attractive and who could be a perfect match for me, you'd say I couldn't be sure and that I needed to know that I could have someone else and not just the first man to kiss me and make me come."

I blow out a breath. Jesus. Iris might not have to kill me because Linnea is going to.

There are people passing by on the sidewalk behind us, cars passing on the street, and I don't hear any of them.

She's my whole world right now.

And probably from now on.

"So I kissed him because I wanted to tell you that I understand I have a choice. And I choose *you*."

I let those words roll through my mind. Through my chest. Through my fucking soul.

Then I drop my head to her knee. "Duchess."

I feel her hand go to my head. "I know...it's complicated."

"So fucking complicated."

"So we'll—"

My head comes up. I lean in. "Let me make something very clear to you." I don't care about the people around us. I don't care about the texts on my phone from my boss demanding answers. I don't care that when we tell everyone we're together, there will literally be a king and a future president pissed at us.

Her eyes go round, but she nods. "Okay."

"Unless you say no right now, I'm making you mine tonight."

She nods quickly. "Yes."

"That means I'm going to fuck you, Linnea. *Tonight*. All night. I'll be your first. And. Your. Last." I enunciate those last three words carefully. Her head continues bobbing up and down, but I keep going. She has to understand this fully. "Once I fuck you, *no one* else will. Ever. So if you have any desire to experiment, to spread your gorgeous wings, to catch up on what you've been missing, tell me now. Because I do *not* share. And once I have you, I'll never get over it. Do you hear me?"

She nods again.

"Say it."

"Yes." She wets her lips. "Yes, I hear you."

"And then we will go back to Cara and we will tell Torin. And...everyone. This is it."

"I understand. I agree."

I'm nearly vibrating with need. And it's so much deeper than physical need. There's no way she can truly understand what she does to me. How can she? She's innocent in so many ways. But I won't be able to let her go. I'm trying to be as up front and honest as I can.

"Make sure this is the cake you want."

That makes her take a deep breath and smile. "It is."

"Make. Sure."

She lifts her hand and places it against my cheek. It's the only place we're touching. I'm in her space, we're sharing air, but our bodies aren't touching. Until she cups my cheek.

"You want to know what I realized about that cake?" she asks.

"Yes."

"The cake that I've been afraid to taste and crave isn't kissing and sex. It's not even love," she says. "It's freedom. It's making my own choices. It's being who I really want to be. *That's* the cake I was avoiding because I knew, deep down, subconsciously, how much I would miss it when it was gone. So I just...didn't let myself have those things. And then you came along. And you saw me. You saw that I was missing *all* of that and...you cared. You wanted to give it back to me."

She stops and takes a deep breath, her smile fading, her expression growing more serious.

"Yes, kissing you in the palace kitchen was a turning point for sure, but my cravings started before that. When Torin came back and made it clear he didn't want to be married. When you were there, actually *listening* to me and caring how I felt and thought about things. I think I started to realize then that things could be different, and I started to want *that*. And then...this trip. This plan. You and Torin thinking that I needed to consider something new. I actually opened my mind to that idea and the cravings got too strong to ignore."

She smiles at me. "That's the cake I want, Jonah. The chance to make my own choices, to have options, to think about things in a new way. And you're the one who has been the biggest champion of that."

She leans in. "So yes, I'm sure that I want this cake. And just like my grandmother's recipe isn't the same when someone else makes it, I know *I* have to be the one making this all come together. Not Torin picking out other men. Not even *you* telling me what else I can have. *I* have to look at what I want, who I am, what my choices are, and decide what ingredients my cake will have."

I swallow. God. In all the times I've been impressed by her and found her stunning and incredible and impossible to resist, this might be the sexiest, the most confident, the most amazing she's ever been.

"I think you are…a fucking queen," I say gruffly.

Her smile is sweet and full of emotion.

She leans closer, her lips nearly on mine. "And I really, *really* want you as one of my ingredients."

Then she kisses me.

It's just the press of her lips against mine, just for a few brief seconds, but it is the most mind-blowing kiss of my life.

So I scoop my hands under her ass, pull her against my shoulder, then stand.

"Jonah!" she exclaims, but she's laughing.

I start for the car with her over my shoulder and my hand on her ass.

CHAPTER 23
LINNEA

On the way back to the hotel, Jonah doesn't let go of my hand for even a second. Our fingers are entwined and I swear the butterflies in my stomach are throwing a dance party.

This feels so right with him. I've never been more sure of anything.

And looking into his eyes as I told him that I choose him, I know that he felt it too. Yes, I do love seeing jealous Jonah, but I hated seeing unsure Jonah. More than anything I want him to know that he can be sure of me. There is no hesitation, no second thoughts. Even though I'm inexperienced when it comes to relationships, I know my own mind and heart.

He lets the valet at the hotel park the car and doesn't let go of me all the way through the lobby and even once we're on the elevator.

I'm itching to break the silence.

Not because I'm uncomfortable, but because I have so much to say.

"My panties aren't wet because of kissing Christian," is what I choose to start with.

His head snaps to the side and he looks down at me. "I don't wanna talk about Christian."

I lift my chin and his gaze. "Okay, we won't. I'll say, my panties are wet and have been wet all day because of *you*. You're the only man to do that to me ever."

He takes a breath and it seems that he's considering how to respond to this. "Thought we took care of that before bowling."

Heat floods through me as I remember the bedroom, the vibrator, his hand on his cock. "Sure. For a little bit. But then you were sweet and funny and charming with everyone at the bowling alley and I got wet for you all over again."

I can practically feel the heat coming off of him.

"I didn't say anything dirty to you at the bowling alley. I barely touched you. I specifically kept from doing that." His voice sounds tight.

"You don't have to be dirty to turn me on, Jonah."

I see his chest rise and fall with a deep breath. "I'm trying really hard to hold it together until we get into our room, Duchess. The things I wanna do to you are not appropriate for an elevator."

I grin. How I feel when he expresses how I affect him is addictive. "There's no one on the elevator with us."

"But there are cameras."

Surprised, I look around.

"Oh, that's right," he says, his voice huskier now, causing a trickle of awareness to dance down my spine.

"You like being naughty in public. Where we might get caught."

I pull my bottom lip between my teeth and nod. The planetarium feels like days ago, but it was just this afternoon.

He lets go of my hand and turns to lean back against the side of the elevator, crossing his huge arms. "Tease me, Duchess."

"How?"

"However you want to. I'm only a few minutes away from being able to strip those clothes off of you and spread you out on the bed, so you can do anything you want. Tempt me."

"I'm not very good at teasing and tempting."

"That's not true. You tempt me by just walking into a room. You make me want you more than I've ever wanted anyone ever."

I swallow hard as emotion hits me. Yes, that turns me on, but it also makes me feel things that are much deeper than lust. Jonah wants me, but he also *values* me and I feel it every moment we're together.

"I want to tempt you, because it feels so good. I love making you feel good. Making you want me as much as I want you," I tell him. "I love this chemistry, this heat between us. I never imagined it could be like this. Just everything you give me, plus this. It's…amazing."

He runs his thumb over his lower lip. "There are so many things I intend to do to you."

"I can't wait."

"You'll do them all, won't you?" he asks.

It's not really a question, but I nod. "Of course."

"No questions? No hesitation?"

"You've never done anything that wasn't good for me, even better than anything I could come up with for myself."

He blows out a long breath, his gaze never leaving mine. "So if I told you that I wanted you to slide your hand into the front of those jeans and give me a taste of how wet you are, would you do it? Even knowing there are people who can watch this on camera?"

A shiver of lust goes through me. "I definitely would. Usually, I don't like being told what to do, but with you..."

One side of his mouth quirks up as I trail off. "When it comes to that needy pussy, you'll let me boss you around all day." Possessiveness seems to come off of him in waves.

I suck in a breath. When he smiles at me like that I want to kiss him so badly. The cocky smugness, the confidence, the sexiness that exudes from him. I love that we have fully put to rest the idea of me ever being with anyone else.

I glance up at the numbers above the door. We have several floors still to go since we're staying on the top floor.

I pop the button on my jeans and slide the zipper down slowly.

I watch as the heat flares in his eyes. God, I love this feeling of power.

Then I flatten my hand on my stomach and slide it down into the front of my jeans. I'm not kidding. I am wet. Have been. And it's all for him.

My hand slides behind the waistband of my panties and then down over my clit and I give a little breathy moan.

"Stay there for a minute," he commands softly.

I watch him, my bottom lip between my teeth as I circle over that spot.

Somehow, he knows where my finger is. His heated stare makes this even hotter.

"Slide your finger inside that tight pussy."

His voice is low, gruff, and I swear it feels like it's stroking over my skin. I do as he tells me. Slipping my middle finger into the slick heat.

"Jonah," I say, soft and breathy.

I watch his jaw tense.

"I want your hands on me so badly," I tell him.

"You're gonna have my hands, my mouth, and my cock right there, sweetheart," he says.

That shiver of lust is stronger this time and I swear he can see me shudder with it.

"Come here," he says.

I slip my hand out from my panties and jeans and take the two steps that bring me right in front of him.

He grasps my wrist and brings my hand up to his mouth. He slowly licks along my finger, then sucks it into his mouth.

My core clenches and I give a little whimper.

"Fucking best thing I've ever tasted." His gaze flicks up to something in the corner of the elevator.

"And mine," he says. He looks at me again. "So no more until we're alone."

I can't believe that I did that, but I know I'll do anything to see that heat and possessiveness on his face.

He looks back to me. "You have no idea how much I want to bury my face between these thighs. It's a good thing you're not wearing a skirt or I don't think I'd fight the urge."

I'm going to have sex for the first time tonight. At least with another human.

And I feel zero nerves about it. I'm excited. So turned on I almost can't walk. I know it's going to be so good. Jonah is the only one I would want to do this with.

I don't really feel like a virgin. I know a lot about sex,

and I've certainly spent time on my own, learning my body. Jonah and I have also been very intimate so far. Still, this is kind of a big step tonight. And there's something amazing about knowing that it's going to be with this man. The only man I ever intend to do this with. That's probably a little cheesy, and some women would think that was sad, I suppose, but this man has always only had me in mind.

Could I have been Christian Waite's girlfriend? Yes. More than that? Maybe.

But, although I think Christian fully respects me and meant it when he said that I would have my own projects, I would be a part of *his* bigger plan as well. Being with me would benefit him. And that's flattering.

But everything Jonah has ever done, said, thought, or planned for me has been about *me*. He would rather give me up, and make sure I was happy, than keep me and have it be less than everything I could want or need.

He's always had me at the forefront of everything he's done.

If I didn't know better, I would think that he loved me.

As that thought hits me, the elevator doors swoosh open.

Jonah grabs my hand and hustles me down the hallway.

His long legs cover ground far quicker than mine and I have to hurry to keep up with him.

I am laughing by the time we get to the door.

"I'm kind of in a hurry," he says, giving me a self-deprecating grin.

"I'm glad," I tell him. "I definitely want you looking forward to this."

He turns to me as the door latch unlocks. "That seems like such an understatement for how I feel about this."

I melt a little. "Oh..."

My phone starts to ring.

I frown. Who would be calling me? It's almost eleven p.m. It's the middle of the night in Cara. It's still fairly early for my sister and brother, so it could be one of them, but there's no one I want to talk to right now.

I pull my phone from my purse.

It's Christian.

And yes, my screen flashes his name. I entered his and James's numbers and names into my phone way back at the energy conference last fall.

"Answer it," Jonah says.

"What? No."

Jonah nudges me through the doorway and says, "Strip. And answer it."

"But..."

He plucks the phone from my fingers. "Strip." His voice is deep, commanding, gruff. Then he hits the button to connect the call and puts it on speaker. He holds it out toward me.

I stare up at him. He lifts a brow. I swallow. "Um, hello?"

"Hi, Linnea. It's Christian."

"Yes, hi."

"I'm just calling to make sure you got in okay."

I shake my head. He didn't need to check on me. "I did. Thanks."

He gives a soft laugh. "Sorry. I know that sounds ridiculous. I just...wasn't ready to say goodbye at the bar."

I bite the inside of my cheek and look up at Jonah. He's just watching me. And holding my phone out.

So I push my already unbuttoned and unzipped jeans down over my hips as I toe off my shoes. I shimmy until the jeans are at my feet and then kick them to the side to crumple on top of the shoes.

"Well, thanks again for coming bowling tonight," I say to Christian. "That was nice of you. It was nice to spend casual social time with you for a change."

Jonah narrows his eyes.

Yeah, I like jealous Jonah. I can't help it.

"I had fun tonight," Christian tells me.

"Me too."

Jonah makes a circling motion with his finger that is a clear *keep going* signal.

"It was sweet of you to check on me now, too." I shrug out of my sweater as I meet Jonah's gaze. He lifts a brow at me calling Christian sweet.

I grin as I let it drop to the floor.

"I'm just on my way to bed," I say. I'm careful not to flat out lie and say I'm going to sleep. But I very much want to be lying on my bed, soon.

"Of course," Christian says smoothly. "I don't mean to keep you up."

"Oh, it's fine," I assure him.

Jonah frowns. I grin. I think I've made it clear that I've chosen Jonah, but *he's* the one who answered the phone.

I reach behind my neck, untying the halter top. Then I pull the top over my head. I'm not wearing a bra.

Now I'm in only panties, standing in front of a fully dressed Jonah.

"I just hope that what I said tonight wasn't too much," Christian says. "I know I came on a little strong."

"Not at all. I appreciated the honesty," I tell him. That's completely true.

Jonah reaches out and hooks his finger in the top of my panties and tugs. I try not to gasp.

He starts walking backward, pulling me along by the pale pink silk.

When he gets to the couch, he sits. He hands me the phone. I take it without thinking. Then he sweeps my panties down my legs. I step out of them as he takes my ass in both hands and pulls me into his lap. Straddling him. Completely naked.

While he's still completely dressed.

I stare at him with my mouth open.

He gives me a cocky grin. Then trails his hot gaze over my body. Slowly. Twice. Before lifting a hand and cupping one breast, running his thumb over my nipple.

I grasp his wrist, but I'm not sure if I'm trying to stop him, or if I'm just holding on.

He mouths, *be good*.

I work on steadying my breathing. And remember there's another man on the phone with me.

One I don't intend to marry, or even date, but who I have to be polite to.

Christian is saying something complimentary about how amazing I am and how much he enjoyed tonight, so I give a soft, "Thank you."

"I was thinking, after we said goodbye, if you think the gala might be too big of an event, too soon, I have a smaller dinner to attend in about six weeks. It's in New York, a local event. Perhaps that would be better?"

Jonah shakes head. He keeps one hand on my breast, teasing my nipple, while he slides his other hand down my side to my hip. He squeezes, then moves to cup me between my legs. I move the phone away from my mouth as a long breath hisses out.

I glare at him. *Stop*, I mouth. It's one thing to strip down and sit on his lap and be cool on the phone, but if he's going to keep touching me, I won't be able to hide my reactions for long.

Jonah gives me a slow smile. And shakes his head no.

"What do you think?" Christian asks.

"Um, maybe—"

Jonah strokes over my clit with his thick middle finger and my thoughts scatter. I glare at him even as I try to press closer to his finger.

No dinner, he mouths.

I wet my lips. "I don't think that's a good idea," I tell Christian. I'm impressed with how normal my voice sounds.

"Oh." He sounds surprised. "Are you all right? You sound a little...off."

Okay, maybe I don't sound so normal.

"I'm actually feeling a little...achy suddenly," I say, watching Jonah's face.

He slides a finger into me. I press my lips together to keep from moaning.

"Oh, I'm sorry. Can I send something over to your hotel?" Christian asks.

Jonah frowns. Clearly with Jonah here I don't need help from anyone else. For anything. He slides his finger in and out slowly.

"No...I'm good," I manage. I grip Jonah's shoulder with one hand. "I'll be okay." I pause. Then I have to say, "Jonah's here for anything I need."

Jonah's eyes are focused on mine as he strokes in and out again.

I swallow the moan that tries to rise up. I might need more practice in staying quiet when Jonah teases me, but I'm very happy to put the time in. It's deliciously torturous.

"Of course," Christian says. "Well, please think about

the dinner. Or the gala. Or both. Or we could also just get together. I can come to Cara, or I'd love to have you come visit again. Here in D.C. or New York."

Jonah's finger continues to move, and I barely register Christian's voice. It vaguely sinks in that if I *did* want to date him, I would love that he seems so eager to see me again.

But it's a moot point now.

"I'll—"

Jonah reaches up and mutes the phone. "Cancel breakfast," he growls.

"Okay."

"Cancel everything with him."

I nod. "Yes."

His thumb brushes over my clit and he curls his finger against the front wall of my pussy. "Good girl."

I take the chance to take a deep breath, then I unmute the phone. "Christian, there's something I need to tell you."

"Okay," he says, sounding hesitant.

I keep my eyes on Jonah's as I say, "What I told you about Jonah earlier wasn't completely true."

"I...see."

"Actually...it was. He is my best friend. My confidant. And sometimes my security. But he's...also the man I'm in love with." I let that sink in.

For both of them.

Jonah's hand stops moving. His eyes get even hotter and his breathing gets more ragged.

Christian clears his throat. "Oh."

"I'm sorry. No one knows. It's a little complicated. But I can't go to the gala. Or any official dinners with you, just the two of us. And I can't spend a weekend in D.C. or New York with you. I can't have breakfast tomorrow either." I pause. "Though I would like to be friends and still talk about ways Cara can partner with you on projects and new ideas. I think you're going to be an amazing leader and we'd love to be your friend and ally."

Jonah doesn't remove his hands from my body, but he doesn't move. He just waits with me. He knows, however else he feels about Christian, that he will be a great ally for Cara.

Finally, Christian says, "Of course. Absolutely. I'm... disappointed. But I absolutely value our friendship as well."

I'm relieved. And I hope he really does feel that way after he thinks about it more. "Wonderful. Thanks for understanding."

"Well, I can't expect you to give up love for politics," he says with a soft laugh.

Hmm. He'd be one of the few. "Thanks, Christian."

"Goodnight, Linnea."

"Goodnight. We'll talk soon."

"Great."

Christian Waite will be fine.

My thumb hits the button to end the call and I toss my phone to the floor.

Jonah's thumb runs back-and-forth over my clit. He makes a noise. "You're not talking to him soon."

I shift closer to him, grinding down against his hand. "I'll have to," I say, breathless. "About other things."

"No one needs to check on you. No one needs to call and catch up. You and Christian Waite will only be having business meetings from here on out. And I will be attending all of them."

I smile and I brace my hands on his shoulders, pressing down against his hand even harder. "Fine. Good. I'm good with that. "

He smirks at me. "You'll say anything I want you to say right now, won't you?"

I nod quickly. "Yes, please, just keep moving your fingers."

He lifts his hand and tweaks my nipple. "The things I could get you to promise me."

I meet his gaze directly. "I will promise you anything. I completely trust you. I know whatever it is would be amazing."

Heat flares in his eyes and I am amazed and touched by the fact that my trust in him turns him on just as much as me begging him to fuck me.

But I'm about two seconds away from doing that too.

"Tell me you're in love with me again," he says. He's not grinning. His gaze is intense.

"I'm madly, deeply, never-get-over-it in love with you," I tell him easily.

"Jesus," he mutters, stroking his fingers faster between my legs.

"Take me to bed," I tell him.

He shakes his head. "You're gonna come right now, right here."

"You're not even undressed. I want more than just your fingers."

"You're going to have all of me tonight, Duchess. I promise. I couldn't keep away from you if I tried. Obviously," he says with a dark chuckle. "But this is your first time. I need to make sure you're hot, wet, and very needy."

I give a whimper and rotate my hips against his hand. "I am."

"Not yet. You haven't even come once."

I tip my head back, feeling my hair spill down my back.

"Do something about that then," I tell him.

He chuckles again. "So bossy, Your Grace."

I smile, even as I'm still looking at the ceiling. I think I could probably talk him into doing anything if I tried hard enough. But the truth is, I want him in charge of this. I want Jonah to take over and do whatever he wants.

I feel his mouth latch onto one of my nipples, and he sucks hard as his fingers thrust up into me.

My orgasm starts to coil low and deep. "Yes!"

I slide one hand into his hair, gripping tightly. I feel wanted and dirty, spread out on his lap, completely naked while he's dressed, having not even taken off his shoes.

But I know this is only the beginning of the wonderful things he has planned for me tonight.

"Okay," he says huskily against my breast. "This pretty, greedy pussy is going to clamp down and come all over my fingers. You're going to make my hand all sweet and messy. Then we're going to work on number two."

"Number two better involve you being naked, too."

He keeps thrusting in and out of me, the pleasure winding tighter and tighter. "What would you do if you got me naked?"

"Look at you. Touch you all over. Run my tongue all over your body," I say, not even really thinking about the words before they emerge.

He gives a low groan. "I don't think you even know what you're talking about, but fuck, I want all of that too."

I rotate my hips against his hand, and he picks up the pace of his thrusts, circling my clit, curling his fingers against my G-spot, and saying, "Let me feel it, Duchess, grip my fingers, spill that sweetness all over me."

I let myself go, feeling the tight coil clench and then release, my orgasm coming from deep within me, spreading out hot and fast and pulling me under.

"Yes! Jonah!"

"Fuck, you are beautiful when you come. I love hearing my name come from your mouth." Then his hand is at the back of my neck and he's pulling me in for a deep, hot kiss.

He takes my mouth, his tongue sliding against mine with rhythmic thrusts just like his fingers between my legs. Slowly, the ripples of pleasure wane and he slips his fingers from my pussy, lifting them to his mouth and licking them clean.

"That's number one."

"How many before I get you inside me?" I ask.

"Jesus, you're gonna kill me."

I lift both brows. "You sure say that a lot for a guy who is sitting here, big and hot and hard and very alive."

He pulls me in for another kiss, a slow, hot one this time. When he lets me go, he rests his forehead against mine. "I don't think I've ever felt this alive, Duchess."

I smile. I love how sweet he can be even in these hot as hell moments.

"Can you please get naked?" I ask him.

"I do love when you beg." He starts unbuttoning his shirt while my hands drop to the front of his pants. I start working on the button and zipper of his jeans. He's so hard behind the fly and I take a moment to run my hand over the huge bulge. He sucks in a sharp breath.

"You're so big," I say with wonder.

"Worried about the fit?" he asks with a smirk.

I tip my head. "No."

He laughs. "No?"

"Of course it will fit. That's what it's all made for."

He squeezes my ass and laughs again. "You're right. It's gonna be a hell of a lot of fun getting into this tight, sweet little cunt. But it's gonna fit."

I swear every muscle in my body clenches. I love the dirty talk.

I stroke my palm up and down his length through the denim, watching my hand. "It's going to hurt a little though, isn't it?"

"It's been a *really* long time since I've been with a virgin. But yeah, a little probably. I promise to make it good for you though, Duchess."

"Of course you will." I look up at him. "You're all about making me feel good and taking care of me."

His grin is gone and he nods. "Fucking right. Always."

I smile. "Let's get to it."

He groans and lifts his hips, shoving his jeans and boxers out of the way. My eyes are glued to the huge cock that is now lying against his stomach, hard and thick between us.

"I love the fact that there's nothing you're afraid of," he says, wrapping his fist around his cock and stroking it up and down the length. The very long length. "You're daring and always up for a new adventure. We're gonna have so much fun."

I'm watching him stroke himself. I've seen him naked, I've seen him touch himself, but now I'm right up against it. And I suddenly want to explore every single inch.

"I want to put my mouth on you," I say.

Jonah pauses, then makes a strange noise that I haven't heard before. I look up quickly. He looks like he's almost choking.

"Are you okay?"

"Just wasn't expecting that. I don't think you really know what you're asking."

"I've never given a blowjob, but I know what one is. "

He makes the choke-cough sound again. "Jesus Christ, Linnea."

I laugh. "If this is what happens when I just talk about it, I definitely want to see what happens when I actually do it."

He slides his hand from the back of my neck up into my hair and then grips lightly. "You want to put your mouth on my cock?"

"I do. I want to lick you all over. I also intend to run my tongue all over your abs, your tattoos. Everywhere."

"We don't have to do that tonight. We can work up to some of this."

"I want to. I've been thinking about your cock since the first time I walked in on you ironing."

His eyes narrow. "Have you?"

The feeling of power that surges through me with this man on a regular basis is absolutely addicting. "I have. Lots of times. Most often when I'm in bed at night alone. With my vibrator of course. But also sometimes just when you walk into a room. Lots of times when we're sitting across from one another at dinner at the palace."

That doesn't seem to startle him as much as I thought it might. His fingers tighten in my hair.

"So we've both been thinking about fucking each other while we were sitting at dinner, the king on one end of the table and your fiancé and my best friend on the other, between us."

My grin grows. "You can try to make it sound dirty, but it doesn't. I've never had feelings for anyone else. Not until you. "

His eyes soften a little at that. But his fingers tighten even more, and he pulls me forward until our mouths are only inches apart. "Same."

"Really?" I'm aware that I am still bare naked on his lap, and that a very important part of him is now there between us, and I'm very interested in getting back to *that* topic of conversation. But at the moment, I really want to follow this particular thread. "You've never been serious about anyone?"

"Never."

"Never met anyone or knew that you *couldn't* get serious?" His line of work obviously has always required that he put the job—Torin—first.

"Maybe both. Never met anyone I wanted that much before Torin. And since him, I guess I haven't really been open to that."

I slide my hands down to his chest. I trace my fingers back and forth across his pecs and over the intricate designs of his tattoos. "You weren't really open to this between us."

"I know. That's how strong it is. I can't fight it. "

"Are you really trying?"

"Not anymore," he says. After a moment he says, "Linnea?"

I look into his eyes. "Yes?"

"I am madly, completely in love with you. There's no one else before you to me. Not even Torin O'Grady."

I suck in a little breath. I was digging for some kind of declaration. I didn't know if I was going to get the L word, but I'm not shocked that he's using it, and it thrills me to my very bones. But the way he said it, the way he made sure I understand that I'm first, even in front of the man who will someday be king, matters. And I know that he knows that it matters.

I swallow. "I'm in love with you too. And I will go wherever you go and do whatever you do. I really think that we are going to make a difference. Somehow, in some way. Together."

He pulls me in and gives me a kiss unlike any other before this. It's soft and deep, and definitely still makes my toes curl, but it is full of so much emotion. It's like he has been holding so much back and is now letting it all pour into me.

Of course, this broody, loyal, sweet-underneath-the-gruff-exterior, amazingly strong man, would not just say I love you. He would make it into something beautiful and amazing that I'll never forget.

I drag my mouth along his jaw and down his neck. I feel him shudder underneath my hands. I keep going, kissing along his collarbone, then down over his chest. I flick my tongue over the designs of his tattoo. I love the heat and the taste of his skin and the firmness of the muscle underneath. His body is so different from mine, and I want to be against it. I want to have it on top of me. I want to be wrapped around it.

I have this deep craving that I know has to do with this man, and I know I need to be as close to him as possible. I slide back on his lap and wiggle down between his thighs to kneel between his legs. He doesn't stop me. I continue kissing and licking down over the ridges of his abdomen, down to the deep V that cuts inside his hip. I lick along that crease to the base of his cock. Then I move to the impressive length. He moves his hand and I look up at him. His jaw is tight, and it looks like he's struggling to breathe.

But he's watching me with so much heat and possessiveness and lust that my entire body feels like it might melt.

I flatten my palms and run them up and down over his chest, then his abs, then his thighs.

"Touch me, Duchess. Wrap your hands around me."

I do as I'm told, wrapping my fingers around his cock, touching him for the first time. He's thick and heavy, and I love the feel of him in my fist. I do what I watched him do to himself, squeezing and stroking from base to tip, then down again.

He sucks in a sharp breath. "Duchess," he says, ragged.

I love affecting this man.

I stroke up to the top, then lower my head and put my tongue against the base of his cock. I drag it up to the very tip, slow and steady, tasting him, loving the low guttural groan it pulls from deep within him.

His hand cups the back of my head and his fingers tangle in my hair.

I look up. "Tell me what to do. "

"Anything you want. It all feels so fucking good."

"I'm supposed to take you in my mouth, right?"

He swallows hard. "You're not going to be able to. Not fully. Just explore, baby. You can learn my size and how I feel this way. It'll be less intimidating when I get between those pretty thighs."

"Does this feel as good as if I could take you all the way in?"

He groans and tips his head back. "It all feels good. Just fucking seeing you on your knees in front of me is almost enough to make me come."

I am intrigued by all of this. It seems so easy to turn him on. I love that.

I understand it too. Just watching his hands grip a coffee cup is enough to make heat swirl through my stomach. Just hearing him laugh is enough to make my pussy clench. Just having his hand against my lower back or grasping my elbow is enough to send tingles through me. I once watched him shrug out of his suit jacket, loosen his tie, roll the sleeves of his dress shirt up, and then climb a ladder to retrieve some old vinyl records from a high shelf in Diarmuid's office. I swear my body temperature went up ten degrees just observing all of that.

So I understand how seemingly little things can be a turn-on when you're crazy about someone.

I lean in and lick his length again. "Is this enough? Tell me something else I can do."

His fingers thread through my hair, and he gathers it back at the base of my head into a ponytail, holding it in one fist. "Suck on the tip, Duchess."

I like that idea. I lick him again, and when I get to the top, I suck gently on the head.

He groans and tugs gently on my hair. I lift my head. "Like that?"

"Yeah." He sounds like it's hard to talk. "Just like that. You can suck harder. You can squeeze me harder too. "

I do. I squeeze him tighter as I stroke him harder and then lick him again, sucking on the tip firmly. I lick the head, suck, then drag my tongue down his length, before repeating the whole pattern again.

"Fuck, Duchess," he praises. "I love your mouth. That sassy tongue of yours, that says the most amazing, brilliant things, up against my cock, sucking me like you can't get enough is a filthy fantasy come true."

I pull off of him. "I want you to feel good. I want to do *everything* that makes you happy."

He chuckles, but it sounds almost pained. "Oh, honey, you fucking do. And we're going to have so much fun."

"We're going to do more? You'll teach me more?"

"Yes. I am going to teach you so many things."

"I want to do it all."

He shakes his head as he pulls in a breath. "Dream girl." Then he tugs on my hair a little harder as he leans forward. His mouth is nearly on mine. "But now I need to make you come again so that I can fully, finally, make you mine."

"Oh yes." I press my thighs together, already feeling the buildup of heat and tingles.

"Just tell me what to do," I tell him.

"Bed. Now."

CHAPTER 24
JONAH

I yank my pants up so I can follow Linnea into the bedroom, but I shed my shirt, dropping it next to the couch.

I watch the sway of her hips, the confidence with which she carries herself, even bare naked, across the room.

She sits on the edge of the mattress and then lies back as I stalk toward her.

Without looking away from her, I pull out my wallet and retrieve the two condoms I carry before shucking out of my jeans and boxers. I toss the condoms on the bed next to the gorgeous brunette who is too damned good for me but who I am going to take and claim and make mine and to hell with the rest of the world.

I kick my jeans toward the door, then put one knee on the mattress next to her, leaning in to stroke my hand from her ankle to her hip.

In the back of my mind, I realize that as of tonight, both Linnea's and my life are going to get so much more complicated. But looking down at the woman who is gazing up at me with a mix of lust and love, I don't care.

Not only am I going to make her mine, but I'm hers.

Whatever that means to my future.

If I have to leave my post with Torin, I have to trust that Iris and the rest of them will be sure there's someone there to take care of him.

I have to trust that our friendship is strong enough that Torin will still reach out to me when he needs me.

And I have to trust that once he's king, he'll bring us both back. I know Torin values us. He'll fight for us.

And as much as I want to believe that Diarmuid loves Linnea enough to let her go if she truly falls in love, I know that Torin will do the same for me. He'll help me figure this out.

My big, main boss on the other hand, is another story.

I could very well lose my job. At least for a while.

But there's nothing that's going to keep me from this woman.

She's lying on the white sheets, her dark hair spilling around her like ink on paper, creamy skin, hard pink nipples, wet, pink pussy all ready for me, all mine.

I am not going to think about anyone else anymore right now. I have a woman to love.

"Dammit you're gorgeous. I can't believe you're mine."

"All yours," she says softly.

I love when she's sweet and soft and compliant.

I also love when she's loud, feisty, and confident.

She's an amazing mix of submissive and siren and I get to see it all. Only me. Forever.

I lean over and kiss her. Then I scoop my hands underneath her hips and turn her onto her stomach, and up onto all fours.

"Jonah," she moans.

With my hand between her shoulder blades I press her chest down onto the mattress, but keep her ass in the air. I run my hand over the gorgeous curves, squeezing, marveling at how huge my hand looks on her body. "One of these days, I'm going to pink up this pretty ass," I say almost to myself.

She moans again and wiggles. "Yes."

The fact that she'll say yes to nearly anything I say and will let me do anything to her is the biggest fucking turn-on. But that's not something we'll get to tonight. We have so much time. All the time in the world.

Still, my pink handprint on her ass, nipple clamps, butt plugs, blindfolds, and silk ties all trip through my head. She'd love them all. She'd turn that control over to me without a thought. She'd know that it's all for her and that I would take care of her at every step. I'd be able to bring her to new heights that she hasn't even imagined.

I run my hand over her ass and up her back. "Not yet," I murmur, for both of us.

I lower my mouth to her back, kissing down her spine. I slip my hand underneath, sliding through the slickness of her recent orgasm. I circle her clit before slipping two fingers inside. Her inner muscles clench around me, and she gives another breathy moan.

I fuck her with my fingers for a few seconds, winding her a little tighter, but I want to taste her release.

I lean over and give her a long lick, then suck on her clit. She cries out, then presses back against me harder. I lick and suck not giving her any time to talk or really even think. I slide the other hand underneath her to play with one of her pretty tits, teasing and pinching her nipple.

She groans. "Jonah, I'm so close."

"That's it, Duchess, give it all up again. I want to taste you on my tongue." I suck harder. "Come on, sweetheart. Be a good girl and fuck my face."

She presses back against me, seeking the pressure she needs. I lap at her and the next moment she cries out.

I don't give her time to come down. I flip her to her back and climb over her. I brace on my elbows on either side of her face, staring down into those gorgeous green eyes.

"You're magnificent. In every single way. Thank you for letting me be here with you like this."

She gives a little laugh and pushes her fingers into my hair. "I could never be like this with anyone else."

My heart clenches in my chest. I love how she trusts me, how she knows that everything I do is for her. I want her to always feel that way.

"I'm gonna take you now. It's gonna be tight, but it's gonna be good. Talk to me, okay? Tell me how you're doing and what you need."

She nods. "I'm so ready."

She's as ready as she can be. She's hot and wet and relaxed and turned on. I grab one of the condoms, rip it open, and roll it on. Then I hook my arm under one of her knees and spread her open.

I look down. "So damned pretty." I look up and see her blushing. I chuckle. "Shy now?"

She smiles and shakes her head. "No. Just...I don't know."

"Don't be shy. This is so fucking hot. Here..." I kiss her, then push back until I'm kneeling between her knees. "Watch me take you."

Her eyes widen but she looks between us where my cock rests at her entrance. I rub it through her wetness, then up over her clit.

"Oh, God," she breathes.

"Watch," I tell her, pressing forward. I slide in about three inches, and she takes me, a sweet, sexy mewling sound coming from the back of her throat.

"That's so..." She stops. "I feel so full."

"This is just the start." I press my thumb to her clit and circle slowly. "Play with your nipples."

She cups both breasts, rubbing over the hard tips before she pinches them. I feel the flutter in her pussy and she sighs.

I press forward, sliding deeper.

She's so fucking tight that I have to grit my teeth and force myself to go slow. "Jesus, Duchess, you feel so good. You're so perfect."

"Jonah, don't stop," she begs, arching closer.

"Never."

I slide in a couple more inches. "Tell me you're with me, sweetheart," I pant. I flick over her clit faster and spread her thigh farther.

Her eyes look a little dazed. "So. With. You."

"Are you in pain?"

"Just really...stretched."

I give a short laugh. God. She's so hot, and she doesn't even know it.

I pull back a little, but she quickly wraps the leg I'm not holding around my thigh. "No!"

"I'm not going anywhere," I promise. "Just need to move." I pull back, then slide forward.

"*Oh*," she breathes.

I grin. "Yeah. Oh." I do it again and when I slide back in, I go deeper.

"*Jonah*."

I take that as a green light and do it again, then again.

The next time I get deeper and she suddenly tenses. I freeze and she frowns.

"I'm okay."

"You sure?"

"Yeah. Just...move again."

I do, more easily this time. She winces slightly, as if she's not sure if she's okay or not.

"Duchess," I say through gritted teeth. "Talk to me."

"I just...I'm good. I'm just a little...I don't know. I feel so *full*."

"Okay." I start to pull back.

Again she clamps her leg around me. Her gaze finds my directly. "Please," she says. "Just..." She pulls her bottom lip between her teeth.

No. I reach up and free her lip. "Talk. What do you need? Anything, Duchess. We can stop right now if we need to."

She swallows. "Fuck me, Jonah. Please. Don't hold back."

I suck in a quick breath and squeeze my eyes shut. Damn. She has no idea what that does to me.

But then I open my eyes and study her. *Really* look at her.

This woman knows herself. She's new to some experiences, but that doesn't mean she's naive or stupid. She knows what she's asking me.

"Yes," I say simply.

She gives me a huge smile.

"Hold on tight, love." Then I lean over and kiss her deeply.

She wraps her arms around my neck. I slide one under her ass, lifting her slightly, then I pull my hips back, then thrust forward, sliding deep.

She gasps. Then moans, "*Yes*," against my mouth. "I feel you everywhere."

I set up a steady, slow but deep pace, loving the feel of her in my arms, her tight heat around me, the way she presses her face to my throat and moans and gasps.

I start picking up the pace as I feel her pussy starting to flutter around me.

"Duchess," I say gruffly against her ear. "I need you to come on my cock. Make me yours too. Cover me in all that sweetness again. Grip me tight with this perfect pussy."

She moans into my neck, and I feel her pussy clench harder around me.

"That's right. Take me in. Damn, you are perfect. I am going to take you over and over. You're not going to be able to take a step tomorrow without thinking about me between your legs, filling up this sweet, hot, tight cunt."

"Oh, God, Jonah," she gasps.

"I love that you saved this all for me, Duchess. I'm glad no one else has ever been able to see, touch, taste this pussy. It's all mine to worship forever."

"Yes, oh, *yes*."

"That's it, let it go, love."

And then she clamps down around me as she cries out my name and comes hard. I'm only two thrusts behind her, unable to hold on as her pussy grips me.

My hips continue to thrust as I empty completely. I kiss her, my hands running all over her body, not able to get enough of her, even on the heels of my orgasm.

Finally, I stop moving and lift my head to look down at her, breathing hard.

She gazes up at me with a goofy, happy smile on her face.

She runs her hand over my face and through my hair. "Wow."

"You okay?"

She shakes her head.

I frown.

"I'm still horny."

I shake my head, chuckling. "Are you?"

"I think so. I feel *something*. I'm...tingly all over. I feel amazing. But I just want...*you*. More of you. All of it. Everything."

I run my hand over her head, brushing hair back from her forehead. "You have me. All of me. From now on."

Her smile softens. "You've gone completely rogue now."

I sigh. "Yeah."

"Sorry."

I grin down at her. "No, you're not."

She giggles. "No, I'm not."

I reach down and pinch her ass. "I'm going to make *you* tell Torin."

She nods. "Okay. But..."

Suddenly she's pushing me to my back. Because she catches me off guard, it works. She looks down at me, a mischievous look in her eyes that I'm immediately addicted to.

"I don't think we should go home until Tuesday."

"What are we going to do until Tuesday?" I ask, my hands settling on her ass.

"Add *a lot* more items to my Like It list," she says.

I slide a hand to the back of her neck and pull her down for a hot kiss, my cock already stirring again.

We will be together in Cara. I won't be able to stay away from her.

But it will be a lot easier to be uninterrupted for hours

on end...not to mention nice and loud...right here in this hotel room.

"You're brilliant, you know that?" I ask her.

"I've been told that a time or two," she says smugly. "So you can come up with a few things for us to do if we stay a couple extra days?"

"Oh, Duchess, I'm your man."

CHAPTER 25
JONAH

"Well, you look downright radiant," Torin says to Linnea as she approaches his desk.

I asked for a meeting with him the moment we returned. We've been back on the island for only about an hour.

He was eager to see us as well, to get a full report on our trip. Especially since I've been ignoring his calls and only sending texts that say *I'll fill you in when we get back* for the last few days.

Linnea takes a seat in one of the chairs facing his desk, leans back, resting her hands on her crossed leg, and gives him a smile. "Thank you. Astrid says it's all the hot sex I'm having."

I cough slightly as I take my seat beside her.

Torin's eyebrows arch and he gives her a half smile. "I see. So the trip to D.C. ended up going well, I take it."

"Yes. I furthered the relationships between Cara and Dr. Hill as well as the senator. And I learned how to bowl."

Torin chuckles. "Good for you fitting hot sex in, too."

She smiles. "Oh yes. I also did end up falling in love with someone."

Torin's smile widens, and he sits forward in his chair, resting his forearms on the desk. "Really? That's wonderful. And he feels the same way?"

I lean toward her and slide my hand to the back of her neck. "He does. Very much so."

My best friend's gaze comes to my face. Then he looks back to Linnea. Then to me again.

Understanding dawns. His eyes widen and his gaze rests on me for several long moments.

Then he slowly smiles. "Well, damn."

I just watch him. But he's looking at me with an expression I haven't seen before. He looks...proud of me? It's not quite that, but it's close.

"You okay?" I ask him.

"I'm *very* okay," he assures me with a sudden, wide grin. "I'm so fucking happy for you."

That hits me hard, directly in the chest. I swallow hard. "Thanks." I look at Linnea. She's watching us with a soft smile. "It's really, *really* good."

He's nodding as if inordinately pleased. "It is. It really is," he agrees.

"You think so?" Linnea asks.

"Of course. I get to keep you both this way, and *we* don't have to get married," he tells her. His smile is bright. "And Jonah will be *so* much more pleasant if he's in love *and* having hot sex regularly."

I give a surprised, choked laugh. Linnea blushes but also laughs. "I'm so glad I can be of assistance, Your Highness," she says.

Torin laughs and I squeeze her neck. I love when she's sassy.

Then he pauses. "But I guess you are *not* going to see Waite again socially, then?"

"I'd prefer the woman I love to not date other men," I say.

"Right. Okay then. I'll have to let my grandfather know the invitation to have Waite come stay for a week needs to be revoked."

I frown. "When did that happen?"

"When the podcast talked about the social media posts of Linnea and Waite together at a bowling alley in D.C.," Torin says, reaching for his phone. "I didn't want to spill that they were on a date but thought it was a good first step that we could point to later when we explain to Diarmuid that she and Christian were in love." He taps his phone screen a few times, then hands it over.

We both lean in and read...

Wait 'Til I Tell Ye
PODCAST EPISODE 737 TRANSCRIPT

Lindsey: So we got this question submitted this morning and I have to say, I'm asking the same thing: Is Linnea Olsen dating Christian Waite?

Jen: I mean...surely not?

Lindsey: Why not? She's gorgeous, smart, classy. And she travels for Cara all the time. He was here visiting a few months ago. And he is *hot*. And single. I mean, he would be exactly her type, right?

Jen: Yeah. Actually, he would be.

Lindsey: And look at these photos of her and the senator.

Jen: I know. He really is hot. And they're bowling. *Bowling*? That doesn't seem like a business meeting thing, right? It wasn't a charity thing or something, right?

Lindsey: Nope. Looks like a date to me.

Jen: Interesting...

F ucking great.

My frown deepens. "Your grandfather listens to the podcast?"

"He does," Torin says. "He's also the one the staff comes to when the podcast and other media outlets ask the palace for statements and comments. He came to ask me what was going on."

"What did you tell him?"

"That Christian invited Linnea to D.C.," Torin says with a shrug. "And that she wanted to go."

"Dammit Torin!" I snap.

"I was planting seeds for what I *thought* our plan was," he says. "I didn't know what was going on with you two."

Right. Of course. The fucking plan. One of several I haven't been following.

I shove a hand through my hair. "What did your grandfather—or rather the palace—tell the podcast?"

"That Linnea and Christian had met before about mutually beneficial programs and that she was in D.C. following up."

I sigh. I suppose that works.

"Believe me, he played it down." Torin leans in. "*He* obviously doesn't want anyone speculating that Linnea and Christian are romantically involved."

"Then why did your grandfather invite Christian to Cara?"

"He didn't. I did," Torin says. Then he shrugs. "Mostly to annoy the king. But judging by the fact that you all looked to be having a good time bowling and that *you* hadn't told me anything about *your* relationship, I thought maybe you'd appreciate me inviting him here."

I feel Linnea's hand on my thigh and I look over at her. She gives me a smile. "This isn't Torin's fault."

I take a breath. She's right. He assumed everything was going according to plan. That I was doing my job. As always.

"I didn't even realize there were social media posts," she tells Torin.

"I take it you weren't spending these last few days scrolling your feeds?" He gives us both a knowing look.

Linnea doesn't even blush. "No. We gave the outside world very little thought, actually." She squeezes my thigh. "But we realize that now we're back to reality and we need to face the fact that things are a little complicated now."

"They are," Torin agrees.

I stroke my thumb up and down along Linnea's neck. "This wasn't my intention when I got on that plane," I tell him. "I did fight it." I look at Linnea. She gives me a smile that wraps around my heart. "I just couldn't do it. Seeing her with other people was too much. The idea of not being there if she needed me, when she was upset or hurt or sick, was worse than anything that can come of us being together." I take a breath. "I'm willing to do whatever it takes, Torin. I'm even willing to risk pissing Diarmuid off. Or... giving up our friendship as it stands. Though I certainly hope that doesn't happen."

After a moment, Torin nods. "I should have seen this coming."

Linnea and I exchange another look.

"Really?" I ask him.

"Of course. You're both fantastic. Given a few days alone together, of course you'd realize that."

"Oh...well...I realized it long ago," I say.

"Me too," Linnea adds.

I love that now when I feel love and warmth for her fill me, I can act on it. At least in some situations. I grasp the leg of her chair and pull her close to me, the chair scraping across the stone floor. Then I cup the back of her neck again and kiss her temple.

I won't be able to do that in every room, with every group of people. Not for a while anyway. But it's a fucking relief to be able to do it now in front of Torin.

Torin studies each of us, one at a time. "I'm not surprised now that I see you together. You've always been easy around each other. Sharing looks, comfortable together. I know you stay up late talking when Linnea is here."

"We've been resisting it for..."

"Months," Linnea fills in.

I nod. "Months."

She's leaning on the arm of the chair closest to me. I want badly to scoop her up and hold her in my lap, but that's probably a little too far even though Torin seems to be taking this news well.

"Of course you did," he says. "You know very well that this jumbles things."

"It does," I agree. "Even if we think the king will go along with the idea that Linnea is in love with someone else and let her out of the arranged marriage with you without disowning her, or banishing her from the island—" I feel her stiffen under my hand.

We both know it's a possibility though we're hoping it's a slim one, but she doesn't like talking about it.

"He won't be pleased that she's in love with *me* rather than someone like..." I sigh. "Christian Waite."

"The king is not going to love this," Torin agrees.

No, no, he won't. I appreciate the fact that my best friend doesn't try to bullshit me, though.

And I'm very definitely thinking about Iris's black belt in...well, everything. And that she's ex-FBI. And that she has a lot of well-connected friends.

I could easily end up much more than "fired". I could disappear and no one would ever find me...

"Your grandfather is not a completely unreasonable man," Linnea protests. "He loves us. He respects Jonah."

"But he loves Cara," Torin says. "More probably than he loves us. He has to."

I squeeze Linnea's neck reassuringly. "That's the job. You're the one who was willing to marry Torin without love because being king and queen was bigger than what each of you individually wanted," I remind her. "Diarmuid might deep down want to tell us this is fine, but the truth is, you would be better for Cara as queen than as the wife of a bodyguard."

Her eyes snap to mine at the word *wife*. We haven't talked about marriage, but it's a given. To me anyway. She is mine. For good. That means eventually I will make her my wife. But I want to claim her publicly afterward. I want her to wear my ring. I want the world to know. I want everyone important to us to know. For her, that includes the king. So for now, we have to lie low.

"We need a new plan," Torin says. "I know we'd all hoped the project with James would be the thing to show my grandfather how well we work together, regardless of marital status. We just need something else like that."

Linnea nods. I filled her in on the fact that James had informed Torin he'd decided to take the project to Canada instead of Cara. She was disappointed and initially felt guilty, assuming that he'd pulled the project from Cara because she didn't want to date him. Of course, I quickly reminded her that if that was the only reason he was giving the project to Cara in the first place, he was an asshole.

"We'll come up with something," she says. "Your grandfather needs to see that you can be an effective and caring king even without me as your queen. We just need to show him what our partnership will look like regardless of who we're married to."

He agrees. "We need to do some research. Reaching out. Networking."

"Maybe there's something else with James. Something on a smaller scale. Or maybe Christian will have some ideas." Linnea's wheels are clearly turning. "At least there's no hard deadline."

I frown at that. "Maybe there's no specific date. But I don't want to hide this. The last six months being in love with you and unable to show it have been hard enough."

Torin looks at me. "That long?"

I nod. "At least."

He swivels in his chair and sits forward. He studies me for a moment. "I thought I knew you better than that. I didn't realize you'd be able to hide these kinds of feelings from me," he says.

I lift a shoulder. "Maybe I'm better at my job than you realize. It's possible I hide all kinds of things from you, Your Highness."

He rolls his eyes.

I can feel Linnea's gaze on me, but I continue looking at Torin.

I'm not speaking to him as my boss right now. Now I need my friend.

"I want her, Torin. For real. For good. I don't want to leave you. I don't want to take her away from here, but..." I look at her and she nods, despite the tears in her eyes. I look back at the prince. "But I will. We'll leave. Even though it will hurt."

He takes a deep breath. "We're going to figure this out. You've done a fuck ton to make sure that I am happy and safe and where I'm supposed to be and doing what I'm supposed to be doing. I will do the same for you."

My chest tightens and I lean forward, extending my hand. He shakes it. "Thank you, Torin."

Then I stand and pull Linnea to her feet.

"Thank you," she says quietly to him.

"Take care of him," Torin tells her.

"I promise."

I feel possessiveness and love and desire like I've never known hit me.

I need to get her alone.

It was a long flight.

I start to escort my woman out of her now ex-fiancé's office, mentally reviewing how we can spend the night together without anyone knowing. It helps that our rooms are right next to one another.

"But can I give you a little advice?" Torin calls out.

I look back. "What's that?"

"You need to not look at her like you just did for a bit longer."

"Oh?" I ask.

He laughs. "It is very obvious how you feel about her now. Everyone's going to know if you're not careful."

I look down at Linnea. She's looking up at me with heat and happiness. I want to see that look on her face for the rest of her life.

Not looking at her as if I'm madly in love with her is going to be the hardest thing I've ever done.

CHAPTER 26
IRIS

> FYI: I fell in love with Linnea. She won't be marrying Torin. We've already told him.

> I'll understand if you need to fire me.

I read Jonah's text again.

FYI? *FYI?* Is he fucking kidding me with this?

I eye my coffee cup. Then I look at the clock. It's a little early to add amaretto but...

FYI, with this job it's never too early for liquor.

I pour in a shot, take a drink, then read his message again.

He fell in love with Linnea.

Of course he did.

It's not just the royals going rogue now. Perfect. Just what I need.

But why wouldn't he?

Linnea is amazing.

Of course she is. She's. Supposed. To. Be. A. Queen.

I lean back in my chair, cradling my cup between my two hands.

I've been doing this job for ten years. I'm *damned* good at it. But I do wonder on a weekly basis if I missed my calling to be an accountant. Or an architect.

Something where things make sense, where facts line up, where things behave the way they're *supposed to*.

I swear the brilliant plan to support benevolent billionaires, and leaders who truly want to use their positions to serve the people, and influencers with platforms for *good* sounded so simple when Alfred Olsen laid it out for me.

Which is why I'm still here, taking care of Declan O'Grady and wrangling the rest of these guys.

I wasn't Declan O'Grady's first bodyguard. Not by a long shot. The man drove off and/or fired six before I came along.

He's fired me three times. I just won't leave. He needs me.

Just like Torin needs Jonah.

I'm not going to fire Jonah. Even though he's now further complicated everything.

Nope. I'm going to fix it. Like I do everything.

Step one—Do. Not. Tell. The. Boss.

At least, not until I have a solution that will be even better than the original plan.

Because he will definitely fire Jonah. Instantly. And while I completely understand the sentiment, it won't solve anything. It's not like we can get Torin a new advisor/best friend/bodyguard who he'll suddenly start listening to.

And if Jonah leaves, he'll take Linnea with him, and we definitely need her brain and loyalty and talents.

Fuck.

I lean over and grab my bottle of amaretto, pouring even more into my cup.

I take a long drink.

Then I text Jonah back.

> FYI, I do not like these kinds of texts.

> Also, can you just not do anything else stupid, or let Torin do anything stupid, for the next few weeks? Please?

Define stupid.

I start to type but then realize that the list I'd have to send is way too long.

I take another drink and think.

Finally I respond:

> How about this? Don't tell anyone about you and Linnea. Just status quo. And don't leave Cara again.

For how long?

> Until I say so.

I wait for him to respond with an *I understand* or *yes, ma'am* or even a *fine*.

After nearly two minutes I type:

> Got it?

Finally I get,

yes.

I don't feel very confident in that yes.

I'm also now too tipsy to come up with a better plan than to just lock them all in their rooms. Separately, of course.

But then I'd have to change my phone number because God, the *whining* would be intolerable.

CHAPTER 27
LINNEA

"Diarmuid?" I say, peeking around the edge of his door.

He looks up from what he's working on at his desk. "Linnea," he says, a smile breaking across his face. "Come in, come in." He pushes back from his desk and rises, coming around the end of the enormous piece of furniture to meet me partway across the room.

He enfolds me in a hug, and I draw in the familiar scent of the cologne he's worn my entire life. It reminds me of leatherbound books and cedar. It's comforting and makes my stomach dip at the same time.

I don't want to disappoint him.

I know what he expects from me. I've always known. It's never been the slightest bit vague.

And now I'm completely rejecting it.

When Jonah found out the king had asked to see me, he'd been nervous.

"We can't tell him about us yet."

"I know." But I'd said it with hesitation.

Jonah had taken my face in his hands. "Duchess. He can't know yet. It will panic him. He might believe separating us is the best way to fix the problem. This isn't the plan and we don't have a better alternative to offer. We need more time."

I know this. I'd agreed in D.C., I'd agreed after we spoke to Torin, I agreed an hour ago, and I agree now.

But being face to face with the man who is as much a grandfather to me as my own was, and the wave of missing my grandfather in that moment, makes it hard.

I have *always* done what was expected of me. Always. I'm the one people can count on. It's who I am. I'm not a doctor or a lawyer or a teacher or a soldier. I'm the someday queen. The reliable one. The one who knows what must be done and will do it. I've taken pride in that. Even when everyone else—i.e., the O'Grady princes—were running around and worrying everyone, the king and my grandfather knew *I* would be here, doing my duty.

I swallow against the tears that suddenly tighten my throat and manage a wobbly smile for Diarmuid.

"Here. Sit." He gestures toward the sitting area in front of his desk.

I've spent hours of my life in this space. I've drunk gallons of tea while sitting on that cozy sofa, drawn pages of maps and pictures and "decrees" with my colored pencils while listening to my grandfather and Diarmuid talk business.

I didn't understand it all, of course, but I understood their tones. I knew sometimes it was serious and solemn, and sometimes it was celebratory.

They both loved this country and loved leading it. It

was a source of joy and pride and sadness and pain. And they shared it all together.

I know that the weight of everything has felt heavier for Diarmuid since my grandfather's death. Actually, even before that, as my grandfather's memory and mental acuity faded.

I've been able to step in and help, and it always made me feel good to do so. But I am no replacement for my grandfather. Their friendship was decades old. Their affection for one another was always obvious. My grandfather was the one person who could truly argue with the king.

Diarmuid has always felt that he needs to protect Cara and its people. He wants it to be a haven. My grandfather, on the other hand, wanted Cara's influence felt beyond its shores. He wanted Cara to be recognized, and to be proof that even a small country can be a big leader.

Emil, Diarmuid's butler and assistant, brings in a tea service and sets it on the low coffee table in front of the couch.

It's early June and in D.C. that means the weather is nice and warm, but here in Cara, it's still cool and today is a cloudy day with wind and rain, so there's a low fire burning in the stone fireplace.

Diarmuid takes a seat in the chair perpendicular to where I'm seated on the sofa.

To keep busy, I sit forward and begin preparing our cups the way we both take our tea.

I'm glad the king wanted to chat. I love our talks and it gave me a reason to stay today. Jonah and I have discussed how it's going to be more difficult to see one another now that we're back. I live two hours from the palace and though I do spend a lot of time here, it is usually at the request of the king.

Torin needs to start asking me here more often. It will start to show Diarmuid that he and I are working together on projects.

Of course, we need to figure out what those projects will be.

"How was D.C.?" the king asks.

This is the first I've seen Diarmuid since Jonah and I returned yesterday. I don't know what Torin has told his grandfather about the trip, so I smile and say noncommittally, "Very nice."

Diarmuid lifts his cup to his lips and takes a sip. Then he says, "I have to thank you."

I sip, trying to figure out what he might be talking about. I swallow and ask, "For what?"

"For representing us so well all the time."

I smile. "You know I love doing it."

"And you're a natural. I also know that we haven't always given you a choice."

I sit a little straighter. Diarmuid and I have never discussed my role in terms of choices. In fact, he's never asked me to do anything. It's just always been assumed that I would. He has simply informed me of what needs to be done.

"It's never felt like a burden," I tell him honestly and it hasn't until recently. Maybe at times in college when I was irritated with the indecision and lack of specifics around my future. But I had never not expected to be a part of the palace.

"Well, I have to thank you for your approach to everything with Torin. I know that hasn't been easy and we haven't discussed it and I've never thanked you."

I try not to show my surprise. I take another sip of my

tea. Then set my cup on its saucer on the table. "What do you mean?"

He gives me an affectionate look. "I know very well how frustrating my grandson can be. But you have been patient and gracious waiting for us to announce the engagement."

I feel my spine stiffen and work to not show my sudden tension.

"Christian and I got off the phone about three hours ago and I had no idea that you would handle that situation the way you did. But I thank you."

The mention of Christian starts my heart pounding. But not in a good way. Christian knows about me and Jonah. He's the only person we've told besides Torin in fact. And that's just now occurring to me. Someone does know about Jonah and me. Someone who talks to people we don't want to tell yet.

I wet my lips. "You and Christian were talking?"

"Yes. Torin told me that James Hill has decided to take his research facilities to Canada. Torin has invited the senator to visit, and I decided to call him ahead of that visit and see if he could give us any assistance in making Cara more appealing to the professor. Thought maybe there was something that could be added to sweeten the deal. I knew the men got along well when they both traveled here a few months ago."

I blow out a tiny breath, feeling a little bit relieved. That all makes sense, though I wish that it was Torin who had made that call to Christian asking for help. "What did Christian say?"

"That he believes there are things Cara could offer that Canada can't and that the U.S. would like to be involved. Canada is an ally to the U.S., but Cara can be as well. We're smaller but easier to work with."

I nod. "Less red tape is what James and I spoke about when I had dinner with him as well."

Diarmuid smiles. "Wonderful. Perhaps we'll invite Dr. Hill again as well."

"That might be a good idea." I pause. "The conversation with the senator was productive? Friendly?"

"Very much so." Diarmuid smiles. "And when he told me that he was looking forward to working closely with you, I wasn't surprised. However—"

My heart thuds against my rib cage. I give him a shaky smile. "However?"

"I *was* surprised when he told me that he wishes he could be working with you on a more personal level."

Oh no.

Diarmuid laughs softly. "I'm not surprised by *that* of course. You're lovely. I'm certain there are any number of men who wish they could get closer to you personally. I was surprised that Christian told me that you and he had discussed that and that you had informed him that you were spoken for."

Oh. *No.*

My mouth goes dry.

It hadn't even occurred to me that this would ever get back to Diarmuid. The night when I was on the phone with Christian, I was *definitely* distracted. And I wanted Jonah to hear me claiming him, not hiding him, or feeling the need to keep us a secret. But it hadn't occurred to me that Christian would ever tell the king that he wanted to date me.

"I'm surprised Christian would bring that conversation up," I finally say, hoping my voice sounds normal to Diarmuid.

"I'm glad he did."

My palms are sweating.

Diarmuid doesn't seem angry with me. But I'm prepared, I realize, to say that yes, I'm in love with Jonah and that if the king insists on us no longer seeing each other or Jonah leaving the country, I will put my foot down. I will not deny my feelings.

"I know this has all been frustrating, but it makes me so happy that you consider Torin your fiancé, even though we haven't made a formal announcement and even though he has been difficult."

I freeze. I stare at the older man. I feel the air rush out of my lungs.

Christian had not mentioned Jonah. He only said that I told him I was spoken for. Not by who.

My adrenaline is pumping and I feel a little dizzy.

Diarmuid leans in and takes my hand. "I love you. And I know that your arrangement with Torin is not because you're in love. I need you to know that I understand that. Better than you know."

I let him take my hand and I even squeeze his back. I try to focus on his words instead of letting my mind spin with the close call we just had. And the fact that Jonah's name could still be a part of a future conversation with Christian.

"You were fortunate to meet Roisin," I say.

His smile is full of affection. "Yes, Roisin is an excellent queen. She is a lovely woman. She has been an amazing partner for all these years. And I am a better king for it."

I frown. There's something about what he says that feels off.

Or rather...what he doesn't say.

He doesn't talk about how much he loves her.

"When did you fall in love with Roisin?" I hear myself ask.

He takes a breath. He squeezes my hand again. "When

our son was born. I walked in and saw her holding him and the love I felt in that moment was...unmistakable."

I feel my mouth open, but then I shut it. I shake my head. "You...didn't love her when you married her?"

He meets my gaze directly, which I appreciate. "Like you and Torin, ours was not a love match. Cara needed a queen like Roisin. *I* needed a queen like Roisin. It was not an arranged marriage like yours and Torin's. But I do know what it's like being in a marriage based on duty versus love."

I stare at him. I didn't know any of this. Roisin is a proud, independent, confident woman. Cara loves her, though she is quiet and is not described with words like 'warm' and 'approachable' and 'relatable'. She's looked up to. People trust her. She has equal power with the king, and she oversees initiatives and policies for education and women's rights. I've heard the staff discuss the fact that they've never seen the king and queen disagree. If they do, it must happen only behind closed doors.

"So you've never dated and fallen in love?" I ask tentatively.

"I didn't say that," the king tells me.

I realize I've never looked up much about the king prior to him taking over the throne. It happened when he was only thirty-nine when his father died of a sudden heart attack.

"You did date? Did you ever meet anyone special?"

"I met the love of my life." His voice is soft, his expression wistful. Almost sad. "But I needed a queen."

That makes my heart hurt. "I didn't know that," I say quietly.

"Not many do." He sits straighter. "Because it doesn't

matter. As you've seen for yourself, we rule very well together. You and Torin will be the same."

My heart drops. I'm suddenly breathing faster than I should be.

On one hand, it's good he doesn't know about me and Jonah, yet.

I don't have to face Diarmuid's disappointment today. Or anger. I don't have to let him down. I don't have to tell him that everything he's counted on me for is not going to happen.

But, this hurts. I feel like I'm denying Jonah by staying silent in this moment. Diarmuid has been where I am. In love with someone, but in a complicated position, torn between love and duty. And I hate that I'm misleading Diarmuid when he's right in front of me and I have a perfect opportunity to tell him what happened in D.C.. He's my family. He loves me. And this conversation is leading me perfectly to what I need to say.

But...

My breath lodges in my chest.

The realization fully sinks in and I feel my head spinning and I have to blink to clear my vision.

It won't matter.

Yes, he'll understand falling in love with someone else, but...

That love won't be enough for him to let me out of the arranged marriage.

Everything we thought, everything we planned on... won't happen.

We were wrong.

Just because he loves me, just because I might have fallen in love with someone else, won't mean that he will understand me turning my back on my duty to Cara.

To him.

"Are you all right?" Diarmuid is looking at me with concern.

I realize I'm gripping my hands tightly in my lap and I haven't said anything for nearly a minute.

"You know that I love Cara," I finally say. It's the only fully truthful thing I *can* say.

Diarmuid smiles. "Of course I do. You've never given me any reason to doubt that for a moment."

CHAPTER 28
JONAH

"Then he said I've never given him any reason to doubt that for a moment, and I almost burst into tears."

Linnea takes a shaky breath and I have to grit my teeth to keep from cursing about the king.

He didn't lay a guilt trip on Linnea on purpose. He meant everything he said. He values her. He loves her. It's all genuine, and part of me appreciates that. She deserves to be valued and loved.

But she needs to be valued and loved when she's doing what makes her happy, not only when she's making everyone else happy.

Everything he said to her, from telling her she's exactly what Cara needs, to informing her that he himself has lived in a marriage that was designed for the good of the throne versus his own personal happiness, has only piled on to her feelings of guilt since we've gotten back.

It doesn't help that I'm also feeling guilty as hell. Iris

wasn't happy, but at least I was able to handle telling her via text. I didn't have to hear the disappointment and anger in her voice. And thank God she didn't say anything like I've failed or let them all down.

I haven't. Yet.

Once Torin is on the throne, and we can prove to everyone that he is capable, and that Linnea will still be here, advising him, helping him, and supporting him, they'll all relax and realize that this is just a bump along the overall path.

But that means that I can't take Linnea away from Torin and Cara.

Which means I can't get fired. Or if I do and I'm asked to leave the country, I can't take her with me.

That's unthinkable.

So for right now, we have to lie low, and not let the king —or anyone who would tell the king—catch on.

I know she hates misleading him though.

When we were in the happy haze that surrounded us in D.C., far from Cara, far from all the expectations and responsibilities, when we could just get lost in one another, and were finally able to admit, talk about, and express our feelings for each other after hiding them for so long from one another, it was easy to believe it would all work out.

But now we're back in the real world. Where the people we care about are telling us that we've messed things up.

We're back in the real world where the people we care about have to help us fix this.

Linnea and I are the ones who fix things. We are the ones who take care of all of *them*.

It's hard for both of us to lean on them instead.

We're sitting at the counter in the kitchen where we've shared so many late-night talks.

"I know this is going to be hard for a little while," I tell her, stroking my thumb across the back of her knuckles.

She lifts those gorgeous green eyes to mine. "We thought he would understand if I fell in love. We thought he'd let me out of this if he knew Torin and I would never really be in love. But now...he's going to expect us to marry anyway."

I try to hide how hard my heart squeezes, but it almost takes my breath away. The king has sacrificed for Cara and he believes Linnea is the right answer for his country going forward. She might be right.

"He can't force you to get married, though," I say. "You're an adult. A grown woman. He won't march you down the aisle at gunpoint."

She swallows hard and her eyes drop to our intertwined fingers. "No, he won't do that."

My heart squeezes, even harder.

Diarmuid might not have to force her. Linnea's sense of loyalty is deeply engrained. They started telling her what was expected of her when she was a young child. All she's ever known is a future that includes serving this country. Diarmuid is as close to her as any member of her family. Her parents have been, at best, distant and, at worst, neglectful. She's close to her siblings, but she's always taken care of them. The only people who have been at all nurturing toward her were her grandfather and Diarmuid.

Her affection for the king is real.

It will take a lot to get her to do anything she perceives as betraying him.

"You can serve this country, and fulfill everything Diarmuid needs from you, but not be married to Torin," I remind her.

She nods. "I know that deep down."

I lift my hand to her chin and tip her head up so she's looking at me. "You deserve to be happy."

"I know. So do you."

"Nothing makes me happier than you do."

"Same for me. *You* are what I want."

Relief rushes through me.

"That's why I hate hiding this," she continues. "You're always in the background. You're always in a supporting role. No one really thinks about how important you are. I want them to know how important you are, to *me* at least. I want Diarmuid to know how important you are. To me and Torin," she says, squeezing my hand. "I want *everyone* to know."

"I only need to be important to you, Duchess."

She sniffs and I run my hand over her hair.

I have to trust Iris. She's angry with me, but she'll help. I know that the past twelve years with Torin have not been for nothing. She knows that I've done my job and have helped Torin get this far. She wants me at his side. I have to believe she'll figure out a way to keep the boss from firing me.

Torin and Linnea both need me. And I need them.

"Just a little longer. We'll figure something out. We have time," I tell her.

Linnea takes a deep, shaky breath, then she slides off her stool and steps close. I widen my knees so that she can step between them. She runs her hands up the back of my neck and into my hair, then pulls my face close and kisses me.

My hands automatically drop to her ass, pulling her against me.

"Show me how the last time we were together in this kitchen should have gone."

I look into her eyes. I know what she needs. She needs to feel the passion, the chemistry, the love that we have that makes us both willing to shirk our duties for the first time in our lives. She needs to be reminded that what we have is more important and worth sacrificing for.

I can show her that.

I can show myself that.

I am fantastic at my job. Will someone else do it as well as I can? Doubtful. But someone else *can* come along and protect and advise Torin O'Grady.

What I know for certain is that no one will ever love my Duchess the way I can.

I slide a hand to the back of her neck and look directly into her eyes.

"You mean the night that I wanted to put you up against the wall, pull these silky pants down, and sink deep into this hot, greedy pussy right here without a thought to anyone or anything else?"

She sucks in a little breath and her eyes dilate. "Yes."

"That night, that kiss, that was just the start."

She bites her lip in a flirtatious way that immediately makes my cock harden. She looks at my mouth and I want to put it all over her sweet body.

I tip her head back. "Kiss me," I tell her. "Show me with your mouth what you want mine doing to your sweet little cunt."

She needs to get out of her head. She needs someone who can obliterate all of these worries about our responsibilities that won't leave her alone. She needs to be reminded that she is a woman with needs, wants, and emotions that matter. Things that she shouldn't have to suppress and ignore.

I am that man.

I'm *her* man.

Her kiss is hot and deep. She slides her tongue along the seam of my lips and when I let her in, she strokes over my tongue boldly. She circles and sucks and strokes and yes, I can definitely do all of that to her pussy. Right now.

Except that we're in the kitchen.

I drag my mouth from her and along her jaw.

"Do you know how much I would love to spread you out on this counter, strip you out of these pretty little pajamas, and make you beg for my cock?" I say gruffly against her ear. "Having you back here in Cara reminds me even more what a perfect, classy, queen you are, and I'd love to eat your royal pussy right here on this countertop where you frosted cookies for me."

She takes a deep shuddering breath. "I'm not perfect," she says.

"You are to everyone here. You are to me."

"They have no idea how dirty and needy you can make me." Her fingers dig into my hair as I drag my beard along her throat. "I didn't even know."

"There's a huge part of me who would very much like everyone to know the effect I have on you. That would love to have these palace halls echoing with the sound of you screaming my name," I tell her. "And there's an equally big part of me that loves keeping that to myself and being the only person on the planet who knows what a naughty, sexy, dirty girl you are."

"I've replayed that night," she tells me, running her hands over my shoulders and down my arms. "The way you lifted me up against the wall and pinned me with your body. But it definitely goes further in my daydreams."

I stand swiftly from the stool and pick her up. She gives a delighted little squeak and wraps her legs around my waist. I stride toward the wall where I first pressed her. I trap her between the wall and my body, then kiss her deeply. Our tongues tangle and I squeeze her ass, then I drag my lips from her mouth and down her throat. I suck gently on the skin. I so badly want to mark her, but it has to be in places she can easily cover.

"I need to suck on your pretty tits and bite your thighs and make this pussy drip," I tell her gruffly. "But I would also love to unzip, pull these shorts and panties to the side, and just sink deep right now. I know you can take me hard and fast, Duchess. You put in a lot of work while we were gone getting this sweet pussy ready to take me over and over, and you're going to feel *all* the reward of that here at home."

She moans and writhes against me. "Do that. Now. I'm not wearing any panties."

I groan. "Naughty girl. Were you hoping to get fucked in this kitchen tonight?"

She laughs and some of the tightness in my chest that's been there since we touched down in Cara loosens. "Yes. But I've never worn panties down here at night."

I pull back to look at her. "You've never had panties on? All those times we were in here flirting?"

She shakes her head and I realize maybe it's good I didn't know that. It was always hard enough to say goodnight to her.

But then she asks, "Were we flirting?"

I smile and lift a hand to cup her cheek. My cock is like granite settled between her thighs and she's wrapped around me like I'm a life preserver and she's floating in the ocean, but I also feel an overwhelming sense of affection. "Yeah, Duchess, we were flirting."

Her smile is bright. "I didn't think I knew how."

"Well, you're actually quite good. You wrapped me around your finger in about two minutes."

"And you've been flirted with a lot I'll bet," she says, lifting a brow.

I chuckle. "I don't remember."

"What?"

I lower my head until our lips are nearly touching. "I don't remember any women before you."

She sighs happily. "*That* was flirtatious. But I love it."

I kiss her sweetly.

She reaches down between us and cups me through the cotton of my lounge pants, not sweetly.

"You're so hard."

"Always with you."

I feel her toying with the tie of the pants and pull back. "We can't do this here. Someone could walk in."

"No one ever walks in on us. They give us our privacy to talk."

"Maybe," I concede. "But someone could easily hear us *not talking*."

"Then I'll need to sneak into your bedroom. Someone might need to be able to find you so you can't leave your room for the night. No one will come looking for me. Or if they do need me for some reason, they'll come to you to come get me."

She's right.

I run my hand over her hair from the crown of her head to the middle of her back. "You're willing to sneak into my room? And stay the night?"

"Of course. I'm already addicted to sleeping with you." A sad shadow passes over her face.

We've talked about how she'll have to leave the palace

and go home at some point and that the time between her visits to the palace is out of our hands.

"I'm definitely willing," she goes on. "But I hate sneaking around. I don't like hiding this. I want to be with you. I want everyone to know."

"I know. Soon."

"You promise? Soon?"

I have no idea how long it will take to get to the point where we can safely make our relationship public. It would be ideal to wait until Torin is on the throne and in charge. But that could be years yet.

"Yes," I say anyway. I lean in and kiss her deeply. When I lift my head I say, "But for tonight, I'm going to fuck you in the bed where I've dreamed of you so often. I'm going to make you come apart in that room where you first walked in on me naked." I drop my voice to that low, gruff timbre that I know she loves. "And you're gonna have to be a good girl and be quiet."

She shivers in my arms and gives me one of those sweet, sexy smiles. "Okay, I think I can do that."

"If you can't, I'll have to find something to stuff in your mouth."

She gives me a grin and I know that we're good. At least for now.

But yeah, staying quiet, in all the ways, is going to get a lot more difficult the longer we have to wait.

CHAPTER 29
LINNEA

"We'll have to throw a party, so make a list. We can talk about a menu next week."

"Your sister and brother will need some notice to plan to be here, so we need to set the date."

"Six months isn't very long, you know."

No, six months isn't very long.

But it's now, apparently, how long Torin and I have until the king is going to announce our engagement.

At least according to my sources.

Who are my mother, Torin's mother, and Queen Roisin.

I think they're pretty reliable.

I'd sat smiling and nodding at tea with them as they told me this news and that Torin and Diarmuid were discussing the official engagement announcement in the king's office at the same time.

They figure we can have the wedding within the year.

So much for having time to figure out a new plan.

So much for not panicking.

I knock on Torin's office door but don't wait for an answer before I open it and walk in.

"Can you just fu—" he starts before he realizes who I am.

I cross to stand in front of his desk, trying to stay calm.

That lasts until I open my mouth. "We have a timeline now?" I ask, planting my hands on my hips. "Six months is no time at all! You *have* to get us out of it, Torin."

"It's fine. I've got it under control," he mutters, sitting back in his leather chair.

"How? What are you going to do?"

"I'm going to...convince him that I'm serious about the title. That Cara is my number one priority and that I'm committed and giving it my whole heart."

'Him' is obviously the king. That all sounds great to me. "How are you going to do that?"

He finally looks up at me. "It would really help if *you* could stop being amazing. Maybe you could piss him off. Make my grandfather a little less enamored with *you*."

That surprises me. I smile despite the situation. "Sorry."

He rolls his eyes but returns the smile. "It's really too bad we have no interest in one another."

God, it's so true. If only *we* could be crazy about each other. But that's never going to happen. "I know. It's annoying how much I *don't* want you."

"Not to mention how much I *do* want her."

I swing toward the sound of my favorite deep voice.

Jonah is crossing the room with long strides.

My stomach flips seeing him. It's only been a couple of hours, but I feel better simply having his gaze on me.

"How'd it go?" he asks.

"I have six months before my grandfather announces my engagement to Linnea," Torin tells him.

Jonah stops next to me as his brows slam together. "Excuse me?"

"We're working on a plan," I tell him.

Jonah looks at Torin with an eyebrow up. "Work faster."

The prince chuckles. "It's been ten minutes."

"Yeah. Exactly. That's about nine and a half minutes longer than I'm comfortable with people contemplating how to announce that my girl is marrying another man."

My heart flips at that. His hand goes to the back of my neck in a gesture that always makes me feel grounded and tingly at the same time.

"I'm not marrying anyone else," I say. Then add, "Probably" just because I like to poke at jealous Jonah once in a while.

He gives a low growl, and his hand tightens on my neck. He leans in and says, "Do I need to remind you who you belong to?" softly and gruffly against my ear.

I swallow hard. "Um, yes, please."

"Good girl," he says, kissing the top of my head, then straightening.

"Am I interrupting? Would you like me to leave you alone?" Torin asks, watching us with amused interest.

"Actually—" Jonah starts.

"Of course not," I say over him.

I would *never* have sex in Torin's office.

Yuck.

But I do have a pretty desk in my room at home...

Jonah chuckles and the sound dances down my spine, sending sparks of heat along each of my limbs.

I clear my throat. "We were discussing how Torin is going to show the king that he's fully committed and going to give Cara his heart," I tell Jonah.

Jonah's thumb is stroking up and down the side of my neck now.

"What does that mean?" Jonah asks Torin. "Fully committed and going to give Cara your heart? You're here. You're stepping up. What the hell else does he want?"

"He wants proof," Torin says. "He wants to see *evidence* that I'm here to stay."

"Okay." Jonah says, clearly still confused by what that means exactly.

Me too.

"But I think I know how to prove to him that I'm here to stay," Torin says thoughtfully. "That I'm putting my *heart* into Cara."

"Okay. How?" Jonah asks.

"I need a wife."

Jonah's answer is immediate. "No."

I feel a little shiver go through me. I love his firm, commanding voice. And that, combined with that touch of jealousy, makes me want to haul him up to his room right now.

Torin frowns. "What?"

"No. You're not marrying Linnea even if it's fake."

Torin's not talking about me. I open my mouth to respond.

But Torin answers first. "I'm not talking about Linnea."

"Then who?" Jonah asks, still scowling.

"Someone special." Torin seems to be thinking out loud. "Someone who will see Cara for the amazing place it is, with lots of potential for more. Someone who will commit themselves to our country in a way that will impress my grandfather the way Linnea has. Someone so incredible, that I can convince my grandfather, and the media, she is the reason I've been going back to the States so often for the past two years. Someone who I can seem so in love with that the king will believe I've brought my *heart* here and that I'm ready to settle down, put down roots, and truly stay."

He picks up the bottle of lavender oil and takes a long inhale.

Both Jonah and I are watching him with wide eyes.

"But..." I start. "You *are* ready to settle down here and put down roots...right?"

"I am," Torin answers. "But the king isn't seeing it. Me saying it is obviously not enough. So I need to give him something more apparent to prove it."

I look up at Jonah, then back to Torin. "So you want to find someone to fake marry you?"

"No. *Real* marry me. It has to be real."

Right. The king would be able to verify if a marriage was real or not. But wow. This is big.

"So you need to find a girlfriend and get her to fall in love with you and agree to marry you in the next six months," Jonah says.

"Sure," Torin agrees. "Let's try that." He finally looks up at us. "You think this is a good idea?"

"I think you being king is a good idea," I say honestly. Then I decide to tell him why. I've been thinking about this a lot since I've decided I'm not going to be queen. "Your grandfather needs to step down. He deserves to rest. He also deserves the peace of knowing that his beloved Cara is in good hands. He deserves to see *you* being a good king. You deserve the chance to show him that. I'd love to see the two of you mend your relationship. But I don't think that will happen until he steps aside, and you have the actual chance to lead. So yes, if you're ready to fall in love and get married then I think this plan is...not terrible."

Torin looks incredibly pleased by that. He claps his hands together as he rises. "Wonderful. Then let's go get our princess."

"Wait," Jonah says. "You have someone in mind?"

Torin grins, then leans over and clicks on a file on his desktop before he steps back and points at the monitor.

Jonah and I both lean in.

Then Jonah looks at Torin. "Uh...that's Abigail Landry."

"Yes, it is."

"Abigail Landry doesn't like you."

"That's a bit of an overstatement," Torin protests.

"Well...she didn't seem to really be into you," Jonah amends.

Torin doesn't seem concerned. "That will change when she finds out that I have something she wants."

Jonah straightens and faces him. "And what's that?"

"Her dream job."

"What's her dream job?" I ask.

"Eliminating world hunger," Torin says.

Oh, well, just *that*.

He grins. "Specifically, she wants to build indoor farms in food deserts and supply fresh food to people, especially children, year-round regardless of climate and terrain."

I just blink at him. Because that sounds amazing. Almost too good to be true.

"Cara is a food desert," he continues. "We can't grow anything here! Our soil is too thin and rocky, and our weather is too cool and windy. We import everything. It's terrible for our economy and our ability to be independent and have strong national relations."

My heart rate kicks up. This sounds like a perfect project for Torin to bring to Cara. Exactly the kind of thing to show Diarmuid that Torin understands what being a leader really entails.

"So you think she'll want to come here because this is the perfect place to do her work and you, as the prince, can give her all the resources she could possibly need," I say.

"Exactly," he gives me a smug grin.

Okay, I'm catching on. If Torin is in love with a woman who is fully committed and really good for Cara, then Diarmuid would have to take that seriously. Diarmuid is not sympathetic to giving up love, but what if that love was *also* an amazing queen? What if she's capable of doing impressive, impactful things for the country? And what if Torin just *married* her? Would the king make a spectacle out of forcing Torin to *divorce* her?

He definitely wouldn't.

If we can convince the country that Torin is in love and show them that this Abigail is perfect for *them* too, then Diarmuid wouldn't dare go against public sentiment.

"If it will keep the king and the country from looking at Linnea as the next queen, then I'm on board," Jonah says. "The sooner *you* are on the throne, the sooner Linnea and I can come out and be a couple in public without worrying about how the king will react."

Exactly. Diarmuid might still be upset when he finds out, but if Torin is king, Diarmuid won't be able to really *do* anything about Jonah and me.

I'll still feel guilty, I'm sure, but I can deal with that later.

"Then we're all in agreement," Torin says.

"We are," Jonah says. "And if we leave in the next two hours, we can get there just in time."

"Where are we going?" Torin asks.

"Louisiana. For a wedding." Jonah grins. He rounds the desk and takes my hand, starting for the door.

"Torin's wedding?" I ask.

That wouldn't surprise me. The O'Gradys are very... impulsive at times.

And hey, I'm ready to get this plan going. Right now. I've waited long enough to tell everyone that I'm in love and I'm sick of having all of this secrecy and worry hanging over my head.

Jonah looks back at Torin. "Maybe. But first...Amelia Landry is getting married this weekend."

I'm in. I don't know who Amelia is, but her last name is Landry. Just like Abigail's.

And I saw the way Torin looked at Abigail's photo. She has to be the woman he danced with two years ago. The one he's still thinking about. The one that made him believe a king could actually have true love.

I look over my shoulder just before Jonah pulls me out of the room.

Torin is still at his desk, looking at his computer screen.

Yeah, that has to be her.

So it looks like we're on our way to Louisiana for a wedding. And to get Torin a princess.

6 Months before the Engagement Announcement...

CHAPTER 30
WAIT 'TIL I TELL YE

EPISODE 741 TRANSCRIPT

Lindsey: So our illustrious prince has once again jetted off to the U.S. for the weekend. Ugh!

Jen: For a friend's wedding! That's sweet.

Lindsey: Yes, we wouldn't want his duties as prince to get in the way of a good party.

Jen: What duties? He's not really doing that much. <laughs lightly> And did you hear? Linnea Olsen went with him.

Lindsey: Wait, what? I love Linnea.

Jen: Everyone does. I mean people have always talked about how perfect they would be together. Okay, at least since Torin first came back two years ago. Their families have been friends for a long time. They've known each other since they were kids.

Lindsey: No question. Linnea is one of us. And she's definitely princess material.

Jen: For sure. So maybe their getaway is more than just a weekend of partying in Louisiana. Oh! Maybe he's introducing her to his friends there! And his brother and sister are there! They know her too, but it's been a while. It's a good thing for them to all spend time together if Torin and Linnea are dating!

Lindsey: Okay, I'm not so mad about this trip now. But, Torin, if you're listening, we're going to need to hear something concrete soon! Spill the tea, Your Highness!

Jonah: I am very displeased with this particular turn of events.

Torin: There's no turn of events. It's just gossip. They'll figure it out once I'm with Abigail.

And when the fuck is that going to happen? She walked out after dancing with you. Again. Then got on a plane the next morning without saying goodbye. And now we're in fucking Shreveport and you've only been texting. This doesn't feel like an epic romance, Torin. This isn't even dating.

I have a plan.

> You also have a best friend who would really love to not have podcasts speculating about his woman being on a romantic getaway with another man.

> Why are you texting me instead of coming down here to my room and talking to me?

> Because, unlike you, I managed to win over the woman I love, and I now have her curled up next to me in bed. Naked. I'm not leaving this to come talk to you.

> I'm happy for you, you know.

> You should be. Linnea's amazing. I'm a lucky son of a bitch.

> She's lucky too. Hey, gotta go. Abigail just texted me.

> Get your shit together, Your Highness.

EPISODE 749 TRANSCRIPT

Lindsey: He's *still* in the U.S.? What the hell is going on? It's been over a week since the wedding.

Jen: Yep. He's still there. But so is Linnea. It seems that the prince has been taking the duchess out to dinner and enjoying the local culture in Shreveport.

Lindsey: *Shreveport*. What's in Shreveport? When he lived in Louisiana, it was down around New Orleans, right? And I always forget Linnea is a duchess.

Jen: Right. Her grandfather, besties with King Diarmuid, was given the title and all that land way back. She looks amazing in that green dress in those photos from their night out.

Lindsey: She does. But *why* Shreveport? Anyone know? If you have a theory, call in or comment on one of our social media posts. They've been seen entering and exiting the Magnolia Hotel, which is *very* posh. They're in the penthouse. Jonah Greene, the prince's longtime friend and bodyguard, is there with them so this must be palace-approved, right?

Jen: Oh, it is! Didn't you see the statement from the palace?

Lindsey: Wait, there's an official statement?

Jen: Yes! And I quote, "The Prince and Duchess have known each other since they were children. That they have a close friendship should be no surprise and their families are delighted that they enjoy spending time together."

Lindsey: Okay, that sounds like the royal family is on board with this trip...and all it entails.

Jen: It really does. Oh! What if he *proposes* to her while they're in the U.S.?

Lindsey: Instead of doing it *here*? He should propose in Cara, don't you think?

Jen: I know *I'll* be disappointed if it happens somewhere else. Even if the U.S. is meaningful to the prince, *this* is their home.

Lindsey: I agree. Okay, listeners, let us know what you think.

> Mother: Linnea, we are delighted about the news we're seeing regarding you and Torin! The king is getting restless, but this trip is helping. Well done. But please remind Torin that a proposal cannot happen anywhere but Cara. That would be in terribly poor taste.

T

wo hours later...

> How many bridesmaids are you planning on?

Two days later...

> I had lunch with Queen Roisin and Princess Ábria. I really need to know about the bridesmaids. Please respond.

Three days later...

> I really need you to respond. Diarmuid and Roisin have asked us to let all statements come from the palace for now, but once your engagement is official, our family can issue some kind of release. I would love to hear from you. And remind Torin about the proposal. And I need to know about bridesmaids. More than six would be tacky.

EPISODE 757 TRANSCRIPT

Lindsey: Okay, you all had *a lot* of opinions about Prince Torin proposing to Linnea in the U.S. rather than here. I'm not surprised. I feel the same way as eighty-two percent of our listeners. That would be crappy.

Jen: I get it. I do. They're from here. They're two of Cara's most beloved public figures. But what if there's some special spot in Louisiana that's really meaningful to him? That could be really romantic. The U.S. was part of his life for ten years!

Lindsey: He did not live in Louisiana the whole time. And *Cara* is his country. And he's not just some guy. He's our prince! No. The engagement needs to happen *here*.

Jen: I guess we'll see. They've been over there for a long time. You don't think...never mind. I don't even want to put that out there.

Lindsey: Well, now you have to. What are you thinking?

Jen: You don't think they're considering *staying* there, right? Or buying a house or land there?

Lindsey: Why would you say that? He's our *prince*. How could he stay there?

Jen: I don't know. I just saw a report that he was on a ranch outside of Shreveport two days ago. Maybe that was just...for fun? But he has a ranch here that he loves and I was just wondering if he's staying there this long to look for property? Maybe just someplace to stay when he's there?

Lindsey: I don't even know what to say. Why would he need a place to stay? Especially in Shreveport rather than near New Orleans where his family and friends are? And he needs to be *here!* Oh my God, Torin, Linnea, one of you has to be listening to us! You need to come home! Tell us what is going on!

Jen: This is why I didn't want to bring it up. But on the bright side...at least we'll have a royal wedding to look forward to, right?

Lindsey: Well, we'd better!

Jen: The palace has released another statement! Quote, "The royal family already considers Her Grace a part of the family and are enjoying seeing the reports and photos of the prince and duchess together as much as everyone else is."

Lindsey: I swear to God, I'm more invested in this than I am my own dating life.

Jen: Oh, hold on, *you* have a dating life? Now you need to start talking!

Lindsey: And that's a wrap for us today! Tune in tomorrow! Just wait 'til we tell ye!

Henry: Okay, I know the podcast listener Rogue123 is you, Jonah. And that's hilarious.

Colin: How do you know that's him?

Henry: That's the ONLY commenter who insists Linnea and Torin have no chemistry and that he doesn't see them as anything more than friends and everyone is clearly getting ahead of themselves with all these dating and proposal speculations.

Colin: He wouldn't dare.

Jonah: He would fucking dare. And that podcast is really starting to piss me off.

Henry: <high five emoji> <laugh-cry emoji>

Colin: <eye-roll emoji>

Jonah: You look gorgeous.

Linnea: Thank you.

Is your pussy still throbbing for me?

Yes. Not finishing what you started was really mean.

We only had twenty-seven floors. We got to the lobby too fast.

You shouldn't have started that in the elevator.

Do you need help with that now?

> I might just go into the restroom and take care of it myself.

NO. Meet me in the empty back hallway on the east side.

> Now? We're here to listen to Abigail speak to this crowd and then support Torin when he goes to talk to her.

Don't care. Some of these people have heard that podcast and think you're here with Torin. Need to stake my claim, Duchess. Right now.

> We need to be supportive of Torin.

Torin who?

> Lol! Stop.

My woman is standing next to me with no panties on, a wet pussy, and thinking that she's here to support another man. Get. In. That. Hallway.

> You told me to take my panties off!

Yep. And you immediately pulled them off, flashed me that gorgeous pussy as you did it, tucked them in my pocket, and begged me to finger you from floor twenty-seven to the lobby.

> ...

...

> The east hallway?

Yes.

> Give me two minutes.

You've got one and a half.

"Hey, Torin, can we talk for a second?" I ask as he, Abigail, Linnea, and I stop outside the bank of elevators at the hotel. We've just come back from dinner and I need to have a word with him. Not the prince. Not my boss. But my friend. "Alone?"

He nods. "Of course."

He's probably assuming that I have a message—or seventeen—to pass on to him from Cara. Which I do. But this isn't the time. None of that matters as much as what is happening between him and Abigail.

"I'll meet you upstairs," Abigail tells him as the elevator doors swish open.

"I'll be right up," Torin says, watching as Abigail and Linnea step into the elevator together.

I know Linnea senses my tension, but I haven't filled her in on my concerns. I don't want her to know I'm worried about Torin and Abigail.

Abigail is supposed to be the solution to...everything. To Linnea and me being together.

If Linnea knew I was having second thoughts about them, she might think I'm having second thoughts about us.

I'm not. Not at all. I want her. She's mine. We're going to make this work. There is no question in my mind.

But I can't deny that I'm not one-hundred percent convinced that this is the way to do it. I don't like how long it's taken Torin to talk Abigail into this. I don't like that she needed so much persuading. And I don't like that they've made only a temporary arrangement.

Still, I give my girl a smile as the elevator doors slide shut.

Torin turns to me. "Is there something from Cara?"

"No. Well, yes, but that's not what I want to talk to you about right now."

"Are you going to congratulate me?"

I'm not. I slide my hands into my pants pockets and just meet his gaze. "Should I congratulate you?"

"The woman of my dreams proposed to me," he says. "She's going to be the princess. I'll have the throne within the next year. Her farm will make a number of positive changes for our country. Isn't that all cause for congratulations?"

"Yes. I heard her lay out all of the practical reasons why the two of you getting married was a good idea."

He sighs and leans back against the wall. "What's the problem, Jonah?"

Well, there are a few. "I just want to be sure that you still think this is the right idea."

He frowns. "Of course. This was the plan when we got on the plane in Cara. I'm crazy about her. You know that."

I pull my hands from my pockets and cross my arms. "I do know *you're* crazy about *her*." That's clear. I've never seen him like this. "That's what concerns me."

"You're *concerned* that I'm crazy about the woman I'm going to marry?"

I don't have to beat around the bush with this man. No one knows him as well as I do. "You're in love with her."

He doesn't even hesitate. He nods. "Yes."

"And does she love you?" That matters, dammit. Yes, her marrying him would take care of the arranged marriage situation, but *fuck*. He's my best friend. He wants true love. And if he's already fallen for her, then by God, she needs to love him too.

It takes him a second to answer. He takes a deep breath. "What are you asking me exactly?"

"Abigail has laid out all of the good reasons why you should get married. No one can really argue with any of them." She practically used bullet points. And she was very clear about the timeline being one year. Only one year. "It is, in fact, a very good, *practical* idea. But was one of those reasons, at any point, in private between the two of you, because she's in love with you, too?"

"No," he admits. "But I haven't said it to her either."

Dammit. "Why not?"

"Because she's not the whirlwind romance, head-over-heels, follow her heart kind of girl," he says. "It's been fast. And it's all a little crazy."

"Exactly," I agree.

"And that concerns you. You think she's marrying me for my money? Or to get what she needs professionally from me?"

I want him happy. I want him to have everything *he* wants. *He* is my concern. Abigail seems like a nice person. I agree that the things she can do for Cara seem very promising. That's all great. But not at the expense of my best friend's heart.

"I think the reasons she's marrying you are not...the same reasons you're marrying her. But," I add. "I think she *thinks* she's marrying you for the same reasons. So I can't really fault her."

Torin sighs. "I'm marrying her for the same reasons she's marrying me, *too*. The farms, Cara, Linnea, my grandfather."

I shake my head. "But you're making a mess of this."

"Because I haven't told her I'm in love with her?"

I drop my arms and take a big breath. "I'm talking to you as your best friend now. Not your bodyguard. Not a member of the royal staff. Not even just a guy. But as someone who considers you a brother."

"All right."

"I don't want you to get your heart broken. And I think there is only one thing, and two people, in the world who can do that. Your country. Your grandfather—who has repeatedly done it, especially over the past year. And now Abigail Landry. Who is going to come to Cara with you, and potentially break your heart over and over again every day."

That twists my stomach into a knot and I fucking hate it. It's not Abigail's fault, but...fuck. Can I let him go through with this? I feel selfish. If they get married, Linnea and I are free to be together. I want that. I *need* that. But I can't live with the idea that Torin won't have what he wants.

He replies after several long seconds. "She and I are an amazing team. We can do really amazing things."

I agree. If hearts weren't involved and he was just hiring her, I'd be fully on board with bringing her back to Cara with us. "I think that's absolutely true. I think Abigail should come to Cara."

He looks relieved. "Good."

"But I don't know if you should *marry* her."

"It's the best way."

I give him a single nod. "In a lot of ways, I think that's true." I pause. "But, if you do it, you need to remember it's a *solution to a problem*. You're going to be king, Torin. You're going to be faced with difficult decisions every damned day. And you're going to sometimes have to make choices that really suck, that are going to break your heart. I don't want your personal life making you feel shitty too. You deserve to be happy. And if you're happy, you'll be better for Cara."

Torin pulls in a long breath. "Abigail *is* the right choice for Cara. I thought you understood this was the plan all along."

"Making a *deal* with her to be princess. Sure. I actually thought the plan was exactly what Abigail seems to think it is," I say. "And seducing her? Sure. I saw how you looked at her clear back at Charlie's wedding."

Torin shifts and clears this throat, then nods.

"But falling in love with her?" I ask. "Especially without anything reciprocal from her? That's...dangerous."

"I think she really likes me," he quips, clearly trying to lighten the moment.

I don't smile. This matters to me. "Everyone likes you, Torin. Even your grandfather *likes* you. He still makes you fucking miserable because he doesn't give you anything more than that," I say bluntly. "I like Abi. She's brilliant. And yes, I'm sure she *likes* you. But she proposed and specifically said she doesn't want it to involve any emotions. And she said she wants it to only be for a year."

He's frowning. "So you're trying to protect me."

"Well, it's kind of a habit now after eleven-plus years," I say with an eyeroll. Of course I'm fucking trying to protect him.

"It's because *you* love me."

I look at him for several seconds. I've told him this

before. But once I was drunk and once he was in a hospital bed with a broken arm and a concussion.

I want him to be happy. He won't be every single second. I know that. His life is going to be complicated and there's going to be a lot of pressure and unavoidable heartache ahead. But I want him surrounded by love to help him through all of that. Because yes, I love him. "I do love you," I say without a hint of humor. "And you deserve to be loved and appreciated a fuck ton more than you are."

He stares at me. Then has the audacity to look a little choked up. He leans over and claps me on the shoulder. "Thank you. And, just so you know, I think I can make her fall in love with me."

Well, I won't be surprised. But I'd really like it if she was head over heels right now. What's wrong with her? "Should you maybe wait for that to happen before you marry her?"

He grins. "Maybe."

"Really?" I ask. Maybe I got through.

"How long do you think it will take?" he asks.

Not long if Abigail is as smart as everyone claims she is. "A month. Maybe two," I say, with a shrug.

He actually chuckles at my answer. "Thanks, man. I was going to say six months."

I roll my eyes. "If it's going to happen, it's going to happen."

"A month," he muses. "That's nothing. So no, I'm not going to wait for that to happen before I marry her."

Well, hell. I groan. "I just want her to be as into you as you are her. That's not so much to ask."

"I'm going to make her a princess. Give her a crown. Jewels, a palace, a private jet."

I give him a *seriously?* look. "Yeah. Too bad none of that really matters to this particular woman."

He smiles. "I guess I'll have to throw in some fruit trees and green rubber boots."

I shake my head. I've said my piece. He heard me. I reach over and stab the elevator button for the penthouse. "Well, if you're going to make her fall for you, I guess you better go up and get started."

He laughs and we both get on the elevator.

We head to our respective rooms, both with a beautiful woman behind the door.

I pause at my door. "Torin?"

He looks over, his door already open. "Yeah?"

"I do want this to work out. I want you to have everything you want. You deserve that."

"Ditto," he says, looking at my room door.

"Thanks."

We both step into our rooms.

Linnea is there immediately. She's in a tiny silk night gown under a silk robe that hits her mid-thigh. "What's wrong?"

God, she's so fucking beautiful. I toss my key card onto the table and gather her into my arms, breathing her in. "I just needed to be sure he's okay."

She pulls back. "And is he?" She looks concerned.

"Says he is."

"You don't believe him?"

"I believe he thinks he is."

She frowns. "What's going on?"

I blow out a breath. I have to be honest with her. "I just need him to be happy, Duchess. I need Abi to love him."

Linnea presses her lips together. But she nods. "I know."

"I don't like this one-year stipulation. I don't like that she's making it a deal, or a job, instead of a real marriage."

Linnea takes my hand and leads me to the couch. She pushes me down and climbs into my lap. My hands settle on her hips, and she links her fingers behind my neck. Just being close to her like this calms me. *This* is also the reason this needs to work out.

"But her job is part of this. For Cara and for her," Linnea says.

"I know. But...he's in love with her, Duchess."

She doesn't seem surprised. "Oh." She wets her lips. "And you're afraid he's going to get hurt."

"Yeah."

She nods. "Okay. Well...is he afraid of that? Did you talk him out of getting married right away?"

I hesitate but then tell her honestly. "I tried."

"Oh."

I study her face. "Are you upset?"

"No. Just..." She frowns as she trails off.

"I know that feels like I'm putting him before us. Before you. But that's not true. I just..." I break off. "Fuck. I don't know. If he gets married, even temporarily, that leaves us free and clear to be together. The arranged marriage is voided. We can tell the king about us right after they get married. If we're together, even if they break up, the king can't expect you to marry Torin."

"But you don't want him to get his heart broken," she says. She runs her fingers through my hair. "I understand that. He's your best friend. And it makes me love you more. You are the least selfish, most amazing man I know."

I squeeze her hips. "But I want *you*. I want to be with you, Duchess. I do."

"I know. And all Torin needs to do is make Abigail fall in love with him, and then *everything* works out." She gives me a little smile.

I try to return it. "Yeah, just that."

She leans in and presses her lips to mine. "I love you."

"I love you too. So damned much, Duchess."

"And it's okay with me that other people matter to you, Jonah," she tells me, stroking her palms over my beard.

God, I hope that's true. Because I'm going to be a real asshole when Abigail Landry breaks my best friend's heart and leaves Cara at the end of this year.

EPISODE 759 TRANSCRIPT

Lindsey: What the hell just happened? Oh my God!

Jen: Um hey, everyone! We're here at a special time with an extra episode because...we have some news!

Lindsey: That's an understatement! We have THE news! Probably the biggest news of the year!

Jen: I would agree. And we got it from Lady Linnea Olsen herself! So, whatever you're doing, wherever you are, stop for a second, take a breath, and turn the volume up.

Lindsey: Okay, everyone ready? Here we go...<takes a deep audible breath> We were right! Prince Torin *was* in the U.S. to get engaged!

Jen: <laughing> But that's about the only thing we got right! He not only *got* engaged, he's also getting *married!* And it's *not* to Linnea!

Lindsey: No, it's not.

Jen: Oh come on, don't look so upset! Clearly Linnea is fine! She's the one who sent us this story and these *photos*. And they're so great! Our producer is posting them right now so you can all go take a look!

Lindsey: Upset? I'm devastated! Heartbroken! I'm *outraged*!

Jen: Okay, okay. Calm down. We have a new princess! Our prince is *married*. Lindsey, this is *great!* Okay, everyone, our new princess is Abigail Landry. She's from Louisiana and is a super brainiac scientist. How amazing is that? They met at her sister's wedding. Not the one he was just at, but one a couple of years ago. So this has been going on for *two years*! That's so sweet! No wonder he hasn't dated anyone else! And no wonder he and Linnea haven't been anything but friends! And...now they're back! They're coming home today!

Lindsey: Yeah. But tell them the *rest* of the news.

Jen: But we should be happy for Torin!

Lindsey: Sure, sure. But what about *our* happiness?

Jen: It's not about us!

Lindsey: It should be a little about us! Everyone, we don't get to have a wedding. They're getting married *today*. In Louisiana! Before they come home!

Jen: Yeah, but...we have a new princess! And just look at these photos! She's beautiful and just look at the way he's looking at her. He's clearly in love!

Lindsey: Well, I can admit they *are* really cute together. Okay, so...<heavy sigh> Welcome to Cara, Princess Abigail. We can't wait to meet you, I guess.

Astrid: Ooooh Myyyyy Goooodddddd. Torin got MARRIED??!!! Mom is losing her shit!

Linnea: I figured. <grimace emoji> But I couldn't tell her what was going on.

I think she's even more upset that you're not upset.

Yeah. Jonah and I are staying at the ranch with Abi and Torin for a while. Need to give her time to cool off. And I need time to sell everyone on Abi.

Will that be hard? What's she like?

She's just shy. But amazing. Perfect for Torin. And, maybe most importantly, willing to be princess. <winking emoji>

And how's Jonah??

Amazing. Perfect for me. And willing to keep hiding this for a little longer until the king loves Abi and realizes that she's going to be a wonderful queen and that Torin is ready to be king. Then we'll tell him about us.

Happy for you! You deserve it! Hope it goes fast though, for your sake.

Thanks. But…turns out sneaking around can be hot <winking emoji> <blushing sweating emoji>.

King Diarmuid: My dear, I just wanted to say that you are still very much a part of this family. We love you. Everything will be okay.

Linnea: I know that. <heart emoji> Thank you. I love you too.

And I want to assure you, I am very happy for Torin and Abigail. She's lovely. She is so good for Torin, and she will be wonderful for Cara.

We'll see.

Linnea: Do not talk to your grandfather before we get home. He's…upset. I think it would be best for you to talk in person when he can meet Abi.

Torin: Why in the world would I want to talk to him before we get home?

Okay, good. Wait, you are going to talk to him when we get back to Cara, right?

We'll see.

Iris: What the FUCK just happened???!

Jonah: Um…

Henry: So…once upon a time there was this handsome prince and he met this sweet, beautiful nerdy scientist…

Iris: How did you get on this text? Dammit. I didn't mean to message the group.

Henry: Hey, did I tell you that Cian got called to a fire the other night?

Iris: What?? He's still doing that? Henry! You cannot let one of the princes DIE! That's like number one on the list of your duties.

Henry: <confused face emoji> Got called to a fire. Not almost died in a fire. <fire emoji> <plus sign> <water droplets emoji> <equal sign> <firefighter emoji> <happy face emoji>

Colin: Is that what you use <water droplets emoji> for? That is not what Cian uses that for when he texts.

Henry: Well…

Iris: Him being a firefighter is not okay, Henry. You need to talk him out of that.

Henry: No can do. Now that he's a big hero, he's getting a ton of attention, and baked goods (who knew… you put out a kitchen fire and other people use their kitchens to thank you), there will be no talking him out of this.

Iris: Henry…

> Jonah: Thanks for the diversion, man, I owe you.

> Henry: No worries, mate. I've got you. Or rather, Cian does. There's always something. That fire actually happened three weeks ago. I've been saving that story.

> Linnea: Where did you sneak out to last night? And why aren't you in bed with me this morning?

> Jonah: Abigail needed to go find Torin late last night so I went with her. He was down at the pub. And then I promised him I'd stay outside her room in case she decided to leave.

> LEAVE?! What happened? Are they okay? Omg! I'm coming to find you! Torin and I have to be at the farmer's market this morning!

> Everything is perfect, Duchess. The princess has realized that the prince truly loves her. And I believe she's realized she loves him too.

> <wide eyed emoji>

> What?? Really????

> Really.

<heart eyes emoji> <heart eyes emoji>

<crying emoji> So it's all good? They're good? WE ARE GOOD??

More than good. Torin declared his feelings for her from on top of a table in the pub to a huge crowd. Abi heard the whole thing. And she's now been challenged to make a public declaration of her own at the market today.

<gasping emoji> Omg! Yes!!

You ready to tell the whole damned world we're madly in love too?

So ready! I love you so much.

I love you too, Duchess. So fucking much.

WAIT TILL
I TELL YE
PODCAST

EPISODE 822 TRANSCRIPT

Lindsey: Okay that was amazing. Who was at the farmers market yesterday? I want to hear from anyone who is an eyewitness!

Jen: I know! I've seen some video, but I'd love to hear from someone who was there. On the heels of the huge public declaration of love at the pub, this was something!

Lindsey: The pub was so great! Seeing Torin get up on that table and declare his love for Abigail was awesome. And yes, *we* do take credit for getting Abigail to the market yesterday.

<sound of hands slapping in a high-five>

Jen: Darn right we do! We challenged her to come kiss her prince in the middle of the square and *dang!* She showed up!

Lindsey: I wanted to make it down there, but the crowd was huge. I have, however, watched Abigail and Torin's speech five times!

Jen: And most importantly...the kiss! The first public kiss between the prince and princess! <squeal>

Lindsey: I know! Not only did Abigail do an amazing job and win us all over in her first public appearance, but she is so clearly in love with Torin, and the kiss was absolutely perfect. So, you're welcome, Cara!

Jen: I know! <happy sigh>

Lindsey: Also importantly, we've had some people write in and tell us that Torin and his grandfather had a very nice discussion that was overheard by several bystanders. Diarmuid told Torin how proud he is of him, and apparently, they're both preparing for Torin to take the throne within the next several months!

Jen: We're all so happy about that!
Lindsey: And...

Jen: And what?

Lindsey: You're not going to tell them?

Jen: OH...that... <giggles> <takes deep breath> We're going to have a WEDDING!!!

Iris: I'm coming to the wedding.

Jonah: Thanks for the warning.

You are so lucky the king loves Abigail.

Most importantly, TORIN loves Abigail. We're all lucky. It's all working out.

You think this just lets you off the hook, right?

It does. Abigail is the answer to everything.

3 Months before the Engagement Announcement

CHAPTER 31
JONAH

"Oh God, Jonah!"

"That's it. Take what you need, Duchess," I urge her, my hands gripping her hips, her pussy tightening around my cock.

She's on top, riding me, but she's still wearing her bridesmaid's dress, so I can't see her gorgeous tits. Or anything else. Her bodice is in place and her skirt is bunched around her waist and hips.

She's the one who pulled me up here to my bedroom and climbed on top. She claims to not like being in charge, but she's a gorgeous liar.

She convinced me that this was the best position to keep her dress from getting too rumpled or messing up her hair.

I don't fucking care. I will take this woman in any and every position she'll let me.

She also insisted we come to my room because no one

walks through my door uninvited. Well, except for beautiful duchesses who get lost on their way to the guest room.

She leans forward, resting her palms on the front of my tuxedo shirt. She moves her hips faster. "I'm so close."

"Fuck me, love. Take it all."

Then she's gasping, clenching around my cock, coming with a cock-hardening little gasp.

She has gotten better at staying quiet when we make love. Unfortunately.

Now that I've taught her that, I'm going to have to teach her to let loose and be loud again once we're free to be in love and living together.

"I love you so fucking much," I tell her as I pull her in, kissing her deeply as I come hard.

While there's never a bad reason to get this woman in my bed, today feels like a special celebration and we just couldn't wait another minute once her bridesmaid and my groomsman duties were over and we didn't think anyone would miss us.

It's all over now. The plan has worked. Downstairs our families and friends are celebrating Torin and Abigail's wedding.

Abigail Landry is the solution to all of our problems.

Tomorrow Linnea has a meeting with the king for early tea. She intends to tell him all about us—that we fell in love, that we want to be together, and that we intend to marry.

The king loves Abigail, and it's clear to everyone that she's perfect for Torin, and incredibly good for Cara. But we've also shown over the past few months that Linnea is still a loyal and effective advisor for both Torin and Abigail and that I can continue fulfilling my duties as Torin's security and advisor.

Truly, everything is working out. There's a tiny niggle in the back of my mind that says that my boss doesn't know about me and Linnea and may feel differently, but Abigail and Torin's wedding was not stopped, and I'm certain he's aware of it. Iris is here, after all. So are Henry and Cian, Colin, and everyone else. He's the only one missing, in fact. If he didn't want this to happen, surely he would've intervened at some point.

So everything's over, and Linnea and I can be together.

After a few moments of cuddling, she pushes up.

"We should get back downstairs," she says.

I chuckle. "I suppose."

The rest of the guests have already left, but the family and friends are having a late dinner. Everyone is gathered in the dining hall, and I am sure they're going to be looking for Linnea soon. I probably should've said no when she asked me to sneak off with her, but I've learned that I have no self-control when it comes to her.

We clean up quickly in my en suite bathroom, and stealthily leave the room. Her sister is sharing Linnea's room while the family is here for the wedding, and I'm grateful. Astrid knows about us and won't mind—and won't tell—when Linnea sneaks out to my bed overnight.

"I can't believe you didn't let me put my panties back on," Linnea tells me as we head down the upper hallway. "I don't know how you expect me to walk around normally."

"I am—"

"There you are," a voice interrupts.

We both freeze.

But a second later the British accent sinks in. It's Henry. I relax. "What are you doing up here?"

"Looking for you. The king wants to address everyone in

the dining room. I noticed when you left. I don't think he did. But he's going to realize shortly that you're the only two missing." He gives Linnea a wink.

I only frown at him for the flirtatious wink. I'm more concerned about why the king wants everyone gathered. "Do you know what's going on?"

"I am sure he just wants to make a toast, or give a blessing, or something," Linnea tells me. She takes my hand and squeezes. "He's so happy today."

I agree. Diarmuid seemed overjoyed. I saw him wipe a tear as Torin and Abigail exchanged vows.

The three of us head back to the main hall, Henry and I falling back to walk behind Linnea, so it looks like we're escorting her.

Fortunately, it seems that we slip into the room without anyone noticing except for Astrid. She gives Linnea a wink like the one Henry gave her.

Yes, Linnea's attempt to keep her dress from being too rumpled from our little liaison was unsuccessful.

I should maybe feel worse about that than I do.

Linnea takes her seat next to her sister and I join Henry and Colin on the other side at the opposite end of the table.

It's been making me itchy all night to be in the same room, near her, but unable to touch her, sweep her into my arms, or kiss her.

I can't take much more of this.

Since we accompanied Torin to the U.S. and then stayed with him as he worked to woo Abigail, then were able to spend a lot of time on his ranch here in Cara as he and Abigail took their time enjoying their honeymoon phase, we've been spoiled with alone time or at least time with people who know our secret. It's making it harder and harder to keep our relationship quiet now that we're back at the palace.

The king is talking to Queen Roisin and his old friend, Oisin. Oisin was Diarmuid's friend and advisor for decades, before visiting the U.S. and spending time in Louisiana, where he fell for a feisty Cajun woman, Cora. Cora was widowed for years, but Oisin won her over and he's now living there with her and the rest of the Landry family.

I watch as the king scans the room and notice when his gaze lands on Linnea. I straighten as he says something to Oisin and then excuses himself. He heads straight for the love of my life.

I don't know why, but this makes trepidation trickle down my spine.

I lift a cup of something—I don't even know what I'm drinking—as I watch him lean over and say something to Linnea, and then her nod. She casts a glance in my direction. She looks worried.

Fuck.

My protective instincts have me fighting the urge to push up out of my chair.

She slides her chair back, then takes Diarmuid's hand as he leads her out of the room.

"You okay?" Colin asked me.

Obviously, I have not perfected hiding how I feel when it comes to that woman.

I shake my head. "No. Diarmuid just took Linnea out of the room."

"They're close, right? Is that a sign of problems?"

I take a breath. "No. Not necessarily." I typically wouldn't have thought anything of it.

But things started being atypical about three months ago.

Because until then, Linnea had never done anything that would even slightly upset the king.

But for about three months now, she's been doing a lot of things that would upset the king very much. With me.

CHAPTER 32
LINNEA

I don't think that I have ever talked to King Diarmuid without underwear on.

I also realize that that should not be the first thing on my mind.

But I'm feeling uncomfortable and that is not helping.

"The wedding was so lovely," I comment before he can say anything. I have no idea what would cause him to pull me out of the family dinner into the hallway.

"It really was." His smile is full of love and happiness.

I have no question that Diarmuid is happy about this wedding. He loves Abigail and knows that she's very good for Torin. Good for Cara. Torin and Diarmuid have mended some fences. I believe that Diarmuid truly believes that Torin is on his way to being a wonderful king.

I was there when Diarmuid told Torin that he expects to be able to turn the crown over within the year.

I'm very happy for them both. I am happy for Cara too.

"You have been such a wonderful friend and advisor to

them both." Diarmuid sighs. "Thank you so much for welcoming Abigail. For helping her feel more comfortable here. For teaching her all of the ins and out of our country. But also for letting her truly find herself here."

I smile easily. I love Abigail. She's very different from me. We have very little in common. But I think she's wonderful. She's brilliant, sweet, and she loves Torin in the way he deserves to be loved. "I am so happy they found each other. I really think she's going to be a wonderful queen."

"I agree. And with you by her side, she has nothing to worry about."

"I'm glad you feel that way. And you know I'm always here for Torin."

"I do. But that brings me to what I wanted to talk to you about. I wanted you to hear this from me directly. Before I tell the entire family."

I frown. The butterflies in my stomach start swooping. "Okay."

"I want you to know that the promises my family—" He stops and shakes his head. "The promises *I* made to your grandfather mean a lot to me. I am not backing out of those."

I frown. I'm not sure what he's talking about. "I don't understand."

"The agreement Alfred and I made was serious. Just because we were playing poker at the time doesn't mean we didn't mean it. It mattered to both of us."

Oh...no.

My stomach feels sick suddenly.

"That night, that poker game, was not the first time we'd talked about uniting our families. That's what we wanted. We wanted to establish a shared bloodline.

Initially, of course, we assumed that my grandson in the agreement would be the king. But it doesn't have to be. So, you have nothing to worry about. You will still be an O'Grady."

My entire body goes cold. I stare at him, unable to form words. I had no idea this was what he was going to say. And I have no idea how to respond.

I didn't know...any of that.

I was under the impression the arranged marriage they concocted that night had been the result of a lot of whiskey, and the late hour. I didn't know it was something they'd discussed previously. Did anyone else know that?

And what did he mean *shared bloodline*?

You will still be an O'Grady.

He said that as if he thinks I'm *concerned* about not being an O'Grady. That somehow he feels he's broken a promise to *me*. That I am upset or disappointed.

My initial reaction is to shout *no*! But of course, I can't do that.

He steps forward and wraps me in a hug. His familiar scent, that normally comforts me, now makes me want to cry.

This is bad. This is really bad.

"I love you, Linnea," he says against the top of my head. "You are very dear to me. I feel like you are one of mine. Watching you grow into the woman you've become has been a great joy to me."

"I love you too," I tell him. "You're very important to me."

"I know that. You *are* my family. I want you to know that. I want everyone to know that. The Olsens *are* my family."

I feel tears stinging and I wrap my arms around him in

return. I can't *not*. This man *is* my grandfather in every way but blood.

Suddenly, I freeze. That thought goes through my mind again.

In every way but blood.

Then again.

In every way but blood.

Then what else he said—*we wanted to establish a shared bloodline.*

My eyes widen. I pull back and look up at him.

He looks down at me with love and pride.

My heart pounds. I wet my lips.

"How will I still be an O'Grady?" I already know the answer, but I want to hear it.

He smiles. "I have two more grandsons. Though I would never ask you to deal with the eldest."

Oh, God.

He still thinks I'm going to marry one of his grandsons.

That's clear as day now.

Why didn't I see that this might happen? How did I not anticipate this?

Because this is nuts.

But they changed Declan to Torin on you.

But that was because Torin was in line for the throne!

Yes, I truly thought it was about me marrying the future king.

But...it's far more than that.

I know that Diarmuid and my grandfather were as close as brothers. Closer, really. My grandfather had two brothers and he never saw either of them as far as I remember.

They're not dukes. They don't have any titles. That title, the land, the influence and power were given to my family by Diarmuid. My grandfather moved my family to Cara. The rest of his family is still in Denmark.

Diarmuid is the king. He could have chosen *anyone* to be his advisor, to bestow titles and power, to confide in. But he chose my grandfather. And my grandfather chose Diarmuid, chose to be close to the O'Gradys, over his own flesh and blood.

So he and Diarmuid came up with a plan to actually create a shared O'Grady-Olsen bloodline.

Oh. My. God.

This isn't about the throne. This isn't about leading Cara. This isn't a 'job' for me.

That was all just a perk.

What they really wanted was for me to become the *mother* of an O'Grady-Olsen child.

The first.

The beginning of an entirely new branch of the family tree. A powerful one, for sure. But also, a very meaningful one. One that mattered deeply to these two men whose bond was purely in heart and that they wanted to, somehow, make more.

I'm stunned.

I have no idea what to say.

This is so much bigger than me. This is really, in some ways, bigger than leading Cara.

Clearly, someone else can do that. Abigail can do that.

But not just anyone can create an O'Grady-Olsen heir.

"Come. We have to reassure everyone else."

My mind is spinning.

I let him turn me and lead me into the dining room. What am I supposed to say? How can I tell him no? Alfred is gone. His friend is *gone*.

This is his only hope for hanging onto that bond and for fulfilling that promise. That dream.

I feel like I'm moving in slow motion. The sounds around me are muted. I feel like my body is detached from my thoughts.

Diarmuid leads me to the head of the table and everyone slowly quiets. Oh, God. This is going to be so bad.

Finally, I look at Jonah.

The man I love. The man I want. The man who I can see an entire future with.

The man who knows me, cares about *me* and what I want. Who sees me. Who has always seen me.

The man who is my dream.

When I was a little girl imagining marrying the prince, I was imagining Jonah. Not his face or name, of course, but the way he makes me feel. The way he treats me. The way he looks at me.

The way he loves me.

I wanted love.

Before I understood what was really happening and that it was a *duty* that only I could fulfill, I did want love. I wanted what Torin said he wanted—to have it all.

Then I thought I could have it all.

When Torin and Abi said "I do", that was supposed to be it. Abigail was going to fulfill the duty of queen. Diarmuid was happy with that. Everything was good and right and everyone was happy. That was supposed to leave me and Jonah free and clear. Free to do what *we* want to do. Free to consider *our* happiness and not what everyone around us needs.

But now…there's still a duty. And I'm still the only one.

Abigail can give Torin an heir. But it won't be an O'Grady-Olsen heir.

I'm staring at Jonah.

He looks beyond concerned. In fact, he looks like he's about to come across the table.

I wish I could give him a reassuring smile. But...I just shake my head.

I watch as Colin puts a hand on his arm, and I realize Jonah did just try to stand.

"Everyone!" Diarmuid says, holding up his hands. "This is such a happy day!"

Everyone turns their bodies toward him. There are lots of smiles and several murmurs of agreement.

"And I want to add to the merriment! Since everyone is together, this is the perfect time to tell you all what's next before you all jet off back to the U.S.."

I look around the table. Almost everyone looks confused. Except for my parents and the queen, who look thrilled.

Oh, great. They already know about this.

Of course, they do.

"Diarmuid," I say softly. "I don't—"

He takes my hand, cradling it against his chest. I feel his heart beating against the back of my hand and I have to swallow hard. A wave of grief over my grandfather suddenly hits me hard.

"As you all know, I've always expected this day to include this lovely woman."

Oh, *God*.

There are now looks of secondhand embarrassment reflected back at me. Except from my mother, who looks ready to burst with happiness.

And Jonah, who looks ready to murder someone. Now Henry has a hand on his shoulder too. He and Colin are clearly keeping him in his seat.

"We absolutely *adore* Abigail." Diarmuid gives Abi a huge smile.

She returns it, though she is blushing and gives me a look that is a combination of embarrassed and confused.

"But what many of you don't know is that when Alfred and I entered into our agreement—"

There are some soft snorts from around the table now. References to the drunken poker game always elicit laughs.

If only everyone knew that the whiskey and gambling that night were simply what finally pushed them to make their plan official.

Diarmuid gives the table a frown and everyone quiets again. "As I was saying," he continues. "Alfred and I wanted our families to be united. Alfred had only one granddaughter at the time." He smiles down at me. "I had three grandsons. Contrary to popular belief, our agreement had nothing to do with the throne. It was simply the assumption that it would be a union of our first grandchildren. Then Declan left, and the agreement moved to my second grandson."

My breathing is faster now and I can't look at Jonah.

"But now that my second grandson is married to another, the arrangement will move to my third grandson."

He stands smiling.

Everyone else in the room is completely quiet.

The clock ticks five times.

Then Cian says, "Hey, I'm your third grandson."

Diarmuid nods. "Yes. *You* and Linnea will marry. We'll announce the engagement in three months."

Now my gaze flies to Jonah's.

His jaw is tight, and his eyes are hard. He's watching me. Waiting for me to do something.

Because...I have to do something.

Of course I do.

I feel a little dizzy.

"*I'm* going to marry Linnea?" Cian repeats. "Just like that? Are you kidding?" He looks at me. "No offense."

Diarmuid nods his head. "Yes. The O'Gradys and Olsens will be united."

"That's cra—" Cian starts.

"No."

I feel like someone else says the word, but I know it came from me.

I suck in a deep breath. Then I shake my head and say more firmly, louder, "No."

I feel Diarmuid stiffen beside me. I turn to him and pull my hand from his.

I take a deep breath when I look into his eyes. He looks completely confused.

"Linnea?"

I know what I have to do.

I have to stop this.

They arranged my marriage when I was *four*. On a playbill.

Then they swapped out my fiancé when I was seventeen because my original one left home, never to return.

Then that one left home and spent ten years playing around in the U.S..

Then he came home and decided *not* to marry me because he just didn't want to.

Then he fell in love with someone else and got to marry her and live happily ever after.

So they're going to just trade out my fiancé *again*? And because they want me to have a baby for them?

What. The Actual. Fuck?

The shock is wearing off, and the anger is setting in.

I loved my grandfather. I love Diarmuid. I respected and loved their relationship. I understand, on some level, their dream to unite the families.

But...I'm not a pawn.

They can't just keep moving me around their chess board.

Everyone else is getting to make choices.

It's my fucking turn.

CHAPTER 33
LINNEA

I take a deep breath and meet the king's eyes directly. "I adore you," I tell him, with sincerity. "You are so important to me." I turn to look at the table full of people. "All of you are. The O'Grady family is so important to me. I'm so happy to be a part of it. And I hope I always can be, in some way, but..." I take another deep breath.

I clench my fists at my sides and lift my chin, and yes, raise my voice. "You all make me *crazy*. You have been messing with my life for...well, my whole life. Everything about *everything* has been about you all. What you want. Or don't want. One minute I'm engaged. Then I'm not. Then I am again, but to someone else. Now I am again to *another* one of you? No. Just *no*."

I turn back to Diarmuid. "I know what you and my grandfather wanted. I understand. And I've done everything you've ever asked of me until now. I've made Cara better. I've helped you. I've helped Torin. I've helped

Abigail. And it's been my pleasure. It always will be. But… no. I'm not going to marry Cian. I'm not going to be an O'Grady. I'm in love with someone else and I'm going to marry *him*."

I turn to look at Jonah. "I'm finally going to do what *I* want and…I want Jonah. I love him and want to marry *him*."

His eyes go wide. But then he stands up, Henry and Colin's hands falling away. "Yes. *Fuck* yes." He starts around the table and comes toward me.

I grin, my eyes filling with tears, my heart pounding, and relief coursing through me.

"Jonah? Jonah Greene?" Diarmuid asks from behind me.

I nod, staring at Jonah. "Yes. I fell in love with him a long time ago. And I want to be with him. No matter what."

"I love you too, Duchess," he says, loud and clear, in front of everyone, coming to stand in front of me. He cups my face in both hands. "That was regal as fuck." Then he kisses me softly.

I feel light and free.

For the first time inside this palace.

I just defied the king, went against my family's wishes, and I feel *lighter*. I can't be everything to everyone. I can't make everyone else happy all the time. But I can make *me* happy. And when I'm happy, I'm a really powerful ally and friend and supporter for the people I love and believe in.

"Well, I'll be damned," Diarmuid murmurs.

Jonah lets me go and I smile up at him. Then I turn to Diarmuid. "I'm not going to apologize," I tell him. "But you do want Jonah and me to stay."

"Of course I do," he says, looking confused by the notion that might not be true.

I'm relieved, I can't lie. But I step close to the king, lift up on tiptoe, and press a kiss to the king's cheek. "Our families will always be united in heart and spirit, and in the good works we do together."

"Oh," he says, patting my cheek. "Of course. But we can still be united by marriage, *and*," he says, looking around at the group again, "by blood."

"What the hell does that mean?" Cian asks, looking concerned.

"A child, of course," Diarmuid says.

"Fiona has a child," Cian says, pointing at Saoirse.

Saoirse grins at him.

Diarmuid smiles at his great-granddaughter. "Yes, she's an O'Grady. Potentially an heir to the throne. But not an Olsen."

"The agreement doesn't say anything about an O'Grady-Olsen child," Fiona says.

"We assumed that would naturally come of the marriage," Diarmuid says. "And more than one child would be lovely. But yes, at least one."

"So…" Henry says. "That's all moot now, though. I don't think Jonah's going to let Linnea have Cian's baby."

"Oh my god, no!" I exclaim.

"Damn right," Jonah growls.

"Don't be weird," Cian tells Henry.

Henry just shrugs.

"Of course not," Diarmuid says over the noise. "Obviously Astrid and Cian will marry and produce the heir."

All laughter immediately ceases and five seconds pass before Cian and Astrid say at the same time, "*What?*"

They look at each other, then back to Diarmuid.

Then everyone stands up and starts talking at once.

And that's when I realize what I need to do.

I probably *should* do something about the fact that Diarmuid is manipulating my sister into an arranged marriage and planning to make *her* the mother of the O'Grady-Olsen baby but...you know what? I've spent a lot of time worrying about my siblings and making things happen for them and Astrid can now wait ten minutes. Or twenty. Or longer.

She can fix this.

Or Cian can.

Or Miles can. Or Henry. Or Torin.

I've got something else that's a little more pressing at the moment. Because it's about *me,* for a change. There's something *I* need to do.

Actually, there's something I *want* to do.

I slip away from Diarmuid and turn to Jonah.

I grab his hands, face him squarely, look him directly in the eyes, and ask, "Will you marry me?"

He doesn't even blink. "Yes. Absolutely."

"Tonight? Right now?" I ask.

His eyebrows arch but he says, "Yes." The answer is firm, clear, without an ounce of hesitation.

My heart swells and I'm filled with a sense of rightness and warmth unlike anything I've ever felt before. There's not a single butterfly fluttering its wing. There's not even the tiniest niggle of doubt. There's not a millisecond of *what will people think* or really a thought about anyone else but Jonah. And me.

This is about *me*. My happiness. My future.

And *I'm* making this choice.

This decision is the easiest, the most obvious, and the surest I've been in my life.

I smile at him with love and...relief. "Then come on."

There are three other people in the room that I need help from and who don't need to be involved in the discussion about Astrid and Cian's possible engagement.

I lean over and say softly to the minister who performed Torin and Abigail's wedding, and who is staying the night at the palace as a special guest, "Could you join us in the next room for a moment, please?"

He looks around, shrugs, and stands up.

Then I motion to Abigail. "Help," I mouth.

She also doesn't hesitate. She nods and grabs Torin's hand.

They all follow Jonah and me into the sitting room just off the formal dining room.

I turn to them. "Jonah and I are getting married. Right now. Before anyone in that room decides that we're fair game to be hitched to someone else."

They all laugh.

But Abigail turns to me. "Are you certain you don't want to wait, just a day, to have a ceremony with everyone present? You can do it tomorrow while everyone is still here. You deserve that, Linnea. You've always been there supporting everyone else. You've helped Torin and me so much. We wouldn't be here without you and Jonah. And you've both been in the royal shadow for so long. You deserve to have your day in the spotlight."

But I'm shaking my head before she even finishes. "I don't need that." I look at the man who stole my heart. Even from the royal shadows. "I've actually had too much attention on me and who I should and would marry for way too long. I love the idea of just doing this my way with no fanfare." I grin. "When they're *not* looking."

Abi smiles and nods. "Okay then."

Torin gives me an affectionate smile as well.

Then Jonah leans in and says in my ear, "You're such a fucking queen."

Yes, I am. Being a queen isn't always a title. It's an attitude.

Jonah looks at Torin. "Will you be my best man?"

The prince nods, looking a little choked up. "Always."

It's a simple, straight-to-the-point ceremony.

But after years of formality and glitz and everyone's eyes on me but nothing being straight-forward about my future, that's exactly what I need.

Five minutes later, I say "I do" to the first and last man I will ever love.

"You may kiss your bride," the officiant tells Jonah.

His big hand settles on the back of my neck, and he moves in close. "Wife," he says gruffly, his hot eyes touching every part of my face.

"Husband," I answer breathlessly.

Then he tips my chin up with his thumb. "I love you."

"I love you too."

And when Jonah kisses me, I feel more wanted and loved and valued than I ever have. It's slow and sweet, hot and deep, and it's a perfect reflection of our relationship and love.

It started slow. It was sweet. And then it got hot and deep.

And I never want any of it to end.

I sigh happily as he lifts his head, because I know it won't. My future is *finally* set. I know what tomorrow will bring. And the next day. And the next.

Jonah.

Love.

Purpose.

Happiness.

The noise from the dining room has gotten louder and we all exchange looks as we turn toward the door.

"So...I guess we have to go back in there," Torin says. He doesn't look ready for that at all.

Jonah's arm slips around my waist. "Actually, Your Highness, *we* don't."

Torin looks at him. "What?"

"*You* are the royal prince and princess." Jonah looks down at me. "We're just the behind-the-scenes staff." He inclines his head toward the door. "I think that mess is above our pay grade."

I start giggling.

Abi looks up at Torin with a stricken look.

Torin looks...resigned. "And where do you think *you're* going then?" he asks.

Jonah's hand slides down to my ass and he squeezes. "The kitchen, I think. I'm in the mood for a late-night snack."

I blush, but also eagerly nod my agreement.

Torin rolls his eyes.

But he takes a step toward the door that will lead back into the dining room. Abi is gripping his hand tightly.

They open the door and I lift on tiptoe to peer into the chaos.

Everyone is on their feet, talking, gesturing, and arguing. Except for two people.

Iris is sitting at one end of the table, her legs crossed, typing into her phone, seemingly oblivious to what's going on around her.

Henry is lounging at the other end of the table, tossing what look like grapes into his mouth one by one.

I look up at Jonah. "Kitchen?"

"Yes," he says, turning me toward a door on the opposite side of the room. "I guess I don't need to remind you who you belong to now." He lifts my left hand to his mouth and presses a kiss to my fourth finger. "Though I do need to get a big, shiny ring on this finger."

I smile up at him. "Oh, it wouldn't hurt to jog my memory every once in a while."

His return grin is almost predatory. "It's a good thing you don't have to be quiet about it anymore."

CHAPTER 34
IRIS

> You need to find Cian's girl.

I'm texting Henry even though we're both in the dining room at the palace surrounded by the new O'Grady chaos.

No one can overhear this conversation.

And I don't really feel like getting up from my chair, where I have a piece of some amazing Danish layer cake in front of me, anyway.

I watch Henry pause in tossing grapes into the air and glance at his phone. He doesn't even look in my direction. His fingers move over the screen.

> Cian's girl? You mean his Cinderella??

Adding a new girl to the situation is not ideal, but Cian can *not* marry Astrid. Not even temporarily.

They certainly can *not* have a child together.

How did I not know that having an O'Grady-Olsen *baby* was a part of the arrangement?

Maybe because the entire 'arrangement' was written on the back of a whiskey-soaked playbill by two drunk guys while playing poker almost three decades ago and it had never occurred to either of them—or apparently the men with them who acted as 'witnesses'—that anyone else needed every detail. Or that they would ever be questioned.

I suppose kings and dukes are like that.

Maybe they just assumed a baby would come along, so it didn't need to be spelled out.

Whatever.

This not-so-little discovery definitely has my mind spinning. This could be very…interesting.

But Cian needs to stay away from Astrid.

I take a big bite of cake.

Damn, that is good.

I need to figure out how to sneak some of this into my suitcase.

> Yes, the woman he met two years ago or whatever. The one he made you try to find.

> How drunk are you?

Not drunk enough.

I cannot go home and tell the boss that Linnea is off the list, so Diarmuid just went on down the line and decided Cian and Astrid would be the O'Grady-Olsen couple.

He might be okay with it.

At least he'll *think* he's okay with it.

Or he'll tell me, and himself, that he's okay with it.

But that can't happen.

So yes, Henry needs to find this woman who enchanted Cian, then snuck out the next morning and disappeared.

Henry looked for her for a couple of months but came up empty-handed. But Cian has not forgotten about her.

> You can use our full resources.

Henry did the basic things to try to find her but ran into dead ends. We all discouraged him from looking further. We figured Cian would get over it as he always did when he 'fell in love' and there was no reason for Henry to chase down some strange woman who didn't want to be found.

Until now.

> Why is this suddenly okay?

> Because I said so.

> <eyeroll emoji>

> Astrid is not an option.

> I would ask why you're getting in the way of a king, and what is supposed to happen with this O'Grady-Olsen family thing if Cian doesn't marry Astrid, and what happens if I can't find this woman...but that seems like a lot of words I don't really want to type. Or read.

I'm going to need to pull out my notes about why I think Henry is the perfect person to be Cian's bodyguard, because it's very easy to forget why I keep him employed.

> Good boy.

> I'm on it.

I sigh. I love when Henry just does what I tell him to do.

That's happened exactly three times, including right now, in the ten years I've known him.

So now I'm suspicious.

And preparing for this to turn into a huge headache.

And worried about...well, all of the questions he "didn't ask".

And running low on amaretto.

So, I do what I always do when I'm stressed and annoyed by men.

I text my favorite friend-with-benefits.

> I need you to come over after I get home.

> Am I bringing chocolate mousse cake from Sandtons, condoms, or amaretto?

> Yes.

EPILOGUE

EPISODE 851 TRANSCRIPT

Jen: More huge news! As if the royal wedding wasn't big enough.

Lindsey: I know, this group is going to make me into a romantic before they're done.

Jen: <laughing> We've just found out, from the happy newlywed herself, that Lady Linnea has gotten married too! To none other than Jonah Greene. Prince Torin's hot bodyguard and best friend!

Lindsey: And all this time, we were going on about how

Linnea was traveling in the U.S. with Torin. All those podcast episodes where we were theorizing that Torin and Linnea were together and all that time he was there for Abigail and Linnea and Jonah were together!

Jen: I know. Imagine what they thought reading our transcripts! They must've been laughing their heads off!

Lindsey: We're lucky they even speak to us anymore. <laughter>

Jen: Well, I'm so glad they do. I am thrilled to hear about Linnea and Jonah. She sent over the message telling us they've been madly in love for months and even when she was in the U.S. and we saw those cute bowling photos of her and Senator Christian Waite, she was actually there with Jonah!

Lindsey: She's a sneaky one. She's going to be great for the palace when it comes to keeping their secrets.

Jen: I know. We cannot count on her to be an insider source, obviously.

Lindsey: <laughing> But we still adore her. Congratulations, Linnea and Jonah! We can't wait to see you out and about, holding hands, kissing in public now. We're thrilled for you!

Jen: So, do you think all the romance and gossip and intrigue are over for the palace and the royal family?

Lindsey: I hope not! There are still two single princes! And these bodyguards are surprisingly hot and romantic!

Jen: True! Even though we *never* hear anything about Declan.

Lindsey: I know...We've got to figure out a way to get news about him. And hey, Linnea surprised us with a juicy story! Astrid and Alex are both single...

Jen: Ooooh...you're right.

Lindsey: Stay tuned! You know we'll tell you ALL!

*Thank you so much for reading **Reluctantly Rogue**!*
I hope you loved Jonah & Linnea's story!
And I hope you're ready for so much more from this world and the royals (and their friends!)!

Cian's story is next!

A small-town single mom like me has no business believing in fairy tales.

But the very handsome, charming, dirty-talking *prince* (yes, seriously) I met nineteen months ago now has his fine ass and panty-melting grin planted on my front porch.

He's been searching for me ever since I snuck out after our hot, fantasy-filled weekend together.

And, dammit, that's a little romantic.

Find ALL of my books at **ErinNicholas. com**

And the best place to find out all the news about that (including upcoming books and more!) is right here!
bit.ly/Keep-In-Touch-Erin
Be sure you get those dashes and upper case letters in there!

And this is your personal invitation to my Facebook group, Erin Nicholas's Super Fans where you can get first looks, behind the scenes peeks, and daily fun with fellow romance lovers (including me!)!

CONNECTED BOOKS FROM ERIN NICHOLAS

All of these can be read as stand-alones, even though they are part of interconnected series! Jump in anywhere and enjoy!

Want to know more about Torin's sister Fiona, his brother Cian, and their bodyguards, including Henry and Colin?

Check out **Kiss My Giraffe** (a grumpy-sunshine, princess-in-hiding, small town rom com!) and **Better Safe Than Safari** (a bodyguard-rockstar, curvy-girl, steamy rom com)**!**

Find all of these and so much more at www.ErinNicholas.com!

About Erin

Erin Nicholas is the New York Times and USA Today bestselling author of over sixty sexy contemporary romances. She's known for her blue-collar book boyfriends and big, boisterous found families in small towns. Her stories have been described as toe-curling, enchanting, steamy and fun. She loves to write about reluctant heroes, imperfect heroines and happily ever afters.

She lives in the Midwest with her husband who only wants to read the sex scenes in her books, her kids who will never read the sex scenes in her books, and family and friends who say they're shocked by the sex scenes in her books (yeah, right!).

Find her and all her books at
www.ErinNicholas.com

And find her on Facebook, BookBub, and Instagram!

Copyright 2024 Erin Nicholas

All rights reserved.

No part of this book may be reproduced in any form or by any electronic or mechanical means, including information storage and retrieval systems, without written permission from the author, except for the use of brief quotations in a book review.

This book is a work of fiction. Names, characters, places, and incidents are either products of the author's imagination or are used factiously, and any resemblance to actual persons, living or dead, business establishments, events, or locales is coincidental.

Editor: Lindsey Faber

Cover design: Qamber Designs

Digital ISBN: 979-8-9908220-1-6

Paperback ISBN: 979-8-9908220-3-0

Special Edition ISBN: 979-8-9908220-0-9

www.ingramcontent.com/pod-product-compliance
Lightning Source LLC
LaVergne TN
LVHW041645070526
838199LV00053B/3564